The Undying Man

Book Two of
The Whisper Prince

Todd Fahnestock

F4
PUBLISHING

For Tami,
Who has been waiting forever

For Steve,
Who left beer on my doorstep as an incentive.

CONTENTS

THE UNDYING MAN

PART I: BETRAYALS

PART II: THE FALL OF THE FAIA

PART III: THE DREAM BEAST

PART IV: THE EIGHTH FAIA

Mailing List/Social Media

MAILING LIST
Don't miss out on the latest news and information about all of my books. Join my Readers Group:

https://www.subscribepage.com/u0x4q3

FACEBOOK
https://www.facebook.com/todd.fahnestock

AMAZON AUTHOR PAGE
https://www.amazon.com/Todd-Fahnestock/e/B004N1MILG

Part I

Betrayals

Prologue

REE WAS GOING TO BETRAY THE MAN who'd saved the empire. She could feel him on her tongue as he approached, a light tingle, and she could taste him, the coppery tang of blood. Her pulse beat faster in her neck. Her stomach twisted like a knotted rope.

As a Ringblade, she had faced duty and death without flinching. She'd fought warriors to the bloody end with her weapons, her wits, and her training. With borrowed clothes, a smile, and a handful of lies, she had worn identities like hats, slipping among enemies who would have quickly knifed her if they'd but known the truth. She had made love to men, spending her body upon them, only to cut their throats an hour later while they lay dreaming. A Ringblade was trained for these things. A Ringblade moved events. It was her purpose.

But she feared the coming of the Whisper Prince.

She turned her face toward the door where Grei would emerge. The royal infirmary housed two dozen beds. Azure curtains hung on wooden poles between the patients to give a modicum of privacy. Moans and soft crying of the victims of the Phantom War filled the room as healers moved from patient to patient. A pungent concoction of medicines rode the air, not quite covering the smell of blood and injury. It smelled of spiced chicken soup, vinegar, and open wounds.

It had been an hour since the Ringmother had visited and made her promise.

"You betrayed us," Selicia had said. "But you can return to the Sanctum. You can stand alongside your Ringsisters once more, if you can prove yourself."

"What must I do?" Ree had said.

"The Whisper Prince must be bought under control…"

Throughout her youth, Ree had been invulnerable. Out of all the other young girls in Moondow, she'd been chosen to receive Ringblade training. Out of the fourteen girls inducted to Sanctum that year, she was one of only two who'd survived the training. After, she had risen to prominence among her Ringsisters. Ree had been a model for all Ringblades.

Then she had fallen from grace. She'd betrayed her order to save her birth sister, Salandra. She'd braced the Slink Lord Kuruk in his own domain.

That was the moment Ree lost her implacable sense of invulnerability. Her fighting prowess had been laughable against Kuruk. Her mental strength had crumbled like a castle built on sand. He had chewed her arm off, chewed into her mind, and driven her near to madness. He'd driven her like a stubborn beast, beat down her will. When Grei had finally set her free, there had been almost nothing left. Now, the only pain that remained was her severed arm, and it was a blessed relief by comparison to Kuruk's mental flames.

One of the twin doors opened at the end of the long room, and Grei entered. When she saw him, the tingling and the taste of copper on her tongue vanished. A lifetime ago, in that fate-filled Lateral House in the wet city of Fairmist, she had kissed and cut the Whisper Prince. After, she had licked the blade as she had been taught, cutting her own tongue as she invoked the blood bond. Her blood had mingled with the blood of the Whisper Prince, and now she could track him wherever he

2

went when she thought of him, concentrated on him. She would always know when he was near. Even in the grips of Kuruk's torture, she had felt him coming. His approach was the tingling, coppery taste of hope.

He had been her mission in her first lifetime, before her soul had aged a thousand years, before she'd known what loss and sacrifice truly was. Now, he was her mission again. That was all it was. That was how she had to look at it.

The Whisper Prince must be bought under control. Selicia's final words floated in her mind. And he will not listen to me. You must become his confidante. You must use every talent available to you....

Grei stopped at the foot of her bed. He looked like nobility. He wore baggy gray pantaloons, a green doublet of Thiaran make, and his right hand was covered with a green glove. She'd gotten a glimpse of that hand at the Temple of the Faia, when she was half-mad and desperate to give him the secret knowledge to defeat the slinks. It had been horribly burned, shrunken into a skeletal claw. Both of them had sustained grievous injuries to their right arms. Grei, at least, could still use his.

"How are you feeling?" he asked.

"Free," she croaked. She cleared her craggy throat and managed to speak in a more normal tone. "Kuruk is out of my head."

He sat down on the edge of the bed. His nearness was like a cool, comforting cloth. He'd saved her. He'd saved them all.

Grei held an oak branch, absently gripping it, turning it, gripping it again. It was about two feet long and pocked with smooth nubs where smaller branches had been, almost as though they had been filed off. As she watched, he whispered softly and brushed his hands over the rough bark. It crumbled away like dried leaves, revealing the smooth bronze wood underneath. For a moment, she couldn't speak. What he could do was miraculous. She wondered if she'd ever get used to that.

He'd just been a brave boy when she'd kissed him in Fairmist. Now he was something different. He had faced down living nightmares and sent them running. He had walked the Dead Woods and emerged alive, communicated with goddesses, overcome Highblades, and outmaneuvered Ringblades. He'd captured the loyalty of the imperial champion, two princesses...

...and at least one crippled, emaciated Ringblade.

She wanted to help him. It was a pressure in her chest, a debt that needed paying. She wanted to defend this boy who had saved her life and her sanity. But instead, she was going to manipulate him.

She was a Ringblade, and she had a mission.

"You're a hero, Grei," Ree said.

"Ah," he said. "Like the emperor?" The mild words were gilded with rebellion. It was the official story about the Phantom War: Emperor Qweryn had died to unmask the slinks, opening the way for the Whisper Prince to banish them. The empress wanted the people to see that. So did the Ringmother.

Ree forced herself to focus. She must lead him gently. Grei was smart; he would catch her if she wasn't careful.

A sweet lie, then. They were more easily swallowed. She had done this a hundred times, but an unbidden thought broke her concentration.

He would hate her for this. If he caught her lying, she would become the enemy. The slinks had enslaved the empire for seven years with a lie, stealing sacrifices under the cloak of a terrible deception. Grei had shattered their hold, sent their leader running. He'd also fought his way out from under the lies that kept Thiarans compliant with the slinks, lies crafted by the emperor and the Ringmother. Grei despised them for that.

Ree swallowed, trying to calm herself. It didn't matter what Grei thought of her. She was a Ringblade. She had a task to perform.

Grei ran his hand over the wood a second time, whispering, and the thick branch bulged at one end and sloped to a slender width at the other.

"You *are* the Whisper Prince," she said. "A hero to all

Thiara. You saved us." She said it with conviction because that part, at least, was from her heart.

"It's on the lips of every citizen," he replied evenly. "So it must be true."

"The emperor played his part, as did—"

"The emperor bought peace with lies, with bloody sacrifices, then he created abominations to fix his mistake. Now the empress wants to start all over again."

He didn't look up at her, but instead concentrated on the branch. Which, frankly, she didn't understand. Was shaping the wood a type of meditation? At the slender end, he coaxed the branch into a round knob. It looked like the beginnings of a fence post.

"The empress is a liar," she agreed, calculating. Ree knew how to change a person's mind. All Ringblades had studied influence and seduction. Agreeing with Grei to start would pull his angry emotions to the surface. There, she could acknowledge them, touch them, mold them. "The people are stunned, scared. They needed strength. She gave them a lie. What they really need is *you* to tell them everything is okay again."

"And if everything is not okay?" he said.

She gave a breezy smile. "Well, first things first."

Grei kept shaping the wood.

"She is their leader." Ree shrugged. "She wants to show them strength. They need to see strength. Should she weep and tell them how close we are to ruin?"

"She wants power," he said. "She doesn't care about the people."

"Powermongers always want power." She agreed again, looking for some way to soften the ground around his distrust. "But the empire bleeds from its wounds. If someone doesn't stand up, give the people strength, they will panic. That's what people do."

"I should probably join forces with Via," he said softly. "Do you think that might mitigate the lies?" He stopped, stared at the branch, and remained quiet.

That was exactly the answer she wanted, the answer she'd been told to secure. But it was too quick, too calmly given. Grei was baiting her, so she cocked her head, thoughtful, and said nothing. It was best to wait, best to draw out his anger.

"When I first met you in Fairmist," he said, "I wanted to stop the lies. I wanted to stop the sacrifices. What good is it to win the Phantom War if we start all over again? One lie, two, three... How soon before we justify a 'necessary evil'? And after that, what? A 'necessary sacrifice'?" He shook his head, began working at the branch again.

Logic wasn't working. It was time to bring fear into the mix.

"Have we really won the Phantom War?" she asked as though it was a philosophical question. "Yes, we learned the truth. We drove Kuruk away. But I saw the heart of his deception, and I *still* have nightmares about it. About his imaginary slinks," Ree said. "Everyone else, they didn't see what I saw. They were only *told* the slinks weren't real. That's almost impossible to believe without proof. Whispers run throughout the city: 'Is the empress lying about the slinks? Do they still roam free in the shadows?' Panic, like I said. Panic will bring ruin as surely as war. Standing next to someone you dislike for five minutes..." She paused for effect. "Maybe that's a small price for security."

He smoothed the knob as flat as a fan, then drew four lines from the center to the edges. The lines became crevices, then splits in the wood, creating five smooth sticks poking out from the center. It was as though the branch was made of clay to him. "Truth cannot be built atop lies," Grei said.

"And what about trust?" she asked softly. "Taking counsel from those you trust."

"Those I trust..." he murmured, not looking up. "Like you, I presume?"

His acerbic tone was a lash across her face, hot and stinging.

She'd been inside his head, and he'd been inside hers. He'd seen her naked soul: She believed in him. She had sacrificed everything to come to him and give him the secret he needed to defeat Kuruk. He had trusted her then. She'd felt it, seen it.

Now she tried to push the pain away and made her face appear as it should. But he wasn't looking. He didn't see the smile she crafted for him.

"Selicia told me you were awake," he said.

Her smile faltered.

"I presume those are her words coming from your mouth."

Ree swallowed, a cold feeling settling into the bottom of her stomach. She wasn't manipulating Grei. The Ringmother had manipulated her. From the moment Ree had begun speaking, Grei had known her real purpose. He'd seen through her poor performance because he'd been warned. With every word, she'd shown him she was the last person he should trust. She'd shown him she was bought and paid for.

She lowered her gaze. Selicia didn't want Ree to convince Grei to join forces with the empress. Selicia had wanted to isolate him, to show him that he had no friends here.

Ree was a fool. There was no place for her back at the Sanctum; not now or ever. The dream had been dangled in front of her to achieve a purpose, and Selicia had accomplished it. Grei looked at Ree and knew she was false. If he'd ever had faith in her, he didn't now.

Ree's first, desperate thought was to spin a new web of lies. She'd been trained to take a situation like this and create a new lie, a believable one....

But if he saw through her second deception—and he would see through it—there would never be another appeal. She would brand herself as his enemy forever.

She trembled. Exposed and vulnerable, like that girl she'd been when the Ringblades first came for her, she did what she had been trained over and over not to do. She let go of the trappings of the Ringblade, and she told the truth.

"You...you saved my soul," she said hoarsely. Her heart felt like it was breaking. "I would do anything for you."

He paused in his work and looked up, into her eyes now,

as though he could smell the truth like a wolf scenting game.

Her eyes burned with tears, but she held his gaze. She let him see her remorse.

She wasn't a Ringblade anymore, and she never would be. She was a maimed, starved nobody with no home. "I…I'm sorry," she whispered. "I'm so sorry."

He watched her without speaking, like he was considering making room in his heart for her. Then he turned his attention back to his work. He massaged the sticks on the branch, making each longer, thinner, and she suddenly saw the shape of a human hand emerge, fingers of wood. The entire branch was an arm from the elbow down. It took her breath away. That was the same shape and length as the arm she'd lost.

"W-What are you doing?" she said.

"Give me your…stump," he said.

She hesitated, then slowly held it up. It was short and awkward. White bandages wrapped it, and he gently unwound them. The burned wound was scabbed and red. Flakes of black flesh still clung to it.

"I'm so sorry about this," he said softly, looking at the damage as though he could see every raw nerve. His compassion pushed at her like a hand on her chest, and she dared to hope. If he could see the deception in her heart, could he not also see her devotion?

She watched as he lifted the wooden forearm to her elbow and lined them up. The wood felt hard on her wound, then he whispered, and a cooling sensation spread over her flesh.

"Grei…"

He ignored her, kept whispering, closed his eyes. A numbness spread through her severed arm to her shoulder.

She suddenly gasped as her flesh separated at the end of the stump like the tentacles of an octopus, then grasped the wooden forearm. The sight made her dizzy, and she bit her lip to keep from crying out, but there was no pain. The tentacles of her flesh grew, creeping like water down the wood until it covered the fingers.

He let out a pent-up breath. It felt as though a hundred

needles suddenly stuck into her flesh and bone, as if he had been holding her pain back and couldn't anymore. She hissed, clenching her teeth as she clenched her fist—

She stopped, stunned, and the pain became an echo in the back of her mind. The fist on her new hand had clenched. She raised it up and unclenched it. She could control it. By the Faia, she could *feel* it.

"Baezin's Blood..." she breathed.

Grei recovered himself, but the wrinkles around his eyes were tight.

"I don't want to help the empress," he said. "Or Selicia. I don't want to fight their war of lies. I want to heal the wounds they've made."

He left the infirmary and closed the doors behind him. Ree curled over her new arm and cried.

Chapter 1

GREI

GREI TURNED AWAY FROM REE. He had hoped she wouldn't side with Selicia, but Ree was a Ringblade, after all. Despite Selicia's heartfelt speech about being his friend, not for a second did he think she was being honest. He'd walked that path before, and Selicia was the ultimate Ringblade. Lying came as easily as breathing. She had fooled Grei for weeks when they'd traveled together. He hadn't known her ultimate plan until it was too late. It didn't matter that Grei had saved her from the tree spirits, from the Highblades, or even that he'd convinced the Green Faia to heal her from a mortal wound. Selicia rewarded his trust with betrayal. When she'd told him Ree was awake in the infirmary, he'd known what to expect.

But it stung. Ree had been kind and fierce and mysterious when he'd first met her. She'd endured unimaginable torments to do the right thing, to give him information that saved his life and the lives of countless others. He had hoped she would keep faith with him.

Oh, she'd sounded sincere at the end. Even the whispers coming from her were sincere, but Ringblades could block his empathic abilities. Selicia had managed to keep her heart hidden from him for days while they traveled together. You couldn't change a snake. You could only keep them at a safe distance.

He shook the dark thoughts from his mind. He'd done what he'd come to do. He had healed Ree's horrible wound. Let it end there. He need not visit Ree ever again.

Grei was adrift in a sea of enemies. That was his true problem. He had no plan, and he needed to find a way to outwit them before one of them struck again.

He reached the door of the infirmary and heard the whispers of two Highblades awaiting him on the other side. Old fear rose inside his chest, hearkening back to when he was a helpless boy, when the Highblades had yanked him from his home, and tortured him until he stopped speaking about the Debt of the Blessed.

The memory and the fear came and went. A warm anger rose in its place.

Put your hands on me, he thought. I dare you.

He opened the door and walked into the hallway. They were both bigger, physically stronger than Grei. They were Highblades. They thought their muscles made them right. One moved to stand at his right side, the other on the left. Leftie reached out to take Grei's arm.

"Touch me and I'll melt your fist," Grei said softly.

The Highblade yanked his hand back.

"I'm guessing the empress would like to see me," Grei said.

"Yes, my lord," the Highblade said, using Grei's new title. That was a new development as of yesterday. Via had announced that Grei, as the Whisper Prince, was to be accorded all the deference of a noble. Another way of trying to suck him into her scheme. A bribe of elevated station.

He considered turning away without a word, but he calmed himself. He had too many enemies. Keeping a strained peace with Via was better than a fight, at least right now. It would give him more time in the royal library, more time to prepare for Kuruk's return.

The murderous slink lord was still out there, seething, and Kuruk was unthinkably powerful. He'd ensorcelled everyone in the Thiaran Empire; Grei could barely wrap his mind around that. How did one person have the strength to do that? Grei had barely managed to send Kuruk running with Vecenne and Blevins fighting by his side, and that had been mostly luck. He couldn't count on such a perfect storm again, especially now that Blevins was dead.

And then there was ancient Emperor Lyndion, the man who had orchestrated the false prophecy and Adora's intended sacrifice. Grei had stopped Lyndion's plan, and had narrowly brought Adora back to life. But that lying bastard was still out there, and he had to be exposed before he did to someone else what he had done to Adora.

And finally, if that wasn't enough, Grei suspected there was a greater threat than either Kuruk or Lyndion. There was a mighty creature in the shadows behind Kuruk, perhaps even the source of his power. This hidden monster, Velak, was stealing bodies and walking them around, forcing them to do his bidding. Grei had turned one of Velak's minions, the Archon Dayn Felesh, to stone. That wouldn't go unnoticed. Velak would come for Grei, too.

So no. Grei didn't need the empress trying to throw him in a dungeon. A strained peace was the best he could hope for, a way to push her off his back until he could get a grip on everything else.

So he went with the Highblades. They took him up two flights of stairs and down an opulent hallway. Oil paintings lined the walls. He stopped and looked at one with a great, white cat skulking at the edge of the Jhor Forest. The trees stretched so tall they were lost in the frame above, and their trunks divided the huge cat into four parts, its red eyes peering directly at the viewer.

What Grei really needed was help, but neither the empress nor the Ringmother could be entrusted with Grei's knowledge.

Via had served Lyndion, either with full knowledge or unwittingly. It didn't matter. The Ringmother was a scheming, backstabbing snake. Ree had just shown where her true allegiance lay. Blevins was dead. Vecenne, as helpful as she had been during the Phantom War, was still the princess of Thiara. And Adora…

Well, Grei would trust Adora with his life, but she had been through so much. He couldn't put a new burden on her right now. When she was ready, he would tell her everything, but for now…

No. Grei was alone, and he had to figure his own way out.

"My lord?" the Highblade said respectfully at the delay. Grei noticed these bloodthirsty bullies had impeccable manners when they were afraid of you.

Without a word, he followed them again. They continued to a room at the end of the hall, guarded by two more Highblades in short gold kilts and X-shaped harnesses bordered in red. Grei's escorts opened the double doors and bid him enter.

The room had four chairs in a semicircle around a half-moon desk. The dark mahogany of the desk matched the red stone walls. On the table sat a little bell and a cask overflowing with scrolls.

The doors behind Grei closed, while his escorts took up positions on either side. At that moment, Empress Via swept into the room dramatically through another door. Her red and black gown had a heavy sash tied at the waist that hung down her front. She had Adora's beauty, and she looked as if she had just come from a portrait sitting. Every fold of her dress was perfect. Her black hair had been combed to a shine, and her crown of woven gold bands sat perfectly atop her head. It would be easy to believe she was a goddess. He shook off the feeling that he was the small one in this room.

"Leave us, please," she said to the two Highblades. The Highblade on Grei's right started for the door, but the younger Highblade on the left—the one who'd initially tried to grab Grei's arm—paused. "Your Majesty, but he is—"

"Thank you for your concern, Arendon," Via said. "Leave us." Grei noticed her hand was wrapped in a subtle bandage. The material was thin and the same color as her flesh. Underneath that bandage was the little square of flesh that had turned to stone while she'd played cryptic word games with him. He thought about healing it for her, but waited to see how the talk progressed.

"Your Majesty." Arendon bowed and removed himself, closing the door after.

"They worry," she said to Grei conversationally, like they were friends. She moved behind the half-moon desk, leaving him the choice of one of the four supplicants' chairs.

He looked them over, then stayed standing. After a brief pause, in which her easy smile seemed a bit strained, she also remained standing.

"My Highblades fought the slinks firsthand, you see." She continued as though she'd never stopped speaking. "The monsters were invincible. Yet somehow you defeated them. To a Highblade, you are the most dangerous man in the empire, and not someone to leave alone with their empress." She paused. "But if the Whisper Prince wanted me dead, I would be dead. Isn't that true?"

"I don't kill people," Grei said.

"But you'd make an exception in my case." She quoted what he had told her when they'd first met, when Adora's life was at risk and the empress wanted to play games with him. "Isn't that what you said?"

"I needed to get to her quickly," he said tightly. Not for the first time, he wished he could hear the whispers of her emotions, but whatever trick Lyndion had taught to Adora to block him out, he'd taught it to Via, too.

"So it was an empty threat?" she asked.

"What do you want?" He listened to the whispers of the room and was unsurprised to discover a Ringblade crouched in an alcove behind the crimson drapes. In addition, Selicia waited in the room from which Via had just emerged. Via wasn't as brave as she would like to seem.

14

The empress leaned forward, her hands splayed on the desk. "I wish we had been able to start in a different place, Grei," she said, her voice full of sincerity.

"I wish that you weren't a liar willing to sacrifice your own daughter," he said.

Her lips tightened, but she kept her frozen smile in place.

"I don't have the time or stomach for more games," he continued. "What do you want?"

"I am working to accommodate you, Prince Grei—"

"Are you?"

"But you make it difficult," she continued. "I realize you see things—know things—that I do not. But I see things, know things, that *you* do not. Let us to be allies. Let us stand together for the good of the people. They need us. Help me protect them."

"The last time I trusted the empire, it threw me into a cell and tortured me because I wanted the truth. If you're offering me a chance to support new lies, I decline."

She sighed, looking like a tolerant-but-exasperated parent. "I don't want to order you to help me," she said. "I would rather that we be allies—"

"You won't be ordering me to do anything," he said in a low voice. Deep-seated rage bubbled inside him. These arrogant royals. They believed they owned everything, that it was somehow their due. But they'd given up their right to rule when they sacrificed children.

"You are a citizen of this empire," Via said. "Are you really so arrogant to think you are above the law?"

"You perpetuated the atrocity of the Debt of the Blessed for seven years. You created the Slink War. Tell me one decision you've made that is a good one, and I will follow you."

"The crown is not accountable to the Whisper Prince."

"Not long ago," he said, "you and your Highblades could force me to do whatever you wanted. Not anymore."

"Don't make me your enemy," she warned.

"If you act the villain, I'll treat you like a villain." He turned to go.

"Don't open that door without my consent," she said quietly.

Grei's heart beat fast, and he paused. He heard the whispered emotions of the hidden Ringblade. Tight. Obedient. Ready to kill.

He turned. Was he ready to humiliate the empress in her own chambers?

"You have delivered the empire from a great evil," Via said evenly. "That buys you flexibility when talking so brazenly to the crown, but only a little."

"I don't need your flexibility."

Tendons stood out on Via's hands. "Grei," she said calmly. "Understand that I hold you in the highest regard, and if I had the luxury of time, I would indulge you. But I don't and I can't. I don't have the time to teach you the nuances of leadership. Your empire requires your service now. I have already given you days I don't have, and my generosity is at an end. You will publicly ally with the crown. I have informed my nobles that you and Mialene have my blessing to wed. We will announce the betrothal tonight, and you will become a prince in reality as well as name."

"No."

She closed her eyes, bowing her head, then opened them again and looked at him. "I thought this would be welcome news. You do not want to marry Mialene?"

"Her name is Adora." Mialene was the princess that Via had sacrificed. Adora wasn't that person anymore. She didn't belong to them. Via didn't have the right to paint that name on Adora again.

Via's lips turned down in a frown, and she swallowed hard. "Very well. Adora. Don't you want to marry Adora?"

"Tell your citizens the truth about the Phantom War," he said. "Tell them your husband murdered Faia, that he eroded the foundation of the lands to grasp at power. Tell that truth, and we can begin a trust between us."

"The empire does not ask for trust. It requires obedience."

16

"The citizens of the empire do not live at your sufferance."

Her expression finally turned stony. "Your naiveté is dangerous, Grei. The empire is fracturing. Will you let it fall?"

He turned and opened the doors without answering. She didn't call after him again, and the Ringblade hidden in her clever little alcove didn't move. But Selicia had vanished from the other room.

The Highblades stood at attention as Grei left. He kept searching for Selicia; she would be near. Once he reached the end of the opulent hallway, he picked up her slippery, emotional whispers once again. She detached from the shadows of a doorway several feet behind him, soundless.

He stopped.

"Your dagger won't make it to my back," he said.

She moved up alongside him. "If I was going to kill you, I wouldn't be so loud."

"I can hear you even if you make no sound. You realize that, don't you?"

"Only a fool boasts about his advantages," she said.

"I think I hate you."

"Whatever will I do?"

He glanced at her, searching for the smile, but her face was impassive.

"You're playing the fool," she said. "If you're doing it on purpose, you're forcing a dangerous game that everyone will lose. If you're doing it by accident, then I'm even more fearful. Power and stupidity are a deadly pair."

"The empress wants us blind to what is actually needed."

"Her words are the law of this land."

He glanced at her. "You agree with her?"

"It is not my place to agree or disagree. It is my place to obey. I serve the empire. That is what serving means. You are her subject, but she treats with you like an ally. This is a gift. Don't spurn it. Either you are her ally, or you are a threat. Surely you can see this."

"She is unreasonable."

"She has been unbelievably lenient with you. You have

committed treason, yet she has but sent me to talk with you, nothing more."

"Treason? She is a—"

"Tread carefully, Grei," she warned. "If you were any other traitor, you would be in irons right now. Or dead."

He stopped and faced her. Her diminutive size, rather than making her seem weaker, somehow made her seem more deadly. Like a thin dagger. He whispered in his mind, asking the air to go hard as stone between them. He knew how fast she was. "Or what? What will you do?"

She said nothing.

"What will you do, Selicia?" he pressed.

"Stop thinking with your anger and start thinking with your head," she said.

"Don't you see what is happening?" he hissed. "This is how it all started in the first place. She wants me to bow to—"

"To the empire that has protected you," she interrupted. "To the empire that has nurtured you into adulthood."

"To an empire that tortured and beat me into submission." He could barely keep from snarling. He let out a breath and spoke in a calmer tone. "When she sees reason and speaks truth, we'll talk about making an alliance."

"You mean when she agrees to do your bidding?" Selicia said. "When she allows you to rule her, then you will allow her to rule the empire?"

"That's not what I'm saying."

"You are holding her hostage until she changes her decisions to match your desires. That is not reason, Grei. That is a coup."

"You're all insane." He continued walking.

Selicia did not keep pace with him this time, but her voice floated up to catch him. "You cannot spit in the teeth of the empress and expect no consequences, Grei."

"Is that a threat?" he called over his shoulder.

Her next words were soft, under her breath. He couldn't tell whether she meant him to hear them or not.

"Ringblades do not threaten," she said.

Chapter 2

VIA

VIA SNATCHED A SCROLL from the table and ripped the ribbon off. The Whisper Prince was going to give her fits. She needed him, and he knew it. Damn it! This thing with Grei was shaping up to be a disaster. She couldn't afford another disaster.

She looked down at the scroll she was crumpling, then inwardly counseled herself to divert her mind down another path.

Read the scroll. Handle some other issue that isn't the Whisper Prince.

With practiced calm, she gently unrolled the scroll and read it.

It was from her son at the war front. The emperor's death and news of the Phantom War had reached the troops. Morale had been crushed. The Benascans had just won a major battle and pushed her army back to the Sere Plains.

She threw the scroll at the wall.

Stop it. Just...breathe.

She needed to get hold of herself. The accumulation of the past days' events were overwhelming, but she couldn't afford to lose her composure. It was nearly time for the celebration *she* had orchestrated to reassure the people. In less than two hours, she would stand before them, smile, and assure them that the empire wasn't falling apart when, in fact, it was.

The damnable Whisper Prince had saved the empire, but the rescue had come at a high cost. And the recovery was brittle. In the aftermath, problems grew like Venishan kelp, and her resources dwindled.

She'd wanted to dispel the shock of the Phantom War with this seven-day celebration, but people hadn't yet gone back to work. They were as skittish as does poised to flee. According to Captain Tellick's report, many were even still leaving the city, calling it cursed. Many more didn't believe there was only one Slink. When intangible phantoms were scuttling about left and right, it had been easier to convince her people of the lie, to show them firsthand. But now that everyone could only trust their faulty memories and active imaginations, doubts sprang up.

In addition, just when she needed a strong policing force, the prison was full of two dozen of the Archon's traitorous Highblades. It would take only a handful of sympathizers among her loyal Highblades to effect a jailbreak. Perhaps even a coup.

To add insult to injury, her head cook was missing, likely fled to her daughter's house in Felesh, and the royal kitchen was in disarray. Via had straightened that out personally. The last thing she needed was the perception that there was a food shortage in the palace.

There was a way to set these troubles right, but it all came down to the Whisper Prince. With just a few well-placed words, he could cement her tenuous rule. But the little hothead wouldn't listen to her. The empire teetered on a cliff, and he went on about the importance of "truth." She had extolled his exploits in proclamations and in song, had elevated him to lordly status, had given Mialene's hand in marriage to him. To a shoemaker's son! But the Whisper Prince, for all his power, was nothing but a belligerent boy. He wanted to fling her offers back at her to show his power.

Via suddenly realized that this latest news of the collapsing war front might be the final blow to her tenuous hold on the empire. If her rule began with a pile of failures—the loss of her husband, her credibility, and the Benascan War—it would be a short rule indeed. She needed a victory, and she needed it fast.

She let out a long, frustrated breath and watched her hands until they stopped shaking. If she showed despair, others would see it. Her poise was, literally, the only advantage she had.

There was a knock on the door. That would be Arendon.

"Enter," she said.

Arendon poked his head in. "The Duke of Felesh to see you, Your Majesty."

Her heart lurched. Dayn Felesh... But the Archon was dead!

She kept her poise, and her reason finally caught up to her panic. It was not Dayn, of course; it must be his son, Biren. Her panic turned to anger.

Thousands had left the city and thousands had returned in the wake of the Phantom War. But not all of those returning had fled the slinks. Some were opportunistic nobles looking for advantage in the chaos. That could be the only reason Biren was here.

"I told him you were not to be disturbed, but he claims it is urgent. Shall I send him away?" Arendon asked.

She was tempted, but Felesh was the largest duchy in the empire, and the most powerful family save the Doragons. Better to deal with this quickly than have it wait. Besides, she longed to unleash some of her frustration upon him.

"See him in."

Arendon disappeared and, a moment later, Biren entered the room. He threw a nasty glance at Arendon as he passed. The young Highblade followed, positioning himself inside the open door, obviously with no intent of leaving.

Biren had not lived in the city of Thiara for half a decade, and Via remembered him as the mischievous son of the Archon who had played with her daughter Mialene by the Sunset Sea. The once handsome boy had expanded into a rough-looking, pudgy young man. He was barely twenty years old, and already twice the weight his father had been. A scraggly, patchy beard darkened his jaw, making him look uncouth. His lips looked wet, and his pink tongue slithered out to lick them as his tiny, dark eyes flicked a glance around the room.

This is my most powerful noble. Perfect, Via thought.

"I require a private audience with the empress," Biren demanded, glaring at Arendon. The Highblade kept his gaze forward as though he hadn't heard.

"You may address me, if you have a request," Via said. "You may also show your allegiance to the empire now," she reminded him pleasantly, as though he had simply forgotten.

Biren's eyes widened, and for a moment she thought he might decline, in which case this would be a short interview indeed. Arendon was ready to kill someone, and she was in the mood to let him. Consequences be damned.

With flames in his eyes, Biren went to one knee. He crossed one arm over his chest, fist on his heart, and gave a quick head dip, fulfilling the motion if not the sentiment. He rose to his feet. It had not been Qweryn's custom to make his nobles bow in private, but until Via had a firm grasp on who was her ally and who was not, she intended to make sure that they all knew who was empress in Thiara.

"Your Majesty," Biren said in a low tone. "I would have private words with you."

"Concerning?"

"You wish to hear this privately."

"Are you so certain of my wishes, Lord Biren?" she said, skipping his new honorific. With the Archon dead, Biren was the duke, but only after the official ceremony conducted by his empress, if formalities were to be observed. It was a low cut, but she was feeling low.

He showed his teeth, but kept his voice genteel. "If you please, Your Majesty, I beg a private audience."

Behind Biren, Arendon lightly shook his head.

"As you wish, Lord Biren," she said, ignoring her Highblade's concern. "Arendon, give us the room." Arendon didn't look happy, but he obeyed, closing the door behind him.

"Please, take a seat," Via gestured to one of the overstuffed Venishan chairs.

Biren flicked a glance at the chair, but he did not sit. Just like the damned Whisper Prince.

"Well, my Lord Biren, what can the empire do for you today?" Via asked.

"The empire can fulfill its promise."

How Qweryn resisted the urge to stick a fork in the eyes of some nobles, Via didn't know. If she'd had a fork, she'd have used it. She worked to keep her voice even as she spoke.

"Perhaps you have not heard, Lord Biren, but we have just finished fighting a war within these city walls. Your father was one of the casualties, and he has not yet been interred. We shall bestow your rightful title upon you in due course."

"I am the Duke of Felesh. I do not need *you* to tell me."

Via paused for half a breath, mystery and anger fighting for control inside her. She managed to keep her temper. "Then please enlighten me, Lord Biren. To which promise do you refer?"

"Mialene."

She opened her mouth to retort, and cut herself short. She suddenly realized why Biren was here. He and Mialene had been betrothed weeks before the first Slink War, when Mia was eleven years old. It had been a political move, a gesture of goodwill from Qweryn to Dayn Felesh. It was also a betrothal that had been completely forgotten in the wake of the horror that followed. Mia had died, after all.

Except, she hadn't.

Biren's greasy lips curved in a smile as he watched Via struggle with the realization.

"I'll need to know your mind on the timing of the

wedding," he said in a smug, growling tone. "I would prefer it at Felesh Keep, but if you wish to hold it in Thiara, I will consider it. I am a reasonable man."

"Biren, this isn't—"

"Duke Biren," he corrected her, showing teeth.

Via paused, fighting to come up with the correct words to navigate this. "Duke Biren," she said with effort. "You might wish to reconsider your position—"

"I do not wish to reconsider my position. I will have my bride."

"New factors have come to light."

"Such as, you have promised Mialene to another?"

Her voice caught in her throat. She should have seen this coming. Qweryn would have. He'd always been prepared for every eventuality. He always seemed to know just a little more than his opponents, and he'd managed his nobles seemingly effortlessly. Before the Phantom War, Via had considered herself a master of politics. Since then, she had spent most of her time running to catch up. She needed to be quicker, to think of these things before they happened.

"We have been through an ordeal here, Duke Biren," she said in a placating tone. "There are many pieces about which you are unaware. The Whisper Prince has arisen."

"I know about your problems, Via," he said, and his temerity at addressing her so brazenly made her stiffen. "You have sold my betrothed to another man, and you have done so publicly. You are making enemies when you should be courting friends."

"It was not my intention—"

"I spit on your intentions. I will have what is mine, one way or another."

"Do not interrupt me again, Duke Biren," she said in a cold voice. "Or—"

"Or what, Via?" he asked. "You will have one of your pet assassins slay me? Let me tell you your options, since you persist in pretending to be the new emperor. Your gates are wide open. A great many people left the city today. A great many arrived. Do you know each of them?"

She felt a chill across the back of her neck. Biren must have brought his Highblades, perhaps even soldiers from his army. How many fighters would that be? Hundreds.

"Now," he said calmly. "As I said, I am a reasonable man. I came for Mialene. You tell me I cannot have her. Very well. What other wife are you prepared to offer me?"

Via wouldn't wish this man upon a Benascan snow snake, but pretending to acquiesce could buy her time. A verbal pact behind closed doors could be undone later.

"You wish to marry Vecenne in Mialene's place," she said reluctantly, and made certain to pause, as though swallowing a bitter medicine. "Qweryn was hoping for a match in the wake of a war victory. But if this is your desire, a union between Felesh and the crown is a smart one—"

"Do you think I will meekly stand third in line behind some mongrel from the wetlands of Fairmist?" He shook his head derisively. "This is why women should not rule."

Biren's gaze fell to Via's breasts, her hips, then moved back up to her face as though appraising a horse. Via felt exposed.

She swallowed down a tight throat. It was as though she was running backward and tripping over every stone.

"You have lost a husband," Biren said. "I have lost a wife."

"I cannot—"

"Think well before you let your next words fly," Biren said darkly in his growling voice. "Think well, Via."

Marry this worm-lipped boy, the bastard son of her late husband and the Archon's wife? Via wanted to retch. Her thoughts flew to the Ringblade hidden in the shadows near her balcony. At a gesture, she could end Biren's sleazy ambitions right here. His body would never be found.

But Biren was now the most prominent noble in her empire. If he came to the palace for an audience and never emerged, even a child could deduce what had happened. Via wouldn't last another week as empress.

What standing orders had Biren's army been given? Where were his soldiers? Surely not clustered all in one convenient place. They would be spread out. Some could have a knife at the throat of each of her loyal nobles. She could not afford to swing blindly in a fight Biren had so obviously planned.

With effort, she cleared her throat. "I am honored," she said. "Allow me to give this some thought—"

"I will have your answer now. You are fond of making quick decisions, freely giving one man's wife to another when it suits you. Now you can make a quick decision for me."

She hesitated. What she needed was time, and he knew it.

"Which will it be, Via? A new husband to rule by your side? Or a war you are in no position to win?"

"Or a dagger through your eye as you stand in this room," she said.

He smiled thinly, but she could see his fear. He knew that the Ringblades answered only to the empress. He knew it was possible one could be right behind him. Biren obviously loved his fat life too much to risk it. "You could kill me," he said, trying to sound uncaring. "If you do, blood would run through the city. Is that what you want?"

"That is the last thing I want," she said softly. Of course, Biren cared nothing for her people and what they had just gone through. He didn't care about the crumbling empire. "Very well," she said. "I will take you as my husband on the seventh day of the celebration."

"No. Tonight," he said. "At the celebration."

"Brilliant," she said. "You sweep into the city and force a marriage days after my husband has been slain. Shall I claim to have fallen madly in love with you? You, a boy who could have been my son? How long do you think the Imperial Highblades will follow a nearly incestuous union under the threat of war? What kind of empire would you command? And for how long?"

Biren chewed his greasy lip. "Then you make the announcement tonight."

"Tonight, you stand at my side," she said. "Let them see you with me. It will be a small thing, but it will guide perception. Tomorrow, I will declare the union of the Felesh and Doragon houses to be celebrated side by side with the Lost Princess and the Whisper Prince, five days hence."

Biren frowned.

"Come to the royal wing tonight, an hour before the celebration," she said, then she looked him up and down. "And dress in something befitting an emperor. We will walk out together."

He hesitated. "Very well, Via," he finally said, nodding. "It shall be as you say." He went to the door, paused there, and looked back at her. "Don't make me regret my generosity. Betray me, and your children will feel the sting first, before I take this city down around your pretty ears."

"It was such a pleasure to see you, Duke Biren," she said.

He left. At a gesture from Via, the hidden Ringblade, Esylle, slipped from her concealment.

"What is your will, empress?" Esylle asked.

"We need more information," Via said. "And we need the damned Whisper Prince on our side."

"If you announce Duke Biren as the next emperor, he may as well be the next emperor," the Ringblade said. "He will seize the power he wants."

"Then we have one day to find his soldiers and render them useless."

"Yes, empress."

"Bring me Selicia."

"Yes, empress," the Ringblade said, then faded into the shadows.

Chapter 3

VIA

VIA STARED AT THE WALL after Esylle had gone, feeling vulnerable. There was only one Ringblade protector in her room, and she'd just turned her into a messenger.

She smelled the ocean breeze from the open balcony. She loved the sea. The very thought of sailing made her heart feel lighter. She'd sailed a great deal when she was a girl in Venisha, back when she wasn't bound by crushing responsibilities.

Now the thought of going back to her box of scrolls and picking out another problem made her stomach queasy. She needed a moment.

She glanced at the water clock, dripping her life away one droplet at a time. A quick nap, perhaps, to regain her composure—

A knock sounded at the door.

She let out a little sigh. "Come in," Via said.

Arendon poked his head in. "It is Lady Aylenna to see you, Your Majesty."

It took her a moment to remember who that was. There

were no nobles named Aylenna. Then it came to her. Aylenna was the daughter of Dayn's other son Bennor, the one who'd had given his life as the second Blessed. Was this the dead Archon's revenge, sending his spawn to harry her?

"Tell her I am busy," Via said. "I shall speak with her at a more convenient time."

"I did, Your Majesty. She says she has the answer to your current problem," Arendon said.

The girl was seven. No, six. What could she possibly know of court intrigue?

Via paused. Then again… She might be close enough to Biren to have overheard something, some bit of information.

"Send her in," Via said.

Aylenna entered. She wore a light green dress, short in the current fashion and belted with a white sash. Her dark hair was oiled back as the youth of Thiara wore it, with a startling lock of snow white flowing from her brow, over the top of her head and down her back. She was stunningly tall for a six-year-old. The girl could have been mistaken for twice that age!

"Your Majesty." Aylenna curtseyed.

"You have information for me?" Via asked, wanting to get through this quickly. She'd be able to tell in the first few seconds if the girl had anything of value, and she didn't have time to coddle children.

"Yes, Your Majesty." She looked over her shoulder at the closed door, as though someone might come charging after her. "My uncle has come to the city and he has brought an army with him."

Via kept her gaze on the child.

She swallowed, then swayed a little. "He came here to threaten you, didn't he? To make you…do things?"

"If you don't know more than that, child, then you have no information I can use." Via began to wonder if this was some kind of ploy by Biren himself. Send a child with false information. Discover if Via really intended to honor her word.…

"He plans to attack regardless, Your Majesty," she blurted.

"Whatever he asked of you, it was only to make you think you are safe today."

Via felt faint. It made perfect sense, to make Via believe the attack was political, something she could control, something she could slow, when in fact it was simply to make her wait while a military coup got into position. That would have taken her completely off guard. "How do you know this?"

"From his own lips, Your Majesty. I received word he was coming, and I hastened to the inn where he and his advisors are staying. It is called the Rusty Anchor." She swayed again, and this time stumbled.

"Child?" Via moved from behind the desk.

"It is nothing." Aylenna held up a pacifying hand and composed herself.

"My own Ringblades did not know Biren was here. How do you know where he is staying?"

"He sent for..." She swayed again. Her face lost its color, and her eyelids drooped. Aylenna fell. Via grabbed her hand and knelt, gathering the girl into her arms. "My tongue," Aylenna murmured. "Tastes funny...."

The girl was sweating, ashen.

"You have been poisoned," Via said. "Hold still. I will call for a healer—"

"No," Aylenna protested. "There is more...I must tell you before..." She hooked her hand around Via's neck. "It is..." she whispered, trying to muster the strength to continue. Via leaned down.

The girl's hand became a claw, yanking Via into a kiss. The girl parted Via's lips, licking her teeth and tongue.

Via yanked her head back. Fire burst through her mouth. She lurched to her feet. It was as if the girl had shoved a torch into her mouth! Her teeth burned, then her face, then her head. She heard laughter in her mind.

A presence pushed into her thoughts, and suddenly a panorama of knowledge swept through her like a prairie fire.

The empire was under attack. The powerful slink named

Kuruk and this girl, Aylenna, were puppets who served a being of staggering power: Velak. He had been conquering the empire one person at a time, and now he had snared its empress.

The fire spread throughout her, and Via fought. With every desperate ounce of herself, she fought him.

But she was only a minnow trying to fight a sea serpent.

Her audience chamber, its desk, chairs, windows, all of it vanished, and she stood in a glowing red room that she realized was the inside of her own mind. Velak stood with her, a handsome man with wide, slanted eyes and horns curling up from his brow. Fire swept all over his body. He smiled at her, then grabbed her by the throat and shoved her against the red wall.

"You are now Axika," he said in a deep, rich voice. One of the flames that flickered about his body formed into a roughly human shape, detached from Velak. It danced on the air, then leapt into Via. She screamed.

"Axika," he repeated.

"No!" Via wailed, feeling that fire take her over like an infection.

"You will be overjoyed to serve me," Velak said.

And then…the burning stopped. And Via *was* overjoyed. Happiness blossomed inside her chest, and she stopped struggling.

"Axika," she said with the same inflection Velak had used.

"That's right."

The red glare of the room faded away. Axika opened her eyes, and the empress's throne room came into focus.

She was lying on the marble floor, mere feet away from the beloved Aylenna, who did Lord Velak's bidding with staunch dedication. Axika stood up and smoothed her black dress. There was work to be done.

The Ringblade Esylle would return soon with the Ringmother. Axika must make sure nothing seemed amiss. Axika picked up Aylenna, took her into the antechamber, and laid her on the couch. On the shelf lay a long wooden box that contained a very special dagger, and Axika smiled. Yes. That would do nicely. She picked it up and tucked it under her arm. She left the antechamber—closing the door tightly so that no one would see the unconscious Aylenna—and returned to the audience chamber in time to see Esylle step out from the hidden door behind the tapestry. Selicia followed, and the Ringmother's dark gaze surveyed the room.

"Welcome Ringmother," Axika said, exactly as Via would have.

Selicia nodded.

"Thank you, Esylle," Axika said. "You may return to your post."

The Ringblade stepped back behind the shadows of the curtain.

"Biren Felesh has come for his betrothed," Selicia said to indicate that Esylle had reported the details of Via's conversation.

"And he brought his army," Axika replied frostily. "Through my city gates. It would have been nice to know that ahead of time, Ringmother."

"No army passed through the gates, Your Majesty. If Biren Felesh brought them, they were dressed as beggars or merchants. I think he is lying."

"Hmmm," Axika said, keeping up the pretense a moment longer because that was what Via would have done. She waved a dismissive hand. "What's done is done. In the end, Biren is a small concern. I will handle him. What concerns me is the Whisper Prince. His brazen disrespect cannot be tolerated."

"Grei was stubborn when he was a boy tripping over his own feet," Selicia said. "Now he is a boy with great power. He can see deceit like smoke rising from a fire, and he hates deceit. He is naive enough to believe truth should be told always, and powerful enough to try to make his point."

"Has he revealed anything to you about this Kuruk that Ree spoke of, this supposed slink lord?"

"He feels betrayed by my near capture of him. It will take time for him to confide in me again, but it can be done. He discovered a great deal, I think, during his fight with the slinks, but for now, I can only guess at what he discovered."

"And Ree?" Axika asked. This might be easy if Axika moved quickly.

"She has divided loyalties, feels a kind of kinship and indebtedness to Grei. She's been circumspect about revealing everything she learned from Kuruk, but I will get her to talk today."

There was nothing in Selicia's words or motions that indicated she knew about Lord Velak at all. That was good. But the Ringmother was far too talented at sniffing out information. When Aylenna recovered, Selicia must be the next to join Velak's ranks.

"Can you think of a way to bring the Whisper Prince to our side in time for tonight's ceremony?"

Selicia hesitated, then said, "Given time, he will see that—"

"Tonight," Axika said.

"No, Your Majesty. It will take time."

"Then he must be eliminated."

Selicia's brows came together ever-so-slightly. "Your Majesty… He is the Whisper Prince. He vanquished the Slinks. He is as powerful as…well, as a Faia. We need him. "

"You're right. We need him as a loyal friend right now." Axika shook her head. "And we absolutely cannot afford him as an enemy right now. Whichever he is, in this moment, is how we must treat him."

"Your Majesty, I advise against this."

"I know you've grown close to the boy," Axika continued. "But the empire comes first, and right now, the empire stands on a knife's edge. Tell me I'm wrong. Grei will oppose us if we use another version of the truth than that which he approves."

"Your Majesty—"

"Ringmother," Axika said in an even tone. "Tell me I'm wrong."

"I cannot."

"And we cannot hold together this city, let alone the empire, without creating a story our subjects can believe in."

Selicia did not answer.

"We must use our years of knowledge to guide and serve our subjects, even if it means deceiving them. Unless we can change Grei, right now... Unless we can make him see the necessity, then he is our enemy. The people love him. He owns the loyalty of at least one of your Ringblades, the awe of the Highblades, and the devotion of both my daughters. Wherever he goes, others fall under his sway. He is a torch poised over dry grass."

"There must be another way," Selicia said.

Axika opened the box she'd taken from the antechamber. Inside was a crude, jagged dagger. Power hummed inside it. She extended the box to Selicia.

"If there is another way, tell me," Axika said. "We cannot allow him to wander free, touching his fire wherever it suits him, and we cannot contain him. He could join up with our enemies at any moment and double their strength."

Selicia gazed at the knife, her lips set in a thin line. "This was the knife His Majesty used to slay the Faia," she murmured.

"Take this dagger and serve your empress."

Selicia looked at the dagger with no expression.

"Do you still serve the empire?" Axika asked softly.

"Yes, Your Majesty."

Axika held out the box to her.

Selicia gripped the hilt of the dagger. Axika kept the wince from her face. She could feel the dagger's hunger. That twisted metal wanted Axika's blood; it wanted Velak's. It longed to tear through magic, to rip Velak away from Via's mind and send the construct of Axika screaming back to Velakka.

"The story will be that it was Biren's assassins who robbed us of the Whisper Prince," Axika said. "Do you understand?"

"Yes, Your Majesty," Selicia's voice was a dead monotone. She stood.

"You have the day and the night to prepare. Return at sunrise with your report," Axika said. "You may go."

Selicia drew her own dagger from its sheath, laid it on the

table, then deftly sheathed Qweryn's dagger. With one last look at Axika, the Ringmother turned and went to the tapestry. There was a whisper of heavy fabric, and she was gone.

Chapter 4

VELAK

VELAK HATED HIS DEAD FATHER, may the turn of the centuries grind his bones to powder. But he hated Mother more.

When Velak had first woken to the world, he'd been connected to it like he was connected to his own heart and veins, to the fire that ran through them like liquid. He remembered clearly the day he'd emerged from Mother's body with his seven sisters, born just like a mortal. The cold air had been a shock to his wet, newborn skin. He'd banished the cold by instinctively calling upon the element of fire. It had been his first act of magic, though he hadn't known what magic was yet. He also hadn't known the difference between himself and humans, hadn't yet known he was a god.

It had become clear quickly enough, though, as Velak observed the world. He had watched for years, first understanding how the elements worked, then understanding the relationships between sky, forest, stream, and animals. Then he had intimately learned the limitations of the so-called dominant animal: humans. Next, he had tried to understand why his sisters fawned over their weak, mortal father. Finally—and Velak had spent the most time on this—Velak strove to understand why Mother doted on father.

If Velak was a god, Mother was a goddess of gods. And yet, she became a weakling when Velak's *human* father raised his voice.

Velak had watched her behavior for half a decade before he realized Mother was weak. That had stymied him. It simply hadn't made sense. He had fought the notion at first. But the more he had watched Mother, the more she had cowed to Father, the more Velak's anger had grown. Mother had refused to let Father know that Velak's sisters were his children, that Velak was also. Mother was ashamed of them, ashamed she had brought a god and goddesses into the world because some stinking Venishan mortal might turn his nose up at them!

Only out of respect for Mother had Velak stayed his hand. As his anger grew, he had wanted to kill all the humans on the continent of Devorra and have done with it, but he had continued watching. He'd convinced himself that he'd missed something. Surely there was some hidden wisdom that had escaped him. Soon, he'd understand the secret and Mother's behavior would make sense.

Then one day, Mother had come to him, distraught. She had been in a rage at Father's unwillingness to accept the ways of the Benascans. Father had declared war on the Benascans, then Mother had declared war on him. Her fury had mirrored Velak's own, and she'd commanded him to burn the city of Thiara to the ground.

Finally, he'd felt aligned with Mother. Finally, something she wanted had made sense. He'd thought maybe her preoccupation with Father had been similar to his own desire to quietly watch until he understood something in its entirety, that she'd finally seen her folly, and that she was through with Father.

With relish, Velak burned the arrogant buildings that Father and his followers had built. He laughed as he flew over the city, bringing fire down in sheets, killing any who tried to flee. He'd thought he and Mother had bonded at last.

He had been naive.

As Velak had reveled in his natural place in the world, Mother had changed her mind. She had flown up to meet Velak in the sky and commanded him to stop.

That was when Velak saw the truth. There was no wisdom in her pandering to Father. She wasn't just waiting so she could divine some secret of the lands. She was simply weak. It had galled him, and Velak's life had changed in that moment. He had spat derisively and continued burning Thiara.

Shockingly, Mother had fought him. And, to his great shame, she had bested him. Weak of the mind she might be, but weak of magic she was not. With the power of the blue roses, which she held as a carefully guarded secret, she had cast him down and humiliated him, all to protect a pile of worthless mortals.

After the battle, she had imprisoned him, locked him away for eternity.

Velak let the memory flame furiously in his mind. It was with him always. It was his guiding passion.

Flames rose around him, each forming a face that laughed or raged or babbled. They were his Velakkans, birthed from Velak's own mind to stave off madness. He'd created them by infusing bits of fire with will and intelligence, so that he would have someone to talk to. There were originally a hundred of them, each with its own name and personality. Eighty-four of them had gone into the bodies of the Blessed through an arduous spell worked by Kuruk to poke a tiny hole from Mother's lands of Devorra into Velakka, Velak's world. Then the creation of Aylenna had made Kuruk's spell irrelevant, allowing the eighty-fifth and eighty-sixth Velakkans to go directly into the Whisper Prince's brother and into the Archon with no spell at all. The eighty-seventh, Axika, had just slipped into the body of Empress Via. What a fine fit that was…

And it was one more taste of freedom. Kuruk may have failed to open a portal, but he had achieved the marvel that was little Aylenna. Seven years ago, as an experiment, Kuruk had bid the very first Blessed to return to his human wife and make a child. The spirit of Kuruk's brother Turoh had been taken from Velakka and pushed into the Blessed's unborn daughter. Nothing had happened at first. For the next five years of the child's life, Aylenna had seemed like an ordinary child. Kuruk thought he had failed and gave up the experiment. But Turoh's personality had surfaced mere weeks ago, and an unexpected wonder suddenly became possible. Aylenna could poke new holes into Velakka, giving Velak access to new bodies with just a kiss.

When Mother had first imprisoned Velak in this place, he'd tried to escape again and again, but the barrier was simply too strong. But it was weakening. And soon, even with the help of his sisters, Mother would not be able to hold it. And if Velak could somehow undermine his sisters, the entire battle would change. He'd had plenty of time to think about his first and last fight with Mother, and he would not make the same mistakes when they faced each other again.

But first, he would have to take away her allies.

Each of Velak's sisters pulled their power from different elements—some from water, some from air, some from plants, or even the earth itself. And each, except little Uriozi, had attached themselves to a haven. His sisters gave power to their havens, and the havens multiplied that power for them to use: The Jhor Forest for Pyll. Fairmist Falls for Jevare. The Valley of Lilacs for Lankoli. The Mine for Besni. Cliffpoint for Sherim. The Vheysin Forest for Deilli. And while these havens gave them power, they were also a weakness. As Mother was bound to the lands, so too were her progeny.

But the element of fire belonged to Velak. It always had, and Velak was the strongest of his siblings by far because of it. Fire was alive, a force that moved outside and inside all things. Fire was not bound to one place, and so neither was Velak. And here, trapped for a century with nothing but fire at his fingertips, Velak had learned far more about his element than Mother could guess.

There was a secret to fire, and he doubted even Mother knew it. It wasn't one element, it was two: Velak called these complementary elements the *shkat* and the *dasha*. The *shkat* was the destructive power of fire, the raging force Velak loved to wield. It could consume Pyll's Jhor Forest or lay waste to Lankoli's Valley of Lilacs. It was the only part Velak had known, and the only part he'd wielded against Mother that first time.

The *dasha* was the light of life itself, something far more subtle. At first glance, Velak had thought it weak. But the *dasha*, he finally learned, was the stronger of the two. It could overcome the inner fire of a living creature, subvert their will, and make them a slave. It could multiply Velak's hands from two to two thousand.

Velak's education about the *dasha* had begun with Kuruk and his brothers. Nearly two centuries after Velak had been imprisoned, seven Benascan boys were thrown into his realm by the arrogant magics of the human emperor called Lyndion. The mortal boys would have died instantly in the searing heat, but Velak shielded them, then pushed his divinity into them in an attempt to save them, transforming the boys. Velak saw the opportunity the instant the boys came to Velakka. They were his doorway back to Devorra.

Infused with Velak's power, the Benascan boys became similar to his Velakkans, but they retained some of their humanity, a crucial difference Velak hoped to exploit.

Velak had experimented upon them with the *dasha,* bending their minds, perfecting what he'd learned. Six of the seven boys had fallen to Velak's dominance immediately. They had been scared and malleable. The seventh, Kuruk, was not. He had questioned Velak's knowledge, fought Velak's dominance. He had made pitiful attempts to protect his brothers.

Velak had almost destroyed Kuruk in those first years, but each time his frustration rose, he'd found himself admiring the boy's strength. It reminded him of himself, standing up to greater odds and never giving in.

Their contest of wills had eventually become a working relationship. They'd raged at each other. But they had also bantered, shared ideas. Soon, they had plotted their escape.

Seven years ago, they had made their attempt. Together, he and Kuruk had ripped a rift through to Devorra, quick and fierce. Kuruk had wanted to escape with all seven of his brothers, but only he and two others had made it through before Velak's damned sisters had slammed the rift shut, trapping the remaining four brothers in Velakka.

Of course, to sell his plan, Velak had made a show of trying to force his way out with Kuruk, Malik, and Bahktish. It had been important for Mother and his sisters to believe this mad rush was intentional. And they had taken the bait.

Though Mother and his sisters had shoved Velak back into his prison, they had taken pity upon the abused Benascan boys and let them remain alive and loose in Devorra.

But Kuruk, Malik, and Bahktish were brimming with Velak's *dasha*. Their very existence on the other side of Mother's barrier created the first pinholes between Velakka and Devorra. The pinholes allowed Kuruk and Velak to communicate mind-to-mind. It also allowed Velak's plan to take shape.

The remaining four of Kuruk's brothers remained hostages to keep Kuruk working on the plan. Of course, Velak had commiserated with Kuruk that the portal had been shut. That's when he told Kuruk about the plan of creating the Debt of the Blessed, about putting pieces of Velak into Devorra one little pinhole at a time. He had assured the boy that if he helped Velak break free, Kuruk's brothers would also be freed.

And Kuruk had set to work, using Velak's lessons in use of the *dasha* to create the attack on Thiara, what the humans now called the Slink War, until he forced the emperor to accept the Debt of the Blessed. Once the humans began sending a Blessed every month, Kuruk performed the spell Velak had taught him. Kuruk created pinhole after pinhole by infusing humans with Velak's *dasha*. Gloriously, these pinholes were so small and subtle, like the *dasha* itself, that Mother did not notice. Velak's sisters did not notice. And so the Blessed had become Velak's eyes, ears, and hands in Devorra.

These Blessed blended back into society, being the filthy little humans they were, until Velak was ready to use them.

Then something unexpected happened. After seven years, Aylenna, the physical progeny of the very first Blessed, developed a startling skill. She could effect the transfer of Velak's *dasha* with just a kiss. Suddenly, the Debt of the Blessed was no longer needed. Velak need not wait a month between transfers while Kuruk recovered. With a single kiss, Aylenna could make a pinhole, could bring through another Velakkan, and her exhaustion from the process only lasted a matter of hours.

Before, Velak had been looking at years of building his Velakkan army before he could hope to threaten Mother or any of his sisters. But with these new developments, the time of his eventual escape was much closer.

And, of course, the emperor Qweryn had killed two of Velak's sisters already. Oh, each had been thrilling, fulfilling. Watching Besni strapped down and drained of her power by the blade that had been created to slay Velak. Delicious. Watching Deilli dwindle to nothing as her haven was devoured by the *shkat*.

The barrier was weaker than it had ever been, and Mother paid less and less attention. She was tired and mournful, longing to don the guise of a human, to live out her fantasy of love.

Then the damned Whisper Prince had appeared. Somehow, he had learned how to use the elemental powers. The Whisper Prince had exposed Kuruk's work and threatened Velak's. Velak had waited for Mother and his sisters to swoop down, to finally see what Velak was doing, and block him.

But they had done nothing....

Instead, the empire was left in chaos in the wake of the Phantom War. And the Whisper Prince, who could have alerted the humans to Velak's deeds...

Also did nothing. The boy had kept this crucial knowledge

to himself.

It was a delicious advantage, and Velak had no intention of wasting it. He steadied his thoughts and pushed his desires through to Axika. He watched through Via's eyes, spoke with Via's tongue, and gave the order to have the Whisper Prince slain.

Velak moved away from that pinhole to look through his new favorite pinhole, the child in Adora's belly. This bit of *dasha* was special. There wasn't much to see yet, just a warm reddish light, but this little body was going to change this fight. This child would be Velak's new form in the land of Devorra, born of his *dasha* and the royal blood of Thiara. And as its will grew, Velak would submerge himself in it like Turoh had been submerged in Aylenna. Velak would be born again into Devorra and claim what was rightfully his.

And then, dismantling the barrier would be just a matter of steps.

He just needed a little more time....

Chapter 5

GREI

GREI WOUND HIS WAY through the palace to his room in the royal wing, third floor, at the end of the hall. He opened the door and looked at the enormous chamber they'd prepared for him. The air smelled of lilacs and the humid scent of the ocean. The bed was easily four times the size of his own bed back in Fairmist. And it had curtains. What kind of bed had curtains around it? The tall, arched window looked out over the sprawling city of Thiara and its thick red wall in the distance. A balcony spread out beneath the window, for sipping tea and gazing at the sunrise or the stars, he supposed.

The left half of the room was square, with two wardrobes. Honestly, who had so many clothes that they needed two wardrobes?

The right side of the room was shaped like a half shamrock, with two round alcoves and a slanted ceiling that was supposed to give the alcoves a cozy feeling. But Grei found those dark recesses vaguely ominous. His first order of business when moving in had been to tug one of the tables out of an alcove and put it closer to the window.

That small, round table was now stacked with thick tomes. Grei let out a weary sigh, thinking of all the reading he had yet to do, then shut the door and went to the table.

According to what Grei had seen in Ree's memories, Kuruk was more than a century old. And according to histories in the royal library, an Emperor Lyndion had ruled in Thiara a century ago. Add this to the vision the Green Faia had shown Grei, of an arrogant emperor throwing Kuruk and six other children into a flaming rip in the air, and the coincidence was too conspicuous. Lyndion and Kuruk had met before.

Click...click... The pieces connected, but they didn't form a full picture. Were Kuruk and Lyndion in league together? It seemed unlikely. They were combative in the Faia's brief vision. And where did that rip in space go? Where had Lyndion tossed Kuruk and his brothers? Grei didn't know for certain, but his guess was that the Benascan boys had gone straight to the fiery dimension where Velak resided. The question was: why? At Velak's behest? Against his wishes? What was the connection? If there were secrets to be had about Kuruk, Velak, and Lyndion—a trio of immortals—then far in the past was a good place to start looking.

So Grei had spent every spare moment scouring books that dated back to the beginning of the empire. He needed to know more about Velak. If Grei could find even one mention of Velak in a written passage, it could give him the clue to illuminate this entire picture.

Grei sat down at the reading table and ran his hand across the embossed leather cover of *The Chronicles of Thiazin's Rule, Volume 6*, smearing a layer of dust. He gently opened it. Emperor Baezin, who founded the empire, had been a conqueror, and his journal writing was spotty at best. There were a few accounts of his early years, but not many. He and his empress, Thiara—after whom the empire had been named—had only ruled for a decade before Baezin's mysterious disappearance.

Empress Thiazin, their only child, had ruled for fifty years after them and—perhaps in a direct response to the frustrating lack of information about her parents—had been a prolific chronicler. She'd written down the smallest details of her rule and her personal life. In her old age, Thiazin had then become obsessed with recording the brief history of the empire before her time. According to Thiazin, Baezin had spent his rule taming wild things, which included his own Benascan wife. They'd met during Baezin's exploration of the continent, and all accounts described them as tempestuous lovers, passionate and fierce and irrevocably drawn to one another.

Grei flipped to the next page, scanning for any reference to a man or creature named Velak. He flipped to the next, and the next, and the next. When he finished that tome, he opened *The Chronicles of Thiazin's Rule, Volume 7*. It took him half the day to finish it, scanning feverishly for any mention of Velak. When he finished that, he opened the next.

He was halfway through volume eight when the sun began to set. Orange light leaked into the room. It lulled Grei, and his eyelids drooped. He blinked and tried to focus on the words, but soon, his eyes slid shut.

He jolted awake when his head hit the book, and he realized he'd fallen over. It was dark outside now, and he could hear the music and revelry of Via's celebration below. He took a deep breath, shook the sleep from his mind, and stood up.

Get the blood moving. That's the trick.

He walked briskly to the balcony, flexing his fingers to pump some life into them. The ocean air was warm and seductive. *Sleep*, it breathed.

He longed to go to that ridiculously huge bed and put his head to the pillow, let himself recover, but he couldn't. Doom hovered over him just as it hovered over every person down there obliviously dancing. He needed his strength, but he didn't dare close his eyes again. There was no time.

The empress's celebration would run long into the night. Thiaran citizens were accustomed to turning their gazes away from the distasteful, whether it was the Debt of the Blessed or the threat of another war. They were hungry for Via's pacifying lies, and it was difficult to sell truth to those who wanted lies.

Grei quailed at the thought of returning to the histories, but he could think of no quicker way to arm himself. He let out a resigned breath and whispered to the candle on the table. It happily flamed to life. He returned, sat down, rubbed his eyes, and tried to find the place he'd been reading. He didn't recall anything from the text in front of him, and was forced to flip back a few pages.

He began reading again, his eyes moving quickly over the writing, flipping the page, scanning it again, flipping the page, scanning...

There! There it was! That was Velak's name.

Grei's heart sped up, and suddenly, he was wide awake. He blinked, drew a breath, and backed up to the beginning of the page to read more carefully the words that Thiazin had carefully penned two centuries ago:

The number of my remaining days shall not outlast the year. The healer says it is my heart, and so I rush to complete my history. I've delayed chronicling this particular story for too long. I realize now that, if I'm to write it at all, I can no longer wait, and I cannot in good conscience let it be buried with my body.

Here is the truth: I am not the firstborn of my father Baezin and my mother Thiara. Of this I am now convinced. Though my mother recorded nothing, and my father not much more, his sporadic notes and my memory tell a tale that no one knows but me.

My mother was with child once before she gave birth to me, and possibly twice. Two years before I was born, she became pregnant and vanished just before she came to term, only to return later with no babe. This spurred a rare journal entry by my father, in which he raged at her.

After reading father's journal entry, it called to mind my final memories of my parents: their last argument, just before my mother vanished and my father went to look for her. I was only four years old, but I remember it vividly. It was the day before the Night of Raining Fire, when all of Thiara burned. My parents thought me asleep for my nap. But their shouting woke me, and I crept close to their door to listen.

Mother said Father had a son named Velak. He called her a liar. She screamed at him, saying he was a short-sighted fool. Father broke furniture. Mother begged him to be merciful. I stayed at the door, listening until Father went coldly silent and Mother began sobbing.

Velak, if you are the brother I never knew, I pray to the Faia that you are alive and well. I pray that you bear me no ill will for taking your rightful place on the throne. I would like to have known you—

A low scrape of stone on stone caught Grei's attention, and his head snapped up. A cool prickle spread over his scalp. Someone was in his room.

Had Kuruk finally come?

Grei forced himself to relax, and he opened his mind to the whispers. He beseeched the candle and its wide, round holder to rise in the air and float toward one of the alcoves.

Adora stepped into the candlelight. She wore a simple cotton nightdress, sky blue, thigh-length, and sleeveless, and it hugged her curves. The sight of her took his breath away. She squinted at the candle, looking for its bearer, her hands hovering at her sides.

In Fairmist, Adora and Grei had been twisted and shaped, abused and betrayed. But they had pushed through their hardships. Despite it all, Adora had emerged radiant.

"Will you toy with me, then?" she asked, squinting at the darkness.

"No," he said, bidding the candle return to the table. "I was just...dazzled," he said.

Adora turned toward his voice, finally spotting him. "You're reading in the dark?"

"Why aren't you at the celebration?" he asked.

"Because you aren't."

"How did you convince Via to let you go?"

"'Mother,'" Adora mimicked herself, dramatizing her words. "'I'm feeling a touch of fatigue from being dead. Will you please excuse me?'" She walked to his table, and he watched the curve of her smile; he watched the sway of her hips.

"She didn't tell you to visit me, though," he said.

She gave a mock curtsey. "There are hidden passages in these walls."

"I'm envisioning a Highblade outside your door, guarding an empty room."

"Two of them."

"How frustrating for them." She stopped next to him, her belly level with his face. He swallowed, looked up at her. Her nearness filled him, and suddenly he wasn't tired anymore. "You should be resting," he said. "We don't know all the effects of—"

"Have *you* slept since the Phantom War?" she interrupted him.

"A little. That first night. The people of the empire need protecting. I can sleep later. There are…" He trailed off. He'd almost started in about all of his studies, but Adora had been through too much recently. He couldn't put those troubles on her head. Not yet. Not right now. He cleared his throat. "I slept just last night."

She shook her head in disapproval. "Really, Grei? A lie?" she whispered. "From the Prince of Truth?" She said the words with a serious tone, but her smile was playful. She reached down and touched the top of his hand where it rested on the table.

He let out a breath, shook his head. "I'm sorry. I don't want to burden you."

"With what?"

"A great many things that need doing." He waved it away. "You should rest. You've been through more than me. And that's saying something."

She seemed about to speak, but instead, she pulled him gently to his feet, put her arms around him. "Grei," she said, looking up at him. "I have spent my life on what 'needed doing'. I've donned so many roles it's as though my face is just a place for one new mask after another. I have used my wits, my body, my very life to protect the empire. And now, the prophecy is done. For the first time, I am free." She paused. "And when I look in the mirror, I don't know who I am. Am I the Lost Princess the minstrels now sing about? Am I Adora the vixen bartender? Am I the prophecy's sacrifice? Am I…the betrothed of the Whisper Prince?"

He opened his mouth to speak, but she put a finger on his lips.

"Let me finish," she said softly. "I have been this shifting creature, but one thing has remained constant: From the moment I saw you, even as a child, I loved you. With no hope or agenda, I loved you. You stood over me, protected me from that slink with the rainbow eyes. You went through tortures I can't imagine…" Her gaze fell on his gloved hand. "…traveled the length of the Thiaran Empire to find me, to protect me once again." She traced his cheek with her finger. "In a life that has changed so many times I don't even know who I am anymore, I have one certainty: you. I may not know who I am, but I know who I *want* to be when I'm with you."

He glanced at the pink scar on her cheek where Selicia had kicked her, at the velvet stubble on her shaved head. She was battered by their harrowing adventures, and she was still the most beautiful woman he'd ever seen.

"Don't we deserve to be selfish?" she asked. "Can't the rest of our lives be about what *we* want, not about what 'needs doing'? Can't we run away at first light and leave everything behind, let my mother twist in the web she weaves?" Adora paused, her eyes so blue and so large in the flickering light. "You told me that one life is enough to sacrifice. You told me to save the next for myself, for *us*."

There was so much Adora didn't yet know, so much he needed to tell her.…

But this was the moment Grei had longed for. At last, he and Adora were together, wrapped in each other's arms. And did anyone else really matter? There would always be problems in the lands—let them fend for themselves. She was the one he trusted. Let the rest of the people in this slinked empire drown in their lies and their sleazy compromises. The magic he wielded opened entirely new vistas for a new life. They didn't need the empire. They could go wherever they wanted, become whatever they chose.

She was right. They'd earned the right to be selfish, and

then some. He wasn't going to bring his dark worries down on her head. In fact, why should he have to shoulder them at all? He knew what he wanted: Adora. In the morning, they'd just disappear together. Let the empire swim in its soup without him.

"Tell me you want me," she whispered. "Tell me you want to build that life with me."

"I do." His voice came out husky. She watched him, looking from one eye to the other, waiting for something. Slowly, a smile crept across her face.

"What?" he asked.

"This is the part where you kiss me," she whispered.

"Oh!"

He lifted her up, and she wrapped her legs around his waist. He kissed her, and her lips moved hungrily to his jaw, to his neck.

"I love you, Grei Forander," she whispered in his ear. "You're the only good thing in this world."

They fell to the bed, and her kisses pushed away his doubts. He would tell her everything. Soon. Tomorrow. In the morning, after they'd abandoned this place, he'd tell her everything while they rode toward a new life far away from this cesspool. When the dangers could no longer reach them, when they'd danced away from all the hands that could grab them, he'd tell her all.

Slowly, she undressed him. He pulled the thin nightdress over her head, running his hands up her sides. She leaned down and kissed him: a long, serious kiss. He laid her down on the bed.

Let us be the ocean, he thought. Rolling and crashing together, uncaring of the world around us. This night belongs to us, not to the empress. This night, and every night after.

Her tide swept him out to sea, and they left the shore far behind.

Chapter 6

GREI

GREI AND ADORA'S LOVEMAKING eventually gave way to talking. They lay in each other's arms, sweat cooling on their bodies. They spoke of common things, pretending for a moment they were normal people. He complained how he hadn't wanted to spend time with anyone in this cursed palace except her, but that ironically he'd been spending time with everyone *but* her, a long stream of people who wanted to talk to him, to make him do things for them.

She bit his shoulder playfully. "Ah, to be so needed…" she said in mock wistfulness. "It's been the opposite for me. I died. I was mourned. Now I'm back. No one seems to know what to do with me. Only Vecenne has come to visit me."

"I'm fond of your sister. Brave woman."

"She's my true family. When she looks at me, she doesn't see a political piece on her game board. She doesn't see the tragic little princess sacrificed to the slinks. She sees me. She saved me when I returned to the palace, when I was…" She hesitated. "She saw the real me. It meant everything."

"I want to hear that story."

Again, that hesitation. A dark look passed over her face like a cloud in front of the sun, but it was there and gone in an instant. Adora smiled. "That tale and many more. But…not now, okay?" She looked up at him, and her eyes were so beautiful, rich blue sparkles that shone with her soul.

"No," he said. "Only good thoughts tonight."

She smiled. "I have a good thought."

"Oh?"

"Our future life together. I had a daydream. We lived in a house," she said. "A little house. No palaces or mansions."

"I like this already. Where?"

"Near Fairmist. The Lowlands, I think. I see mist in the air, but not the big droplets inside the city proper. You're a farmer."

He laughed. "I'm a farmer?"

"With chickens in the yard."

He made a face. "Is it okay if they're something else? I don't like chickens."

"The great Whisper Prince, afraid of chickens?"

"Chickens are terrifying."

She laughed. "Fine. It could be pigs. It doesn't matter."

"Oh pigs. Good. They don't stink at *all*." He wrinkled his nose.

She pinched his side, and her voice got quiet, serious. "The point is…it was simple. Simple and lovely. We leaned on each other. We did simple things, made a life for each other. We didn't care about anything outside of our little house, and we…" She trailed off.

"We what?"

"We had a little girl. I saw her…knew her…as though she was already alive. She had your wavy brown hair, my blue eyes, and I saw her riding your shoulders, hanging onto your ponytail, laughing. And I knew we were safe. Nobody knew where we were. No one knew I was an Imperial Princess, nor that you were the Whisper Prince. It was just us. Us and our daughter. A family."

"What was her name?"

She slid her leg over his, hugged him. "I don't know."

"She didn't have a name?"

"I thought you might want to have a hand in naming our imaginary daughter."

He chuckled drowsily, and she snuggled into him. For a long time, they just lay together, holding one another. He started to drift off when she spoke softly, almost so softly he didn't hear her.

"Do you know why I love you?" she asked. Her hushed, serious tone brought him back awake. "Because you choose the right thing, Grei. No matter what I or anyone else says. No matter if you're terrified or exhausted or facing impossible odds. You never consider the easy way, only the right one."

"Maybe that's why I get beat up so much," he joked.

But she didn't let him lighten the mood. She pushed herself up on one elbow, and he could see her blue eyes in the dim light. "I need to say this," she whispered. "I spun lies for you in Fairmist because I thought it was my duty. But I want you to know the truth. I want to say to you what I've longed to say for seven years. I was torn and bleeding, beaten down and betrayed by everyone I loved when that slink emerged from the forest. *You* stood up, fought for me. *You* gave me hope when I had no hope left. I'd seen great men with great power run from their fears, but you—one small boy—stood up against impossible odds. Seven years later, you did it again. Except this time, you gave hope to everyone, not just me. Grei, we didn't need Highblades or a prophecy or an emperor. We needed you."

He didn't know what to say.

"Some say there is goodness inside every person." She shook her head. "I don't believe that. But I believe in the goodness inside you. It's the only thing I know for sure. You are what a hero should be."

She curled into him, and he hugged her fiercely. He could feel her heart beat against his chest, and he wanted to stay like this for the rest of his life.

"I love you," he said huskily.

"You're the only one I trust," she murmured. "I love you forever."

"Forever," he echoed.

Her tense body relaxed. It was as though, once she had released her words, she could rest, and as her tension slipped away, it took his troubles with it. If Adora loved him, everything else was going to be okay.

He let his mind drift, and his eyes slid shut. Exhaustion surrounded him so completely it was like he'd fallen into a deep pool with no sight or sound.

And for a time there was sweet, life-giving rest.

Then the dream took hold.

He became a child's tattered doll, tossed upon fierce winds, and he flew east along Baezin's Road to Fairmist, moving so fast his mind could not keep up. Pressure squeezed his head, and he shouted soundlessly.

Far below him, long rifts opened the earth, streaking like lightning along Baezin's Road. Fire flared upward, spilling out of the cracks and burning the earth, the trees, and the sky. The inferno raged across the land.

In the center of the maelstrom, a giant male face rose. It looked like Emperor Qweryn, but elongated. He had flaming hair, enormous eyes and horns sweeping back from his hairline. Grei shouted denial, but the fire was relentless and continued to race across the land.

Then, a thin light split the sky overhead, illuminating a blue rose hovering in the midst of the flames. Its shining presence slowed the inferno, held it at bay. But its protective power seemed fragile, like glass ready to shatter.

The fiery dream vanished, and Grei was abruptly standing in the South Forest. Adora curled near his feet, a child again, the sodden little Forest Girl. The horned and deer-faced slink that had threatened them stood mute before Grei, its long arms hanging low, gnarled knuckles almost touching the ground. Waves of rainbow color radiated from the slink, shaking the trees like they were an illusion. It seethed power, as though it could destroy Grei if it but opened its mouth to speak.

Then it did:

"Baezin and Thiara broke the world," it boomed like thunder.

The slink lowered its finger, pointing at Grei.

"You must heal it."

The invisible wind yanked him upward again, into the sky.

Grei flew north to a forest of enormous trees of ice. Before he could catch his breath, he went down, plunging into the largest of the trees like a ghost. Inside the tree was an enormous room with a group of people in thick robes, most of them old men. Grei's ghost-self veered, then slammed into the body of a beautiful blond Benascan woman. He sank into her skin like he had sunk into the white tree in the Dead Woods. He felt her body, felt the cold of the air on her skin like it was his skin. He felt the hot rush of blood in her veins like it was his blood. He heard the noise of the men talking around her, and he heard her thoughts. The woman was thinking about Blevins.

Her thoughts became his, and Grei was no more. He was a Benascan woman named Cavyn…

Cavyn felt her Beloved's death at last. He'd been hacked with swords, scorched with fire, and encased in a stone box. The Thiarans had buried him days ago, but only now did the last traces of the blue rose seep away from her Beloved's body.

His final, inaudible breath raced across the lands to her, over the Jhor Forest, across the Sere Plains, past the Thiaran war front. His death slammed into her, forcing her backward into the white wooden wall.

She dropped like a felled tree. The Council of Seven leapt to their feet, but she was barely aware of their shouts around her mortal body. Her head hit the hardwood floor with a sickening thud, and her heart stopped.

She and her Beloved were linked together, down through the centuries. When a sword pierced his body, when fire blasted into him, she felt it. When he died, so did she. She had bound herself to him because of love. Human love. Ecstasy and agony together. He had brought her higher than she could have imagined, had made her real. He had sliced her open, left her insides bright and bleeding. Forever.

Cavyn reached out a long, ethereal hand to the sacred field in Benasca that none could find but her. Her ethereal fingers were thicker than Frost Trees and longer than Baezin's Road. She reached into the field her mother had left in her care…

…and destroyed another blue rose.

Its potent essence burst through her, and she repaired the damage to her mortal flesh. Blue roses were little hearts, pumping magic through the veins of Devorra. Cavyn channeled the stolen power through herself and past herself, retracing the path of her Beloved's final breath, back to the city of Thiara. She drove that potent, life-giving blue into him.

He fought her.

"Let me die…" he begged her.

She reminded him of when she had begged, when she had opened herself, laid her heart at his feet and asked him to be merciful. She let that image linger, then took his memories of her—his memories of who he really was—and forced life into his body. The lands had bled for him. Now he could bleed for her. Forever.

Grei gasped and thrashed awake. Loud voices thundered in his mind like a crashing wave. His thoughts jammed together in his head like logs: the deer-faced slink had…sent him a dream. But there were no slinks. Not really. There was only Kuruk. And the deer-faced creature wasn't Kuruk. So…what was he? The woman, Cavyn, had the ability to bring the dead back to life with some force that Grei had never seen nor heard about. He had no idea a blue rose contained such power! And Cavyn's beloved…

…was Blevins. What did that mean? In Cavyn's thoughts, she'd mentioned they'd been linked together for centuries. She'd created an immortal, an undying man—

Adora laid a hand across Grei's tense arm, startling him.

"Grei? Are you okay?" she asked, worry in her voice. She sat up, slid her hand reassuringly across his back. Her fingers were warm, and he wanted nothing more than to turn from the bizarre dream and lose himself in her embrace.

But he moved off the bed, put his feet on the cool stone floor, and listened to the loud rush of noise in the room. He tried to make out the words, tried to understand where these overwhelming voices came from, but he couldn't. The elements of the world whispered their purpose over and over. But these voices just…sang of nothing…nothing he could understand.

Was Cavyn like Grei, another Whisper Prince? A Whisper

Princess?

"What is it?" Adora asked.

"Something's happening," he said, wincing as the voices grew louder still. Two streaks of blue light lanced into the room, piercing the north wall and shooting into the west. They crisscrossed the room and held their shape like a pulsing blue river.

"Do you see that?" he asked. He reached out a hand to touch one of the blue rivers, then stopped himself.

"It's dark, Grei, I... What are you looking at?"

She didn't see them.

"I have to follow." He grabbed the billowing pantaloons that Thiaran men used for breeches and pulled them on. "I don't have time to explain. I have to—"

"No!" she said.

Her sharp tone brought him up short. He spun around, surprised. "Adora, it's okay."

"Don't go," she said desperately, as though she was that vulnerable Forest Girl again, wretched and drenched and huddled into herself.

The bright blue river of light began to fade.

"Don't," she repeated. "Our new life... Let's start it now. Right now. Stay. Let you and me decide what happens to us next. *We* decide. Not the needs of the empire or the empress. No Ringblades or slinks or...or whispers. You and I. Together. Please."

He hesitated. The glowing river faded more with every instant. "Adora, if I don't follow it, I'll lose it. This is the piece. I need to know it, but it's only here right now. We can talk in the morning. And I promise you we'll start our new life. We'll make our decisions together." He turned to go, but she called out again.

"Grei, please..." Her voice was forlorn, like he was abandoning her.

"It's fading," he said. "Adora... It's just this one thing."

She rose to her knees, naked on the bed, her hands at her sides. "We could chase them endlessly. The next catastrophe.

The next prophecy. The next mystery…" She bit her lip. "And if that's what you want, I will do it. I'll walk those paths with you. I'll chase those mysteries, I promise. But let's decide together. You and I." She held out a hand to him. "Please."

The glowing river was almost gone. "Adora…" His dream had stirred up the pieces of this puzzle with a fierce wind. They spun all about him, and it could all make sense if he could but grab the pieces, put them together. He could make Adora safe for all time. Velak, Cavyn, the blue roses, the deer-faced slink. This last was the piece that would bring the whole picture together. He was sure of it. He stood there, frozen in indecision for a breathless moment.

"I'll return," he promised. "Minutes only."

"Grei—"

He dashed out the door.

Chapter 7

GREI

THE BLUE RIVER OF LIGHT pierced the stone walls of the palace, angling downward, through the floor. Grei leapt down the stairs, past the Highblades on watch.

"My lord—!"

"Not now."

He raced to the first level, trying to keep track of the lights, but they had started to fade, like water in a stream drying up. He raced down the hallway, swung left, then right, then left again, taking frustrating minutes to weave through the corridors until he burst into the east courtyard where he had fought Kuruk.

He gasped. A hundred streams of blue light arced over the horizon, twisting every direction as they shot into the palace walls, converging on something beyond. Something to the west, by the coast.

The air blurred. Pressure squeezed Grei's head, and the ground shook. A high-pitched keen pierced his ears, like wind blowing through a crack. His Faia-touched arm burned.

Clenching his teeth, he raced around the edge of the palace to the west, and it was deserted. It was long past Deepdark, all the revelers had gone back home. As he rounded the palace, he saw the last trickles of the light flow and disappear…

…into the royal graveyard.

Grei slowed to a walk, breathing hard, his heart beating fast.

The resting place of the Thiaran nobility was a maze of obelisks and tombs between the palace and the ocean. Rows of white marble obelisks stood like sentries, cold testament to those who had died in service to the empire. Some were statues carved in the likenesses of those buried beneath. Others were tall pyramids of stone. Still others were carved into icons to indicate the lives of the dead: swords, crowns, books, a howling cliffcat, a sea serpent on a cresting wave.

A wide canal bordered the graveyard, and Grei jogged across the bridge, then slowed to a walk, then jogged a little more. The blue streams of light were gone, but he felt a growing knot in his stomach. They'd buried Blevins in this place, and Grei was all but certain that's where the light had gone. Blevins, the beloved of some magic wielder. It staggered him. The man had been a mystery from the first moment, and the mysteries surrounding him were growing even after his death.

Grei wove through the tombstones until he reached Blevins's tomb, officially the tomb of Jorun Magnus. Grei stopped, his breathing nearly normal now. He had crafted Blevins's tomb the first day after the Phantom War, once he was certain Adora was awake and healthy. The tomb was topped with a heavy slab of marble that no one man could lift. Grei had whispered to the stone, creating raised symbols of Thiara's sun, Fairmist's raindrop, and Baezin's Blade. The actual sword had been returned to the empress to bestow on the next imperial champion. Grei felt it belonged in Blevins's resting place, but he wasn't consulted on the matter.

The cacophony of whispers vanished, leaving dead silence. It was the same kind of silence Grei always felt when he had listened to the whispers of Blevins's body.

"She's the reason you don't die," Grei murmured to himself. "Cavyn. Who is she?"

Cavyn's facility with the whispers made Grei feel like a rabbit under a crackling lightning storm. He didn't even know there was power to be had in blue roses. Bringing Adora back from the brink of death had nearly killed Grei, but Cavyn had resurrected Blevins again and again and again. How many times? Over how many years? Cavyn had said centuries.

A piece of the puzzle slammed into place.

"By the Faia..." Grei whispered as he realized what that meant.

If Cavyn had been resurrecting Blevins for centuries...she could have been resurrecting him since the beginning of the empire nearly three hundred years ago.

Click, click, click...

Thiazin's chronicle said Velak was the son of Baezin and Thiara. Baezin had been Venishan, come from across the Sunset Sea. Thiara had been Benascan, pale-skinned and blond.

Cavyn was Benascan, pale-skinned and blonde. Thiara. Cavyn.

By the Faia...

Grei's mind whirled. Could Cavyn *be* Thiara, three hundred years later? Were those two the same woman? His brain stuck on that. Humans didn't live for centuries. It wasn't possible.

Except...Emperor Lyndion had lived long past a normal human lifespan, and he was of the Thiaran royal line, descended from Baezin and Thiara. What if there was something fundamentally different about Baezin's family? Unnaturally long-lived... Or at least some of them? What if Cavyn, specifically, had brought something magical to Baezin's line?

Then the obvious struck Grei. He raced down the line of logic like beads on a string, and he gaped at the tomb in front of him. Cavyn had called Blevins her beloved.

If Grei's guess was somehow true...if Cavyn was actually the legendary Thiara...

Grei put a hand on the tombstone next to him, a carving of cliff cat, and steadied himself.

"You're Baezin," he whispered to the tomb. The emperor's champion Jorun Magnus, who had masqueraded as the drunk Blevins in Fairmist, was neither. He was Emperor Baezin, the first emperor, the founder of the empire.

There was a soft scrape and clunk inside Blevins's tomb. Grei jumped back, then marshaled his thoughts and listened for the whispers. The stone vibrated its thudding mantra: Solid. Immovable. *Stone…stone…stone…* But, as before, Blevins's body inside the tomb was silent.

Move, Grei requested of the lid he had created, and it obeyed him, sliding soundlessly aside as though the granite had become slick.

Grei! A shout burst in his mind. It was Adora's voice. He felt her emotions through the sudden connection. She was terrified, in pain. She screamed.

"Adora!" Grei spun toward the palace—

Selicia stood behind him, a slender shadow in the deeper dark of night. Her shoulder jerked, and she stabbed him in the stomach. The knife plunged deep, angled up under his ribcage. Adora's screams were cut short, replaced by a hiss.

"Selicia!" he gasped. White-hot pain filled his chest.

"I warned you," she whispered, her voice tight. "Foolish boy. Now the empire shall have to—"

A great crash jolted the Ringmother, and she let go of the dagger. Grei staggered away. He hit a headstone and spun, grappling with the hilt sticking out of his stomach. He choked. Hot blood ran down his chin. He couldn't breathe.

Get the blade out. Mend the wound, he thought.

He yanked at the dagger's hilt. Agony shot through him, but the blade didn't budge. He pitched forward, slammed into another headstone, spun again, staggered sideways, somehow managing to stay on his feet.

The dagger wouldn't come out. It wouldn't come out. Worms of fire pushed through his veins. The hissing in his head grew to a keening wind. His hands were wet with blood where they clasped the dagger.

Can't…breathe…

"Magnus!" Selicia shouted.

Grei peered back the way he'd come. Standing up in the tomb was a naked Blevins, but not the Blevins Grei had known. This was the formidable champion Grei had seen in his vision in the Dead Woods. Blevins was now a six-and-a-half foot tall muscled slayer with giant shoulders and hands that could snap a tree trunk. He towered over the Ringmother, who dropped to a fighting crouch with another dagger in her hand.

"Selicia," he hissed, lowering his head.

Selicia launched herself like a spear. Her blade should have sunk into Blevins's stomach, but he twisted, grabbed her wrist. She lashed out, striking his chin with her heel. His head snapped to the side and he dropped her, growling. She rolled gracefully to her feet, flinging a second dagger, a metal sliver in the moonlight. Blevins snatched it out of the air by the blade. He flipped it, catching the hilt.

"Where is my sword?" he growled.

Grei's mind went numb, and he stumbled backward. The whispers had vanished. He couldn't breathe. Everything was cold. So cold. He heard rushing water, mixing with the keening hiss in his head.

"You won't escape a second time, Magnus," Selicia said.

"Do I look like I'm running?" Blevins growled. He lunged at her. Her ringblade flew.

Grei tripped on the short, decorative fence around the graveyard and fell backward.

He splashed into moving water, then he sank…sank into soft darkness…

Chapter 8

ADORA

ADORA STARED AT THE DARK BALCONY, the bed sheet wrapped around her. She had tried to stop him. The moment he had flown out of bed, she'd wanted to grab his arm, make him understand… His leaving struck a kind of terror into her, like if she could just keep him in the room, just keep him from going, he would be safe. She would be safe. But she couldn't explain the doom she was feeling, and so he was gone. She'd begged him, but it hadn't been enough.

She tried to sort through her unreasonable fear, but it didn't make sense, even to her. She felt like she and Grei walked a ridge with a steep drop-off on either side, hands clasped and leaning out dangerously, each balancing the other. Below them an unknowable horror, and only if they walked the knife's edge together could they stay safe. If either one of them let go, they would both fall. The only time she didn't feel it was when Grei was near. In her skin, in her heart, in the very marrow of her bones, she knew that together—only together—they were safe.

She tried to calm herself, tried to tell herself she was being ridiculous. She distracted herself by looking around the room. This had once belonged to her brother Paryvil, who had died in the first Slink War. The austere furnishings he'd favored had been replaced with red and gold silks bordering the balcony. There were two paintings by Mochere, small figures in sweeping landscapes, always with reds and golds of the setting sun. Her mother had brought in stuffed silk chairs and a vanity with a full-length mirror. There was, of course, a small room with a bath inset in the floor. In the wake of a disaster, Mother had made readying this room a priority. She had done everything she could to make the Whisper Prince her friend.

But she didn't understand that Grei's friendship could not be bought. He didn't want opulence, didn't need comfort. He wanted truth. And he wasn't going to get that from Empress Via. She was too much like Adora's father.

Adora ran her fingers over her naked arms, breathing in the salty scent of the ocean. A hint of overripe sea fruit wafted up from the remains of Mother's celebration below.

Adora had opened up to Grei last night, had given all of herself to him. She had been vulnerable with him in a way she'd never been with anyone else. The thrill of letting go of her strict control had given her a dizzying pleasure. Not once did she think that he might betray her, not once did she put up her guard. It was just…honest. Two normal people, loving one another.

It was the way life ought to be.

Her reminiscence, like the sea fruit below, turned cloying. Yes, she'd opened to him, let her guard down with him, on all points except one.

Adora was pregnant with another man's child. And she hadn't told him. How was she possibly going to tell him?

She put a hand to her belly. The Archon Dayn Felesh's foul image rose in her mind. He'd been a liar and a manipulator, and she had been tainted by his touch, infected with his seed.

Her face went hot with shame.

When Adora began studying the prophecy under Lyndion's tutelage, she'd sworn to pay any price to save the empire. And she had stayed true to her word. She'd done her job, had followed Lyndion's orders, had given herself up as a sacrifice.

But she hadn't expected to live. Now she had a chance to look at a possible future aside from death. Now she had a chance to regret her choices, and the weight of them was crushing her. When Grei looked at her, his eyes glowed with love. He saw a dynamic, driven woman. And under his gaze, she felt like that woman, worthy and desirable. But could Grei, even as good-hearted as he was, want her once he knew the truth? Her heart seized at the thought of telling him about a baby inside her that didn't belong to him. She imagined his face twisting in disgust. That loving glow in his eyes would die, and her soul would shrivel.

And once Grei cast her aside, who would she be?

She felt the burn in her belly, a low stoking of coals that heated her blood and had begun to move outward into her arms, her legs, her chest. It was a reckoning she'd not anticipated. It was—

"You have succeeded, my daughter," a deep voice said from behind her.

Adora whirled, her heart in her throat.

"Lyndion!"

The white-haired Speaker of Baezin's Order stood in her room as though he had just appeared, his white robes like the garments of a temple keeper. How was he here? How had he sneaked past the guards?

"What are you doing here?" she demanded, thunderstruck.

"I have come at the completion of the prophecy. You saved the empire, my daughter. You have exceeded all my expectations. Did you think I would not find you, not thank you?"

His sudden statement hit her harder than she expected. She tried to push it down, but a blush crept into her cheeks. For seven years, all she'd wanted from this man was a scrap of approval. To see his smile, to see that approval all over his face, flustered and confused her.

"Well…you're welcome," she said. "Except I did not fulfill the prophecy. Grei did not sacrifice me. He said that your prophecy was broken."

Lyndion laughed. That startled her almost as much as his sudden statement. She couldn't remember him ever laughing.

"It was. *He* broke it," Lyndion said. He held up a hand in a pacifying gesture as she was about to defend Grei. "And then he fixed it," he continued. "He, too, has surpassed all of our expectations. He learned what we, in the end, did not know. But we were right about one thing."

"That he was the Whisper Prince."

"Yes," he said. "You and Grei worked together better than we could have guessed. You revealed what even the Order could not foresee. You exposed the slinks."

"Well…" She nodded, suddenly remembering she was naked except for the bedsheet clutched to her breast. She felt exposed, twisted the fabric tighter in her fist. There was a robe draped over the changing screen next to the bed, but he was between her and it. She didn't want him to see that she was uncomfortable, so she stayed where she was. "Again, you're welcome."

"I know we have been hard on you," he said. "To transform you into what was needed, it was necessary that we constantly test you. There was no room for error. I didn't dare let my compassion become a weakness in you. But at long last I can apologize for that. Please know that every single hardship you endured was a knife in my heart, but you had to accomplish the impossible. We couldn't, even for a moment, let up on you for fear of failure." He gave an apologetic look, head bowed, eyes focused on her. "But now, I need no longer be your taskmaster." He paused, then held out his arms to her. "Will you accept the hug of an old man?"

Adora blinked, then moved forward into his embrace, keeping a tight, self-conscious grip on the sheet. It was odd. For years, all she had wanted was a bit of kindness from this man. Now that she had it, it felt alien. She tried to make herself feel differently, but she couldn't.

He looked down at her. "You have earned a reward and then some. My only wish is that there was something that we, the Order, could give you for your courageous service," he said.

She didn't say anything.

"Is there anything you wish to have, my daughter?"

"No," she said finally, measuring her words. "But there is something I would be rid of."

He cocked his head, curious. "The Order's resources are formidable. Will you tell me what this thing—"

"I'm pregnant," she said. "With the Archon's child."

Lyndion narrowed his eyes, like he had when he'd first assessed her as a child. "We are in Thiara. Did you perform the Falarynne Ritual?"

The Falarynne was a spell cast upon Thiara long ago, a simple but powerful aspect of the city, and a reason for its often sensuous lifestyle. Women did not become pregnant in Thiara without the Falarynne. If a couple wished children, they performed the ritual, a simple, slow dance in specified timing. Like a key, it unlocked the Falarynne, and a child could be conceived.

"Of course not," Adora said. "I had no need of a child. Somehow the Archon circumvented the Falarynne. When I…chose to lay with him, I did so because I knew it would not make a child, not in Thiara. I thought to manipulate him, but…that didn't work.…" She wiped at her eyes, hating that she was crying in front of Lyndion. She had not shown this much weakness since the first year at the Order House. "And then, Grei returned." She cleared her throat. "There was hope for the prophecy again. I threw myself into its fulfillment, certain I would die and the pregnancy wouldn't matter, but Grei changed the prophecy. He defeated the slinks and brought me back to life, and now… Now I…"

Lyndion held her hands, watching her with compassion.

"I don't know what to do, Speaker," she said, using his honorific for the first time in years. "There is no prophecy for this."

Lyndion narrowed his eyes and, for a moment, it frightened her. He looked like he did when he was thinking of a new, rigorous test for Adora. "I see..." he mused. Then suddenly, he smiled as though he had come up with the answer. "Very well. I will take it out."

She looked up at him. "What?"

"You have saved us, Adora, and Baezin's Order takes care of its own. After your sacrifices, I would do anything to make a happy life for you."

"You can do that...? How?"

"There are ways."

Her heart leapt at the thought that she could be in Grei's arms, free, her horrible choices a part of someone else's life, floating downriver where she would never have to face them again. She could be the woman Grei thought she was. She could be the woman he deserved. "That is what I wish," she said.

"Then come with me." He stepped toward the balcony, letting go of her hand.

She blinked. "Right now?"

"The sooner you have it out, the easier it will be."

"Yes," she said, pushing past the abruptness. Yes, the sooner the better, certainly.

She went to the wardrobe and opened it, pushing through the scanty fashions that flooded the Thiaran streets. She chose a pair of riding breeches and knee-high leather boots. "Where will we go?" she asked as she changed behind the Venishan changing screen.

"Not far," he replied. "I will have you back in time for your breakfast."

"That quickly?" She emerged from behind the changing curtain, ready. Lyndion remained by the balcony.

"It is a simpler process than you might guess."

She joined him on the balcony. The lamp posts were lit in the deserted courtyard below. Lyndion placed a tiny box made of thin steel rods on the ground near the balcony's rail. She'd seen this artifact in his study at the Order House before, next to similar trinkets. She'd always wondered what it was.

"Take my hand," he said.

"Is it a spell?"

He shook his head, smiling. "Trust my directives, Adora. You were ever difficult in that regard. Let me help you. Take my hand."

Hesitantly, she reached out. His cold, bony fingers clasped hers tightly.

"Close your eyes and clear your mind," he said.

She hesitated, and he arched an eyebrow.

She closed her eyes. The whispers that had quietly filled her head since Grei had brought her back to life came faster, as though responding to something Lyndion was doing.

She opened her eyes.

A square of light nearly as tall as Adora hovered before them, bordered in glowing silver patterns. It grew up from the artifact. Outside the glowing square was the normal world. The stone rail of the balcony, the city below spotted with lamplights, the moon and stars in the dark sky overhead. But within the square was blackness.

"Lyndion! That's amaz—"

He stooped and lunged through the opening, yanking her with him. She careened into the portal and darkness enveloped her.

She stumbled on uneven ground and fell, cutting her hands and knees on the sharp rocks. She hissed, craned her neck backward. The square portal now framed Grei's room at the palace, and all around it was night sky and dark, craggy shapes. The giant moon shone down, and the stars burned bright and cold overhead.

"Where is this?" she said. Prickles of fear ran up her spine. This was not Thiara. This was nowhere near Thiara. Whispers clamored in her head, and she looked desperately for Lyndion.

He towered over her, a dagger raised high.

"No!" She scrambled backward to the portal. She almost reached it, but Lyndion seized her arm with a growl. Her foot kicked the little box, and it skittered through the portal into Grei's room. The portal vanished.

Lyndion roared his frustration and yanked her toward him.

"Lyndion, don't!"

He brutally clubbed her with the pommel of the dagger.

Pain burst in her head like he'd split her skull. She collapsed to the jagged ground, and her body felt like a sack of sand. She wanted to push away from him, but she couldn't make her legs work.

Through blurry vision, she saw him lean over her, blotting out the bright stars.

"Now, you little bitch," he said. "You're finally going to give me something of use."

The dagger came down again.

Chapter 9

ADORA

ADORA AWOKE, shivering uncontrollably. Her clothes had been stripped away. Her arms and legs had been shackled, and her naked body had been pulled tight over a cold stone slab. Each of her heartbeats was like a hammer striking her head.

Thoom, thoom, thoom!

She looked around with her right eye, but she felt the other eye flop in its socket, blind. He had cracked her skull! Terror squeezed her throat. She couldn't think.

Thoom, thoom, thoom!

She yanked against the restraints. Iron chains rattled, but held her tight.

"You're awake." Lyndion's voice came from above her. Panting, she leaned back, saw him. "You always were tougher than you looked," he said, touching her shoulder as he moved to the side of the stone slab. "Of course, you always looked like a hundred-gold-a-night courtesan. Even as a girl, you had that look." He chuckled. "You don't look like much now, though. Bald and, well..." He cocked his head, appraising her, and let his sentence hang.

"W-W-W..." she tried to speak, but her tongue lolled about, clumsy.

"You didn't need to be awake for this, just alive," he continued. "But I'm glad you'll bear witness."

"W-W-W..." She tried again, louder this time. It felt like she was chewing on a root. She couldn't form the words. She knew what she wanted to say, but her mouth didn't seem to be connected to her brain anymore.

"Ah," he said, as though he understood her. "Sometimes when the head is damaged, people lose the power of speech. I confess there might have been more passion than purpose to my blow. The crack is...impressive. I feared for a moment I had overdone it." He gave an oily smile. "Where are we? Is that what you're trying to say?"

She panted, looked past him with her good eye, to the side, searching for escape.

"We are on the Night Mountains, if you must know. This is where you'll pay me what you owe me."

She tried to shout, but it came out as, "M-M-M!"

Her strength ebbed, and she lay back against the table, struggling for breath. Warm liquid crept beneath her shoulder blades. Blood. Her blood. She craned her neck and saw that the stone was covered in it. Tears blurred her vision.

"It would have been simpler if you'd just done what I asked," Lyndion continued. "I trained you. Shemmel trained you. By the cursed Faia, *everyone* trained you, and you failed so miserably I could barely believe it. You were a waste of seven years. All I wanted was Grei to release the spell I created at the Temple, the spell the damned Faia closed down. Was that so hard?" He brought his bearded face close to hers. She tried to pull away, gasped at the pain of moving her head. "But through your glaring flaws, you always carry little gems, don't you? And this last one, well, it may make up for all of the efforts wasted on your behalf."

"P-P-P..."

He watched her like a cat watches a fish. "It's galling, really, that you would have power over my destiny, that I would have to cater to you for years only to have you fail me in the end. You and everyone else in this shuddering empire are mice. Terror of this, horror at that. Run, run, run. You're so frightened you can't see a gift right in front of you. This is no child, Adora. This is power, a seed of fiery Velakka. Do you feel that warmth?" He put a hand on her belly, pushed lightly. "Here. That is Velak himself, filling you, making you larger than the mouse you are. He is the Eighth Faia, the most powerful of all, growing inside you. And you would throw it away." He shook his head. "You don't deserve it."

"V-V-V..."

"Who is Velak?" He pulled a long knife from a sheath at his side. It had a wicked curve to it, coming to a needle point at the end. "The Faia are female, all seven of them. Except there was an eighth. Their brother, stronger than all of them combined. A god of fire, banished by the cowardly Baezin at the dawn of the empire. He is trying to return through you, and you want to throw it all away." He shook his head. "You're a mouse, Adora. Just like the rest of them."

She felt heat under his hand, deep in her womb. It responded to his touch, growing, reaching out to her extremities. The cold vanished.

"Yes," he murmured. "Bring it up. Bring it out." He said something in a strange language she'd never heard before. Then he lifted his flat palm off her skin, as though coaxing the heat to rise.

He touched the dagger to her skin, right on her belly button, then sliced her down the middle. She screamed, a guttural, ragged cry.

Grei! She fought frantically, chains rattling. *Grei!*

Lyndion dug deeper, cutting a semi-circle in the bowl of her hips.

She thrashed, her throat raw as she howled like a beast.

Red mist wafted up from the cut. Lyndion held out his fist, a ruby ring glimmering on his middle finger. The mist flowed into it.

She tried to watch, tried to fight, but her strength was gone. Her head thudded back against the slab. The sudden warmth left her, and icy cold flowed into her.

"Farewell, my daughter," Lyndion said.

"Grrrrei..." she said, and her good eye slid shut.

Chapter 10
ADORA

ADORA WAS DYING.

She felt her life sliding away. There was blood on her thighs and back and head, and she sank into it, into the slab and through it. The blood closed over her head, enveloping her arms and legs as she sank downward into a pool of red. Lyndion's mutilations no longer hurt. The pain curled into whips of light, writhing above her in the crimson sea. The only thing that burned her now was her shame. She had *trusted* Lyndion, just like she'd trusted her father and Jorun Magnus.

She shouted her rage into the sea of blood, but there was no sound. Dead women didn't make sounds, but she shouted until the sea of blood rippled.

Images flowed past her, moments from her life: Playing with Biren Felesh as a child, stomping through the waves. Mother laughing, her raven-black hair flowing in the sea breeze. Father tossing her into the air, that happy smile on his face. Father's stony face—as though he had never smiled at her in her life, as though he didn't even *know* her—when he condemned her to be the first Blessed. The Faia rescuing her from the shale slope as the slink grabbed for her. Grei standing before the horned, rainbow-eyed slink of the forest. Lyndion laying out the rules of the Order House. Grei on the Blacktale Bridge, his lips on hers. Magnus's anguished howl as he stabbed Adora through the heart. Grei's face hovering over her as she awoke from death.

Grei…

Adora had envisioned herself as a pivotal figure in history. Not known to most, of course, but having saved the lives of every citizen in Thiara. Yet that was one more lie Lyndion had fed her. He'd had his own personal, selfish reasons for sending her to die. And, in the end, nothing she had done had helped Grei defeat the slinks. It had all been Grei's actions—his decisions—that shattered the slinks' hold on the empire. From the moment Lyndion had found her—the moment Baezin's Order had set her on their insidious path—she'd been nothing but a pawn.

But she had loved Grei. That had been real. As she felt herself dying, the thought of Grei was a small warmth inside her. She regretted so many things, but she didn't regret that…

A figure coalesced in the endless blood sea. For one brief, hopeful moment, Adora thought Grei had come to save her from death again.

But it wasn't Grei.

The figure was taller, slender. He was handsome and yet…he wasn't entirely human. Horns sprouted from the edge of his hairline, curling back over his head. His straight, sharp nose was long, jutting down from his fierce brow all the way to his wide, flat mouth. His chin came to a point sharper than any person she'd ever seen. He wore armor, squares of glistening crimson metal from waist to neck. It formed to his body and flared into points above his shoulders. On his head, waves of flames formed a fiery mane that flickered down past his ears.

"You're dying, Adora," the flame-haired man said.

"Yes," she said, resigned at last to her fate. At least now she wouldn't be able to continue making horrible choices. At least here, it would end.

"Your heart has stopped. I have slowed this moment, just a little, so we may talk, but it will not last. In seconds, there will be nothing even I can do."

"You slowed my death?"

"And I can save you, if you let me."

"Who are you?"

"I am your uncle," he said.

"Uncle..." She sank deeper into the thick, red sea. The man descended with her, eager.

"Stay with me, Adora," the man said. "This brief moment is so important for us both. Something has been stolen away from each of us and, together, we might make it right. Apart, we are nothing. Apart, you will die and I will remain imprisoned."

"My uncle died in the Slink War," she said, and her words sounded slurred in her ears.

"Oh, I am your great-great-great-uncle, from long ago. Baezin's blood runs in my veins. And it runs in yours. That makes us kin."

"Who...?" she said, meaning to finish her question, but it just didn't seem important.

"My name is Velak."

"Velak..." she said it. She didn't know that name. The man looked like a slink. How could she be related to a slink? But her emotions seemed to have floated above her, mixed in with the bright whipcords of pain she could no longer feel.

"I've never heard of you." A flicker of memory rose, then faded.

"My name was erased from history, because I was betrayed by those who said they loved me. I was lied to," he said.

A slither of rage raced through Adora. "So was I."

"I know."

The memory returned. Lyndion had been talking about Velak as he killed her. An eighth Faia. "Lyndion said he wanted to free you, to use your power," she said.

Velak sneered. "Lyndion is a fool who dreams of greatness.

79

He is a liar and deceiver. He sneaks about, pretending to be something he is not. Deceivers are small, and I despise the small. My power will burn Lyndion to a cinder. When I am free, he will be the first to die."

"But you're…a slink. Like Kuruk?"

"Slinks are imaginary horrors, Adora. There is no such thing as a slink. Kuruk is just a Benascan boy I filled with power. The slinks were Kuruk's invention, a shadowy fright to force his *dasha* on the weak-willed. But I am real. The Faia keep me trapped, barred from entering your world. I need your special help to escape."

"Why would I help you?"

"Because I will never lie to you," he said. "Because together, we can both live free. If you consent to let me inside you, and if you fight to stay alive, I can heal you. I will give you the immortality I gave to Kuruk. And I will give you the power to destroy all those who ever betrayed you."

Adora felt her clarity ebbing. The red sea sucked her farther down. Velak descended with her.

"You have only seconds, Adora. Will you let me help you?" He held out his hand.

"I love Grei…" she mumbled.

"I know you do, but you cannot have him if you do not let me help you. You must let me in. You must reignite your will to live and fight! Once you do, I can fill you with fire and repair the damage Lyndion did to you. I can keep you alive."

She tried to hold onto her thoughts, but they began to fragment. She saw Grei's face superimposed over Velak's.

I love you, Grei.

Clarity came again, like a wave rolling onto the shore. This wasn't Grei.

"You want to use me," she said.

"Yes," he said.

"No."

"But you will use me as well," he said. "You have unfinished business. I will give you the power you need, the power to avenge yourself…the power Lyndion sought. I will make you so mighty no one will ever betray you again."

The red around her darkened as she sank. Her thoughts began to break apart again.

"Justice…" Velak's voice closed over her like hands, pulling at her. "You can have justice, right the wrongs that have been done," he said. "Bring Lyndion to his knees. Kiss your lover again."

"Grei…" she said. A flash of their lovemaking buoyed her up for a moment.

"Will you give me permission to join with you?" Velak asked. "Adora, we must be one in this, or it will not work, and you will die."

"I will see Grei again?"

"You will."

"Yes…" she said.

"You give me permission to join with you?"

"Yes."

Velak smiled. "Brave girl," he said. "Brave, brave girl."

"Yes..." she murmured.

He stretched toward her, becoming a red gleam, and went into her.

For a moment, there was nothing. Adora desperately wanted to sink into oblivion, but she fought it. She summoned her strength and looked upward, toward the brighter aspect of the red sea.

Light flared in the red sea, turning it orange.

"By the Faia!" she shouted, her mind and emotions burning to life.

Velak's laughter echoed everywhere, ebullient.

"By *me*!" he exclaimed.

Adora rose quickly upward through the bright red water. She broke the surface and opened her eyes.

The expansive, starry sky stretched out above her. All around her, hillocks of misshapen rocks crouched like giant, hunched figures. Before her, the sharp landscape ended in an abrupt cliff.

She sucked in a deep, shocked breath and looked down at

her body. The vicious cuts Lyndion had made were gone. She could see through both eyes. Her skull had mended.

"I've made you free of pain," Velak said inside her head. "Free of the rotting shackle of mortality."

She looked at her hands. Flickers of flame ran over them and vanished. Her nails were translucent like glass. She felt a raging fire inside her. "Free of mortality?"

"Forever."

She stood up from the bloody, rough-hewn bier Lyndion had laid her upon and walked naked to the edge of the cliff. The drop was dizzying. Dark clouds drifted below her, and the ground was so far away the Fairmist River looked like a silver thread.

"We're on the Night Mountains," she whispered.

"Yes," Velak replied. "A powerful spot for making magic. It is why your great-grandfather took you here."

"Great-grandfather?"

"Yes."

Her stomach felt sick at that.

"We have a twisted family tree," Velak said.

She touched her belly with both hands, where the core of the raging fire resided. Somehow, it didn't burn her, it made her feel...powerful.

"Lyndion is a thief," Velak said. "He always was. He captured a spark of me by ripping open your body. I have given you a bonfire."

"Thank you."

"If you want to thank me, take your vengeance," Velak said. "Make your life right. Make him suffer for what he did to you."

"Grei..." she said, looking to the west, toward Thiara.

"Yes," Velak said. "You will kiss your lover again. But first, Lyndion. He betrayed you. He betrayed your lover. Will you return to Grei with empty hands? Or would you rather return triumphant? Show him you are worthy of his love. Destroy his enemies."

"I love him," she said.

"Yes. So let us give him a present. Even now, Lyndion seeks his next victim. He is free to use others as he used you, to slice into another victim. You could save that person. What would Grei think of that?"

Adora clenched her fists, and fire blazed through her. She opened her mouth and flames roared out. It shocked her, and she stumbled back a step. Flames leapt out of her skin, rippling over her body. "What have you done to me?"

"I have given you power…" he breathed. "You are the sword that can behead the monster."

"I…" She looked down at her hand, wreathed in flame, and imagined Lyndion. She pointed at the bloody bier. A blast of fire erupted from her finger. The crude stone bier exploded in a shower of molten stone. Burning chunks rained down around her.

"Yes," Velak said. "Yesss."

"You want me to kill Lyndion," she said.

"*You* want to kill Lyndion," he corrected. "I will make it possible."

"Yes," she said.

"Everyone who has ever hurt you," he said. "Make them burn."

She turned to the edge of the Night Mountains and looked down. She saw the thread of the Fairmist River to the east, the Badlands, and the Deadwoods. She could see startlingly clear, inhumanly far, from this height. She saw Fairmist, engulfed in its white shroud of floating water droplets. "How do we get down?"

"Think of Lyndion. Think of how he hurt you."

She did, of how he had deceived a little girl, sent her to her death and, when she'd escaped that, came to gut her with a knife. Flames snapped and popped in her belly, in her chest. The nimbus of fire grew around her.

"More," he whispered.

She imagined Lyndion twisting, screaming, begging for his life as she burned him. The flames around her leapt higher.

"More!" Velak shouted.

In her mind, she incinerated Lyndion, watched his flesh turn to crumbling ash. She saw Shemmel burn as well, then all of Baezin's Order. She saw her father curling into himself as he blackened. She saw Magnus in flames.

A firestorm whirled around her.

"Now fly!" Velak shouted. "Fly! Fly!"

Adora leapt into the sky.

She streaked down, cutting the air like a meteor, and slammed into the ground with an explosion, but it did not kill her. Velak's excited laughter danced around her as she stood up in the crater she had made.

"Burn!" he said. "We will burn them all…" A picture of a thickly wooded forest with huge trees flashed through her mind. It wasn't the South Forest, where Lyndion and Baezin's Order lived, and at first Adora was confused.

"They are there," he assured her. "Our enemies are there."

Her concerns burned up in the flames of her hatred, and Adora walked toward the Jhor Forest.

Part II

The Fall of the Faia

FAHNESTOCK

Chapter 11

GREI

"WAKE, WHISPER PRINCE!" an old man hissed in his head.

White-hot pain stabbed in and out of him, leaving behind a harsh hissing that filled his ears. Grei cried out and blinked open gummy eyes. High above, a shaft of light lanced down from a triangle window, but it did nothing to illuminate the blackness. He couldn't tell where he was. It was so dark, and it smelled like dust. Where was the old man who had spoken? Or had he imagined it?

He tentatively touched his belly. The dagger was gone, and bandages had been wrapped around his middle, but his stomach was a ragged slice of agony. As he came more awake, the agony intensified so that he could barely stand it. It felt like a giant spider had burrowed into him, forcing thin, sharp legs into his veins. He clenched his teeth and bit down on a whimper.

Memories flooded him. Selicia, stabbing him. The crude dagger glinting in the moonlight. The Ringmother's impassive eyes like glittering chips of onyx. Blevins, rising like a dead emperor, grim and ready for violence.

And Adora's scream.

"No!" Grei shouted. She'd screamed in his mind. He'd left her alone, and she was suffering.

He tried to push himself to a sitting position, but the spider in his belly twisted, dragging blades through his veins.

"Stop it!" a woman commanded, loud. Thin hands grabbed him and held him still.

"Adora is hurt! She's…"

"*You're* hurt. If you move, you'll pass out again. You pass out, you die. Stop thrashing."

He stopped. The overwhelming agony receded a little.

The woman let go tentatively, as though testing to see if he'd lurch again. He reached up, grappled with her hands. One was normal; the other was as hard as wood.

"Ree," he croaked.

"Baezin's Blood, Grei…" she murmured, exasperated. "Here. Drink this." She lifted his head and put a flask to his lips. Water trickled into his mouth, and he coughed. The spider contracted its vicious limbs, and he moaned, laid his head back against the flat stone floor. He couldn't see Ree, only the bright stab of moonlight from above. That light was eerie. How could it be so bright, but fail to illuminate anything in this room?

"I can't see," he said.

"You can," Ree said. "It's just…weird in here."

"Where are we?"

"The Slate Temple."

"Slate Temple?"

"A crazy cult raised it a hundred years ago to the god Venisha, but they were run out of Thiara by Empress Lymeera. She tried to tear this place down, but the stones are immovable and hard as steel. So they abandoned it. Nobody comes here because it's… Well, it freezes the blood. Things don't work right in here. I thought it would be a good place to hide you." She cleared her throat. "Now, if you must move, do it gently. You're losing blood. The Faia only know how much you left in the canal. And wounds soaked in canal water are...never good. You might have an infection."

"I can't lie here," he said. "Adora is...hurting. She might be dying."

"*You're* dying, Grei. I bandaged you up as best I could, but you're not going to help Adora or anyone until we deal with that wound. So don't pass out. Fix it." He felt her lean near, felt the heat of her body. But he still couldn't see her.

"Selicia stabbed me," he said.

Ree went still, and he suddenly wondered if he should have told her that. Ree was a Ringblade. Would she feel obligated to finish Selicia's job?

"I saw the dagger," she whispered. "It's one of the emperor's artifacts."

"You know about those?"

She didn't respond to that. The hissing in his head was still abominably loud, and it was driving him mad. He couldn't hear the whispers of the elements around that damnable hissing.

And he couldn't work magic if he couldn't hear the whispers.

He tried not to think about how that terrified him. Without magic, he was just a boy from Fairmist, helpless all over again. If his enemies caught him like this, whatever they wanted, they'd get it.

His enemies... They were everywhere. The only person he could trust was Adora.

And yet, here Ree was...tending to him.

A new thought struck him: Selicia. The dagger. Ree to the rescue.

It was all too convenient.... Selicia had taken great pains to keep Grei alive during their journey across Thiara, even though she could have killed him. It made no sense for her to suddenly assassinate him, unless...

...unless it was part of her plan. What Selicia wanted was Grei's trust; she wanted him to follow her lead. And now that he adamantly refused to trust her—and he'd told her as much—how could she possibly find a way to turn that around?

Maybe by worming one of her Ringblades into his confidence by, say, helping him when he most needed it?

Yes. It seemed suddenly and abundantly clear. Selicia was a hardened assassin. She could have killed him instantly with that thrust.

And Ree might have been at the ready in the graveyard, ready to stage a fight with Selicia to protect him. But they hadn't counted on Blevins. No one could have expected him to rise from his sarcophagus, not even Selicia. The surprise on her face had been real.

So Ree had improvised, watched him fall into the canal, fished him out downstream, and here they were.

"Selicia stabbed you…" Ree said pensively. "Selicia doesn't miss on purpose." She echoed his thoughts.

"Ringblades *are* meticulous in their planning," Grei said. He had to get away from her. But he could barely sit up. If only he could use his magic!

"We have to get you out of Thiara, away from here entirely," Ree said.

"That sounds convenient," he replied, unable to hide the anger in his voice.

Ree paused. "Convenient?" She sounded surprised. By the Faia, they were so good at lying. It made him hate her just a little more.

"Yes. Like how you found me," he said. "Convenient."

Ree paused. "You think Selicia sent me…" she said, as though she was just piecing that together.

"I know she did. I just want to hear you say it."

"We don't have time for your suspicions, Grei. You're dying. What you think of me doesn't matter. You need to heal yourself. After that, we can play the trust game all you want."

"I'm not putting my life in your hands," he grunted. "Even if it kills me."

"Wow," she said, and she let out a little breath. "Okay. Let's play this out. First, Selicia didn't send me. But if she had, why would I help you now? Why not finish the job for her?"

"To gain my trust," he grunted. "To put me…into an

impossible situation, push me under the water until I'm almost drowning, then throw me a line."

"I see," she said flatly.

"You can spin whatever story you want—"

"Shut up," she cut him off. "If you insist on being pig-headed, then let me tell you this. I've done nothing but think about you since you healed my arm. I've done nothing but think about my place in this world. I thought being accepted back into the Ringblades would make me feel whole again, but it didn't. The Ringmother manipulated me to isolate you. She used me like…like an outsider. And when I saw the betrayal in your eyes, when I realized what I'd done, it felt like I'd lost my arm all over again. My training told me my allegiance was to the Ringblades, but my heart told me that what you're doing, what you're striving for, is the better path. So after lying there in conflict all day, I made a vow. I'm not going back to my sisters, Grei, even if they would let me. I give my oath to you. And my life."

He clenched his teeth. He'd heard this speech before from Selicia's lips outside the Dead Woods. This was exactly the same charade—playing subservient, throwing herself in front of danger. Selicia had slowly lowered Grei's guard, bit by bit, and made him believe she was a real person with real feelings. Then she'd betrayed him.

He cleared his throat. "I don't believe you," he said hoarsely.

She was silent for a moment. "That's just stupid," she said in a frustrated voice.

"Fine. I'll trust you. Let's start with this. Tell me how you found me."

She hesitated, confirming his suspicions. Then she said, "We're…connected."

"Really? How?"

"A kiss and a cut," she said, echoing her own words from a lifetime ago when she'd kissed him in the Lateral House in Fairmist. Right after her soft lips had pulled back from his, she had cut his ear with her knife. "I bound you to me."

"You used some kind of spell on me?" He'd thought it was simply a cryptic warning, Ringblade style.

"I took your blood and mixed it with mine so I could track you, to find you for Selicia. So tonight, when you were stabbed, I felt the knife go in because of our bond. I came looking."

It was a perfect explanation to make her presence here plausible. "Really?" he said flatly. "What kind of magic is that?"

"The kind we can talk about when you're not bleeding out," she said. "Will you really let yourself die to prove I'm trying to betray you? That's the most ridiculous kind of idiocy. Why don't you let me help you? You can interrogate me after."

He was starting to feel light-headed, and he hated that she was right.

"Dammit…" he said.

She put her hand to his forehead. "Hate me later. Heal yourself first. Heal this thing."

It wasn't a suggestion he could argue with. He closed his eyes, reached out, strained to hear the whispers, but all he could hear was the damnable hissing that filled his mind.

"Grei," Ree said urgently.

"I'm trying." He ignored her and tried to reach past it all, straining to catch the whispers. But the hissing was like a wall of sound. The whispers were out there; he could feel them, but he couldn't hear them.

He tried to push through the wall, imagined himself breaking it. Nothing worked. He finally gasped, opening his eyes.

"I can't…" he said.

"You can't what?"

"I can't hear the whispers."

"What does that mean?"

"I can't…use magic."

"What?" she asked incredulously.

"It's… There's something in the way." The worst of the hissing seemed to come from his left side. "Maybe it's this temple. Maybe it mutes the whispers like it sucks away the light."

He tried again, but the hiss only grew louder.

He gasped and set his head back. "We're going to have to…" He labored for breath. "Going to have to get out of here before I can do anything."

"Bad idea," she said gravely. "A normal person wouldn't even be awake. I don't even know how you're doing it. If we move you…I don't think you'll survive it."

"I'll try again." He laid there for a moment, trying to catch his breath. Breathing hurt so much; he couldn't seem to get enough breath.

He rallied his thoughts, then pushed his awareness into the hissing. This time, he didn't try to fight it, or fight his way through it. He tried to take hold of it, to draw it into himself. It was painful, and the spider of agony tightened inside him. He gritted his teeth and kept pulling. The hissing became so loud it was painful, then suddenly, he heard a voice. It wasn't the voice of the floor or the air, not the voice of any element he'd ever heard. This voice sounded ancient, like an old man rasping his words, and he could barely hear it through the hissing.

Let me help you, Whisper Prince.…

The scrape of metal on stone came from his left.

Grei gasped and let go of the struggle. Steel on stone. Steel. The dagger.

"Grei?" Ree asked. Her hand alighted gently on his shoulder.

"Ssst!" he said urgently. "The dagger. Where is the dagger?"

"Here." He heard that same scrape of steel on stone as she picked it up. "I could barely get it out of you. I thought maybe it was barbed, but it was just…tenacious."

"That's what it is. That's what's making the hissing."

"Hissing?"

"Get it away from me," he said. "Put it somewhere else. On the far side of the room."

Her soft footsteps moved away, and the hissing died down. He took a deep breath of the stale air, and he thought he could hear that creaky voice beyond the faded hissing, but he couldn't make out the words.

"Is that better?" Ree asked, suddenly right next him.

"By the Faia, yes. Give me a moment." He strained, and he managed to pick out the whispers over the hissing. But they were different now. The whispers rippled, like they were tumbling down a churning river.

He encouraged them to grow louder, trying to coax the voices from the whispers, encouraging them to define themselves. But instead of a chorus, the whispers resolved into a dissonant clash of caterwauls.

Listening to the whispers was never just listening. That was just the best way he could describe it to himself. In truth, hearing the whispers was like hearing, seeing, feeling, tasting, and touching all at once. So as the eerie voices became clearer, they also became palpable. At first, they were feathers on his skin, then they became a thousand tiny ants crawling under his skin.

He gasped. They'd never done that before.

The ants went deeper, into his muscles, into his bones, following the same path as the agony-spider's burning legs. They crawled into his chest, behind his heart, his organs. He felt them behind his eyes, crawling, searching.

His body lurched. The tiny ants tugged at his organs, at his muscles, like they were trying to create space there, trying to pull his skin from his muscles, trying to push his organs apart.

Grei envisioned grabbing the ants, harnessing them.

Heal me.

The rippling caterwauls warbled, as if confused.

Heal me. He forced the flesh, the blood, the tendons and muscles of his stomach to be as they were before he'd been stabbed, to knit together whole, just like he had beseeched his body to become flesh after Julin had turned him to stone.

When Grei had recreated his body from stone, his muscles, veins, rushing blood, bones, brain, each piece of him had a different song, and each knew what to do in concert with the others. He'd given them his request, and they had done the work. They had sung together, rising in a chorus of natural power that he hadn't had to manage.

But this time, the voices didn't work together. Each was confused. They clashed.

Do it, he demanded. *Put my flesh back the way it was.* He envisioned them sewing him up.

The discordant voices rose, and he felt that power again, but this time it felt unnatural. Like blind soldiers ordered to rush down a corridor, they slammed into each other. The magic burned through his veins, through the cut in his stomach. The burning sewed his middle like a glowing hot needle. It plunged into him, then out, again and again, lacing up the damage. Grei screamed.

"Enough!" he shouted, but his command was weak. The magic wouldn't obey him. It stabbed into him, pulled out, plunged in again…

His screams became distant, and he slammed back against the floor. He felt Ree on top of him, pushing, holding him down.

The slash of light overhead vanished, and Grei lost consciousness.

"GREI…"

He opened his eyes. The air was humid, and it smelled like wet sand. The triangle window shone overhead. He still couldn't see anything, but he was lying in a trench the shape of his body, a perfect indentation in the stone floor, and it was filled with water. He grunted and sat up. The water—if it actually was water—dripped from his hair and shoulders.

"Is this…blood?" he asked, touching his arms, putting his hands up in front of his face, but the liquid wasn't sticky.

"I think it's stone," Ree said. "Like…Faia stone turned liquid. You melted it underneath you."

"How can you tell?"

"Because I watched you do it."

"You can *see* in here?"

"I see well in the dark. Did you mean to melt the stone?"

He ignored her, put his hands to his middle. The stabbing pain was gone, but his skin felt tight, like a twisted rope, as if his torso had been spun a full turn.

"Take these bandages off." He tore at the strips of cloth.

"Stop it." She grabbed his wrists, her hands like bird talons. "You'll open the wound."

"I healed it," he said, but he felt sick. He needed to know what he'd done to himself, needed to get underneath the bandages. The spider with its hundred thin legs of slicing pain was gone…but what remained wasn't right.

She hesitated, then let go of him. He unwound the bandages and felt along his belly. The smooth skin had become ridged, hard and irregular. The ridges slanted across his middle and down to his hips. Some went straight up, becoming fibrous lumps near his ribcage. He ran shaking fingers over the new formations.

"By the Faia… What happened?" Ree whispered.

"I…" he started. "I…did it wrong." He couldn't see the damage, but his fingers told him his belly had been transformed into a ruined, ridged monstrosity. He rolled out of the watery indentation onto his hands and knees and threw up.

Ree placed a hand on his shoulder.

"Grei…"

"Give me a moment," he whispered. He struggled to stand, and she helped him. But he couldn't straighten completely. The ridges pulled tight, like there were ropes lashing his belly to his ribcage.

"You're not bleeding anymore. If you can walk, we should go," Ree said. "You shouted a lot. If anyone is near, they're coming. Let's get you somewhere you can rest. Maybe you can…" she paused, and he felt a swish of air like she was making a gesture, "…fix this."

Ree was right about one thing. He was no longer dying. He could hear the whispers, could work magic. Grei closed his eyes and tried to push down the horror of his self-maiming.

"You're right," he said. "We've wasted too much time already. Let's go. We have to find Adora."

"Find Adora…" she trailed off incredulously, then she put firm hands on his shoulders. "The only place you're going is underneath the Red Wall and far away. I'm not joking, Grei. Ringblades find people. That's what we do. And when we find them, we finish our mission. Selicia knows you fell into the canal. There's only so much of it to search, and when they don't find a corpse, they're going to search the nearby houses. And then they're going to look here."

"Then they won't be looking in the palace," he said.

"We're— What? No! We're not going to the palace. That's the last place we want to go!"

"Ree—"

"Listen to me. You weren't sneaky before you were injured. Now you're loud as a bear. Even a half-alert guard will catch you. But there won't be any half-alert guards because everyone is going to be *looking* for you. You have only one advantage right now: speed, stealth, and the fact they don't know I'm helping you. I can use all the Ringblade secrets in the city to elude them before they discover what I am doing. But it will not take long for the healers to report me missing from the infirmary. Once they do, Selicia will tell my sisters to check all the places I'd use to escape. We go to the palace, and the few advantages we have vanish."

"Adora is in trouble."

Ree made a frustrated little noise in the dark. "Please, Grei. For once in your life, listen to reason. If I can get you out of the city before sunrise, then I can return without being noticed. I can move freely through the palace in a way you cannot. I can investigate what has happened without suspicion, and the empress will look at your disappearance as another mystery of the Whisper Prince. Then, I find Adora, I bring her out. We all leave Thiara together. If I can't find her—if I need your magic—I'll come get you. We'll make a new plan. Going straight into the empress's arms right now while the Ringblades are hunting for you is suicide. You might as well stab yourself with that dagger again!"

He shook his head. "They're hurting her. I'm not going anywhere except straight to her." He shuffled forward, one hand on his belly and another in front of himself, looking for a door.

"You're so stubborn," she growled under her breath. "By the Faia, let me help you!"

"I don't trust you!" he blurted. In the dark quiet, all he could hear was his own heavy breathing. He cast about, looking for something, anything, that would indicate a door. It seemed like there were no walls in this place at all. The blackness went on forever. "Where is the door?"

"I understand why you don't trust me," she said, her voice low. "But I'm the only friend you have."

"I was wrong about…" he began. He pushed down the helplessness he felt, and the wash of emotion that crashed into him when he thought about how Selicia had saved his life, then he'd saved hers, and then she had poisoned him without a hint of regret. That moment would be burned in his memory forever. And now he had another to put with it: Selicia's cold black eyes as she shoved a dagger into him. "I can't afford to be wrong about you."

"I would give my life for you," she said softly, earnestly. "I'd do anything you ask of me. Please. Give me one more chance to prove it to you. For your sake."

He heard the *kronk* of steel against steel, and sharp moonlight spilled in through the square of the doorway with Ree's silhouette in its center. But the light still didn't illuminate anything inside this horrible temple.

Grei lunged at the doorway, and Ree stood aside. Relief rushed into him as he burst into the real world of light and houses and cobblestone streets. The Red Wall of Thiara sketched the edge of the horizon, and the looming spires of the palace rose to his left, with the seven white towers of Thiara behind it. The moon hung low in the sky, a brush stroke of white with strips of clouds sliding across it. He breathed the fresh sea air and straightened as much as he could, pulling against the strange new strands of muscle in his stomach.

He could see Ree now. Instead of her black Ringblade leathers, she wore a long-sleeved dress that nearly touched the ground—a matronly garment by current Thiaran fashion—but Ree's black boots, scuffed and road-worn, were a Ringblade's boots. The dress hung from her skinny form and was cinched around her waist like a sack on a scarecrow. She began to close the door.

"Wait," he said. "The dagger."

"Leave it," she said. "Let this cursed temple and the darkness swallow it."

"No," he said. "It's…" He didn't want the thing close to him, but he didn't want it laying around for someone else to pick up. "I have to take it with me."

"Didn't you say it fouled up your magic?"

"I can't just leave it." The threat of the dagger was barely eclipsed by the mystery it presented. Grei wanted to understand the kind of magic the emperor had used to make those weapons. He wanted to understand how the Ringblades wielded magic at all. The dagger that had wounded him might be the only key to that understanding. And that understanding might be the only key to undoing the wreck he'd made of his belly.

She sighed. "How have you not died a thousand times before now?" she muttered under her breath. She pushed open the metal door, vanished into the blackness again.

A warm breeze blew across him, but Grei shivered. Thiara had suddenly become a maze with a hundred passages, each more dangerous than the last. This morning, he'd been an imperial hero. Now he was marked for death.

The *krunk* of the door snapped him out of his reverie as Ree pushed the metal slab closed.

"Are you sure?" She held the dagger point down, the hilt wrapped in a ripped piece of her dress like she didn't want it touching her flesh.

He held out his hand, and she passed the dagger to him. The hissing in his mind rose, and the rippling whispers of the ground, the air, and the temple receded to a quiet distance, but they didn't vanish completely this time. Carefully, he slid the blade through his belt. His stomach tightened, as though his muscles sensed the nearness of the thing that had cut them.

Ree slipped her hand into his. "Now, let's get you out of the city, then I'll come back for Adora."

"No."

Her jaw clenched in frustration. "They're going to catch you. Then who will save her?"

"I left her. I shouldn't have. I'm going back to fix my mistake," he said.

"By making another?"

Adora's last words returned to him.

Let's start our new life now. Right now. Stay with me.

"She begged me to stay, Ree," he said through a tight throat. "She begged me, and I left. And now they're torturing her."

"If you really want to save her, you'll be smart," Ree said.

"Be smart and trust you?"

It was like he'd slapped her face, and her silence told him how much he hurt her. But her brows suddenly furrowed. "Fine," she spat.

He yanked his hand out of hers. "I've had my fill of Ringblade 'friends'," he said. "I don't need another. You said you'd do anything for me? Then leave me alone." He strode up the street, pressing his hand to his side as he hunched over.

Chapter 12

GREI

GREI HADN'T TAKEN FIFTY STEPS before Ree fell in alongside him, her mouth set in a stubborn line.

"I said to leave," he said.

"Well, I'm not," she said. "If you're determined to be stupid, then I have to be stupid with you. Maybe when they come to kill you, they'll get me instead." She produced a knife from somewhere and stabbed it through the edge of her dress, ripped away the bottom half of it, and exposed her legs to mid-thigh.

"What are you doing?"

"If I'm going to die tonight, it won't be because I tripped over this ridiculous thing."

She took the lead and turned down a dark alley. He hesitated, and she stopped halfway to the next block and glared at him.

He looked up the street, the way he'd been heading. Street lamps burned on either side. A short distance away, people moved, casting long shadows in the lamp light. Down the alley, he could barely see Ree. He had to admit, the alley was much better for concealment. The only problem was that he didn't know where it went.

And, of course, she did.

She waited as he struggled with his decision. He wondered what she would do if he just kept walking. Probably follow him.

And what if he was wrong? What if she really *was* trying to help him? What if she wasn't a scheming betrayer like Selicia, if she actually was what she claimed?

He thought about using the whispers to listen to her mind, to get the truth, but the horrible botch he'd done on his belly scared him. The magic had gone wild and made his body part inhuman. What would happen if he tried it again?

He clenched his fist and stalked into the dark alley toward Ree.

Without a word, she led him through darkened streets to a thick tree that blocked the moonlight. Just beyond the tree stood the low wall that surrounded the courtyards and gardens. Ree revealed concealed divots in the wall where an agile person could climb up. She helped him up and over, then followed.

They landed inside the palace garden, again obscured by head-high shrubs and bushes. Hunched over, she guided him through the maze until they reached the palace itself. Together, they crouched against the wall next to a tall, arched window.

She nodded to a shadowed place just beyond the yellow light that spilled from the window. In the shadows, a stack of small stones huddled next to a twisted, artful thorn bush. Together, they ducked underneath the window and shuffled sideways.

Ree selected four small stones from the pile and slipped them into her pouch. Behind the thorn bush, she cleared away a thin coating of dirt to reveal a stone slab. Digging along its edge with her finger, she triggered something, and the stone slid aside.

A two-foot by two-foot square hole opened up next to them, dropping into absolute darkness. She motioned him through.

He peered into it. "How far down?"

"About six feet," she said. "Hang from your fingers, and you'll touch before you drop. Go."

"Where does it lead?"

"The palace. Where you want to be. Exactly where you shouldn't be." She rolled her eyes. "Do you want to save the princess, or do you want to stay here and have a lesson in the secret passages of the Ringblades?"

Grei pressed his lips together, turned, and lowered himself into the darkness. His belly started to tighten up as he stretched, but he touched the ground before he had to let go of the lip. A moment later, Ree landed next to him. She ran her fingers along the wall, hooked on something he hadn't seen, and the slab slid shut, walling them off into absolute darkness.

"I suppose you were going to walk through the archway." Her voice floated next to him.

"Can you actually see in here?"

"No."

She took his hand and led him through the blackness.

"Then how can you move through this?" he asked.

"Math."

He started counting their steps, but in the dark, the rippling whispers slithered into Grei. Earth. Dirt. Roots. But they didn't sound like they should. It was like his head was underwater, and the whispers had to warble through the water to get to him.

The dirt floor ended at a stone step. Grei tripped, and Ree held him upright. Together, they began climbing steps in a tight spiral. It was so narrow his shoulders brushed the stone walls on either side. It stopped at a wall, and Ree put her ear to it. After a moment, she ran her hands gingerly along the wall.

A stone slab half Grei's height slid silently to the side, letting blinding torchlight into the tight spiral stairway. She went into the light and tugged him through onto a larger, wider staircase. He recognized it, had always thought of it as the "tree stair" because each ridiculously wide step held a potted tree next to the wall.

He blinked in the dim light, and she held a finger to her lips. To their right, several steps up, was the landing of the third story of the palace. Two sets of boots clomped somewhere above in a bored cadence. A patrol of Highblades.

She pointed at herself, pointed upward. Then she pointed at him, and gave a gesture that was unmistakably, "Stay!" Then she turned and slipped up the steps to the landing, her boots making no sound. Ignoring her, he followed, trying to be as quiet as she was. He turned the corner just as she padded up behind the oblivious Highblades, gaining speed. His foot scuffed the step, and one of the Highblades heard it, turned his head.

But Ree had already leapt into the air. The alerted Highblade's eyes went wide, and he drew a breath to shout, but he never got to use it. She grabbed him around the neck with both hands and used him like a pole to swing her legs around. The Highblade huffed, unable to yell through her grip. He spun off balance and Ree used the momentum to kick the second Highblade, one foot in the throat and one in the chest. He careened backward and slammed hard against the wall, his head making a sickening *thunk* against the stone. He slumped down, unconscious.

She hung on to the first Highblade, letting his staggering momentum pull her with him. She twisted around him like an eel. His legs buckled, and she landed on his stomach with her knees. The air whooshed from him, and he gaped like a landed fish.

She struck, one lightning-quick fist to his temple, and he went limp.

Her breaths came hard and fast, her thin body shook, but she recovered herself and stood up.

"Ree—"

She put a fierce finger to her lips, her eyes blazing, and she shook her head. She pointed up the hall, then to her ear.

He glanced that direction, but didn't see or hear anything.

Ree efficiently and quietly stripped one of the Highblade's

belts and removed both of their sheathed daggers. After she cinched both weapons around her skinny waist, she pointed up the hallway. She grabbed his hand, and they ran. Tendons stood out in her neck and her thin wrists. Her ribcage worked as she sprinted away.

"Slow down," Grei whispered.

Ahead, the hallway opened into a wide room filled with columns at least three feet in diameter. She crouched to conceal herself behind the closest, her body quivering.

"Ree," he whispered. "Your legs are shaking. Slow down."

She put a finger to her lips, pointed at the column as though to indicate what was on the other side, then leaned into him. "Highblades," she breathed into his ear.

He closed his eyes and let the rippling whispers grow louder. He had to do something to help—

She grabbed his arm, shocking him out of his trance. She shook her head, held up one finger, then pointed it at herself.

He mouthed the word: *No!*

She shook him again, sharply, pointed at herself again, more forceful this time.

He pointed at her quivering legs.

She gave him a withering stare. Before he could grab her, she slunk around the column. She melted to it, rested her head against it as she circled it.

She pulled two stones out of her pouch, tossed one from her left hand to her right, and moved into the center of the hallway. Her arm blurred and the first stone flew. There was the sound of rock on skull and a body crumpling.

"Hey—" the second Highblade started, but Ree's second rock was already flying. Another *klunk*. Another body falling.

Grei scrambled after her, just in time to see Ree race toward them. She slid on her knees next to them, gathered her stones, each with a starburst of blood on it, and slipped them back into her pouch.

Grei caught up with her, then knelt to check the pulses of the prone Highblades. "Are they—"

She hauled him to his feet. "Save them or save your lady,"

she whispered harshly in his ear. "You cannot do both." She pulled him across the room and into another hallway.

Ree's gaze seemed to be everywhere at once. She kept checking behind them, in front of them, the shadowy corners in the alcoves of the other doorways. In moments, she stopped at the door to Grei's room. He reached to open it, but she put a hand on his shoulder. She leaned into the doorway like it was a lover and put her ear against it. After a moment, she stepped away and ran her fingers lightly along the top of the doorjamb, then to side, then along the floor beneath the door.

"Okay," she murmured, glancing up and down the hallway again. Softly, she lifted the latch and opened the door. They went inside, closed it silently behind them.

The room was exactly as Grei had left it, the books stacked on his table, the bed rumpled. But there was no Adora.

He peered into the darkened alcoves. No movement.

"We have at least sixty seconds before the alarm is raised," Ree said in a low tone, no longer whispering. "If the Faia are with us, we may have as much as ten minutes. Be quick, Whisper Prince."

He touched the foot of the bed. The soft blanket was still indented where Adora had knelt, where she'd begged him to stay. His guilt burned.

He looked despondently around the room. He wanted to rush back into the hall, racing through the palace to Adora's room to find her sitting there, waiting for him. But deep down, he felt something horrible had happened here. She'd been taken. And it had happened only moments after he'd left. He paced around the room, searching for some sign of what might have happened.

"Tell me what you seek. Perhaps I can help," Ree said.

"I don't know. Something indicating abduction."

"Why do you assume she was taken?"

"Because I heard her scream my name."

Ree moved quietly along the wall, ran a light finger over the books sprawled on the table. Grei went into the darkened side of the room, away from the moonlit balcony. It was from these shadows Adora had emerged. He reached out, listening. What had once been whispers of stone, intoning their permanence, was now a warbling tune, coils being hit with a stick. It took him precious minutes to sort through the new sounds, but he found a passage behind the stone, the tinny clink of air behind the wall. Adora's secret passage—

"Grei," Ree said, breaking him from his train of thought.

He emerged from the shadows to find her crouched by the balcony rail. "Is this yours?" She leaned over a little metal object on the ground, but did not touch it. It looked like the skeleton of a small jewelry box, comprised only of thin spars.

He cocked his head.

"Not yours," she concluded.

"What is it?"

"A Venishan artifact," she said.

"What does it do?"

She shook her head.

He listened for whispers, but there were no whispers. Instead, a light hissing came from it.

"It's like the knife," he murmured.

"The knife isn't Venishan," Ree said. "It's one of the emperor's."

"How can you tell—?"

Ree's head snapped to the side, and she held up a hand for him to stop talking. She focused her hawk's eyes on the room's door. "Our time has run out," she whispered. "They're coming."

"That was barely more than a minute!" he complained. But she was right. Now he heard the faint rush of booted feet.

"I told you. They're on alert."

"Quick," he said. "Adora's secret door." They rushed to the darkened corner—

And pulled up short.

The small stone door was open, and a young, tiny Ringblade stood there. She had black clothes and short cropped black hair. Her narrow gaze flicked between Grei and Ree. She clenched her ringblade, which was painted black except for the glimmering edge.

"You should have fled, Ree," the little Ringblade said.

"I tried to convince him," Ree replied calmly. "He's stubborn—"

"Him, you should have gutted," the Ringblade said. "The Ringmother lies abed, unwaking, broken. They say she will not survive."

"I didn't do that," Grei said.

"Stand aside, Syvet," Ree said.

"He snapped her arms, Ree. He broke her leg." Syvet's eyes were furious, and a flush crept into the tops of her cheeks. "If she lives, she will never be the same."

"The twenty-second, Syvet," Ree said. "We serve the empire, not a personal vendetta."

Syvet showed her teeth. "You dare quote the Seventy-Seven? You are not my teacher anymore. You have forgotten the first dance and so forgotten them all. Attack me, and your betrayal is complete."

"I don't want to fight you," Ree said. "But there is more happening than you know."

"There's only one thing I needed to know, and now I do." Syvet glanced at Grei, then back at Ree, disappointed. With practiced ease, she hooked the ringblade at her side and pulled out two long, thin daggers, seemingly from the very darkness itself. "Once, you were an inspiration to us, Ree," she said. "Now you will be a cautionary tale."

The approaching booted feet finally thundered up to the door. It burst inward, splinters and twisted metal spinning to the floor. Highblades charged in, forming a wedge, short swords drawn. Empress Via strode in behind them. At her side was a tall girl in a green and white dress. The girl had dark hair and a shock-white lock at her brow.

"Well done, Syvet," Empress Via said to the Ringblade.

"Grei," Ree warned, keeping herself between him and Syvet.

"You are a slippery one," Via said to Grei, then her gaze fell on the wrapped knife he'd shoved in his belt. "That should have killed you."

Grei's mind raced, and he fought to think of a way to stop this from escalating. He didn't come up with anything. "It doesn't have to go this way," he said.

"You were too stubborn to have it any other way," Via said.

"I'm willing to talk, but you—"

"I'm sure you are. Now. But you spat in my face, Whisper Prince." She said the title with dripping sarcasm. "We'll talk when you're tied to a rack."

Grei kept his focus on Via, listening to her warbling whispers. He flicked his attention to the girl at her side, and mentally recoiled. Those weren't the whispers of a normal person. He looked at her closer. Her bearing was predatory, like an eagle about to stoop into a dive. Her gaze devoured him hungrily from behind that innocent-seeming face.

The girl came closer.

Let me see inside her, he said to the air. Let me see what she truly is. Show me! The rippling whispers grew louder.

Suddenly, the whispers became the crackle of flames.

He gasped and fell back against the wall. That same magical signature had been all over Julin and the Archon. This girl belonged to Velak!

The crackling sound of flames filled Grei's mind, and he suddenly couldn't hear anything else. Even the dagger's hissing retreated under that crackling, popping assault.

In Grei's magical vision, a flaming silhouette rose behind the girl. It had horns and eyes that glowed brightly. The sound of the flames crackled even louder, like the distance between him and the tall girl was an invisible tunnel that trapped the noise. It reverberated, increasing, louder and louder.

Stop! he demanded.

The noise of fire vanished, replaced by Ree shouting his name.

"Grei!"

He blinked. The raging whispers and the silhouette of Lord Velak vanished. Via's eyes and the eyes of the tall girl now glowed red.

"What did you do?" Ree exclaimed. "What was that flaming thing? Was that…?"

"You saw it?" Grei demanded. Even Syvet had stopped at the sudden spectacle.

"It was as tall as the ceiling! Of course I saw it. And now their eyes…" Ree said. "Did you give the empress red eyes?"

"That's not the empress," he said. "She and the girl have been taken by Velak." Ree knew *that* name. She'd seen it brightly during her time inside Kuruk's mind.

The tall girl launched herself at Grei, covering the distance in an inhuman leap, fingers extended like claws.

Ree lunged in front of him, taking the girl's attack on herself and pivoting like they were dancing. The spin was fast and tight, and Ree threw the girl at Syvet. Both Syvet and the tall girl went down in a tangle of arms, legs and dress fabric.

"Attack!" Empress Via shouted. The Highblades charged forward.

Grei whispered to the air, asking it to become a solid wall in front of the Highblades. The nearest Highblade's sword arced down, on target to behead Ree—

The blade stopped an inch from Ree's neck, clanged and rebounded backward, smacking into the man's own helmet.

The other Highblades beat against the invisible barrier. Echoes reverberated so loudly that Grei winced. The floor wobbled beneath him. The ceiling began to drip. The floor underneath Ree's feet turned to gray water, and she sank straight down like it was a pool. It closed over her head, and she vanished from sight.

"Ree!"

The warbling whispers intensified. One of the Highblades suddenly flew up into the air as if grabbed by an invisible tentacle. Another tripped and slammed into the ground. Half of the Highblades sank into the floor like Ree, but only up to their chests, then the ground hardened. The others slowed, as if the air had become thick.

The magic had gone wild again…

Beneath the cacophony of whispers, he heard that hissing. In horror, he glanced down at the jagged dagger stuffed in his belt. He'd forgotten all about it. He needed to get it away from himself.

He yanked the dagger out of his waist band and threw it at the window. It clanged against the windowsill, spun upward, then clattered onto the floor of the room.

"Noooo!" Syvet shouted.

He spun. The tall girl's hands clutched Syvet's head like they had been kissing, but even as Grei watched, the tall girl's hands went limp, and she fell away from Syvet, seemingly dead. Blood stained the tall girl's dress where Syvet's dagger protruded from her thigh.

Syvet clawed at her mouth, and her yell turned into a choked gargle. She slumped next to the inert girl.

Grei tried to piece together what was happening. Were they dead?

Then Syvet's head rose. She pushed herself to her feet and blinked. Her eyes glowed red.

The realization hit him like someone had smacked his chest. This was how Velak was infecting people. That girl was the source. She had delivered Velak's infection through a kiss. Velak was stealing bodies through *that girl*.

"Get him!" Via shrieked at her Highblades, who continued trying to find a way through Grei's barrier.

Syvet turned sluggishly toward Grei. He had to calm himself, think clearly. Now that he'd cast away the dagger, Velak wasn't the only one with magic. If Velak could push his will into people, maybe Grei could extract it like a poison.

Grei kicked Syvet in the gut, and she tumbled backward, fell again. He only needed a moment of concentration. As Syvet struggled to rise, he called upon the whispers. Now that the dagger was gone, he could hear the whispers more clearly, but they were still warbly. He concentrated on them, heightening the sound of the snapping, popping laughter inside the tall girl until that was all he could hear.

Then he pulled the crackling flames from the girl like he

was yanking tough roots out of stubborn soil. They struggled, and Grei clenched his teeth. He saw the infection as a red octopus inside the girl, writhing in his mental grip, resisting, but Grei was relentless.

You...will...obey me!

He pulled until a thick cloud of red mist seeped out and hovered over the girl's body, thin tendrils leading back to her, clinging to her like Grei's imagined octopus tentacles. With a slash of his hand, Grei beseeched the air to slice the mist away from the girl's body.

Go, he thought. Leave her.

The red mist hovered free, wobbling.

Grei let out a gasp. He'd done it! He'd sucked Velak's influence from the girl. Now he just had to do the same for Via and Syvet....

But the warbling whispers didn't stop. Like before, they reverberated, growing louder and louder. The air rippled, wobbling out and striking the far wall, then returning. He shouted and clapped his hands over his ears at the cacophony.

Syvet slammed into Grei, knocking him against the wall, which gave way like soft dough, forming around him. Panicked, he smashed his elbow across her face, then lurched out of the wall, his body dripping with rock clumps.

The wall and part of the floor shimmered like water, rippling up to his heels like he stood at the edge of a lake. Grei shuffled forward, but he couldn't go far. There was a wall to his left. To his right, Syvet had been driven to her knees. She shook her head and tried to recover her senses. In front of him, Highblades still hacked at his invisible barrier or struggled, chest deep in the floor. Via picked her way across the room, running her hands along the invisible wall and seeking its edge.

Grei's red mist puffed out in every direction. The cloud touched the nearest Highblade, who was laboriously chipping at the stone that trapped him up to his knees, and enveloped his head. He thrashed, falling onto his back, then went still.

The mist moved on, touching another Highblade with the

same effect. By the time it reached a third, the first stood up straight again. He was still trapped in the floor, but his eyes glowed red.

The mist expanded. One by one, the Highblades thrashed and went still. One by one, their eyes glowed red, and they started moving again.

"No!" Grei shouted. Reflexively, he stepped backward, and his foot went straight down into a watery part of the floor. He fell, and the floor swallowed him.

Grei closed his eyes and mouth. He had done this once with Adora when they had escaped the palace during the Phantom War, but he'd *meant* to do it that time. He'd been in control. This time, for all he knew, he would sink down a few feet and the rock would harden, suffocating him—

A hand closed over his ankle. He thrashed, fighting it.

The grip tightened and yanked, pulling him deeper into the thick liquid floor.

He dropped into open air, thumping into Ree's waiting embrace. She staggered under his weight and bore him to the floor.

"Stop struggling!" she said. She pushed him off her, rolled to her feet and peered at the dripping ceiling through which Grei had just dropped.

"Close it or they're going to follow us," she demanded.

He staggered upright. "I've done something terrible," he gasped.

"Turn the ceiling solid again or they'll follow you!" Ree demanded.

"I can't. It's not working. …" He trailed off. Two sets of boots sank through the ceiling. Highblade boots. They *had* jumped after him.

"Do it!" Ree shouted.

Then suddenly, the ceiling became hard again without Grei requesting it. The protruding legs flailed frantically for a long, grisly moment, then twitched and went still.

Shouts rose above.

"What is happening here?" demanded a voice from behind

them.

Grei and Ree spun to see Princess Vecenne in a nightgown emerge from a darkened alcove. She held a bow and a nocked arrow pointed directly at Grei, blinking her eyes as if to clear away sleep. "Prince Grei? What are you doing in my rooms?" she asked. Her gaze flicked over Ree's strange attire, the ripped dress, the daggers belted around her waist. Her target moved fluidly from Grei to Ree.

Ree flipped the dagger and grasped it by the blade, but Grei put a hand on her arm. "She's not one of them," he said.

"One of who?" Vecenne asked. She lowered her bow and cocked her head upward as the thumping above ceased. Booted feet faded away, no doubt heading for the staircase.

"They'll be here in seconds," Ree said, crossing to the balcony and looking down.

"*Who* will be here?" Vecenne asked.

"Something has happened to your mother," Grei explained quickly. "She and her Highblades have been overtaken by an entity named Velak. They're coming for me."

"Save the explanations," Ree commanded. "We're going to break legs if we jump. We need a way down."

"Where is Mia?" Vecenne demanded.

"She's been taken," he said. "I don't know where. I was trying to find out when your mother burst into my room with her Highblades."

A dozen pairs of boots thumped down distant stairs.

Vecenne looked between Grei and Ree for a breathless moment, then apparently made her decision. She strode across the room to the door, picked up a stout wooden plank and dropped it into iron slats on either side. No sooner had the bar fallen into place than those racing feet clamored to a stop outside the door. It shook as someone tried to open it.

"Open up," came the commanding voice of a Highblade. "In the name of the empress!"

Vecenne ignored the command and joined Ree at the balcony, pushing aside the curtains to reveal a full sack nestled at the base of the stone rail. The sack had a rope trailing out of it, fastened securely to one of the wide rail's pillars. She ripped the sack off and tossed the coil of rope over the balcony. It fell until the very end of it tapped the ground two stories below.

"Nice," Ree said appreciatively.

"One moment," Vecenne said calmly, going behind the changing curtain that hung in the corner of her room.

"Vecenne," Grei hissed, trying to keep his voice down. "There's no time to change clothes!"

Her voice floated out from behind the curtain. "I ran through the streets naked once, Prince Grei. I'll die before I do it twice."

The knocking became brutal thudding, as though the Highblades were striking the wood with their swords. Luckily, they didn't have an axe.

Vecenne emerged in a shockingly short amount of time, dressed in tight breeches, soft leather boots and a loose shirt made for riding. She snatched a full satchel from the side of her dresser, tossed it to Grei. He barely managed to snatch it out of the air.

"What is it?" he asked.

"Needful things," she said. Something heavy *thunked* deep into the door. Okay, maybe they *did* have an axe.

"You seem…prepared," Grei said.

"The Archon burst into my room and rendered me helpless in an instant. I was naive then," she said. "I'm not anymore."

The door shuddered with another strike.

"You first, Prince Grei," Vecenne said, nodding at the rope.

"No," he said. "I'll go last—"

"Shut up and listen to her." Ree slapped a hand on Grei's shoulder and pushed him toward the balcony. "You go. Then her. Then me."

"I will go last," Vecenne said.

"Princess—"

"That's an order, Ringblade," Vecenne said with authority. "There are things I can do in this room that may slow them.

Can you say the same?"

Ree gave a wry smile. "Yes, Your Highness." She gave a quick bow, then joined Grei by the rope. "Let's go," she said.

He swung a leg over the balcony as the door shuddered and an axe head appeared, the wood splintering around it.

"Go!" Ree shoved him. Grei began sliding down the rope.

Vecenne went to the door, nocking her bow and aiming calmly. "Mother!" she said. "What are you doing?" She put a frightened tone in her voice that hadn't been there a second ago. The thumping stopped.

"She's giving you time. Use it," Ree hissed at Grei. She leapt lightly to the rail and slid down after him.

"Vecenne, dear?" Via's voice was muffled by door and distance as Grei descended.

"Mother, what are you..." Vecenne's voice slowed sluggishly, then trailed off altogether. Grei gripped the rope, burning his hands and stopping his descent. Ree slid into him, her feet thumping onto his shoulders.

"Something's happened," Grei said. Suddenly, he quailed. The mist! The mist had come through the crack in the door! "No!" he said, his guts twisting at the idea that Vecenne had been turned. "We have to help her!"

"By the Faia, get to the ground!" Ree said, pushing on his shoulders.

Grei heard the thump as the door's bar clattered to the floor above, removed from inside the room. Vecenne was gone.

"This way," Vecenne's voice said. "They're on the balcony." The Highblades' booted feet rushed closer.

Ree drew one of her stolen daggers and sliced the rope, but not all the way. It frayed, the smaller strands snapping.

"Get down or fall!" she said, and they both slid down quickly. Grei hit the ground. The impact jarred his very bones. He half crouched, half crumpled. He fell to his side and managed to turn it into a roll that brought him to his feet. Five feet from the ground, Ree grabbed the rope tight, arresting her fall and giving the rope a fierce yank. It snapped, and she dropped the rest of the way, landing lightly on her feet. The rest of the rope fell, coiling in a haphazard pile next to her.

The first of the Highblades came into view as he slammed into the rail above, growling as he assessed the situation. Vecenne appeared beside him, bow in hand. Both of their eyes glowed red in the dark.

"Into the shadows," Ree warned. "Quickly!"

"Vecenne…" He felt sick.

Vecenne drew the bow smoothly.

Ree yanked on Grei's arm. The arrow sparked on the cobblestones where he had stood a second before. The princess nocked and drew. Ree jerked him into the shadows. Another arrow shattered on the stones just behind them.

They ran.

Chapter 13

VELAK

VELAK WAS STUNNED. A thousand faint pinholes suddenly appeared within his tiny realm, and he gaped at them. It actually took him a long moment to realize what the Whisper Prince had done. Ever before, Velak could only poke through to the land of Devorra by Kuruk's spell, cast upon a living Blessed. Velak saw these connections as tiny holes poked in the membrane of his prison dimension. Through those tiny holes, Velak could reach into Devorra, could push one of his flaming Velakkans inside the Blessed and control them.

But now, Velak could suddenly see from a thousand perspectives, each like a spyglass floating in the room where the Whisper Prince had cast his unbelievable spell.

Velak laughed. He laughed so hard that his flaming Velakkans cackled and cried for joy with him. The Whisper Prince—so recently the one rogue element that could undo all of Velak's plans—had suddenly brought those plans within immediate grasp.

Velak commanded several of the drifting pinholes to float

toward the nearest human, a Highblade hacking at the invisible wall. Velak could not move the pinholes quickly; it was like they were part of a floating mist. It took painstaking effort to force them toward the man. But after a moment, they surrounded the struggling Highblade, and Velak could see the man from a hundred different angles. With concentrated purpose, Velak sank into the man's head and eyes.

A new hole formed in the red wall of Velak's prison, sharp and clear like those of the Blessed, and Velak could feel the Highblade's fiery *dasha*.

"Durak," Velak whispered, and a dancing bit of flame came forward. "Dive," Velak said, pushing his Velakkan through the pinhole. Durak, carrying Velak's *dasha*, raged into the Highblade and dominated the man. "Free yourself," Velak commanded of his Velakkan, and Durak obeyed the order with alacrity, hacking at the stone around him with renewed ferocity.

Velak moved to another Highblade, pushed through another Velakkan and dominated him. Then another and another. He cackled with glee. His acquisition of his great grand niece, Mialene Doragon, was his master stroke. Even now, she marched north to the Jhor Forest for Velak's first reckoning with his first sister, who the humans called the Green Faia. But having Velak's *dasha* floating as a red mist, free to infect however many humans he liked, would be devastating.

Things would move swiftly now. And soon… Oh, so soon, he'd have his reckoning with Mother.

Then the Whisper Prince melted the floor and dropped through it. The boy appeared to be struggling with his connection to the elements. Velak sent the empress, the Ringblade, and the Highblades after the him. All those who'd freed themselves of the floor charged from the room, down the stairs, and to the room below.

They chopped futilely at the door until, finally, Velak's red mist caught up. He pushed it through the crack in the door and took control of Princess Vecenne.

But they were too late.

Velak gnashed his teeth when they failed to capture the Whisper Prince. The boy was unpredictable and slippery. And Mialene had an unhealthy preoccupation with him that made Velak's hold on her precarious. The best thing the Whisper Prince could do for Velak was die.

He sent a dozen Highblades into the city with orders to kill the Whisper Prince, then he settled behind the eyes of Syvet, an exciting new acquisition. Velak had longed to infiltrate a Ringblade for years, but he'd never had the opportunity. They were cagey, secretive, and tight-knit. None would ever have allowed Aylenna close enough to kiss them.

Velak spent the bulk of his attention on Mialene, but she was still making her way to the Jhor Forest, so he allowed a piece of his attention to take special interest in joining Haxx, the Velakkan he had pushed into Syvet. Haxx faded back while Velak took direct control of the Ringblade.

With Syvet as his vehicle, he returned to the Whisper Prince's room to look closely at the wild magic the Whisper Prince had unleashed. Some red mist still hung in the air. The walls and floor had solidified in rumpled, melted shapes. Fascinating. The Whisper Prince had yanked something wrapped in cloth from his belt during the battle and flung it at the window.

Syvet moved to the window and Velak recognized the dagger immediately. It was one of the crude artifacts Emperor Qweryn had made from the deaths of Velak's sister, Deilli. Syvet crouched, touched it, and felt the malice within. She kicked it away. It felt just like the accursed sword Mother had made and passed on to Father—Baezin's Blade.

Then she contemplated the second artifact. Ah, this was Venishan. A Slate Wizard's handiwork and...

No. It couldn't be....

Syvet leaned her head back and laughed with Velak's dark voice.

This was an *argarakth!*

Velak tried to listen to its whispers, but he could hear

nothing. Syvet growled Velak's frustration. Humans were deaf to the whispers of the elements, and no matter how hard he'd tried, he couldn't make them hear. It was why bonding with Mialene had been joyous. Her natural bloodline, born of Mother and Father and unlocked by the Whisper Prince, allowed her to hear the whispers, which allowed Velak to use them, to speak with the elements and, most importantly, to wield the *shkat*.

Syvet picked up the *argarakth*, and it hummed in her hand. A little image of what she must do flickered in her mind, so quickly Syvet would have missed it. Velak, of course, did not. That was the manual of instruction for the artifact, that brief flash. Only one who already knew about it, or one who was attuned to the ways of magic, would have known to look for it. The Slate Wizards of Venisha made their artifacts usable for those who were initiated, or for those who were willing to pay.

Ah... Velak thought at the image's instruction. *It's like that.*

Syvet grinned Velak's excitement. She held the *argarakth*, one hand on the bottom, one hand on the top as the flickering image had shown, and she twisted. In his mind's eye, Velak pictured the giant, frost-lined trees of Benasca, the kingdom where Mother had hidden herself away.

The box grew, and Syvet dropped it to the floor. It clattered, settled, all the while continuing to grow until it was the size of a normal doorway.

Beyond the doorway, a haze of cold hung above winter pathways of snow and crushed black gravel winding between Benasca's giant Frost Trees.

Syvet laughed again. Velak made her rise on swift legs, cross to the hanging red mist, and breathe a deep lungful of it. Turning, she sprinted back to the doorway and leapt through it onto the snow. She swiveled, snatched up the *argarakth*, and the door closed.

Her breath emerged in a fog, and Velak looked through her blinking eyes at the majesty of the Benascan capital city, Iceward. An ice-blue sky with piercing sunlight illuminated the towering Frost Trees, each three times as tall as the Thiaran

palace and as big around as a house.
    I am coming, Mother.

Chapter 14

GREI

GREI FELT SICK as Ree led him away from the palace. Vecenne had become one of them. She'd fallen to the enemy. After a block of numbly following Ree, Grei dug in his heels and skidded to a stop. "We have to go back for her."

"We will," Ree said, jogging to the end of an alley and peeking around the corner.

He looked back at the dark palace, hesitating. After a moment, he took a step back the way they'd come.

She grabbed his wrist; he hadn't even heard her cross the distance to stand beside him. She spun him around. "Don't be stupid."

"We can't just—"

She slapped him across the face, hard. He gasped, scrambled backward, and put his fists up. She stood there, hands at her sides, her eyes blazing.

"It's my fault," he said. He'd made a colossal mess of things. He'd only wanted to find Adora, and instead, he'd turned her sister over to the enemy.

"Yes," Ree said. "It is. And if you'd listened to me, none of this would have happened."

He swallowed hard. She was right.

"And it's my fault," she continued. "I took you to the palace when I knew I shouldn't, and I almost lost you. And we *did* lose Vecenne. We're not returning so we can lose more."

"You didn't have a choice. I insisted—"

She waved away his protest. "I could have knocked you unconscious and dragged you away in a sack. The next time you act like a pig-headed idiot, I will."

He was ill at what he'd done. Velak could absorb people at will now, for as long as that mist lasted. "I…I'm so sorry," he said.

"Be sorry when I get us to safety. Until then, be smart." She turned and started down the dark street again, glancing down at the bag Vecenne had given her. She rummaged through it with one hand. Giving one last, meaningful look at the looming palace, Grei followed. How was he going to undo the damage he'd done?

They quickly moved out of the wealthy part of the city, past the merchant shops and bourgeois houses, down to the Red Wall. It gleamed bloody in the moonlight, rising behind the colorful shops.

Ree took a moment to stop, pulled a cowled cloak from Vecenne's pack, and threw it to Grei.

"Put this on," she said.

He hesitated, then put it on and pulled up the cowl. In Fairmist, everyone wore cloaks. In Thiara, almost no one did. By the Faia, Thiaran Highblades walked around with only X-shaped harnesses across their chests, and women wore sashes across their breasts and skirts so short they would have been scandalous in Fairmist. Still, he didn't question Ree's motives now. More than ever, he was beginning to think her declaration in the Slate's Temple was genuine. If she'd wanted to deliver him to Selicia, letting Syvet have him in the palace would have done the job. He quietly flushed at his horrible treatment of her. She was right. If he'd just listened, Vecenne wouldn't be in thrall to Velak right now, and neither would Syvet.

"Follow me." Ree went briskly down the street for two more blocks, then stopped between a bakery with white walls and blue trim, and a pipe shop with blue walls and white trim. There was space between the two buildings, just enough for a person to fit. Ree slipped into it, and he followed. The walkway dead-ended against the Red Wall.

She knelt quickly, put her hand against the wall of the pipe shop and slowed her breathing. As she had in the Thiaran palace, she pressed herself against the wall in an almost sensual way, cheek and chest against the cool stone. Grei stood in awkward silence. The rippling whispers filled his mind, but he didn't dare use them until he figured out for certain what had gone wrong at the palace. He'd stopped the Highblades with his invisible air wall, but then the ceiling, walls and floor started dripping. How could he wield his magic with such a price behind it?

At least the hissing had gone away when he'd discarded the dagger.

Ree rapped her knuckle against the stone seven distinct times. A crack appeared in the wall, and she grasped the edges with her fingers, pulled it open. A two-foot square passageway appeared.

"It's a slide. I'll go first," she whispered. "You wait for a count of twenty-five, then follow me."

"Of course."

"Twenty-five," she emphasized. "Go later, the door will shut on you. Go sooner, and it will kill you. Understand?"

He swallowed, raised his eyebrows. "Kill me?"

"And me. There's poison down there. It's going to take me a twenty-eight count to disarm it. Once I've done it, the door will close. Count to twenty-five, then you have three seconds to slip through. Understand?"

"Yes," he whispered, tense with attention.

She watched his eyes and seemed to approve of his solemnity. She gave a ghost of a smile and held up three fingers on her wooden hand. "Twenty-five seconds to wait. Three to get through. Don't count too fast." She winked, grabbed the top of the opening, slid her body gracefully into the dark, and vanished.

Grei began counting. At twenty-five, he mimicked her movement, fell on his butt, and scooted awkwardly forward. Just as the door began to slide shut, he found the ramp and slid down so fast it felt like he was falling. He fought his panic and clamped his mouth tight on a shout of surprise.

The slide slowed, and he felt Ree's touch. She slid her fingers along his arm, found his hand, and helped him stand up.

"Can you see?" she asked.

"Not a thing."

"You're not much in the dark, are you?"

"When the whispers are working, I can 'see' just about everything."

She made a noncommittal noise. "We're going to fix that." She took his hand and led him into the dark. It was a short tunnel. No sooner had he started to adopt the rhythm of her swaying walk than she said, "Here." She took his hand and put it on a steel rung. "This is a slide, same as the way we came in, but there are rungs on either side. When you see light, climb toward it. We'll go together. I'll use the other set of rungs. They rise at an angle. Near the top, you'll almost be hanging from the ceiling. It's going to get harder the higher you go, so be ready for that."

"At an angle?"

"If you get in trouble, let me know."

He cleared his throat. "I can climb up a ladder, thank you."

"My apologies, Whisper Prince." Above, a panel slid aside, and light spilled in, illuminating the slide between them and the rungs that curled up toward the opening.

He started up. The first few were fine, but it was a constant strain on his twisted stomach muscles. By the time he'd climbed a dozen rungs, his badly sewn belly flared, painful cords yanking on his abdomen and ribcage. Each step up pulled on them.

"You okay?" Ree asked after his third grunt of pain.

"How far?" he said through his teeth.

"Ten more rungs."

"I'll make it."

"Don't fall," she said with a calm gravity that sharpened his attention.

Poison. Death.

He kept climbing. After about five more rungs, he could see a moonlit wall and a slash of the night sky through the vertical opening. He grunted at the brightness but was grateful that he was almost to the top.

His belly blazed with pain, but he forced himself up, climbing the final five rungs. Ree grabbed him and helped him though the little doorway. He gasped and rolled onto his back on a packed dirt alley, slick with moisture.

As soon as he was through, she pushed the door shut, crouched, and put her face up to it, listening. She brought her fist up and knocked seven times next to her head. The seam in the stone wall vanished.

"Secret Ringblade escape?" he asked.

"You're lying in piss," she replied.

He lurched upright even though his tortured stomach muscles spasmed their displeasure. He gasped and held his side. "Piss?"

"It's not rainwater."

Now he could smell it.

"There's a tavern one house over," she said, giving him a wry smile. "Welcome to Lowtown. Come on." She led him to the mouth of the alley, looked both ways, then nodded and crossed the street. Hunched over, he followed.

The city of Thiara on this side of the Red Wall was wholly different from the fanciful shops on the other side. The inner city boasted cobblestone streets, stone-sided canals, and sparkling towers. Here the streets were packed earth, worn with wagon tracks and cut with trenches of filth running down the center or the side. Most of the buildings were made of wood and showed great use. They had faded paint, broken boards, and mud spattering the base of their walls.

Ree stopped in front of a rundown inn. The wooden sign that hung over the door, once suspended by two rusty chains, now hung forlornly from just one.

"The Fecund Fox?" Grei said dubiously.

"I'll be right back," she said.

"I'll go with you—"

"No. You wait here." That hard, wooden hand clamped onto his arm. "I know what I'm doing."

"But, I—"

"It's far past time for you to see the importance of appearances," she interrupted. She pointed at the ridged scars on his belly, at his skeletal, charcoal-colored hand and forearm. "If I go in there with you, he'll see a shirtless, wounded man and a bedraggled woman." She gestured at her own ragged, dirt-smeared, ripped dress. In his eyes, you're weak and I'm prey. Understand? If I go in alone, unworried, two daggers strapped to my waist, he'll hesitate, ask himself questions: Why does this woman think she can wander these dangerous streets alone? Is she more dangerous than the streets themselves?"

"Weak?"

"Trust me." She winked and went inside. The weathered old door to the inn slowly shut behind her. He sighed and waited in the muddy street.

She emerged a moment later with a key, then led him down the next alley to a squat hovel with a door. Grei raised an eyebrow. "This is the room?"

"The best room they have in a place like this," she said. "But stay wary. I know how to deliver a hard stare, but we may still get a sneaky visit tonight by one of the innkeeper's friends, or perhaps the innkeeper himself."

"Has that ever happened to you?"

"A few times," she said, then she smirked.

"What?"

"There was this crazy boy in Fairmist once. Snuck into my room while I was sleeping. I was stark naked. I almost killed him."

"Hey, you weren't supposed to be there. Did anyone else ever break into your room… I mean, not at a Lateral House, but in a regular place. To…you know…"

"To rape me?" she filled in the rest of the sentence matter-of-factly. "Yes."

"What did you do?"

"I gave him a permanent limp."

"I thought a Ringblade would kill someone for such an attack."

"Well…I made sure he'll take no for an answer next time, which serves everyone a bit better. A dead man tells no tales. A man with a limp can spread the word, give others something to think about." She winked.

She put the key in the cracked door, which had pieces that had been nailed back on, as though it had been kicked down and replaced with what they could find. The handle moved, but the crooked door was stuck in the doorjamb. Ree put her shoulder into it and shoved it open.

She entered the room, and Grei came in behind her. There was a small bed in the center, leaned toward the lower right corner. The floorboards were rough and uneven. A small window with no glass looked out onto the dark street. An oil lamp sat on a tiny table near the bed, the single concession to comfort in the room. Or perhaps a concession to shady dealings that needed a modicum of light. His belly was on fire, and he was so tired it felt like his body weighed three times too much. He desperately wanted to fall over and sleep for a week.

"They won't find us here," she said. "Not tonight." She dumped Vecenne's bag onto the bed, and the contents tumbled out: a pair of soft leather shoes bound together with a string, a small knife, a map of Devorra, two silver forks, a leather bag treated with wax and cinched tight with a drawstring, a Venishan looking glass, fishing line and three hooks, a pendant with the Thiaran imperial crest, two extra bowstrings, a few jeweled baubles, a length of thin rope, and another bag that clinked when it hit the mattress.

"Oh…" Ree let out a little breath of surprise. "The princess doesn't fool about when she packs."

"Is that gold?" Grei indicated the pouch that had clinked.

She glanced at the bag. "Or silver. But I wasn't talking about that. Money is easy to come by. This…" She picked up one of the baubles, a small chunk of onyx with a cap of filigreed silver on one side. "Is not."

"What is it?"

Holding it by the silver cap, she touched the onyx to the wick on the oil lamp. A flame flickered to life. That familiar hissing sound filled Grei's mind. He flinched back, surprised, and the hissing faded.

"Another Venishan artifact," Ree said. "These are expensive. The Ringmother has one, but besides that, I've only ever seen them in the possession of wealthy Venishan merchants." She put it back with the pile on the bed.

Magical artifacts… Grei's fatigue pulled at him as if an anchor had been tied to each of his limbs, but he had to know more about these things. They were cropping up like weeds. How did one fight them? Being stabbed by that magic dagger had fouled up his magic. How could he protect himself against something like that? More importantly, how did he heal himself from this current wound?

"I never realized there were so many of these…devices in the empire," he said. "I never saw them in Fairmist." He thought about the ring he'd seen Selicia use to call her Ringblades after she'd betrayed him outside the Jhor Forest. "Do the Ringblades make these artifacts?"

She shook her head. "Venishans. It's part of their religion."

"Religion?"

"They have a number of those Slate Temples in Venisha, just like the one we were in."

He remembered the creaking, old man's whisper: *Let me help you.…*

Just thinking of it gave him a shiver and made his stomach ache. He leaned forward again, trying to ease that tightness.

"What do they worship?" He changed the subject.

"The god Venisha. And their high holy ones make these kinds of artifacts. They're called Slate Wizards."

"Can they do magic like me?"

"Any magic they have comes through their artifacts. And usually it's just little things, like this flame. I've never even heard of anyone doing what you do. Except the Faia, of course."

"Do the…uh, artifacts talk to people?"

"No." She looked at him through narrow eyes. "Why?"

"I don't know," he lied. "Just curious."

She watched him, obviously not believing his lie, but she let it pass.

Grei cleared his throat and changed the subject. "Can you burn a person with that?" He nodded at the piece of onyx.

She touched it to his hand.

The hissing in his head grew louder, and he flinched away. The moment he drew his hand back, the hissing faded.

"It won't hurt you," she said. "It's cold." She touched it to her own finger. Obviously, Ree didn't hear the hissing. "You could leave it as a paperweight on a sheaf of paper. Unless you hold it by the silver end and imagine something catching fire, it's just a rock." She held it out to him.

He hesitated, then took it. The hissing in his mind grew louder, but he was prepared this time and did his best to ignore it. The craftsmanship was intricate and delicate. Tiny foreign words had been inscribed on the silver cap wrapping the stone.

"Venishan…" he said thoughtfully. "This couldn't have been created in the emperor's workshop?" he asked, though he felt he knew the answer.

"It's Venishan craftsmanship. The few artifacts of the emperor's I've ever seen are…" She trailed off.

"Crude," he finished for her.

"Yes. And…"

"Vile," he added.

"They have a certain feel, don't they?"

"I wonder…was the emperor trying to gain the powers of a Faia by using the techniques of the Slate Wizards?"

Ree cocked her head. "That's an interesting thought."

"Maybe these Slate Wizards can create artifacts because they *do* have powers like mine."

"Maybe. But I doubt it. You manipulate the world like a Faia. The Slate Wizards don't. I don't think they could have been run out of Thiara if they had that kind of power. Also, I was one of seven Ringblades sent to search for the Whisper Prince because there *is* no other like you. No one but the Faia could shape a stick of wood into a living hand. No Venishan artifact can melt the floor into water." She tossed the chunk of onyx into the air and caught it. "Slate Wizards can light fires, send messages, create light. That kind of thing." She began putting all of the items back in the bag. "They don't bring hands back to life."

"I want to meet these Slate Wizards."

"The Slate Wizards were run out of Thiara for a reason. They're insane. All of them."

"How do you know?"

"We study Venisha." She paused. "Ringblades do, I mean. The Slate Wizards have tried to invade Thiara twice, so the Ringmother makes it a point to know everything about them. My lover spent years as a spy in Venisha. She says Slate Wizards are insane, and she suspected the process of making these artifacts warps the mind."

"She? Your lover is a woman?"

Ree gave him a sidelong smile. "You thought I only liked kissing boys?"

"Well…" He searched for words. "I didn't mean…" Her mention of kissing caused a flush to creep into Grei's cheeks, but Ree seemed thoroughly unashamed. He felt like the fumbling young man he'd been in the Lateral House when he'd first seen her stark naked, commanding, and articulate.

He cleared his throat. But he *wasn't* that young man anymore. He'd lived a lifetime since then. "Well, our kiss wasn't real anyway. I was your mission."

"One can enjoy one's work." She winked, and for a moment, he saw the wry, sexy Ringblade from Fairmist in her gaunt face.

He changed the subject. "I wonder if anyone in the empire—besides the emperor—ever created an artifact."

"The Faia," she said, moving smoothly back to business. "But not many. Mostly, they created monuments or wonders that bent the laws of nature, like the Lateral Houses, the droplets in Fairmist, the bridges, the Night Mountains."

"The Faia created the Night Mountains?" he asked.

"Who else?" she said.

Grei wasn't certain about that. After his dream about Cavyn, he was beginning to doubt the Faia were the only godlike beings in Thiara, or even the most powerful. "Maybe the Faia can't build artifacts like the Slate Wizards," he replied.

"The Faia can do anything. They're goddesses."

"What if they're not?" he asked. He felt these artifacts were important somehow in the incomplete tale of Velak, Kuruk, Cavyn, and Baezin. But he couldn't see how.

"I think you're sleep-addled," she said.

He looked longingly at the bed. She wasn't wrong about that. But he felt an urgency, like a pressure building in his mind since they had fled the palace. He'd been buffeted and blasted like a leaf in a hurricane since he'd found that written passage in Empress Thiazin's journal. He'd unearthed so many secrets in the last day. They seemed like they should all fit together, except they didn't.

He should tell Ree all the secrets. If Grei was killed, no one else would know what he'd uncovered. He glanced at her. She *seemed* to be his loyal ally, seemed to be his friend.

But Ringblades could *seem* like whatever they wanted.

She cocked her head to the side. "You want to tell me something, Grei?"

He opened his mouth to speak, and his throat constricted.

When Selicia had wormed her way into his heart, he'd been scared and lonely, just like he was now. He couldn't make the same mistake twice.

"Just…just that you look tired," he lied, and he looked at the bed. "You go first. I'll keep watch."

She chuckled. "How gallant. Are you angling for another kiss?"

Despite his fatigue, he managed to smile. "No. Your kisses are a bit sharp for my taste." He touched the notch in his ear.

"Then I shall make you a deal," she said. She put her hand against his chest and pushed him gently onto the bed. "You close your eyes and lie here for five minutes. If you can get up after that, then you take first watch and I'll sleep."

His back pressed into the lumpy mattress, and it was the softest thing he'd ever felt in his life. "Okay," he said. "I'm not going to fight you."

"That would be nice, for a change," she said.

"Wake me up in the morning," he mumbled.

"The morning is an hour away. I'll wake you when I must."

"Mmmm hmmm," Grei murmured. A final thought rose in his sleepy mind as he began to drift off. "Ree?"

"Yes, Grei."

"What is the first dance?" He murmured. "Syvet said you forgot the first dance, so you forgot them all. What does that mean?"

Ree was quiet for a moment. "We never fight another Ringblade. That's what the first dance teaches."

The silence stretched. "I'm sorry, Ree."

"I have chosen my path. Sleep now, Grei."

Chapter 15

GREI

The slink from the South Forest met Grei the moment he fell asleep. As before, it stood amidst the same trees it had the fateful day Grei had risen to protect the Forest Girl.

"Who are you?" Grei shouted. This couldn't actually be a slink, like he'd always thought. Slinks were creations of Kuruk's imagination. They didn't actually exist. This was something else, and he struggled to wrap his mind around its agenda.

The thing lowered its mismatched antlers and pointed its overly long, shaggy arm at him. Rainbow colors rippled across the air toward Grei.

The dream took him immediately. This time, he saw through Adora's eyes, not Cavyn's, but it wasn't the Adora he knew. Flame flickered over her body, and her hair was a bonfire.

THE GREEN FAIA CRINGED beneath Adora's wrath. Flames rippled over Adora in sheets of orange, one after the other, and her eyes glowed red.

She pointed a finger at the Green Faia, who scrambled backward like a squirrel. The little goddess leapt into the air, her green dress flaring. She landed on the lowest branch of a giant tree, but the limbs above her burned. The trees all around her burned. She had nowhere to go.

"Call them," Adora growled, and it wasn't her voice any more than it was her body. "Call out to them. Bring your sisters to help you."

The little Faia clenched her fists, and the air rippled. The ripples flowed into Adora: one, two, three... Each shoved her back a step, then she hesitated. The snarl left her face, and suddenly she looked disoriented.

"Wait," Adora said in a soft voice, her real voice. She held up her hand as though she was blind, reaching out for something solid. "This is..."

But then her head drooped like someone had cut her neck muscles. When it came back up, her lips bent into a thin smile that Grei had never seen before.

"That might have worked," she growled, "in another life. On some other mortal's body. But she's a Doragon. Our niece, sister. And she welcomed me in."

The Green Faia wilted, and she looked sadder than anyone Grei had ever seen. She leapt to another branch, landing as lightly as a butterfly, but the branch was already on fire. Grei could not feel the heat, but the air shimmered with it. Wolves howled in the distance, desperate, frightened.

The Faia concentrated, and her face took on the same expression she'd worn when she'd talked to Grei mind-to-mind.

"No," Adora replied in her growling voice. "Nothing you can say— nothing you can do—will stay my wrath. There is no concession you can make to me, no promise. What I want from you, dear sister, is everything. I want your life. Your forest. I want to claim every poisoned whisper you've spoken to the lands, every beast you've engorged with your power, every waft of strength you've pushed into these trees. I will take it all from you, just as you took them all from me."

Adora pointed, and the Green Faia leapt away—

—right into the lance of fire shot from Adora's other hand. The Green Faia contorted in mid-air, but the blast caught her. Her gossamer wings burned away in a flash. She hit the ground, arching in pain and struggling to touch the glowing nubs on her back.

"No!" Grei shouted, but neither Adora nor the Green Faia could hear him.

"Now, sister," Adora worked her fist around in a circle, flames dripping from it, "let's find out just how much you can give me...."

"GREI!" Thin, rough hands had hold of his shoulders, shaking him.

Grei shot upright, swinging at whoever was attacking him.

A bony forearm blocked his clumsy swing. Ree caught his wrist, and he gasped. He still felt the pain of the Green Faia in his chest as though he was burning.

"The Green Faia!" he shouted, but the dream was gone.

"What?"

"She's dying. I have to—"

"You were dreaming."

But the dream about Cavyn—the last dream the slink of the South Forest had sent—*that* had been real enough to bring Blevins back from the dead. And Grei dreaded this was the same. He wanted to vomit.

"Dammit, Grei, we're in real trouble," Ree said sharply. "Wake up and listen to me!"

Still disoriented from his dream, he ignored Ree and looked around the room. The crooked door was shut, but light speared through the cracks. Through the dirty window, the yellow sunrise lit the tops of the wooden houses of Lowtown. It was morning.

"What's happening?" he asked. His heart thudded in his chest. *Baezin's Blood, what* else *could possibly go wrong?*

"Get your boots on," she said. "We have to move."

"The Jhor Forest," he said. How long would it take him to run that distance? An hour? Longer? "We have to go there now."

He yanked on his boots, pushed open the crooked door, and stepped into the bright street, blinking against the bright sunlight. To the east, the Jhor Forest burned. A plume of black, oily smoke roiled into the sky. So it was true... Grei's dreams weren't just dreams. They were windows to other places, to events that were actually occurring.

"By the Faia," Ree murmured, looking at the column of smoke. "You saw the Jhor burning in your dream?"

"We have to get there. Now." He started up the street.

She caught his arm. "Grei, there's something else—"

"She's killing the Green Faia!" He spun around to face her. "We have to…" The words died on his lips as he looked back toward the palace for the first time. To the west, a red haze hung over everything. The top of the palace rose above it, as did the glimmering Web of Blades and the seven white towers. But everything below had been swallowed by a sea of bloody mist, and it was moving toward Lowtown.

"That was why I woke you," Ree said. "Is that what I think it is?"

Doom slid into his stomach like a greased stone. The cloud he'd pulled from the tall girl was growing… "It's going to take over the whole city," he murmured. "He's going to make slaves of everyone."

The insidious mist slithered through the streets like tentacles. Already, he heard panicked shouts on this side of the Red Wall as the Thiarans awoke to their danger.

"Undo it," Ree said. "Can you undo it?"

"I…don't know how it happened," he murmured. "I didn't mean to make it in the first place…. I only meant to cut Velak's hold from the girl." Prickles of horror spread across his scalp.

They stood in stunned silence.

"What do we do, Whisper Prince?" Ree asked, her voice flat, calm.

His heart hammered. If he ran into that mist, would it take him, too? If he tried to fix it…would he make it worse?

"It's time to decide," she said. "I will follow you."

"The Green Faia could fix this," he whispered. "She could…fix me, undo what I've done here." As he spoke, his words hardened with conviction. Yes. It was the only real answer. "We save the Faia first, then we come back."

"Let's go." She grabbed his arm and hauled him down the

street just as the red mist hit the Red Wall near them and spilled over like a weightless wave.

"Run, Grei," Ree said. "Run as fast as you can."

Chapter 16

GREI

REE SAID IT WOULD BE AN HOUR to reach the edge of the Jhor, but perhaps she meant herself. Grei told her about the dream as he struggled to keep up with her, and by the time they reached the smoldering forest, it had easily been twice that long. His feet were blistered, he couldn't breathe, and he tasted blood in his mouth. But they'd outrun the red mist. In the first half-hour, he'd told her about his dream, about Adora, the flames around her, the hate-filled voice coming out of her.

Smoke drifted between the green trees, and the plume of fire that had been in the center of the forest was gone. They'd watched the flames die down as they charged up the slope. Grei hoped this meant the Green Faia had defended herself successfully, but as they strode deeper into the forest, his hopes died.

When Grei had first visited the Jhor Forest, it had teemed with life. Creatures had watched him from behind every trunk, between every leafy branch. But now, the trees drooped. He heard the baying of the wolves somewhere in the distance, heartbroken. The grass was dry and warm, as though all the moisture had been sucked from it. No animals moved in the branches or between the trees. In fact, except for the wolves, the forest was silent.

They pushed their way through the foliage, and Grei saw the deadly tree under which he and Selicia had hidden. The fire hadn't reached this far, and the tree's long, paper-thin vines were still shiny. He remembered the Highblade walking into those vines, sword out, ready to kill, when a thin, bony arm had descended and impaled him.

"Don't go near that one," Grei murmured, pointing at the dangling vines.

Ree eyed the tree and gave it a wide berth. The smoke grew thicker as they moved cautiously through the trees. Grei pulled the edge of his cloak up over his nose and mouth and breathed through it.

"How do you know the dream is real and that this isn't just a fire in the Jhor?" Ree asked. "A forest fire doesn't mean a prophecy."

"Have you ever seen a fire in this forest?" Grei asked.

She hesitated. "Not in the Jhor," she admitted. "But it's still a forest. Forests burn."

"Not when they're protected by a Faia."

The thick green trees gave way to burnt trunks and leafless black branches. Smoke curled up, choking the sky with a dark gray haze. The ground was a charred ruin. Grei began running, and the blackened trees gave way to a blasted clearing. In the center was a blackened, human-like shape.

He rushed forward and threw himself on his knees next to it, reaching out to touch it, but it wasn't made of flesh and bone. Instead, a cluster of thorny, charred vines formed the shape of the tiny burnt body. The vines had sunk deep into the ground in many places. Grei gently touched the vines and the thorns.

"No!" Tears brimmed in his eyes. "I'm too late."

The Green Faia was dead.

He remembered her powerful song in his mind, filling him

with grace and power. He remembered her gentle touch on his thoughts, her melodious voice in his mind. He remembered the visions she gave to him, of Kuruk and Lyndion.

Grei held up his right arm, skeletal thin with charcoal-colored flesh all the way up to his elbow. He remembered her final words, just before the Faia had healed this arm, just after he'd mentioned Adora.

Love. It is the human gift. She. You.

"I'm so sorry." He cried softly.

Her powerful song was gone. Its absence was a frightening void in this place. He felt the profound, quiet shock in every living creature around him. He felt an ache in the hand she had repaired.

Ree approached, solemn. Her image blurred through his tears.

He looked down at the thorny corpse of the Faia, wiped at his eyes, then clenched his teeth and reached into her with the whispers. The powerful song of the Jhor Forest was gone, but he fought to hear what life might remain in the vines. The whispers warbled to him, confusing, and his scarred stomach clenched. He pushed past the pain, trying to understand the warbling voices. Sweat broke out on his forehead, but he finally heard what the vines were saying. But despite their heartbreaking shape, they were only vines. They didn't hide the Green Faia somewhere within. She was gone.

He let the whispers go, but like before at the palace, the warbles continued, getting louder. Suddenly, the world rippled like everything was a reflection in the water and Grei was a stone that had been dropped into the center of it. A mighty ripple radiated out from him, touching the trees. The nearest charred tree began to drip, just like the wall at the palace had done.

Grei lunged to his feet. "Stop it!" he yelled, but his command only seemed to shove the ripple outward, making it stronger. The three nearest trees turned to water and splashed onto the ground, creating small streams of black water.

He backed up, horrified, staring at the ripple in the air that continued outward.

"What are you doing?" Ree demanded.

"I…" he whispered. "I had to see… If she was alive, I had to *do* something!"

The ripple continued, hitting a group of charred trees. It turned them to water, then flowed to the next cluster of trees. They sagged like melting candles. The ripple moved on, and he could see a swath of trees sag and fall as it radiated outward, like someone was rolling an invisible wheel over the trees. It kept going and going until he couldn't see it anymore. His heart hammered in his chest, and he felt sick to his stomach. "I have to stop. I can't…I can use it anymore. I thought that maybe—"

"You *have* to," she said. "You have to find a way, undo that red mist. It's going to keep coming. What if it doesn't stop at the edge of the city?"

Grei imagined the red mist rolling over the empire, turning everyone into Velak's red-eyed puppets.

"Baezin's blood…" he murmured. Less than a day ago, he had vengeance in his heart. He had wanted to call Kuruk and Lyndion to task for their crimes, wanted to reprimand Empress Via for her lying ways. He had wanted to *fix* the empire.

Instead, he'd broken it. No. He had created a new scale of disaster. This wasn't just the Thiaran Empire at risk. This wasn't just one person a month in the Debt of the Blessed. If that red mist kept expanding, it would consume every living human it touched.

Grei suddenly felt like he was drowning. He couldn't seem to get enough air.

"Grei…" Ree said quietly. "We're going to find a way through."

"A way through…" he murmured.

"Keep your wits. Breathe."

He forced himself to calm down.

"You're broken," she said. "We just have to fix you. We will find a way," she repeated.

After a moment, he nodded. "Okay. Okay, yes."

"We are currently a step behind," Ree said. "So we move faster, we get a step ahead."

"How?" he said. He managed to keep the despair out of his tone, but only barely.

She held up a finger. "A Ringdance can only be done properly one step at a time. So that's what we're going to do. You said the Green Faia could fix your magic."

"And she's dead," he said, failing to keep the anger from his voice this time.

"Then we find another Faia."

He opened his mouth, then shut it. The simple statement took the wind out of him. "The Blue Faia," he murmured.

"There's a Purple Faia. And an Orange and a Black."

"I don't know where they are. The Blue Faia is in Fairmist."

She shook her head. "It's a start."

"And we have to find Adora. Velak has her. That wasn't her. She was covered in flames and... He's...done something to her. It wasn't her voice that taunted the Green Faia. That wasn't Adora."

"And why hasn't he used these powers before?" she asked serenely. "If he can give this kind of power to those he enslaves, why not blast us with flames from Vecenne's balcony?"

"I...I don't know."

"Then these are the questions. How do we fix your magic? How is he making these attacks? How do we save Adora? Until we answer them, we don't have time for self-recrimination—"

Something moved in the trees, and they both spun. At first Grei wondered which of the Jhor's infamous monsters would emerge. Or would it be Adora, coming back? He'd met the carnivorous tree and the enormous wolves, but if legends were to be believed, those weren't the most fearsome to be found in the Jhor.

The smoke shifted, and a humanoid silhouette strode forward. He emerged, a giant of a man, and he wore the short red kilt and X-shaped harness of a palace Highblade. The hilt of Baezin's blade jutted prominently over his right shoulder.

"Blevins!" Grei blurted.

Chapter 17

GREI

BLEVINS HAD BEEN an enormous man in Fairmist, but he'd also been enormously fat. His appearance had been comical right up to the point when Grei realized he was a hardened killer, right after Blevins had bested Galius Ash, the finest swordsman in Fairmist.

This reincarnated Blevins was a six-and-a-half-foot tall giant made of solid muscle. His shoulders were unrealistically wide, and his bulging biceps sloped into slender forearms, the arms of a natural swordsman. His deeply defined chest was strapped with an X-shaped harness so tight it looked like the leather would snap. His legs were tree trunks, and his sandaled feet crunched over the burnt branches on the forest floor.

His intense gaze took in the clearing, flicking from Ree to Grei to the nearby stream filling with brown water from the melted trees. His gaze stopped on the cluster of vines shaped like a Faia's body, then he glanced at Grei.

"Stormy," he acknowledged, as though they were back at the Floating Stone. He appraised Ree, his lips bending into a frown. "Ringblade," he said in a low voice.

Ree didn't say anything, but she flicked Grei a warning glance.

A thin bandage wrapped Blevins's neck. It was red with blood, and a raw cut raked his cheek just below his eye. Both wounds looked like narrowly-missed kill strikes.

"Is Selicia alive?" Grei asked, remembering what the Ringblade Syvet had said at the palace, that the Ringmother had been broken, left dying after her fight with Blevins.

"It was the third time the bitch tried to kill me," he said. "Should I care?"

Again, coming from Blevins in his obese form, that might have sounded humorous. Coming from this Blevins, it sounded ruthless and deadly.

"How did you know we were here?" Grei asked.

"I'm good at finding people," he rumbled. "I'm *great* at finding you."

"What does that mean?"

"I don't know." Blevins shrugged. "Once I put Selicia down, I went looking for my sword. Once I found my sword, I went looking for you. My feet led me here."

As with most of Blevins's responses, he didn't answer the question.

"That red mist," Blevins said. "You make it?"

Grei clenched his teeth. "It was…a mistake."

Blevins narrowed his eyes. He pointed at the melting trees. "That an accident, too?"

"He didn't kill the Faia," Ree interjected.

Blevins turned his head to regard the Ringblade with contempt. "When I want something out of you, Ringblade," he growled. "I'll use a dagger."

Ree bristled, opened her mouth to retort, but Blevins cut her off, turning to Grei. "She's manipulating you."

"She saved my life," Grei said.

"I bet she did. Saved it right after Selicia put a dagger in you. Pulled you out of that canal. Got there just in time, did she?"

He'd recited exactly what had happened. "She was…cast out of the Ringblades."

Blevins gave a dark chuckle. "Cast out? That's funny. Look at her, so silent, letting you argue for her. That's how they work. They whisper in your ear, nudge you until *their* words come tumbling out of your mouth."

"Blevins—"

"Did you trust her when she first showed up? I bet you didn't. Then she did something self-sacrificing, then did something else, made you trust her a little more. Then somewhere in there, she told you what to do. It was so sensible, I bet you followed her without thinking. Something like: 'Run, Grei!' or 'Follow me!' Just a little thing in the heat of the moment, but a command nonetheless."

Grei clenched his teeth. He couldn't deny it. It had happened just like that, and he'd questioned each of her commands, but each of them had been so…sensible. And yet, the danger hadn't been fabricated. The threats had been real. Would Grei have done anything different if he'd been alone?

Blevins shook his head. "Of course," he rumbled, as though Grei had affirmed everything he'd said. "They fill you with fear or fog your mind with lust. Whatever works best. Think back, Stormy. Did she take a knife for you? Kill someone who threatened you? Kiss you? Fuck you?"

"Stop it!" Grei said.

"Look at her." He shook his head. "Silent as a lake." Blevins swiveled his gaze to Ree. "Nothing to say for yourself, Ringblade?"

She glared back at Blevins without flinching. "Someone *is* trying to manipulate you, Grei. That's sure," she said in an implacable tone. "But it's not me."

"I don't manipulate," Blevins growled. "I don't hide, and I don't cozy up to my enemies." He drew his sword. Empress Via must have stripped off the black paint that had covered it, because the blade gleamed in the sunlight. "I kill them."

Blevins started toward Ree, sword sticking out from his hand like it weighed nothing. She crouched, now holding two daggers.

"Put your weapons up!" Grei shouted.

Blevins stopped advancing. He glared at Ree, then glanced at Grei. "I'm trying to help you, Stormy," Blevins said. "She's a villain."

"Or you are." Grei held Blevins's gaze. "Everything you accused her of, you're guilty of too." Blevins had hidden in Fairmist, pretending to be a fat drunk when he was actually the most dangerous man in the empire. "If you're trying to help, then stop causing problems. The two of you fighting doesn't help me."

Blevins sighed, then he straightened and sheathed his sword. Ree shrugged, then stood up from her crouch. The daggers had vanished again.

"I don't trust *either* of you," Grei said, "since we're being honest. But I don't have time to look for flaws in my allies. I have enough disasters. I don't have time to mediate a grudge match between Highblades and Ringblades." His heart ached at the death of the Faia, and his skin crawled at the thought of what Adora had become. "Now…I'm going to talk, and you two are going to listen, or you are going to leave."

Blevins narrowed his eyes. Ree kept her steady gaze on Grei. "I'm with you," she said. "I told you I was, and I meant it."

Blevins rolled his eyes. "Well, I'm not going anywhere." He crossed his arms over his enormous chest. "I promised to protect you, and that's what I'm going to do, especially with *her* nearby."

"Ree tried to manipulate me," Grei said. "Twice. But she's never told me an outright lie. You have. In fact, I think you're still lying."

Blevins sighed and dropped his hand to his belt. Ree tensed, but he wasn't going for a weapon. He glanced down, like he'd expected something to be there, then frowned. "I need a drink," he murmured, then, "Well, Stormy. Whether you believe me or not, I've been straight with you. Aside from lying about my name and my title and my previous position."

He shrugged. "I *was* Jorun Magnus. But now I'm Blevins."

"That's all you have to say?" Grei asked.

The big man grunted. "I was the emperor's champion. His axe man, his bodyguard, his confidante. I fought the Slinks, protected him during the Slink War. I followed every order he gave to me, slew his enemies. I also stood by his side when he cut apart a Faia. And when he ordered me to sacrifice his daughter to the Slinks, I did it even though I loved her like she was my own child. That's when my loyalty cracked. It started then, and seven years later, when I couldn't stand it any longer, I broke every oath I'd made and cut my way out of the palace. I wandered the empire after that, drinking, waking up in strange taverns or ditches. Eventually, I made my way to Fairmist, intent on drinking myself to death. And then I met you..." He shook his head. "And my goals changed."

"Why? How did they change?"

"After you fell through the stone outside the Delegate's palace, after you turned it to water, you weren't just some crazy boy anymore. I had to protect you," he said.

"Why?"

Blevins hesitated. He opened his mouth like he was about to tell Grei the answer, then he frowned. It was as if he suddenly couldn't remember, like he'd almost had the answer, then it was gone. He grunted, frowned. "I don't know. I can't say why any more than I know where to walk to find you when I need to."

"What else?" Grei pressed. Ree glanced at him, as though she'd caught scent of a secret.

Blevins held his hands out, palms up. "The rest you know," he growled. "I die, I wake up. I die, I wake up. When I wake, I remember my sword, and I go get it. But now I remember you, too. I know I have to find you."

"How?" Ree asked.

Blevins gave her flat glance that could wither flowers. "I don't answer to you, bitch."

"How?" Grei repeated her question, frowning.

Blevins glared at Ree, then he looked back at Grei.

"Because I don't know why I can't die, and I think you do."

"I do," Grei said.

Blevins's hard expression changed into surprise. His thick, black eyebrows raised. "You do," he murmured, and his voice sounded strangely hopeful. "Why?" he demanded. "Why do I keep coming back?"

Grei hesitated. Blevins acted like he didn't know he was Baezin. But was that just an act?

Or had Grei guessed wrong? Was Blevins *not* Baezin?

Grei glanced at Ree. She didn't seem to know where Grei was going, but she nodded encouragingly. He found himself wishing he'd told her his suspicions about Blevins before now. Her Ringblade ability to detect lies would be useful.

"You're not who you say you are," Grei accused.

"I thought we covered this," Blevins said.

"No. I mean you're not Blevins or Jorun Magnus. Both are fabricated."

Ree narrowed her eyes, glancing at Blevins then at Grei.

"And who do you think I am?" Blevins asked laconically.

"You're Emperor Baezin," Grei said, watching Blevins's reaction closely. How he responded could tell volumes.

Blevins's face darkened, and he shook his head like ants were crawling across his scalp. "What? I'm who?"

"That's what I discovered," Grei said.

"No. You said something, but I didn't hear you. What did you say?"

"I said you're Baezin the First. The conqueror. The father of the Thiaran Empire."

Ree's face froze in a neutral expression; Grei suspected that was the face a Ringblade was trained to show when she didn't want her real emotions running across her face. Blevins clenched his teeth, shook his head again. "Your words sound like bees! Speak plainly!"

Grei glanced at Ree. "Did you hear me?"

"I heard you. I just… You can't really think he's Baezin," she said. "Baezin is a three-hundred-year-old corpse. He's not walking around as this muscle-bound man-beast."

"Unless he was resurrected over and over for centuries," Grei said.

Comprehension dawned in her eyes, and she drew a slow breath. "Grei…"

"What are you saying!" Blevins growled. "You think I'm three hundred years old?"

"He can't hear his name," Grei said, suddenly understanding. "Cavyn… The woman who brings him back to life also steals his memory. Maybe she makes sure he can't hear his own name, so that it won't accidentally trigger a memory. It's some kind of spell."

"Oh Grei…" Ree said, finally letting her mask of non-expression slip. She looked stunned. "The first emperor? I don't think—"

"He doesn't know who he is," Grei whispered. "Maybe he never knew."

"A spell? What are you saying? Someone is altering my mind?" Blevins demanded.

"Yes."

"And I'm who?"

"Can you hear the word 'emperor'?" Grei said.

"Of course I can hear the word 'emperor'." Blevins growled.

"Do you know how many emperors have ruled in Thiara?"

"Sixteen."

"And the third emperor was Emperor Vandis."

"Of course."

"The second was Empress Thiazin."

"What are you getting at?" Blevins growled.

"Who was first?"

"The first emperor was…" Blevins's voice trailed off. His eyes widened. "He was…" He shook his head and glared at Grei. "The man. That man. The… The…"

"You can't say it."

Blevins blinked. "I can't say it," he whispered. "I can't even picture it. There's a…a hole there. I imagine… He's… His name is…" His voice lowered to a growl, unable to say the word. "…the first emperor, but there's no picture. There's a throne where a man should be sitting, and there's a hole in it."

"That's because the hole is you," Grei said.

He growled and put his fists to his head. Ree snapped out of her stunned reverie and crouched down. She scrawled the word "B A E Z I N" in the charred earth.

"No," he growled. "I'm a Highblade. I was Jorun Magnus."

"That's what she wants you to think," Grei said.

"She who?" Blevins asked.

"The woman resurrecting you."

Again, he shook his head like he was trying to beat away a swarm of bugs. "I'm Jorun Magnus!"

"Who is your mother?"

"I…" Blevins faltered.

"Who is your father?"

"I come from…'"

"Where did you grow up? What's your earliest memory?" Grei pressed.

"I've…always been a Highblade," he growled.

"No one has always been a Highblade. I'll bet your earliest memory is when you became the emperor's champion."

"No, I was in the ranks before that."

"How long? When did you arrive in Thiara?"

"I…" Blevins clenched his teeth.

"How long have you had that sword?"

"I got it when I became the emperor's champion."

"I don't think you did. I think you've always had it," Grei said. "And when they took it away from you, you went after it. Because it's Baezin's Blade, and you can't bear to be separated from it."

"It's what? What is it called?"

"He really can't hear the name Baezin," Ree marveled.

"The sword is the only part of the real you that's left," Grei said. "That's why you have to have it. Every time you wake up, you have to find it."

Blevins stood there, looking at nothing. He blinked once, as though he was trying to find those most basic memories:

childhood, parents, the place he grew up, his real name. At the end, he roared at the sky and clenched his fists. "I can't remember any of it. Why?" he said.

"You did something. I don't know what. She's angry at you."

"I'm B…" he tried to say the name, but it wouldn't go past his lips. He growled and tried again, failed again "I'm…an emperor," he said instead, then turned away angrily. "How can this woman be controlling me? Controlling my life and death?"

"She's like a Faia," Grei said. "But more powerful."

Blevins rounded on Grei. "Take her out. Pull her magic out of me."

Grei stepped back, but Blevins pursued. Ree jumped between them, daggers flashing.

"Stab me and I'll break your neck," Blevins warned her, but he stopped his advance and pinned Grei with a glare. "Take her out. You said she's magic. So are you. Destroy this hook she has in me. Do what you do."

"I can't."

"You're lying." He lunged forward. Ree's daggers came up. They should have plunged into Blevins's belly, but he grabbed her wrists, snake-quick. He shoved her arms wide and head-butted her. Her legs wobbled, and her arms went limp. Blevins tossed her aside and lifted Grei by the tunic.

Ree groaned on her hands and knees, blinking, trying to get up, but she fell over on her side.

"Her magic is stronger than mine," Grei rasped around Blevins's huge fist. "I'm nothing to her. She could snuff me out with a thought. I think she's…" he trailed off.

"You think she's what?"

"I think she's Thiara. The empress. Your wife."

"Thiara!" he growled incredulously.

"But she's like me. She can hear the whispers, use them…"

Over Blevins's head, deep in the forest, Grei saw treetops ripple. In a swath, the trees turned to water and dropped like a giant, invisible wheel was rolling over them, like Grei's ripple of foul magic had rebounded off something and was coming back toward them.

"Oh no," he said.

Blevins dropped Grei and spun around. The phenomenon was almost upon them. Ree, who'd finally shaken off his strike, also looked at the melting trees.

The nearest shimmered and splashed to the ground, green and brown water flowing downhill.

"Get behind me!" Blevins roared, holding Baezin's Blade in front of himself like he could strike the spell.

Still unsteady, Ree lunged past Blevins and tackled Grei. She took him off his feet, slamming the air from his lungs, and her momentum carried them several paces backward.

"Ree!" he shouted, but his voice was cut off as they plunged into the stream. Water filled his mouth. He tried to stand up, but Ree's arms and legs wrapped around him, and they sank together beneath the water. Grei hadn't had a chance to take a breath before he'd gone under, and his chest spasmed, desperate for air. He struggled, but she held him, arms and feet bound around him like rope.

Bubbles rose up from his mouth, and dark spots swelled in his vision. Above, over the surface of the lake, he saw a shimmering light pass over them, ruffling the water. His magic. His rogue spell had moved on. He struggled to get free, his chest feeling like it would explode, but Ree held on. His jerks became feeble. Just as he thought he was going to pass out, she released him and hauled him upright.

Grei fell over on his hands and knees in the shallows of the stream, coughing and sputtering. The stream was wider, racing faster with the new, multi-colored water joining it. The current grabbed at Grei, threatened to pull him downstream. Ree took his arms, tried to haul him up to his feet, but he batted her hands away, coughing. "You almost drowned me!"

"Protected you," she said, panting and pointing. He followed the gesture. The ripple of magic had cut a new swath to the south. It raced to the end of the Jhor, trees becoming water and dropping to the ground. The ripple continued, water building, rushing, cutting new grooves in the dirt. The entire slope became a torrent of multi-colored rapids churning toward the Fairmist River at the bottom of the hill.

"By the Faia…" Grei murmured, aghast.

"Grei…" Blevins's deep voice came from behind them. Grei spun around.

The giant man stood where he'd been, facing them with sword in hand, dazed. He wobbled on his feet like someone had clubbed him, and he'd refused to go down.

Then the side of his head bent, turning to ooze, and collapsed into his shoulder. His shoulder melted. His arm slid down his side. His whole body fell, turning into clear, shimmering water. He splashed to the ground, a shimmering streak atop the green and brown flows.

"No!" Grei closed his eyes, concentrating and reaching for the whispers. They immediately became loud in his mind. Blevins's body banged like pots and pans, a cacophony of discordant noises.

Ree grabbed Grei's arm and shook him, breaking his concentration. "No," she said. "Don't do it."

The banging noises vanished.

"Ree, he's melting—!"

"Look!" She pointed at the retreating ripple, turning anything living into water as it neared the Fairmist River. "First the mist. Now this. You *can't* save him; you'll create another calamity."

Grei sank to his knees in the colored water. Baezin's Blade and sheath, the X-shaped harness, the red kilt and the sandals quivered in the thin rush that flowed to the engorged stream behind Grei. That was all that was left. Blevins was gone.

"I killed him," Grei whispered. He'd killed the first emperor of Thiara, the undying man, the only one who might have shed light on this deadly mystery of Velak, Kuruk, and Lyndion.

"Grei," Ree warned, her voice suddenly tight as she tapped his shoulder. "Look."

Chapter 18

GREI

ANIMALS OF ALL SIZES and shapes ringed the burnt glade. A dozen towering wolves watched with heads low at the edge of the melted trees, yellow eyes glowing. Deer stood next to them, and flying hares perched on burnt branches that hadn't been melted. A hundred birds of all shapes and colors flapped down through the drifting smoke. Closest was a black cat larger even than the Imperial Wand's mount in Fairmist. It slunk between the trees, back and forth, deep green eyes fixed on them.

Warbling whispers reached into Grei's mind.

"...he can hear us..."

"...he is the new mother..."

"...the new mother..."

Grei looked at the animals, and he suddenly realized *they* weren't speaking. It was the trees, just like the spirits of the trees had spoken to him when he'd fled into the Dead Woods, back when he'd barely known how to listen to the voices of the elements.

"They're looking for the Green Faia," he whispered. He

picked up Baezin's Blade, slowly buckled on the harness, and rose cautiously.

"The animals?"

"The trees. Or…their spirits."

"Trees have spirits?"

"In a Faia's forest they do." In the Dead Woods, each of the spirits had looked like Adora. But he didn't see any figures this time, just voices.

"…the new mother. Come to us…"

"…come with us…"

An invisible force picked at his clothing, lifting pieces and letting them fall. A touch brushed over his magical arm, the one the Green Faia had brought to life again.

In the Dead Woods, the powerful spirits were bent on killing any humans who dared trespass. They were vicious and angry, and they'd only spared Grei's life because he could speak their language. But here, the spirits weren't angry; they were lost. They were…desperate. They wanted their mother back.

The invisible hands tugged at him, pulling him toward the heart of the forest. He lost his balance and stumbled in that direction.

"Stop it!" he said aloud, pulling his arms in. The force on his wrists vanished.

"…come to us…"

"…come with us…"

"…become the new mother…"

"I'm not a Faia! But I will find the one who killed her. I promise. I will make it right."

"…make it right…"

"…Mother…"

The invisible hands caressed him again like a breath of wind, then fastened lightly on his wrist.

"We're in danger," he whispered to Ree, a cold realization settling in his belly. These spirits weren't vengeful…but what would they do if he told them he wasn't going to be their new mother?

"I can't hear what you hear," Ree whispered back, watching the animals standing at the tree line. "What's happening?"

"...*make it right...*"

"...*Mother...*"

"They want me to replace the Faia," he said.

Ree glanced over her shoulder, then pulled Grei toward the swath of melted trees that cut through the forest. The birds went quiet. The cat raised his head at the motion. Its lips peeled back, and it gave a purring growl. The wolves moved forward, silent as ghosts, following Ree and Grei. Several flying hares landed on the ground, noses twitching and teeth chewing the air.

"What does that mean?" Ree asked.

"They want me to stay."

"The alternative being?"

A half dozen of the wolves gave them a wide berth and loped past, fifty paces to the west, circled, then lined up to the south, cutting off their escape.

"...*come to us...*"

"...*Mother...*"

"I don't think they're considering an alternative." Grei slowed. They were surrounded.

"...*stay...*"

"...*Mother...*"

They neared the line of wolves, and the giant beasts lowered their heads and growled. Grei and Ree stopped.

"Ideas?" Ree asked softly, a dagger in her right hand.

He frowned at her dagger. "I don't think we ought to attack a pack of wolves with a knife."

"I'll sheathe it as soon as you give me different plan."

Suddenly, Grei was slammed forward. Huge teeth slid along his back. Ree shouted as the giant cat pounced on Grei. It had been utterly silent in its approach, and it knocked Ree to the ground. Grei was lifted into the air, dangling from the X-shaped harness clamped firmly in the cat's mouth. Ree scrambled to her feet, slashed with her dagger, but the cat bounded away, Grei dangling from its mouth.

It took him a paralyzed moment to realize the cat hadn't bitten him.

"Grei!" Ree shouted, sprinting after them, but the cat was far too fast for her to catch.

The cat launched itself at the line of wolves. At the last second, the cat leapt powerfully to the side, clearing a twenty-foot distance. Grei yelped as they sailed over the heads of the wolves, over the entire melted area, and landed on the great branch of a massive tree. Grei shouted as he jammed his feet against the trunk of the tree. Flying hares and birds scattered in all directions. The tree's trunk was as big around as a house, the branches as thick as Grei's chest.

Frantically, he grappled with the cat's enormous head, trying to grab its ears, its eyes, anything to get it to drop him.

The cat gave a quick shake of its head, rattling Grei to his bones. Baezin's Blade, loose in its scabbard, spun away into the shadows below.

"No!" Grei reached for the magic sword, but it had vanished, and the cat leapt again.

Claws dug into the tree. Shreds of bark flew. The cat leapt powerfully from one to another branch, then launched out the far side of the tree, grabbing on to the next, then to the next. Grei bounced and whipped like a limp rag. Each impact rattled his teeth in his head, but the cat didn't let go. After four powerful leaps, it landed on the melted ground beyond the wolves.

The wolves yipped, wheeled about, and pursued. The cat sprinted down the aisle of cleared ground, running alongside the wild, multi-colored river. Rainbow water flew up from its claws as they dug deep. The wolves howled, loping after them, but the cat was faster. Trees blurred past Grei.

Through watering eyes, he saw a gap in the trees ahead, long green fields beyond. They were nearly upon it when the cat yowled, mouth opening. The whispers grabbed hold of Grei and ripped him from the cat's mouth.

Grei was lifted into the air, spread-eagled as the whispers

tore at him.

"…stay…"
"…Mother…"
"…fill us…"
"…don't leave us…"

Grei shouted, trying to pull his arms together, but the force was desperate, and it was stronger than him.

The cat wheeled around and let out a cat scream. It jumped in front of Grei just as the wolves arrived. They lunged in, biting at the giant cat's legs. The cat spun, swiping and sending two of the wolves sprawling with its enormous claws. The wolves were huge, but the cat was half again as big and supernaturally fast.

The wolves pulled away from the dangerous cat and circled. Grei was utterly confused. Was the cat fighting for him? It had been taking him where he and Ree had wanted to go: to the clearing between the trees and the slope.

For long moments, the wolves circled, looking for an opening, but the cat waited, tense and ready.

Then Ree appeared from the darkness of the trees. She leapt silently from the edge of the forest like a wraith. She must have sprinted this whole way.

One wolf spun in surprise as she leapt into onto its back, using it to launch herself into the air. Its jaws snapped behind her heel as she flew over the cat, flipping in the air as she sailed toward Grei.

And she held Baezin's Blade gripped in both hands.

She swung the magical blade down, inches from Grei's left wrist, then elegantly sliced it past his right hand on the backswing as she dropped. The invisible grip vanished. Grei fell, landing in a heap on the muddy ground next to Ree.

She breathed so hard that her skinny chest pumped like a bellows. She didn't say anything, just grabbed his arm and propelled him toward the break in the trees ahead. He stumbled, gained his balance, then sprinted. The wolves tried to follow, but the giant cat attacked them, scattering the closest two and rounding on the others, which hesitated.

The invisible hands came for Grei again just as they reached the edge of the trees. They lifted him up again.

"...*Whisper Prince!...*"

"...*Stay!...*"

Ree slashed at the air again before Grei got too high, and he fell again, this time tumbling clear of the forest, rolling across grass that was not melted. The spirits of the trees wailed in despair, and he could see a green tint to the air, pulsing, but it seemed unable to reach beyond the tree line.

In a shower of leaves and branches, the cat exploded from the forest and landed on the slope, tearing brown gashes into the verdant earth and looking back the way it had come. The wolves stopped at the edge of the trees. They turned their muzzles turned to the sky and howled.

Grei stared, stunned, at the forest. Next to him, Ree sucked in breath after breath, hands on her knees. He could only imagine how fast she'd had to run to catch up with the wolves and the giant cat. Finally, she gasped between breaths, "Is that...a friend?"

The giant cat watched them, head low. Its glowing green eyes seemed like miniature torches, and Grei could hear powerful warbling whispers coming from the cat.

"I don't know," Grei said. "I don't know what it is."

The cat stared significantly at them for a long moment, looked east toward Fairmist, then the green glow faded from its eyes. They became a normal cat's eyes, golden and bright. The cat looked around, confused. It lowered its head, hissed at them, then leapt up the slope and back into the forest.

Chapter 19

ADORA

THE HUGE STAG Adora rode staggered, lurched a few more steps, then died underneath her. She hit the ground and danced away, keeping her foot from being crushed.

The dying stag jolted her. With an effort, she pushed the rage out of her mind, pushed Velak out of her mind.

She blinked, finally coming to her senses. She stared down at the stag, and her chest ached. She should be sad at its death, shouldn't she? But it was hard to feel anything. She didn't know where she was, how she'd come to be here, why she'd been riding the stag or why it was dead. In fact, she couldn't remember anything about her life before she'd stepped off the Night Mountains or after. She'd streaked to the ground like a comet, then there was only fire. Joyous, vengeful flames had exploded within her and without, filling her mind and body, shooting from her fingertips...

She'd shot those flames *at* someone. But she couldn't remember why. Or who. It was as though it had been...erased from her memory.

She tried to summon the memories, but a thick smoke swirled inside her mind, obscuring everything.

She looked down at the stag, up at the blue sky and its wisps of clouds, then at the gentle hills all around her. She could perceive all of this in startling clarity, but when she tried to remember what had happened during that explosion of fire, she couldn't. She concentrated, tried to peer through that smoke, but her head began to hurt.

She'd lost something important, and she felt ill. Was it about the stag? The stag was dead because she'd ridden it to death, because she'd treated it cruelly. Why had she done that? The stag was...

"...doing what it was made to do." Velak's whisper slithered out of the smoke in her mind.

"Stop it," she said aloud, trying to shove him away. "I want to think my own thoughts."

"You are."

"We killed the stag," she said. "And we killed...someone else..."

"...who needed killing."

"...who needed killing," she finished, using his exact words as though he'd put them on her tongue. She shook her head. "I said stop it! Who was it? Who did we kill?" Lyndion was what mattered to her, not anyone else. *Lyndion* was the one who needed to die, and if she hadn't killed him, what was she doing?

"Who did we kill?" she asked again, frustrated that she couldn't remember. She remembered rage and that it made her feel so good. A figure flashed through the smoke in her mind, there and gone, obscured by the haze. The figure had been small, lithe. "A child? We killed a child?" she asked, appalled.

"Because of Lyndion."

The image of Lyndion's white hair and craggy face emerged clearly in the reddish smoke inside her mind.

Yes. Lyndion. He must die.

"You promised me revenge," she said.

"And I gave you revenge."

Again, her chest ached, but she wasn't sure what emotion she was supposed to feel. Sorrow for the child? Hatred for Lyndion? The smoke swirled thickly, and Velak continued talking in her mind.

"You were imprisoned by Lyndion. He took you, kept you, and finally butchered you."

A red sun rose in the smoky haze. Rage filled her, warming her chest, her arms and legs. Flames crackled inside her mind again. She envisioned Lyndion writhing, burning. He'd used her for seven painstaking years, then he'd gutted her like a fish.

She had trusted others, and they had also betrayed her. She'd trusted her father; he'd thrown her to the slinks. She'd trusted Jorun Magnus; he'd abandoned her on a shale slope with a horde of slinks....

"The Green Faia handed you over to Lyndion."

"She handed me over to Lyndion," Adora murmured, remembering the Green Faia pulling her away from the slinks, delivering her to the South Forest, laying her gently on the forest floor.

"She helped him chain you, conspired with him to kill you."

Now the memory of the Green Faia in the Jhor Forest came to her in full clarity. The little Faia burning, dying. She had a momentary ache, that same illness, at seeing the Faia suffer, but then bright rage covered over it. "She helped him...."

"She has been punished."

"We must punish Lyndion," she snarled. "And Jorun Magnus. And my father."

"And the Whisper Prince."

The ache in her chest returned. "Grei..."

"Yes."

"Grei loves me," she murmured, the words rising from somewhere deep inside her, slipping past the smoke. The smoke swirled more thickly. Flickers of flame rose up, blocking her from her memories, but somehow she could see Grei's face. Sweet, beloved Grei. He was the only hope in this tarnished world.

"He lied to you."

"No."

"You begged him to stay. You felt Lyndion close. Deep down, you knew he was coming to hurt you, to cut you. That's why you begged Grei to stay, but he left you vulnerable. He handed you over to Lyndion."

"I begged him…"

That, she remembered, grasping Grei's arm, begging him. *Our new life… Let's start it now. Right now. Stay,* she had said. She had held her hand out to him. *Please…*

But he hadn't taken it. He hadn't stayed.

"He killed you every bit as much as Lyndion did," Velak said.

The smoke in her mind swirled, agitated, trying to keep her from seeing something, but the memories slipped through. Grei's lips on hers. His body against hers. Standing together with him in the cold waters of the Temple of the Faia. He'd refused to kill her then. He'd defied Lyndion's prophecy, thwarted Lyndion. Grei had brought her back to life.…

"No," she said.

"He betrayed you," Velak said.

"I love him."

"You loved him with all your heart, and he delivered you to a monster. Grei must suffer most of all."

"Delivered me to Lyndion…" Again, her heart hurt, but she couldn't find anything false about what Velak was saying. Adora had begged Grei to stay. He had left her alone in the palace. Lyndion had come afterward. And then he'd taken her to the top of the Night Mountains. And then he…he…

Rage flared. The flames rose higher in her mind. Lyndion must die in agony, thrashing as fire blackened his skin, melted his eyes.

"And Grei."

"Grei…"

"He left you."

"He left me."

"We must have our revenge on both of them."

"I want to kill Lyndion."

"Open yourself to me again. I will give you the power to do it."

"Yes."

She opened herself, and Velak roared into every part of her. She swelled with heat, and it exploded out from her chest and the tips of her fingers.

She let out a long sigh. "Yes."

"We will melt the flesh from his bones. Come. We are nearly there. Just over that rise and we will wreak our vengeance."

She began walking.

The Tullawn Mountains loomed to the south. The rise crested and gave way to a valley with more small hills scattered throughout. Lilacs rose tall, bordering bushes dotted with purple berries. The bushes and the lilacs covered the hilly ground for a mile in each direction. To the east and west, the land flattened out and became grassland. To the south, the grasslands were brief before becoming foothills.

She strode down the slope and among the bush-covered hills, guided by Velak's memories. She rode the fiery wash of his strength as Velak guided her unerringly forward. The hills were small, each only twice as tall as she was, little miniature mountains.

They reached a clearing in the center of the valley and found a little girl waiting for them. She had lavender skin and dark purple hair, and she wore a brief purple dress and no shoes. Velak knew her name, whispered it in Adora's mind: Lankoli. Humans called her the Purple Faia.

Lankoli opened her mouth, and a musical noise emerged, like a bird singing.

"I knew you would come someday." Her voice joined the smoke in Adora's mind.

"And yet you kept me caged," Velak replied, using Adora's mouth. "You should have freed me. Aided me. I would have been merciful then."

"I don't think you know the meaning of the word, Brother." Lankoli shook her head. *"This human does not belong to you."*

"We are working together. A common goal of vengeance."

"The lands have felt your absence, brother. With every passing year, I have felt the balance slip a little more. Mother was convinced imprisoning you was the only way. Now I wonder…"

"Is this where you tell me you were always on my side?" Velak said with Adora's mouth.

"I think it was foolish to try to lock you away. You are a force of the land as surely as we are. It created a void."

"That 'void' will take your life, Lankoli." Velak sneered. "Your quest for knowledge comes far too late. Do you think this introspection will sway me from my mission? Even now, you hold your piece of the barrier that holds me imprisoned."

"If I foreswore Mother and my sisters, would it matter? You were born with wrath, brother. You fool yourself if you think it was your imprisonment that birthed it. It was always your responsibility to tame it."

"Mother has made a wreck of these lands. The humans warped her; it was her insane desire to be one of them. It is time to cleanse her mistakes. It is time for me to claim stewardship of the roses."

"Mother was always broken, but love is not a mistake. Pyll says love is what balances the lands. Mother sought that balance."

"Pyll died, burning in my flames, waiting for love to save her," Velak growled with Adora's lips.

"You killed her.… I felt it…but I hoped…" Lankoli closed her eyes softly, face tight with pain. Her little hands curled, becoming fists, and she hugged herself. *"Oh, sister…"*

"Don't pretend you loved her," Velak said. "If you loved each other, you'd all still be clustered together, crafting your trinkets for humans within the womb of Fairmist. But you can't stand each other any more than I can stand you."

"Come then, brother," Lankoli said in a small voice, barely audible in Adora's mind. *"Finish it."*

"You aren't going to fight?"

"Our deaths will not sate you, but I fear you will only realize this when their bitter taste fills your jaws. Remember that I told you."

He laughed.

She held her arms out. *"Begin your reign."*

A lance of fire shot from Adora's finger. A purple shield

surrounded the Purple Faia, protecting her for a brief moment, then the shield shattered. The fire burned into Lankoli, and she let out a high-pitched keen like a wailing bird. The fire consumed her, and she vanished.

A twisted bush lay where she had been, coiled in the shape of a crouching girl, arms over her head, berries squashed and leaking purple into the charred earth.

Velak reveled in the glory of it. He sang a song that Adora felt she should know, a song she had heard somewhere before, but that she couldn't quite recall. Lost in his revelry, Velak's hold on Adora slipped, and she could think for a moment, just long enough for the realization to fill her, for her to think about it like Adora, instead of like Velak.

"We killed a Faia," she said, her words slow and thick. "We killed two Faia…"

Velak continued his song.

"But…we didn't come to kill Faia." Terror blossomed in her chest. "What did we do?" Panic spread through her. Images of the Green Faia burning returned to her, and she gasped. "What have I done? It is…"

"…*necessary.*" Velak said inside her mind, returning from his victorious song; his voice blended with hers.

"No!" Adora shouted, crying. "You said we were going to kill Lyndion! This is not Lyndion! These are…"

"*…his allies. They made the path upon which he walked.*"

"But he was…" Were the Faia her enemies? Smoke thickened in her mind, and suddenly it was hard to think again. She shook her head, trying to clear the smoke away.

"He took you, kept you, butchered you," Velak whispered.

An image of Lyndion rose upon the smoke, a knife raised high. Rage filled her, and she clenched her teeth. "I want to kill him," she said.

"He lives in Fairmist."

"Fairmist."

"We will find him there. We will make him pay."

"Yes…." For a moment, she hesitated. There had been something she'd wanted to say, something she'd remembered that was important.… Something…

But the thought was gone. All that remained was rising flames and roiling smoke inside her mind. Nothing was more important than Lyndion's death. Nothing else mattered but revenge.

"To Fairmist," Velak said in her mind.

She began walking east.

Chapter 20

CAVYN

CAVYN PLACED HER HAND on the smooth, cold wood of her living room wall and whispered to it. It opened like a mouth, revealing a curving stairway to a warmly lit sanctum below, a place none knew about except her and Velak. She stepped across the threshold, closed the door behind her, and descended the stairs into a septagonal room. The seven corners of the room—one for each of her daughters—represented the forces that created the powerful barrier that kept the lands safe from her firstborn son, Velak.

There were five plants of different colors in five of the corners of the room: A deep blue water lily, a green vine coiled with thorns, a majestic orange aloe plant, a cluster of lilacs surrounding purple berries on a stem, and a thatch of charcoal-black grass. Each was a node of protection, bound within the roots of the oldest tree in Benasca, linked to the five remaining havens of her daughters, and holding the life lights of her daughters, whose presence and power held Velak at bay. Of course, two of the corners were dark, shriveled long ago. They represented her daughters who had died: a broken brown cattail for Besni and the husk of the yellow sunflower for Deilli. It put more of a burden on Cavyn and her remaining daughters, but the barrier held.

The oval mirror in the center of the room wasn't actually a mirror; it was a window to Velakka, the prison that held her son. Cavyn had built the mirror in this place because, if she could not have her Beloved, she could at least see him in the face of their son. Velak could never be set free, of course. He had no care for the fragile mortals of the lands. His anger would consume the lands. But with this mirror, at least she could talk to him, give him the comfort a mother should give.

After all, wasn't that what a mother was for? To bring comfort to her children? Though Cavyn and her daughters had to keep Velak confined—his last tantrum had nearly burned all of Devorra to cinders—Cavyn wanted to ensure he knew she still loved him.

In this room, she and Velak were both helpless; he a captive, she without magic. The barrier made from her daughters' life force not only kept the barrier to Velakka in place, but it likewise ensured that no magic entered this room. In this place, she could not pull power from the blue roses. It was a delicious helplessness. Here, she felt closer to being human than anywhere else.

And with her helplessness reflecting her son's helplessness, it allowed her to relate to him on equal ground.

"Hello, Mother," Velak said from the mirror as she reached the floor of the septagonal room.

"How are you feeling?" she asked, as she always did.

He smiled, but did not answer. His face was more human than any of his sisters, save the horns that curled back from his forehead. His skin was only slightly reddish; it could have passed for human, while Pyll's green skin or Jevare's blue never would have. Velak's long, pointed face watched her, and he smiled.

He was beautiful. She had been beside herself with joy at his birth, watching the tongues of flame run over his little body. The power of him radiated from the very first moment. When he had smiled up at her with his translucent, pointed teeth, she'd felt her heart melt like a mother's heart should. She'd loved him instantly. But even with all that, she knew her Beloved would never have accepted Velak with horns and flames running over his body. And so, father and son had never met. Only her tenth child had been suitable. Only Thiazin.

Velak's red eyes glowed. He seemed happier than she'd seen him in a long time, but it didn't fool her. Like a wild animal, he was ready to attack her.

"How are you feeling, Mother?" he asked.

"Tired," she said truthfully. She always spoke the truth to him. She and his sisters had imprisoned him, and they could never free him. The least she could do was share the rest of her life with him.

"Did you use another blue rose?" he said.

She smiled ruefully but said nothing. When Velak was a boy, she had incautiously mentioned the blue roses to him and his sisters. Velak had immediately been interested. He wanted to know where they were. The blue roses were the source of all magic in the lands. While she shared everything else with her son, she had never told him how to use the blue roses, nor how many existed, and certainly not where that secret field lay. It was the only thing she denied him.

"You always look exhausted when you kill another blue rose," Velak said. "One would think it would fill you with life."

She just smiled, looking at his beautiful face.

"You gave it to someone else, didn't you?" Velak took a deep breath, as though he was about to dive underwater. He was so handsome. "Who would you give such power to?" His gaze smoldered.

"Kuruk has been to Thiara." Cavyn changed the subject. "He started his war again."

"Yes, and he ran from a human."

"Kuruk is a sweet boy. He longs for his lost childhood."

"I wonder what that is like, to have a childhood."

"I have tried to show you," she said.

"The Whisper Prince bested him." Velak ignored her response.

"Whisper Prince?"

Velak smiled wider. "You should have been born a crab, Mother. You do love to bury yourself in the sand."

Whisper Prince. What a curious title. She wondered if it had to do with the voices of the elements. She decided she would have to find out more about him, this Whisper Prince, but not from Velak. He would use it for leverage. He used everything for leverage.

It was her duty to know about important moments in the lands, but Cavyn had never been good at her duty. She had always wanted to live a human life, not hold the responsibility for the lands. That job had been made for her mother, and Cavyn wasn't especially good at it. Her mother had *known* that, but she'd left Cavyn with the responsibility all the same, left her and never returned....

Cavyn cleared her mind of the frustration, lest Velak see.

Little faces of flame flickered in the mirror behind her son, clamoring to see over his shoulder. His little Velakkans. Velak was a destroyer first, but even he had created. The creatures were his thoughts made real, splinters of his soul, and they were like little people in their own right, seeming to have their own thoughts and reactions, independent of Velak.

People would do almost anything to keep from feeling alone. She pictured Velak's splinter-selves doting on him, caring for him. Perhaps this loneliness was something that could be cultivated in Velak. During his tantrum, he'd been determined to exterminate all human life in Devorra. But that would just make the lands into a second Velakka, only larger. If Velak could be convinced to spare humanity, perhaps someday, he could be brought back to live among them.

"I wonder if you..." Cavyn trailed off. Just beyond the mirror, in Pyll's corner of the room, the thorny green vine representing her strength—her contribution to the barrier that kept Velak imprisoned—was withering. Its coils slowly turned brown, dying. Pyll had released her support of the barrier. Or Pyll had…died. A spike of fear lodged in Cavyn's heart, but she kept it from her face. Her gaze flicked around the room, stopped on the purple berry bush that represented Lankoli's power. Two of the leaves were brown. As she watched, a third leaf was slowly turning brown. It, too, was dying.

They'd been killed. Pyll and Lankoli had been killed! She shot a look at her son—

The mirror exploded.

Flames blasted her from her feet, throwing her backward. Shards of glass stabbed her skin, pierced one of her eyes, half-blinding her.

"Velak!" she screamed as her son lunged through, suddenly free of the mirror, somehow free of his prison. He was large and real and right here in the room. Sparkling shards of mirror fell around him as he blurred forward.

The power of his flames should have vanished the moment they came into this room. This room was sealed against magic! How—

Velak snatched her by the neck, picked her up and threw her across the room. She hit the base of the staircase, the hard steps bending her mortal back. She cried out, fought the pain, and flipped onto her belly. Somehow, he had brought his power here, and she was mortal in this place.

The horror washed through her. Velak could kill her. She craned her neck, looking up the staircase toward her salvation. Above, she could rejuvenate her eye and her body with a gesture. She could take hold of Velak and drive him back. With a grunt, she lunged up the stairs. She needed to keep ahead of him. She just needed to reach the door—

She stopped halfway up, breathing hard, her blood dripping on the stair in front of her. One dot. Two dots. Three…

"Go ahead, Mother," Velak whispered in her ear, standing next to the steps.

Blood seeped into her good eye, and she blinked it away, peered up at the door. She could open it. But now it was the final barrier between Velak and the lands. Her heart hammered. The pain of her wounds made her feel like a fawn that wanted to run from a panther. With effort, she pushed back the clamor of agony and tried to think.

"You longed to be human for so long," Velak whispered. "Now you are. Tell me how it feels, Mother. Are you proud? Look at you, running scared from pain and fear. Are you proud of the frightened rabbit you've become?"

"H-How?" she asked.

"All those things you sought with such fervor. Love," he whispered. "Compassion." He shook his head. "Weakness." He laughed then, a strong laugh full of good-hearted mirth. Then he went silent. "I waited so long," he whispered in her ear. "Then you gave it to me."

"I gave you nothing. I *shut* the rift you created—"

"You let Kuruk, Malik, and Bahktish live. You saw them as boys who needed a mother, so you spared them. You didn't see that they were my ambassadors. That's where it started."

She tried to understand how that had created a power imbalance. She had allowed Kuruk and his two brothers to return, but she had slammed the door when her son had tried to follow. He had been contained.

"The Debt of the Blessed," he breathed. "I told Kuruk what he needed to hear, and he delivered to me what I needed to destroy you."

"The Blessed that Kuruk devoured…?"

"He didn't eat them. He transformed them," he said. "He filled them with my Velakkans."

Her blood ran cold. He'd broken the barrier. It must have been so small that she hadn't noticed. Just small enough to push the little slivers of personality through.

Her mouth opened. There were holes in his prison. Somehow, he'd used them to slay Pyll, to slay Lankoli. To weaken the barrier. He'd pulled his power through those tiny holes.… And pulled them into this room. That was how he had his magic, and she had none.…

"Oh," he whispered. "It hurt. Every Velakkan I created

hurt, every Velakkan I pushed into a human body was like a rip in my soul. But every rip reminds me of you, Mother. You gave me the gift of hatred, and it has sustained me through every year of agony."

"I never meant—"

"Oh, please," he interrupted. "Tell me what you *meant* to do." His eyes burned with rage. "You, who caged me. You, who tried to make me small and helpless. You, who stole my birthright."

Cavyn's mind reeled. She had to think her way through this. It was just so hard with the pain, with the helplessness of knowing she had no access to the blue roses in this place.

"So here I am, Mother. I'm going to rip down your barrier. I'm going to kill my bitch sisters. And once you are all dead, I will open that door above." He grinned. "Unless, of course, you'd like to open it now. Give me freedom. Claim your blue roses. Then we can find out, at last, who is more powerful."

Cavyn's mortal heart beat so fast it felt like it was in her throat, choking her.

That open door was her salvation. And it was certain doom for the lands.

"I have dreamed about this for so long," he said. "To give you the helplessness you gave to me. To know that, whatever you do, you lose. If you don't open that door, I will fill that mortal body of yours with so much pain you will scream for death. Then I will kill you to weaken the barrier further. Then I will simply burst through from this side. And if that doesn't work…" He shrugged. "I will wait. Adora is in the world, working for me. She is hunting down my sisters. When I slay enough of them, that barrier will collapse. What will it take? One more? Two? I doubt I'll have to chase them all down. I can feel the barrier weakening already. Maybe all it will require is your death.…"

He stroked her cheek, his long, inhumanly sharp fingernails like daggers. They moved up, tracing a path along her temple, across the back of her head. It sent cold tingles through her.

She breathed hard, blinking away blood, watching it drip

onto the floor. Drip. Drip. Drip.

"Velak, please…"

"Oh yes. Do beg. Very human of you." He tapped his pointed chin with a finger. "But if you let me out the door," he dropped his voice to a whisper, "if you tell me where the blue roses are, I'll make you a deal. I'll let you live as a human, just like you always wanted. I will strip away your immortality, strip away your magic, just as you always wanted, and I pledge that I shall not kill you. You can live out your mortal lifespan and die of old age."

"Velak, there is more that you don't know," she said with a tight voice. She tried to sound strong, but her body hurt so much. "If you'll just—"

He plunged his fingernails into the taut flesh between her ribs, and she screamed. White-hot agony exploded through her.

"Let's find out," he whispered, close to her ear again. "If your death will weaken the barrier enough to let me out."

She clenched her teeth, trying to be brave, but she made a low, squeaking noise.

"A whimper, Mother? Come now. Let us have one of our mother-son chats. Speak for me."

He made a fist, fingers slicing deep into her body.

Cavyn screamed.

Chapter 21

GREI

REE DIDN'T SPEAK as she led Grei down the slope to the Fairmist River. To the west, the red mist had spread over the entire city, a low-hanging crimson haze. It had barely been three hours since they'd fled Lowtown.

Grei felt hollow, staring at the water as he stumbled along behind her, trying to bear the burden of his colossal failures. Blevins was dead... Grei had killed him.

After the Phantom War, Grei had been so confident. He'd come into his power, fought monsters, pierced the grand illusion. He'd done the right thing. But where had it brought him? Could he honestly say this was better than the Debt of the Blessed? Weeds of disaster sprang up wherever he went. He hadn't listened to Adora; now she was Velak's slave, a monster of fire and rage. He'd birthed the red mist, given Velak a way to enslave the city of Thiara in a day. He'd come to help the Green Faia, but left behind a swath of melted trees.

And he'd killed Blevins, his only real friend aside from Adora.

You can't save him; you'll create another calamity. Ree's words bubbled up in his mind again.

He clenched his fists. No. He couldn't wallow in self-loathing. He had to figure a way through this.

Ree led him into the trees near the river and gracefully picked her way through the foliage, never stopping, rarely slowing. He could barely keep up with her. He wondered, not for the first time, if Ringblade initiates were chosen for their inherent strength and stamina. Both Ree and Selicia seemed to have endless endurance.

Not long ago—when Ree had grabbed him in the Temple of the Faia, delivering the secret of Kuruk's defeat by opening her mind to him—she had looked like a spindly fever victim, a single step from death's door. Maybe it was the intervening days of rest and food, or maybe it was the cessation of Kuruk's brutal spell, but she didn't look fragile anymore. She wasn't the svelte and curved Ringblade he'd met in Fairmist, either; a new Ree had emerged from her trials. With her short dress, ripped and ragged and smeared with dirt from her athletics, she looked like a lean, wild animal.

Over the next half an hour, Ree continued east along the river. He kept expecting her to stop, to question him, but she didn't. She drove methodically through the undergrowth, away from Thiara, ducking limbs and stepping through tall riverside grass.

He wanted to trust her, to tell her everything and get her keen mind working on the problems that filled his head.

But Blevins's accusations were simply too accurate to ignore. He'd described her every action of the last day as though he'd been there. Grei even opened his mouth to speak a few times, but stopped himself. Eventually, he remained reluctantly silent, struggling with himself.

Ree led him east for hours. Only when the sun made long shadows across the waters of the Fairmist River did she stop. He was practically blind with exhaustion, and he stumbled to a stop, leaning against a tree.

"Drink," she said, nodding at the river. "Rest."

"You're going to hunt?" he guessed. It was what Selicia would have done.

"To fish, yes," she said.

Or fish. Selicia had also fished. All Grei wanted to do was collapse. "You don't have a hook," he murmured.

She winked at him, shook Vecenne's bag.

"Oh."

"You haven't asked me any questions," he murmured.

"Would you answer if I did?"

He didn't answer that.

"I know you, Grei Forander. If someone pushes you, you push back." She seemed about to say something more, then shrugged. "Rest. With everything happening, who knows when you'll get another chance." She turned toward the river.

"I have to go to Fairmist," he called after her.

She stopped, looked over her shoulder. "Do you?"

"Yes."

She glanced back toward Thiara. The trees blessedly blocked the horrible red horizon. "Well, we're not going back to Thiara."

"Ree, I…"

"Grei, you can barely stand. If you want to talk, we can talk when you wake." She turned, made her way down to the river. He slid to the ground, his back against the tree. Its bark was smooth, and the solid wood felt good. A warm breeze blew over him, mixing with the distant sound of the rushing river. He smelled the moist earth, the hint of the distant sea.

He didn't want to sleep. He had these images, pieces of a puzzle that would form a picture, reveal a mystery. He was so close. He had to figure it out. Every second he let that puzzle lay unfinished could be catastrophic. But…by the Faia, he was tired.

He closed his eyes. It would just be for a second, to rally his strength. But the breeze was so warm, the scent of the river so nice. He kept his eyes closed for a moment longer than he meant to. The sun's warmth on his eyelids turned into a swirl of colors. He suddenly realized he'd had his eyes closed much longer than a moment. He tried to push them open, but they weighed a hundred pounds each.

He slept.

The dream started immediately.

The shaggy beast stood before him with its bloated torso and mismatched antlers, watching him with those crazy, rainbow eyes. Its deer-like head was raised, as if haughty.

They weren't in the South Forest this time, but instead in a valley with little purple hillocks. This wasn't anywhere near Fairmist. Grei had never been here before. The edges of the dream were fuzzy, and it took him a moment to realize the hills were not actually purple, but instead covered with purple berry bushes.

The beast reached a spot that had been charred black. In the midst of the blackened ground was a twisted bush with purple berries, some whole, some broken. The bush was shaped like a little girl, just as the thorny vines in the Jhor Forest had been in the shape of the Green Faia. The beast turned its long, slender head toward him. Its rainbow eyes swirled, and it drew a breath.

"Four are dead now." The beast somehow spoke, though its lips didn't move. "Only three remain. Velak will kill them all. Then he will kill every other living thing in Devorra."

"Who are you?" Grei demanded.

"They tried to hold him," the beast intoned. "But he has found a way through. He has poured himself into a vessel that can carry his wrath to Mother."

"What is your name!"

"She goes to meet him, but she goes unaware."

Grei rose suddenly into the air, then the rolling hills and berries shot far below him.

"No," he gasped, flailing, trying to force himself back down. Instead, the wind took him over the landscape. He crossed the Fairmist River again. The great plains rushed beneath him, then the northern Thiaran city of Wheatreen. The fields gave way to frost-prickled grasses, then a snow-covered forest that stretched to the horizon. The trees became a white blur as Grei hurtled through the air. In the distance, he saw the enormous, bone-white Frost Trees of the Benascan capital city. They towered over the rest of the forest like adults over children. Then he was upon them, rushing

toward the tallest, thickest tree, as big around as the entire Thiaran palace.

He cried out as he hit the trunk, but he passed through it like a ghost. He was reminded of his intense journey through the Dead Woods when the tree spirits had shoved his body into the trunk of the white tree. But this time, there was no pain. His meteoric speed slowed as he passed through the living white wood and emerged into a large room.

It was circular, curving around a center pillar, the wooden walls as white as the snow outside. But the rest of the room's accoutrements were warm. Lively paintings hung all around, landscape autumn scenes in oranges and golds, just like the kinds he'd seen in the palace in Thiara. A red velvet couch made of rich mahogany faced a matching chair over a glass table against the wall. As the curve of the wall continued, the rest of the room was obscured. Grei saw two pans hanging from hooks, but the rest was lost to view.

Cavyn, the blond Benascan woman from his dream at the palace, stood at the center pillar, facing away from him. She reached out a hand, put it on the pillar, and a yawning portal opened. She stepped through, then the mouth closed and she was gone.

"The rift is there," the dream-beast said. "Secured by the efforts of those you call the Faia. But four are now dead. The barrier weakens. Mother goes to talk with Velak, and she thinks herself safe, but the wards are breaking. She doesn't realize what Velak has done here."

"Why are you showing me this?"

"You must go to Benasca. You must warn her. If needed, you must save her."

"Who are you? Who is 'she'? Who is Cavyn?"

But the room slowly faded to black...

Grei started awake. Disorientation clutched at him. It seemed only moments since he'd closed his eyes, but the day was gone. Stars shone between the dark leaves overhead, and Ree sat next to a glowing fire ringed by rocks.

"Another nightmare?" she asked.

"What time is it?" he asked. The dream clung to him. It had been so frantic, so imperative.

"Not yet Deepdark," she said.

Grei had been terrified when he first met the horned slink-who-was-not-a-slink seven years ago, but in the dream, the beast had been the worried one.

You must warn her. If needed, you must save her.

The air smelled like sizzling fish. His mouth began to water, and his stomach rumbled. He couldn't remember the last time he'd eaten anything.

Ree gave a wry smile. "Sit up. Let's get some food into you." She pulled a blackened corn husk from the edge of the coals with her two daggers, balanced it delicately between the two sharp tips, and set it on a flat rock in front of him.

"By the Faia, that smells good," he said.

"All yours."

He leaned forward and took the smoking husk with the sizzling trout inside. It was hot, and he bobbled it from hand to hand as he brought it to his lap, but he didn't drop any of the precious fish. As soon as he could blow it cool, he began stuffing the fish into his mouth.

"Are all Ringblades accomplished hunters and foragers?" he asked around a mouthful.

"The seekers are."

"What's a seeker?"

"The Ringmother sends seekers out into the world, looking for things."

"Like you looked for me," he said.

She nodded.

"Is Selicia a seeker?" he asked.

"Selicia is everything."

Grei looked at his fish, then back up. "Which Ringblades are killers?" he asked.

She cocked her head, and for a moment he thought she wouldn't answer. Finally, she shrugged. "All of them."

"All?"

"Killers. Hunters. Diplomats. Each of us is trained to use our minds, our skills, our bodies in every way we can. A strong mind can push a body through unbelievable trials. We're trained to survive in the wilderness, to go without sleep, to expand our stamina beyond what is considered normal. We're trained to use our bodies to vanish from sight or to capture every eye. We're trained to thrive surrounded by allies or enemies. Whatever is needed, in whatever situation. And yes, we're trained to kill."

"How is being a diplomat about the body?"

"How is it not? People pay more attention to appearance, gestures, facial expressions than they do words. You move with them, they begin to move with you."

"Diplomat? You mean seductress."

"That, too," she said, winking.

Was she anything more than a fluid identity? Did she even have a personality aside from the Ringblade training? "Does it bother you to use sex just to get what you want?" he asked.

"Does it bother *you* to use sex to get what you want?"

"I don't!" he said, then he thought of the Duchess of the Highward, right before he fully discovered his magic, when he'd hated himself and ran around the Harvesthome Festival as The Whisper Prince. What a different meaning it had had back then.... He thought of Neviva, and the Venishan woman beneath the bridge, the Duchess Venderré. He cleared his throat. "Well, not with a goal in mind. I don't set it up coldly. I don't do it like you."

Her mouth curved upward in a smile.

He felt his face grow warm.

"I think I see what you're getting at," she said. "You're equating sex with love?"

"I'm not equating…no."

"It's okay. Most people don't think about sex clearly. It makes their emotions volatile, and Ringblades do a great deal of training on how to control and channel our emotions. Ringmaids are stripped of quaint notions first. Like imagining sex and love as one. By the time we pass the threshold from Ringmaid to Ringblade, we're pragmatic about the body and how to use it. We see the world with clear eyes. Only then can we truly act and move events. Ringblades don't indulge illusions. We cannot afford to."

"Love is not an illusion. Sex can… With the right person,

it's…it's the next step."

"The next step?" She raised an eyebrow, then shrugged. "If that is what you prefer to see, then—"

"It's not about perception."

"It's all about perception. You can use sex to make yourself feel good, or to make someone else feel good. You can also use it for leverage. Manipulation. Domination." She watched him. "It's an act, unspecific until you make it specific." She shrugged. "You can also use it for love, of course, but thinking sex and love are the same thing, that's an illusion. And a person who lives in an illusion can be manipulated. And a Ringblade who sees an illusion like that… Well, we can add to it, shape it, take control of it."

"So you can use your body, let another touch you, be intimate with you, just to manipulate them? It doesn't bother you?"

"I'll use whatever I can to attain my goal," she said. "I will break my own bones. Scar my soul. I would—and have—taken lives."

"Do Ringblades even believe in love?"

"Deeply," she said without hesitation. She glanced down at the fire and, for a moment, she seemed wistful. "We know the truth about love," she said softly.

"What truth?"

She cleared her throat and looked into his eyes again. "That love is more important than anything else."

Her quiet, fervent passion made him pause. "How can you even say that, then sleep with someone to manipulate them?"

"It's exactly because of what I do that I know love. Ringblades are family, Grei. And not just through some accident of birth. We're a family lashed together by feats of physical prowess and tests of the mind, tests of the emotions. We're joined together by intense, common experiences and a deep love and respect. After a month of Ringblade training, Ringmaids are bound more tightly than we ever were to those in our former lives."

"So Ringblades love within your sanctum but kill out in the

world?" he asked.

"We serve the empire when and where it needs, no exceptions. We do not allow ourselves the luxury of exceptions."

He fell into a troubled silence.

"What are you seeking, Grei? Are you trying to decide if I am a moral person?" she asked softly. "What do you really want to say to me?"

"I want…" He hesitated. "I want to trust you," he said bluntly. "But you give me no reason."

"What proof would satisfy you? Saving your life, maybe? Pulling you from a doomed city? Fighting my own sisters to help your cause over theirs? Breaking every oath I ever made in order to keep my oath to you? What would satisfy you?" She gave a wry smile. "Shall I sleep with you and tell you that it's love?"

He frowned. "Ree…" He shook his head. "Everything you've done could have been planned. Selicia might have laid out your orders before I ever came to see you in the infirmary."

"She might also be a purple turkey with no wings. You are jumping at shadows."

"Selicia fooled me once. I believed in her, and she betrayed me."

"I'm not Selicia."

"You're *just* like Selicia! You'll do whatever it takes to achieve your purpose, no matter who you betray, no matter who you hurt."

"*You* are my purpose, Grei!" She raised her voice, and he could see her irritation. "I don't serve the empire anymore. I serve you!"

He hesitated.

"You do what you want, but you know what's happening in Thiara. The empress, Princess Vecenne, Syvet, and who knows how many more by now? All taken by Velak's mist. If you think I'm part of some elaborate scheme, who do you think I'm going to report to? Even if I still served the empire, there will be no empire to serve soon if I don't help you."

"Very well," he said. "I'll tell you what I know."

"That would be good," she said.

"Blevins is Baezin," Grei said.

"I heard that," she said. "But I don't believe it. Certainly, Magnus is a powerful fighter, and Baezin was reputed to be a legendary swordsman... But just because Magnus shares that trait with a long-dead emperor doesn't make him the three-hundred-year-old father of the empire."

"If you're having a hard time believing that, then the rest is going to be even harder..." he said.

He told her everything he knew about Velak. She already knew some, of course. She'd seen Velak in Kuruk's memories when the Slink tried to devour her mind. She knew that Velak had created Kuruk, and that Kuruk had inserted pieces of the fiery lord into the human bodies of the Blessed. He described his encounter with his own brother, how Julin had utterly changed after undergoing the transformation of the Blessed. But Grei added more. He told her about the Archon, and about how Velak no longer needed the Debt of the Blessed to dig his claws into human bodies. He explained what he'd learned about the girl with the white lock of hair, and how the red mist had come to be. Then he mentioned his dreams; the dream of the Benascan woman Cavyn, and the dream in which Adora had attacked the Green Faia.

Once he'd set the stage with all of these mysteries, he told Ree how he'd searched for any reference to Velak or Lord Velak in the Thiaran libraries. And he found one single reference to a Velak in the histories of Empress Thiazin. He described it to her.

"Wait, Velak is Empress Thiazin's brother?" Ree asked.

"And possibly the firstborn of Baezin's line. Thiara was pregnant once, maybe twice, before she gave birth to Empress Thiazin. Thiazin wrote that her mother vanished before she came to term, then reappeared later without a child, and it precipitated a fight between Thiara and Baezin. Thiazin speculated that fight was about Velak...that the child she'd hidden was Velak."

"Baezin's blood…" she murmured.

"Literally," he said.

She frowned.

"But the questions don't stop there," he said. "Like how does Velak have enough power to create something like Kuruk? How does he have the power to take over human bodies, to kill a Faia?"

"Is he a Whisper Prince?" she asked.

"I think he's a Faia."

She blinked. "But…the Faia are female."

"All the Faia we know about."

"Wait." She held up a hand. "You're saying Velak is Baezin's and Thiara's child," she said. "And you're saying Velak is a Faia. Then you're saying…"

"That the Faia are the daughters of Baezin and Thiara," he finished for her.

"That's insane."

"It takes a leap. Just follow me a little—"

"The Faia were here when Baezin arrived," she interrupted, waving a hand. "Before he even made the empire. Even Baezin's journals say so. He couldn't have been their father."

"I got stuck on that, too," he said. "You're right, Baezin was here only a few months when the Faia first appeared and began giving him magical miracles. I almost dismissed the whole notion because of it; I thought Empress Thiazin had misheard or misremembered, or perhaps she'd been talking about a different Velak. But I searched for another reference to Velak, or even a reference to anyone else *named* Velak. There's no mention anywhere. I even checked what few Benascan histories are available."

"A singular name?" she said. "That doesn't prove anything. Maybe there were a hundred Velaks, but none were captured in books."

"Then how about this: You've seen into Kuruk's mind. Velak is imprisoned. With his vast power, who could possibly imprison him?"

"The Faia," she said.

"The Faia," he agreed. "No one else has the strength. And now that Velak's free, who is he targeting?" He told her about his latest dream, about how the Faia were holding some kind of barrier, and that it was weakening as the Faia were slain.

"Adora is the key. If we can free her from Velak, he loses his 'vessel'. He won't be able to kill the Faia anymore. He stays in his prison."

She held up a hand. "That doesn't mean Baezin and Thiara gave birth to goddesses."

"But just—"

She waved her hand in a peremptory gesture. "Listen. Let's say I indulge you for a moment and imagine that a Venishan conqueror and a Benascan woman could miraculously give birth to seven goddesses. Somehow. Let's say some strange magic infected her womb. Whatever. But that's where the fiction has to end. It takes nine months to make a baby. Not a few weeks. You'd have to assume Thiara somehow went to Venisha first, met Baezin and became his lover *long* before he ever sailed to Devorra, and then later, just as he arrived, she bore his babies. There's no record of anything like that. Baezin's own journals say he'd never met her before he arrived on these shores."

"It takes nine months to have a baby," Grei said. "If you're human."

"They *were* human."

"Baezin was. Even if he's something else now, he was human before. There are records of his life in Venisha. But Thiara wasn't Venishan."

"She was a Benascan."

"That's what the history books say. That's what Baezin assumed. But he and his conquerors didn't know anything about Benasca back then. He simply assumed. I don't think she was Benascan. I don't think she was Venishan or Benascan or anything human. I think she was a Faia."

Ree's eyes widened. "What?"

"Not one of the seven. But something else. Maybe

something stronger. The mother of the Faia. I think Thiara is the one in my dreams. I think she's hiding in Benasca and calling herself Cavyn, just like Magnus hid himself in Fairmist and called himself Blevins."

Ree put a hand to her head, like she was dizzy.

"It's a lot," he said. "But stay with me. It starts to come together. Cavyn transformed herself into the semblance of a human. Baezin met her, fell in love with her, gave her the name Thiara. They became lovers. She bore him children, but didn't tell him about it. When he found out about this, they fought about it. Thiara withdrew, then used her power to make sure Baezin never died, either as a punishment or because she couldn't bear to watch him pass away. Or both."

"The mother of the Faia...?" Ree murmured, like she was trying to wrap her mind around it.

"Ree, I felt Cavyn's presence. It was staggering. I've been face-to-face with two Faia, and neither exuded this kind of power. When her spirit fingers roared over me in the palace, I felt like an ant looking up at a bear."

Ree pinched the bridge of her nose, eyes closed. "The mother of the Faia..." she murmured, then she held up a hand. "But it...it takes nine months to make a baby."

"What if it didn't?"

"But it *does!*" She slapped her hand on her leg, opening her eyes, and he could see the fear and anger on her face. He understood it. He'd been feeling the same way.

"With the power I have," he said. "I can ask stone to become water. I can ask wood to come to life." He gestured at her arm. "If Cavyn was a hundred times more powerful than me, what would stop her from creating an actual person? What would stop her from doing it in an hour—or even in a minute—if she wanted?"

Ree watched him, her eyes wider than normal. She didn't say anything.

"If you make that one leap," he said. "It makes sense."

"One leap..." she murmured, then she just looked into the fire, hands on her knees, her body stiff.

"Ree?"

She glanced up at him and swallowed. "I feel very small, Grei."

"That only means you understand what I'm saying."

"It's just…" she began. "Some things are certain. Some things *have* to be certain, don't they? The sun rises in the east, sets in the west. The tides of the ocean roll in; they roll back out. A woman becomes pregnant, carries a child for nine months, then gives birth…" She shook her head. "A mother can't make a baby in a day."

"We're talking about a goddess," he said.

She sighed, looking exhausted. Since he'd met her, Ree had been unflappable and unstoppable, burning with supernatural vigor, but right now she looked like a malnourished refugee, spent and vulnerable. She pushed a breath out between her lips.

"There's more," he repeated.

"Oh. good." She rolled her eyes. "I was worried it was just going to be about these trivial matters.…" she said sarcastically.

"Cavyn had another child," he pressed.

She narrowed her eyes. "Another Velak?"

"No."

"Something worse than Velak?"

"Better, I hope. I think he's trying to help me."

"Not a Faia?"

"Not one of the seven, anyway. I think this creature, whatever he is, sent me the dreams about Cavyn and Adora. He's helping me understand what's really going on. I think he wants to stop Velak, too."

"Why do you think that?"

"He said 'They tried to hold him'. He told me to go to Benasca to help Cavyn. He called her 'Mother'."

"Maybe this creature is feeding you lies. Maybe it's Velak's ally, trying to confound you."

"Everything he's told me so far is true."

"Grei, listen. If Velak is threatened by the Faia, then he's threatened by *you*, too," she said. "This dream beast could be one of Velak's minions. What if he's trying to draw you out, draw you to a place where Velak can attack you?"

"I met this creature when I first met Adora, before I knew about Kuruk or Velak or any of the rest of it. At the time, I thought he was a slink. But he couldn't have been. The only real slinks were Kuruk and his brothers."

"Maybe that's exactly what he was. A phantom slink. And now Velak is using it to manipulate you. You can't just trust it," she said.

He shook his head, looking down. "I think I can. I think I *have* to."

She cocked her head. "Why?"

A shiver went up Grei's back; he looked into Ree's eyes.

"Because I think he made me into the Whisper Prince."

Chapter 22

GREI

REE HAD CHOSEN their camping spot to be concealed. With the moon high in the sky and the cover of the trees, no one could see them from even twenty paces away. Once Grei was awake and full of fish, she left for a brief time and came back with two horses, saddles, bridles, and saddle bags. She'd also found a pair of purple pantaloons to cover her legs underneath the ragged dress. Obviously, it was all stolen.

"Where did you get that?"

"Keep your voice down," she said. "There is a Felesh plantation house just over that rise. You shout, they're going to hear you."

"I suppose theft falls into your philosophy of doing whatever you need for your mission."

She shook Vecenne's satchel. "I left enough coin to buy three horses better than this. And who would wear these that didn't have to?" She gestured at the gaudy pantaloons. "I did them a favor." She tossed him a sleeveless tunic.

"Thank you," he said, promising himself that he would see

the horses returned after this was all over. He removed the X-shaped harness, pulled the tunic over his head, and felt better that he wasn't running around bare-chested. She had also brought him a thick belt.

"You can't carry the sword with that." She pointed at the harness. "A Highblade sees you with that, he'll kill you on sight." She took the harness and, after a moment of working at it, she removed the clasp that held the scabbard and attached it to the belt. She tossed the harness into the bushes, gave Grei the belt and scabbard, and he buckled it on. He had never worn a sword before. It felt awkward to have one at his waist, but it was much less awkward than wearing the damned harness.

"We should ride as far as we can before the sun rises," she said.

They packed up their meager supplies and doused the fire. They rode east toward Fairmist, and during the moments they walked the horses, resting them, Grei shared with Ree every detail of the moment he'd met Adora as the Forest Girl. He told her of the Green Faia standing watch over the injured Adora, then vanishing in a spray of sparkles. He described the tree against which Adora leaned, how he'd given her his cloak and held her. He described when she kissed him, and how he'd stayed with her for days, waiting for his father to look for them. For himself as much as her, he described the dreambeast, both from that first meeting and from the dreams. He told her of its hideous appearance: its bloated torso, impossibly long arms, bark-like skin, uneven horns and deer face.

Ree asked questions like she wished to memorize everything he said. Beyond that, she didn't speak, and once the story was done, they rode hard again. It took them two days to reach the ivory spears of the Badlands, dead trunks like a giant's teeth rising in the moonlight. The Night Mountains hung overhead, shadowy hulks blotting out half the star-dotted sky.

They made camp next to the Fairmist River in the exact same place he'd first camped with Selicia after the Dead

Woods. After they tied the horses to graze, Grei went down to the river. He hoped the gentle flow would settle his thoughts.

He crouched down, let out a long breath, and threw a stick into the water, watched it float downstream.

The sound of the rushing water pulled his worries away, and soon the warbling whispers rose in his mind. But he didn't speak back to them. It took losing Blevins to realize that he couldn't use his magic. It was dangerous to him and everyone around him. He touched his belly gingerly, feeling the ridged, twisted sewing job he'd done on himself. He couldn't fix it. He didn't dare try.

But if Grei was right, the dream-beast had bestowed these powers on Grei. If the dream-beast wanted Grei to "mend the world," then he could bestow them again.

Ree approached and stood behind Grei.

"We will reach Fairmist tomorrow," she said. "Best use this time to sleep."

He nodded.

"Do you have a plan?" she asked.

"Find the dream-beast."

She waited in silence for him to elaborate. When he didn't, she said, "Well, simple plans are the best." She down next cross-legged next to him.

"He wants me to find him," Grei said.

"Says one of your random jumps in logic?"

"What do you mean?"

"You have a tendency to imagine the world as you'd like it to be, then decide it actually *is* that way."

"I don't do that."

She gave a rueful smile and shook her head. "It's your best trait. If you were anyone else, I'd dismiss you as delusional. But you're the Whisper Prince, so you actually do have the ability to change reality. It makes you more of a visionary than a madman. We'd still have the Debt of the Blessed if not for you. But with your magic in question…I'd like to probe a bit further."

He didn't like where this was going.

"What makes you think this dream-beast wants you to find it?" she asked.

"Because I... Because he made me into the Whisper Prince."

"So naturally he can do it again, fix your problem." She nodded. "I understand that. But you think he wants you to find him because *you* want answers."

"He *does* want... I mean, that's not what I'm saying..." he trailed off. That was what he was thinking, actually. But why would the dream-beast send him dreams if it didn't want Grei to find him?

"Okay. Fair enough. Let's say he does want you to find him. You're assuming he wants you to find him because he wants to help you. What if he doesn't? What if he wants you to come to him because it's a trap?" she asked. "What if the dream-beast works for Velak?"

"That's ridiculous. He doesn't work for Velak."

"Again, you think that because you want it to be true. You have no evidence whatsoever," she said. Grei opened his mouth to retort, but she held up her hands in surrender. "Say you're right. Say he's not working for Velak. Let's say he's an ally. Another kind of Faia."

"That's exactly what I think he is. A Faia we've never heard about before."

"And Velak is methodically killing Faia."

"The Faia we know. The seven."

"Why not this one, also?" she asked.

That stopped him.

"You didn't think of that," she said.

"I didn't think of that," he echoed.

"So this creature could be next on Velak's list. Going there could put you right in Velak's path."

"All the more reason to get to the dream-beast first," he said firmly.

"What if this dream-beast knew about Velak, knew he would eventually return and begin killing the Faia. What if he knew about it seven years ago, and he's been waiting all this time for Velak to finally come for him?"

"I think he wants me to help stop Velak, to…maybe join with me to push Velak back."

"What if he created you expressly to be a lightning rod for Velak?"

He opened his mouth to refute her, but he suddenly wondered if she was right. It was something he had wondered. If the dream-beast had turned Grei into the Whisper Prince, the question remained: Why? Was Ree right?

"Maybe this dream-beast keeps sending you dreams so you'll jump in front of Velak, a willing sacrifice," she said.

Grei shook his head. "There has to be a better reason I was given this magic."

"Now you're acting like you know this thing, when actually you don't. You're good-hearted, Grei. But most people act through self-interest. They'll do anything to save themselves."

"A Faia wouldn't do that."

"You mean the Faia who ignored us for centuries, through the Slink War and the Debt of the Blessed?"

"It created the Whisper Prince to help."

"You don't *know* this creature. The dream-beast could be anything. It could be another Velak. It could be worse than Velak."

"Stop it!"

"Fine." She held up a hand in surrender. "I told you I will follow you. So I'll trust your instincts. Maybe you'll make your delusions into reality again." She shifted, pulling her knees up to her chest and resting her chin on them. "We find the dream-beast," she said softly.

"We find the dream-beast," he agreed, but his heart was filled with doubts that hadn't been there before.

Part III

The Dream Beast

Chapter 23

URIOZI

URIOZI FELT THE DEATH of her sister while she was staring at the Sunset Sea. It hit her like a violent wind from all sides, compressing her body. Uriozi fell forward, almost touching the water. She reflexively beseeched the wind to lift her, and she floated back, alighting safely on the shore. Fear and grief tightened all around her. Lankoli. Dead. Pyll first and now Lankoli, both within a matter of hours. Velak was here. He was coming for them at last.

Only two of her sisters remained: Jevare and Sherim. The strain of holding Velak's barrier suddenly doubled, and it made her gasp. Little beads of sweat appeared on her forehead. But she could take the weight. She *had* to take the weight.

She looked to her left at the jagged peaks of the Cliffgard Mountains. Her sister Sherim's haven lay atop them, high up where few humans could reach. Sherim would be feeling the strain, just as Uriozi was. They each had an equal share of holding Velak's barrier.

Uriozi had stood by the sea for more than a day, trying to

muster the courage to visit. She'd stood here so long, another of her sisters had died. Was it inevitable, then? No matter what they did, were they destined to be wiped from the lands one by one by Velak? There was a ruthless symmetry to it. They would die together as they had been birthed together.

Uriozi remembered waking to the world on the day of her birth, so long ago. She remembered being in Mother's human womb, the warmth of sunlight through the layers of human skin and organs, the body that Mother had worn when she birthed her children. She remembered coming into the world to see her mother's face: sadness, disappointment.

For the first several years of Uriozi's life, she'd thought that was the normal reaction mothers had for their children. She hadn't known most mothers were overjoyed at seeing their progeny for the first time, that they showered them with love and affection. All Uriozi and her sisters had known was that Mother was in love with Father, and that these children might not please him. So for that first decade, Uriozi and her sisters tried their best to show Mother and Father how pleasing they could be.

Velak had not. He had kept his own counsel while he made up his mind. In the end, he'd decided Father was an inferior creature and Mother was debasing herself. Everything had changed after that. Velak had gone on his rampage, and Mother had opposed him. And then, the sisters had been forced to choose: side with Velak or side with Mother. It had seemed an easy choice. Velak had wanted fire and retribution, the slaying of humans, and the scorching of the world. The sisters had already fallen in love with the lands, and some had even begun attaching themselves to specific places, like Pyll to the Jhor Forest. Certainly, Uriozi and her sisters hadn't wanted to see the lands consumed in fire.

But as the years and decades and centuries had marched on, Uriozi had often questioned what they had done. Opposing Velak had been sane. But it soon became clear that Mother was not sane. Her solutions caused so many problems. She'd cut Velak away from the lands like a spot of rot from a healthy plant.

Uriozi had contemplated Mother's methods for centuries now. Mother was supposed to keep balance and promote harmony in the lands. Yet her choices made the lands an increasingly dangerous place. She sewed discord, created imbalance. From the moment they'd imprisoned Velak, Uriozi and her sisters could still feel him seething, overflowing with malice. His continuous pain soured everything the sisters did. It was the reason her sisters withdrew from humanity, found less and less joy in the lands. It was the reason they'd eventually withdrawn from each other. She and her sisters hadn't come together in almost a century. Even when Besni and Deilli died, when the human Emperor Qweryn stole their lives, the rest of the sisters had stayed away.

We've made terrible mistakes. What poor stewards we have been. What a poor steward Mother has been....

Still, none of them ever challenged Mother's imperatives. And now it was too late. The lands were so grossly out of balance that Uriozi couldn't conceive of what to do to put them right.

And so Uriozi was here, just north of the human city of Cliffgard, standing next to the deadly Sunset Sea. After Pyll's death, Uriozi had come straight to Sherim's haven without really knowing why. She'd been drawn here as though the very lands were calling. And yet she was too ashamed to float up there and talk to her sister, so ashamed that she'd stood here while Lankoli died. What they'd done to Velak had made them all ashamed. But for a dash of chance, Velak could have been any one of them. They might as well have imprisoned any of their other sisters. None of the sisters could really look into the eyes of their siblings after what they'd done to their brother.

No, Sherim didn't want to see Uriozi.

I will go up, Uriozi thought fervently. I will at least talk to Sherim. And if we cannot stand to look in each other's eyes, then at least I will know that I tried.

But she didn't move. Instead, she gazed at the rolling waves and felt the mighty barrier of Velak's prison like a pressure trying to break her bones, a barrier that was supposed to keep him at bay. A barrier that was failing with every sister who fell.

Maybe that was why she was drawn to the sea. She could also feel the barrier their grandmother had put in place along the coast of the entire continent of Devorra, the one after which they'd modeled their barrier for Velak. Of course, Grandmother's barrier, made to keep Venisha out of these lands, was as strong as ever. It was fueled by the blue roses, an endless source of magical power, and not the life forces of Uriozi and her sisters.

The entire Sunset Sea was a battle similar to the one Uriozi and her sisters fought with Velak. The difference was that their grandmother had won that battle against the god Venisha.

Humans who sailed those waters, seeking trade with Venisha, sometimes ran afoul of gigantic sea creatures living in the deep. It was assumed the rapacious monsters simply lurked there, waiting only for human flesh, but Uriozi and her sisters knew the truth. The monsters had been made by Venisha expressly to kill Mother or any of the sisters who might dare to venture into those deadly waters.

A hundred years ago, the god Venisha had almost had his way. He'd infiltrated Thiara with his wizards and his artifacts, but Empress Lymeera and the sisters had driven him out. Now, from time to time, he would strike at the barrier, but it was ever strong.

But now, the lands are doomed anyway. Grandmother succeeded. We have failed. We need not fear the god Venisha when Velak will devour us from within. And here I stand, afraid to float up and talk to Sherim—

Suddenly, Uriozi heard a new voice, a voice from the sea. Fear jolted through her as she imagined Venisha choosing this moment to attack grandmother's barrier.

But no. That wasn't it.…

She turned all of her attention on the incoming wave and saw a strange, shimmering liquid along its crest. The wave crashed, smoothing out along the black sand and carrying the shimmering liquid almost to Uriozi's feet.

Was this a new monster of the god Venisha? Uriozi waited cautiously on her side of the barrier.

But that was no sea monster. It made no dusty, metallic clanging like the rest of Venisha's handiwork. This shimmering—somehow cohesive—liquid sounded like...

It sounded like the voice of a human.

Uriozi came close, peering at it, and then she did what she had never done before. She stepped into the sea and whispered to it. This would alert Venisha as surely as if she'd yelled in his ear, but she would be quick. Surely none of his water monsters could reach her so fast.

The seawater flowed toward Uriozi, carrying the glimmering slick with it. She urged it farther up the beach, encouraging the coarse, black sand to form a groove of black rock. It complied happily.

She guided the water swiftly past the barrier, up the beach and safely away from the ocean. She made a pool in the black rock to hold the water, then beseeched all of the regular seawater to turn to white steam, leaving only the shimmering liquid with its human voice in the pool.

She shaped the rock into a perfectly round bowl the size of a human bathtub, and listened more deeply to the flickering voice.

Suddenly, she recognized it.

Alarmed, Uriozi floated away from the pool in disbelief. But that simply couldn't be.... It simply...couldn't be!

Father's dark voice babbled incoherently within the shimmering liquid. He growled and railed. She heard the words "Whisper Prince" and "Thiara" and "The Faia."

Uriozi thought Father had died centuries ago. He had disappeared right before Velak had been imprisoned. She'd always thought Velak had killed him, but now a dozen different thoughts leapt to her mind. Was this some clever attack upon Mother by Venisha, a baited trap to lure Mother into the Sunset Sea to take her beloved back? Was this a sick punishment Mother had wrought, for Father to drift upon the sea as a half-sentient slick of liquid forever?

Dark thoughts descended on her. Mother and Father's relationship had always been tempestuous. Was Mother so demented that she would do this to Father?

Uriozi's pulse quickened. She'd not seen a path to mending these torn lands, but suddenly here it was. The rifts in the lands stemmed from the rifts in Uriozi's own family, begun before she had ever been born, before she'd first opened her eyes to Mother's sad disappointment.

Uriozi suddenly saw it as clear as sunlight peeking through the clouds. Whatever the body of the lands required must begin with the body of her family. Whether that meant healing or amputation, they must come together to do what needed doing. And they must come together now. There was no more time to spend on regret.

I have to restore him.

She considered trying to reform him herself. But there were so many elements to consider that she hesitated. She had no doubt she could reconstruct his flesh as it had been, the way his bones went together, the way his organs and his eyes must sit so they functioned. But Uriozi had never done this with a human before, and there were other things to consider when reconstructing a living being. If Uriozi rebuilt Father and did it incorrectly, he might have the form and function of his body, but none of his original spirit or memories.

Each of her sisters had a specialty, just as they had havens. Pyll's had been love. She'd been enamored of humans and their passion for each other. Lankoli had been drawn to the quiet power of human melancholy, and she'd loved the twilight. For Besni, it had been loyalty and the assurance of solidity over time. Jevare was perhaps the most powerful of her sisters; she owned the element of water as surely as Velak owned fire. Uriozi was an adventurer; she prized curiosity and knowledge above all else.

She looked to the high, craggy mountains that were her sister Sherim's haven, and she felt a whisper of luck, what humans called fate. She'd been compelled to come here, to Sherim's haven and nowhere else when Velak began his killing.

Then suddenly Father, one of two people at the heart of this rift, had arrived on the Sunset Sea, of all things, in a liquid form that only two of her sisters might reconstruct into his human self again. Jevare, of course, but also Sherim...

Sherim's specialty was healing.

Chapter 24

GREI

GREI AWOKE DISORIENTED. He'd half slept on the hilt of Baezin's Blade, and he could feel the impression of it on his cheek. He rubbed at it. Half the sun was visible on the eastern horizon, spreading smears of light yellow, pink, and orange. The smell of roasting meat filled the air.

For a bewildered moment, he thought he was with Selicia weeks ago, camping here the first time with his charred arm and a belly full of fear. He rose on an elbow to see Ree slowly turning a rabbit on a makeshift spit over the fire.

"I didn't think there was any game to be had so close to the Badlands," he murmured, blinking.

"There is always game. You slept a long time," she said. "Another dream?"

"No."

"Maybe that is a good sign."

"That smells wonderful." He sat up, looking hungrily at the sizzling rabbit.

She carved off a slice, skewered it on one of Vecenne's

silver forks and passed it over to him. He sat up and stuffed it into his mouth. Even as the warmth of the meat went down, he shivered at the cooling air. In two days of travel, the temperature had steadily decreased, and there were no thick Fairmist cloaks in Vecenne's bag. They'd have to remedy that the moment they reached Fairmist.

They finished their meal in silence, then rode into the Badlands, far enough from the road that they could barely glimpse the spiky pines of the Dead Woods to the south, and that was fine by Grei. He had no interest in visiting that place again. The violent spirits who lived there had almost killed him the first time he'd fled into those forbidding trees. He had no doubt they would happily finish the job if he ever returned.

They rode all day, leaving the Badlands in late afternoon and moving into the flat plains south of the Fairmist lowlands. By the time the sunset spread orange and purple wings across the horizon behind them, the plains had given way to the lush lowlands where most of Fairmist's food was produced. Ree found a camping spot near the river.

"Best to camp now," she said. "It's still a half-day's ride to the city and we're going to start running into farms."

"We could just keep riding," Grei said.

"It will be well past Deepdark before we get to the city," she said. "Let's face this dream-beast in the light of day. It will be easier to spot traps."

"This isn't a trap."

"Then it will be better to parlay with him with an alert mind," she said. "We rest here tonight."

He didn't push the matter. As eager as he was to sort out the problems with his magic, he didn't have the heart to disagree with her. The ridged scar on his belly was flaming like a hot wire pulled tight inside him. Riding all day hadn't helped it, and he was exhausted.

While Grei made a small fire, Ree vanished into the twilight and returned with six ears of corn and a horse blanket. At his disapproving frown, she shrugged, then stuffed four ears of corn into the edges of the coals. She shucked the other two, laying the golden corn to the side and keeping the husks. After, she fished the river. Luck, or a ridiculous amount of skill, was with her, and she caught four trout. He helped her clean them, then she showed him how to wrap them in the corn husks to stuff into the coals next to the corn.

They feasted that night. Grei couldn't remember anything ever tasting so good. He ate one and a half of the trout and an entire ear of corn. Ree ate two trout, and finished off the last of Grei's half.

"Hungry?" Grei asked her, leaning back with his hands on his belly. He noticed that she'd eaten half again as much as he had this entire journey.

"I've been ravenous since you freed me from Kuruk's hold," she said. "I wasn't hungry while I fought his compulsion," she said. "It replaced any other signals from my body. I forgot to drink. Forgot to eat, so much that I passed out from hunger several times. When I woke, I only ate because I knew I should."

She had been skin and bones when she'd grabbed him in the Temple of the Faia, delivered her critical message about the slinks. She had filled out a lot in the past days. She almost looked like the Ringblade he'd first met in the Lateral House.

At his gaze, she gave him a smile, then lifted the horse blanket and tossed it to him. "I saw you shiver this morning. That's for you."

He caught it. "Wake me at Deepdark. I'll take watch."

She nodded. Grei adjusted himself, laid down and pulled the blanket over himself. He rested his head against a small, grassy bump and was asleep in seconds.

The next morning, they packed up and rode through the Fairmist lowlands. After barely half an hour of riding, farming huts and furrowed fields shaped the land all the way to the mist, which covered the hillside like a white cloak. The cobbled width of Baezin's Road and the mighty expanse of the Fairmist River ran side by side until they disappeared into the white. No one could see the city of Fairmist from a distance, but Grei knew exactly where he was. Nostalgia hit him like a wave.

The air was cool, and would get cooler still as they climbed the slope into those floating droplets.

They headed up, past the foot-high wall of rainfall the droplets made as they reached the limit of the Faia's mighty spell. He felt relieved to see the floating droplets. Surely the Blue Faia was still alive if her spell was still in place.

Beyond that, tendrils of mist hovered at knee-height and collected in irrigation ditches and low-lying spots between the farm houses. Soon, the droplets didn't lay in low spots, but floated in the air, glimmering spheres surrounding them. Days ago, Grei might have whispered to them, asked them to move out of the way. Now he didn't dare.

So, after five minutes, they were thoroughly drenched, and he began to shiver. He glanced at Ree. Her thin purple pantaloons and ripped summer dress clung to the curves of her lean body, making her all but naked. Every inch of her was covered in gooseflesh, and tense muscles stood out on her arms and thighs. Still, she didn't shiver.

"We need proper attire," he said. "We'll die of exposure."

"Or embarrassment." She smirked at his prolonged look, then crossed her arms over her exposed breasts. "You look positively indecent."

A flush heated his cheeks, and he cleared his throat. "Okay. Clothes first."

They approached the city wall. Two Highblades stood atop the Wall Road overhead and two stood underneath the arch, which was wide enough to admit four coaches side-by-side.

When Grei had left, he had been bound and unconscious, a prisoner, and an irrational part of him wanted to hide his face from the guards. But even with Baezin's Blade hanging from his waist, the pair of Highblades barely looked at him. Their gazes lingered on Ree. She gave them just enough of a smile to make them grin to themselves. They didn't challenge Ree and Grei as they rode underneath the shadow of the wall.

"One of your calculated smiles?" he asked her.

"Most men have a running fantasy inside their heads. About women," she said. "It's easy to play upon that fantasy if you try. And you can make them look at their fantasy when they should be paying attention to reality."

"How did you know they wouldn't see it as an invitation?"

"Well, there are looks and there are *looks*," she said. "I gave them the former, just a bit of fuel for their fantasy. It makes them feel a little warmer. A little happier. And it keeps them from thinking about how bizarre we appear."

"Hmmm..." he said.

"Hmmm, indeed."

The city wall was wide, and it also served as a road that encircled the city from the Blacktale Bridge all the way to the South Forest, and it took them a long minute to pass underneath its entirety.

Grei fell to thinking about the last time he'd been in Fairmist. He certainly hadn't left as he had planned, and this homecoming wasn't what he'd envisioned either.

He'd been taken from the city a prisoner, unconscious, and had awoken in the Badlands with Adora's gentle fingers stroking his brow. He'd freed Blevins from the wagon prison, opening an explosion of violence. Then there was his harrowing flight into the Dead Woods, his journey with Selicia, her betrayal, and the final battle against Kuruk.

During the adventure, he'd all but forgotten about his original desires to find the truth, to stop the Debt of the Blessed. Everything had become so much larger than he'd ever imagined.

And after the Phantom War, he'd sat nervously at Adora's bedside, waiting for her to wake, wondering if she would be the same person after he'd pulled her life force from the Faia's magical water, which had somehow kept the fire of her spirit in stasis, giving him the time to whisper her life force back into her body. When she'd awoken as herself, he'd felt every mishap he'd had, every wound he'd borne, had all been worth it.

Grei had envisioned himself returning to Fairmist with Adora, triumphant. He'd imagined seeing the look on his father's face as he rode into the heart of the city, the Debt of the Blessed gone forever and Adora radiant at his side. He had imagined his father bowing his head, finally acquiescing that Grei had been right all along, that he'd searched for the truth and found it. Grei had envisioned himself returning home victorious…

Yet here he was again, right back where he started. He was broken. He'd failed Adora, accidentally killed Blevins, and created something worse than the Debt of the Blessed.

Ree touched his shoulder. "Are you okay?"

"No," he said. "I left as a prisoner. I'm returning as a villain."

"You didn't create the red mist on purpose," she said.

"But I created it. Now all of Thiara belongs to Velak."

"You'll undo it—"

"At least we have a direction," he cut her off, not wanting to wallow in self-pity. He banished the image of his father from his mind, sneering and shaking his head in well-worn disappointment. "That's something."

They rode into the section of the city known as Wall End, and Grei knew where they needed to go first. Most visitors had trouble with Fairmist's weather when they arrived, so there were a smattering of shops that made their business selling weather-appropriate clothing to newcomers. He guided them to the nearest. They stopped outside, and Grei gave Ree another long glance.

"Keep up that stare and I'm going to take it as a compliment," Ree said, turning her head deliberately slowly to him, a sarcastic twist to her lips. "Should I just take it off altogether? It might be less alluring for you."

He adjusted Baezin's Blade at his waist. "You're going to attract a crowd."

She gave a mock gasp of surprise and put an exaggerated dainty hand against her lips. "What will the Fairmist gentry say?"

"Let's make this quick."

They dismounted and tied their horses outside the shop.

A rusty bell sounded when they entered. A thick man with

a bushy mustache emerged from the back room behind the counter. "Not from around here?" he said.

"We need clothes," Grei replied.

The shopkeeper appraised Ree, his gaze touching on her thin, mismatched dress and pantaloons, plastered to her skin. But it was quick, professional, and then he looked her in the eye. She held his gaze.

"I'm looking for something a little warmer," she said.

The taciturn man actually cracked a smile at that. "Bet you are. You know, y'ain't the first to come in from Thiara," he said. "Lots o' people fleeing the slinks. You here 'cause of the war?"

Grei cleared his throat. "Yes."

"Some saying the slinks was phantoms." The man grunted. "A bucket o' horse clods, that."

"It's true," Grei said.

The shopkeeper frowned, then wiped one of his big forearms across his mouth. "Well," he said. "I seen what the slinks did the first time 'round. And now they've done for the emperor? Doesn't sound like a phantom to me. How's a phantom kill a man?"

"Not all were phantoms," Grei said. "There were three slinks, in the end, but only three. Two were killed by Jorun Magnus. The last killed the emperor."

The shopkeeper rolled his eyes, then eyed Ree again. "Cloaks and what else?" he asked. "Dress for you, miss?"

Ree pulled out a handful of coins and slapped them on the counter. "Riding breeches. Sturdy tunic. And everything else."

They chose breeches and thick tunics that fit them, waterproof blankets and saddle packs for the horses, then finished with waterproof cloaks. They exited the shop within half an hour and spent some few minutes next door at a grocer's, where they filled the horses' packs with food.

All told, it took an hour, and they started out again. They doubled back to the city wall and up a stone ramp that led to the top. The city wall had been built not only to defend the city against Benascan attack, but also to stabilize the first tier of houses within the city proper. Atop it was the Wall Road, which stretched all the way to the South Forest.

They trotted briskly southward along the wall, passing a few other riders and two guard stations. With their new clothes, they looked just like every other Fairmist citizen. No one accosted them, and at the end of the wall, they rode out into the South Forest.

He led Ree back to the little glade where he'd first met Adora. The blue rose he'd left here still thrived. It glowed softly where he had stuck it into the ground. He dismounted, tethered the horse and knelt beside the flower.

When he'd planted the rose, he'd been beside himself with anger and grief. It had been a useless gesture to stuff a broken stem into the ground. But the rose had lived. As if in response to his tears, it had taken root and thrived. That small miracle had opened his mind, and the nonsensical whispers had finally begun to make sense.

"Is this the place?" Ree asked, coming up behind him

"Yes," he said.

She knelt next to the blue rose. Grei's chest tightened, and it was all he could do not to tell her to get away from it. He knew Ree would never harm the rose, but his protectiveness was instinctive.

"To me, it always represented Adora," he said. "But, if my dreams are to be believed, it means more than that."

"Cavyn," Ree said. "She uses these for magic."

"The power was overwhelming, beyond what I understand."

"But you made this one grow?"

"Either that, or the dream-beast was standing over my shoulder without me knowing, and he healed it." He turned away from her and faced the direction from which the dream-beast had come. After a moment of staring in that direction, Grei clenched his fist and decided to reach into the damaged whispers. Hesitantly, he opened his mind to receive them.

The whispers warbled unevenly to him, and he searched for any trace of the dream-beast. But it was like trying to listen to something through water. He began to feel a pressure building inside him, just like he'd felt when he used his magic in the Jhor Forest. Right before everything became a disaster.

A tiny ripple in the air, barely perceptible, radiated out from him. Immediately, he stopped listening. He clenched his teeth as he watched the ripple. The droplets in the air shivered, and a few dropped to the ground. But no trees melted.

"Grei…" Ree murmured warningly.

He let out a breath. "I stopped. I—" But his frustration cut off his words. He sat down on the edge of his cloak, crossed his legs, and looked into the forest.

"Is there something I can do to help?" Ree asked.

He opened his eyes. "We're going to have to go looking, I think." He quailed at searching every piece of the forest, but if he couldn't use his magic, there was no other choice.

"Which direction?"

"That's what I'm trying to decide. Who knows if the dream-beast circled this glade a half dozen times before he appeared to me and Adora, but if he came directly from…wherever he lives, then maybe we can plot a straight course back in that direction and find something."

"Maybe we could—" She hissed, cutting herself off.

Grei turned.

The huge dream-beast stood between two trees at the edge of the clearing. His arms were as thick around as Grei's waist, and so long they almost touched the ground. His bloated torso was covered with hair and skin that looked like tree bark. His twisted antlers were mismatched, of different shapes and lengths, and his legs ended in hooves as wide as dinner plates. His deer's head was the most eerie of all, its intelligent rainbow eyes peering into the glade.

Ree backed up, her daggers now in her hands. The dream-beast's rainbow eyes swirled. Ree gasped as her hands spasmed. Both daggers fell to the ground at her feet. She crouched, ready, but she didn't attack.

"That's him," Grei said.

A tense, silent moment stretched through the glade. Grei

expected the dream-beast to do something, but it just stood there, watching. A voice slithered into Grei's mind like the whispers of magic, except this voice was loud and crisp, so loud he gasped.

"You should not have come here."

Chapter 25

GREI

GREI'S QUESTIONS SLAMMED into each other in the rush to get out of his mouth, and he said nothing. For a stunned moment, he was back in time, watching the dream-beast emerge from the forest so long ago. Back then, he'd leapt to his feet to defend the Forest Girl. This time, he was simply struck dumb.

Finally, one of his questions elbowed its way out of his mouth. "You did this to me," Grei whispered. "*You* turned me into the Whisper Prince."

"You must leave. He will come for Jevare next."

The words blared his head. Grei winced. "I'm not going anywhere! We need you."

"What's going on, Grei?" Ree asked. He glanced at her. She was still crouched low, but she'd sidestepped closer to her fallen daggers. Her arms hung so that one finger touched a hilt.

He suddenly realized Ree couldn't hear what the dream-beast was saying. "He's talking to me, mind to mind. He wants us to leave."

Her lips pressed into a firm line.

Grei looked back at the beast. "Help me first."

The beast snorted through his nostrils.

"Velak has slain Pyll. He has slain Lankoli. He will come here next, seeking Jevare. He will kill you if he finds you. If he finds me. It is not safe for either of us."

"I need your help."

The beast shook its head. "Go. And do what you were created to do."

"Created to do? What was I created to do?" His heart sank as he realized Ree might have been correct. What if this creature had created Grei to be a lightning rod for Velak? To draw the wrath away from itself.

"Go."

The dream-beast shuffled backward, withdrawing.

"No!" Grei rushed the creature—

The dream-beast's rainbow eyes flashed, and suddenly he wasn't there. The ground lurched as vertigo hit Grei. He staggered to the side, trying to catch his balance.

"Where did it go?" Ree asked.

Grei wobbled, making his unsteady way to the place the dream-beast had stood. Two hoof prints the size of dinner plates pressed deeply into the earth, and the grass was slowly rising from the indentations. To the north, the edge of a bush was flattened and a low tree limb was broken, but Grei hadn't heard it crack.

The dream-beast had used magic to escape. But he hadn't…vanished, otherwise there would be no proof that he'd made a path for himself.

"Which way did it go?" Ree asked, standing next to him. He hadn't even heard her cross the distance.

"North," he said. The dizziness was slowly fading.

"Can *you* do that? Just vanish?"

"No," Grei murmured. "I can't do that."

The dream-beast had just admitted to creating Grei. He'd given Grei the power to change the world, then abandoned him. Grei's anger boiled up. He'd come all this way, pinning his hopes on finding the dream-beast, which had been a longshot at best. Now they'd actually found the creature, but it had simply left them sitting here.

Fine. You want to use magic? Fine.

He opened his mind to the warbling whispers, drew them into his mind, and he reached out to touch the water droplets in the direction the dream-beast had fled. They fell like rain and the tree next to him melted and dropped to the ground in a sudden deluge of brown and green.

"Grei!" Ree gasped. "You can't—"

The dream-beast's powerful voice thundered in his mind, and Ree's voice stopped abruptly. The melting tree stopped melting, frozen in a bubbly mound of green and brown. No more droplets fell like rain, and even the floating ones stopped drifting.

The dream-beast suddenly stood next to Grei, snorting heavily.

"What have you done?" His loud voice thundered in Grei's head.

"The only thing I *can* do," Grei yelled at the creature.

"This is an abomination. I taught you how to listen to the land so you could serve it, not unmake it!"

"Taught me? You taught me nothing!" Grei flipped back his cloak and lifted his tunic, showing the jagged ridge on his belly. "I was stabbed with one of the emperor's cursed daggers, and now the whispers are garbled and everything I try turns to disaster. That's why I need your help."

Grei looked back at Ree and was stunned to find the Ringblade frozen in a lunge. She'd reached out her hand as if to grab him, but she was as still as one of the statues in The Garden, where the Delegate kept all those who had been turned to stone by the Imperial Wands.

"What did you do to her?" he asked. Then he connected it. Everything was frozen, not just Ree. The scant floating droplets in the air didn't drift. The branches of the trees did not rustle. There was no sound whatsoever except his words and those of the dream-beast.

"You cannot hear the voices of the land?" The dream-beast

answered his question with a question.

"Did you stop time?" he murmured, shocked.

"Tell me about the voices. Be quick, Grei. Please."

"I hear them, but they're mixed up, and when I use them…" He gestured at the melting tree. "This happens."

The dream-beast stared at Grei's belly.

"Ah…" he said in Grei's mind, as though he was seeing something finally. *"That is…dangerous."*

"Help me fix it."

The dream-beast held perfectly still. Finally, he snorted turned about. *"Follow me."*

The dream-beast moved farther into the woods, and Grei followed. Grei's swath of destruction, much smaller than in the Jhor Forest, seemed to have petered out about twenty feet from him, as though the dream-beast had contained it with his own magic. The dream-beast snorted in disgust as they moved past the melted trees, then deeper into the woods.

"I shall have to return after Velak is gone to undo this damage. Most of these trees will die anyway. And if I hadn't stopped you, that ripple might have spread throughout the forest."

The dream-beast wound through the forest to where three little streams met, frozen in time where they flowed into a huge, round hole in the ground. Grei looked around. He had been through the South Woods a hundred times. He'd practically grown up here, and he had never seen this place. The little streams turned into nothing but spray before hitting the bottom, filling the circular hole with white mist. But the movement of the streams had all stopped, just like everything in the glade of the blue rose. It was like Grei was in a dream.

"Velak is nearly upon us," the dream-beast said. *"We cannot afford to be caught above ground."*

The wall down the well was granite covered in moss. It created shelves and steps descending in a circle until they vanished into the mist. With an agility that belied his ungainly shape and size, the dream-beast leapt to the nearest shelf, bounded to the next and the next, his wide hooves striking with practiced grace as he descended. Grei leapt after, and immediately, his ill-healed belly sent a flare of pain as he straightened too much. Gasping, he slowed down, kept himself partially hunched as he followed the dream-beast. Curling over eased the strain a little, and he stayed that way until they reached the static mists.

They descended through the mists to the bottom, where the walls that had been shaped and polished in a perfect circle, with a six-foot wide walkway around a pool in the center. There were ten tunnels in the walls, evenly spaced apart, and a colored symbol glowed above each archway. Yellow, purple, blue, green, black, orange, brown, red, and a ninth archway with a rainbow of all eight colors. The tenth had the outline of the same arc of the rainbow, but without a color. Ten small stone bridges arched up from the circular walkway to the center of the pool, where they met and created a circular platform suspended a few feet over the water. Ten tiny streams, frozen in time, trickled out of the pool, each down the center of one of the passageways.

The dream-beast clopped onto the walkway that bordered the pool, let out a deep huff, and suddenly everything started moving again. The pool glimmered in the half light. The mist whirled about them.

"This way."

The dream-beast walked around the pool and into the rainbow tunnel. Grei followed. The moment he stepped into the passage, he felt a pang of familiarity. The tunnel smelled like water, greenery, and flowers in bloom. Designs had been carved on the walls, covered with creeping moss. They were rough pictures, but not crude, as though someone with talent for pictures had drawn them long ago. Again, he was struck with the feeling he been here before.

The dream-beast lumbered down the circular hallway as though it had been created to fit exactly his height. His giant hooves clacked easily on either side of the thin stream, which was about a foot wide, but Grei had to choose one side or the other to keep from waddling forward. He decided on the left side and reached out to brush his hand on the mossy wall. The moss gripped his fingers as they passed, and he yanked his hand back.

The action struck a chord in his mind. He'd done that before, that very action of snatching away his hand from the curious, grasping moss.

"I know this place," Grei murmured, stopping in front of a carving on the wall, half obscured by the moss. The figure of a woman with flying hair stood on the left. To her right were seven smaller figures, each with dresses and flowing hair like the woman. To the right of them, as though standing behind them, was a taller figure, taller than the first woman, and he was wreathed in flame.

The seven little figures had to be the Faia. The flaming man was Velak. The tall woman with the flying hair was Cavyn. This was a family portrait.

Grei moved slowly forward. The next figure in the carving was taller than all of them, large and wide, with twisting horns and a deer's face. The dream-beast.

The final figure, farthest to the right, was a human baby with a crown.

"The children of Baezin," Grei whispered, touching the carving of the baby. Again, that familiarity struck him. He'd seen this before, touched this before, but he hadn't known what it meant then.

Grei turned to find the dream-beast standing in a slash of sunlight at the end of the tunnel. Again, he snorted like an impatient horse, then turned and continued into a blindingly bright room beyond.

Grei followed quickly, and the tunnel opened up into a beautiful glade bordered by a forest of rich maple, beech, ash, and cherry trees.

He breathed faster. They'd descended a hundred feet, and walked no more than a hundred feet through the tunnel, yet this wasn't a glade in some deep crevice. There was the sun, and none of Fairmist's telltale floating mist. It was spring here, and it shouldn't be. There were a blend of budding spring colors and the heady scent of flowers in bloom. The sky overhead was bright blue, and a sun—much larger than the normal sun—shone down. It had been autumn in the South Forest.

"What is this place...?" he murmured. He reached out and put a hand on the nearest tree branch, clasped it like he was hanging over a waterfall. "Where are we? Why is it still spring here?"

"I like the colors," the dream-beast said in Grei's head. "So they stay that way for me."

"But the...the sun! There's no... We're underground!"

"Settle your mind, Whisper Prince. The natural flow of time has begun again, and we don't have much of it."

"I've been here before. You took me here," Grei murmured. "The night I saw you, when I was trying to protect Adora."

The dream-beast snorted. "I saw the danger when Kuruk tore his way into this world, when he whipped the humans of Thiara until they ran all the way to Fairmist. Mother and my sisters saw Kuruk as harmless to the balance of the lands, cut off from Velak, so they let him be. But Kuruk was Velak's creature, as sure as clouds are creatures of the sky. I knew it could not end there.

"Now Velak has found a way to strike from within his prison. Pyll paid the price. Lankoli paid the price. So too will Jevare if you do not stop him. Once she is gone, the barrier will crack. I do not think the others will be able to hold him."

"Velak isn't free yet?" Grei asked.

"No. But his latest vessel allows him to act in this world in a way he never could before."

"Adora," Grei said.

"They are kin. Mother's blood runs in both their veins. Velak can use some of his power through her."

"And you're a Faia," Grei said.

"The word 'Faia' is a human construct."

"Don't mince words. If you're not a Faia, then you're like them. What is your name?"

"Saebin."

"Saebin..." The name rang a strong bell in Grei's memory.

Just like the family portrait. Just like the grasping moss.

"I've been here before," he murmured.

Saebin hesitated. "You were not supposed to remember."

"You erased my memory?"

"I taught you."

"Taught me…" Then it made sense. Saebin's ability to stop time. Grei's sudden year's worth of growth. The appearance of the whispers. His strange familiarity with this place. He hadn't met Saebin for one instant in the grove. He'd spent a year in this place. That was the year he'd lost!

His head spun and he felt dizzy again. He kept hold of the branch. "You…" he said. If felt like someone had knocked the wind out of him. "You stopped time. You took me here."

Yes.

"You stopped time in the rest of the lands so I could spend a year here without anyone knowing?" he asked incredulously.

Saebin snorted, shook his antlered head. "Of course not. I can halt time in the lands above only for a moment. But time does not move the same way in my haven as it does in the lands. And the farther from that tunnel you go… He pointed back the way they'd come. The slower time moves in the real world."

Grei looked back at the archway. "So Ree is…?"

"Time has already begun again for her, but it is moving slowly compared to here in my haven. Only moments have passed for your friend since we left. She probably has only barely noticed you have vanished."

"Why…?" He thought of all of his struggles, trying to discover what the whispers were, fighting to learn how to use them. "Why did you take my memory?"

"To protect myself. But apparently I have failed in that, just as I have failed in instructing you. I assumed you would retain the intrinsic ability to use the whispers. You did not. Every day I hoped, but it took you seven years to wake up again."

Grei's scalp prickled with heat, and he wanted to shout at the creature. "You stripped me of my memories! You wiped my mind and threw me back out into the world! What did you think would happen?"

"I could not afford to have you coming back here."

"They tortured me, Saebin! I flopped about, struggled to understand what had happened to me. Your instruction did nothing!"

"It was…disappointing."

Saebin cared nothing for Grei's trials. Grei clenched his fists and bit his tongue.

"Then I discovered that Velak was making cracks in his prison with the Blessed, and I had no choice any longer. I had to intervene directly." Saebin shivered.

"That's why you sent me the dreams."

"I had hoped you would help my sisters, not come here."

Grei was thunderstruck at the arrogance…the sheer negligence of this creature. "I was just a boy! Why would you choose a boy? They *tortured* me!" he repeated.

"The emperor was a killer. His Highblades are killers. But you were a child with courage and determination.… You saw a fellow human in need and jumped forward to give your life for her. I thought someone like that might do the same for my sisters."

Surprise twisted together with his anger, and then the anger seeped away.

"You were pure," Saebin said. *"You had strength. I chose you because you are a protector."*

Chapter 26

GREI

GREI HAD A DOZEN QUESTIONS, so many he didn't know where to start. In his mind, he kept stepping toward one question only to change his mind, then stutter-step toward the next. He held up a hand.

"Why don't *you* fight Velak? You stopped my rogue magic with a few words. Anything I can do, you can do better, stronger. It should be you."

"It cannot be me."

"Why?"

"It cannot be me."

"Saebin, I'm broken. And I don't even know what I'm doing!"

Saebin turned and shuffled deeper into the glade. Grei followed, angry. At first, he was stunned that Saebin could assume Grei would be some kind of champion without knowing why or how. Then he remembered how the Blue Faia had reacted at Fairmist Falls, recoiling from Grei when Selicia attacked. He'd assumed the Blue Faia was his ally, too, that she

227

would protect him. But she hadn't. She had turned away with as little emotion as Grei might give a riverside pebble.

In a Faia's eyes, humans are just snarling, snapping dogs following our baser instincts, Grei thought. He doesn't think knowledge will help me. I'm just an arrow he shot, hoping it would hit Velak.

"But now you are here," Saebin said in Grei's mind. "And our time is up. Perhaps I was wrong not to leave you with more information. I just couldn't risk you...coming back. But it is all too late for that now. Perhaps your curiosity must be sated before you can act. If that is what it takes, then you may glut yourself on information."

As Saebin lumbered forward, a small stone hut appeared ahead. Grei blinked. It hadn't been there before. But the closer they got, the larger it got. It wasn't a hut at all. It was a domed structure at least two stories tall. There were no discernible blocks or mortar, only an archway and ten high window holes near the top of the arch. The smooth structure looked like it had been made out of one huge piece of stone. Grei marveled as he neared, looking for any indication that the dome hadn't just grown up out of the ground.

They went through the archway into an enormous circular room. Every wall was a bookcase filled with books, rising from the floor all the way up to where it curved into the ceiling. It was reminiscent of the circular room with the pool, except, instead of ten archways, there were ten stone trellises between the rows.

"Baezin's Blood..." Grei murmured, looking at all those books. "This is as big as the imperial library."

Saebin said nothing, but walked to the center of the room. There, capturing the focused light of all ten windows, was a tall round table with three open tomes. Saebin nodded his great, long head at the nearest book. *"Baezin's journals. Our family history. It will tell you nothing more than you already know: Velak comes, and he will kill us all if he can."*

Grei had even more questions now than before, and he moved toward the table like a moth to light. He picked up the nearest book and turned it to look at the cover, keeping his finger between the pages to mark the place. The cover was leather, battered and scratched, and it was partially burned; the top edges of the book looked like it had rested in a fire. But there was no title, no indication of who had written in it. Just an unmarked journal. He flipped the book back open to where it had been marked. The pages crinkled.

The entry had no title, just a date in the upper right-hand corner in the Venishan month and year. This had been written almost three hundred years ago:

Thiara returned to me today after another disappearance. I thought perhaps she had been killed, but she walked through my door like she had simply stepped outside for a pail of milk. I asked her where she had gone, but her lips remained closed to the subject.

What have I done, giving my heart to this woman? Her mystery was once a heady wine on which I stayed drunk for days on end, happily. But there is more at stake now. Thiara's unexplained disappearances are ominous. I met her before I first met any other Benascans, but now I wonder if she could have been a spy, sent far in advance. It would show a cunning that I've not attributed to the savage northlanders, but now that I think on it, it fits with how they see their women as workhorses, existing only to serve and perpetuate the community. I can envision the Benascans sending their most alluring woman to seduce me, to become my beloved, and then use her as leverage later. If that is the case, then I cannot allow myself to be swayed by her any longer.

I came to these shores to build a better dream than old Venisha. Certainly a culture that enslaves their women is not better. I cannot live side by side with such an abomination. I cannot allow my daughter to live in such a land.

And I cannot afford to leave a snake at my breast, if that is what Thiara really is. But perhaps…perhaps I can make her see how important this is. When I look in her eyes, I am certain of her love for me. Perhaps I can turn her to my viewpoint. I pray to the Faia that it is so, and that I need not take further action.

The entry ended there, and a new entry was dated a week later on the next page. Grei kept reading.

We declared war on Benasca today. They took three women from my city, beating senseless the guards who tried to stop them. My mind still spins in turmoil, seeing shadows of betrayal and deceit. I wonder if my beloved

Thiara gave the Benascans information about our defenses so that they might slip past.

It cannot be borne. If strength is the only language Benascans understand, then I shall oblige. I made my announcement, and Thiara took it badly. I cannot tell whether she is a spy, or simply compassionate to her people. I explained that what I do is necessary.

She called me a monster.

I lost my temper. I told her that I am emperor, not her, and she must accept my decision. She knelt before me then, crying, but I would not let her tears change my mind. Then she rose and she kissed me. For a moment, I thought she had accepted my decision, that all was forgiven. I nearly offered apology for my harsh words, but before I could, she began babbling like a madwoman. This incoherent nonsense continued for long minutes as I stood amazed, and for the first time, I suspected my beloved suffers from an illness of the mind.

Then she hissed at me, actually hissed like a cat. She claimed the burning of the fledgling village of Wheatreen, earlier this week, had been the act of our son, not the Benascans. Then she stormed out.

Her insistence that I could have a son by her chills me. The very idea is ridiculous. If such a thing was possible, at most he would be seven years old. He could not possibly have wrought the destruction visited upon Wheatreen. And yet… What of her absences? I did not keep such careful track of Thiara when we first met. During one of her long absences…could she have possibly brought some half-term babe into the world that survived? It is unthinkable, and yet… I am chilled at the thought.

The entry ended. Soot marred the next page, and the writing was nearly illegible, hastily jotted down.

We have been attacked by the Faia. It is the only way I can explain what I saw tonight. I didn't glimpse any of the tiny goddesses, but who else could make rain turn to fire? Veldenus thinks Venishan sorcery is behind it, but we both know there are no Venishan artifacts powerful enough to rain fire. Only the Faia could manage this. Some say they saw a creature made of flames flying in the fiery rain, laughing. Perhaps this is a new goddess, one I have not yet met?

Thiazin is safe, at least, but I could not find Thiara in the conflagration. She left me in anger barely an hour ago, and I can only hope she escaped the city and is not lying dead under the burned-out ruin of one of the houses. The city is almost completely destroyed. So many are dead. I have never seen anything like it.

We must rebuild our fortifications immediately. I have called the army back from its march to Benasca. We are vulnerable here in the city, and, until we can put together defenses, we must have our soldiers at home.

I feel a doom, as if I have made a misstep. Ever before, the elements of this magical new land have worked in my favor. Robust winds carried our ships here. Materials to build came easily to hand. The Faia worked to assist us, to build Fairmist.

Now it feels like anger simmers in every shadowy corner.

I cannot find my beloved. I cannot find her anywhere.

"That's the last entry." Grei looked up at Saebin.

"Does that sate your curiosity?"

"Sate it? It just brings more questions."

"These bits of history are beside the point. There is nothing that can be done now except to stop Velak."

"Where is the rest?"

"Those were my father's last recorded words. My sisters and I believe he died at Velak's hand sometime just before Velak's imprisonment. The next histories are written by Archon Veldenus, who took the throne until my sister, Empress Thiazin, was fifteen years old."

Grei swallowed, and he decided he wasn't going to tell Saebin that his father had not died, that he'd been resurrected by his mother for centuries…and that in the end, it wasn't Velak or even Cavyn, but Grei who had killed Baezin.

Grei cleared his throat. "It was Velak, wasn't it?" he said. "The son Thiara referred to."

"Of course."

"And you were born before Thiazin," he said, thinking of the picture in the hallway.

"Baezin believed Mother was a human woman. She liked that, wanted him to continue believing it. It was the only vision that fit into her love story. She happily mated with him, happily bore his children, but she was only learning what it was to be human. Her pregnancy warped because of the magic within her. Velak and my sisters came to term in two weeks."

"I was right…" Grei murmured.

"You knew this?"

"I guessed. I also guessed that Thiara hid the babies from Baezin."

"She did. When Mother realized her mistake, as her body quickly distended, she fled. She gave birth to my sisters and my brother at Fairmist Falls.

"She returned to Baezin, leaving my sisters and brother to grow up by themselves, and she continued to play out her human love story with Baezin. She tried to do as she thought a human mother might. She led him to Fairmist to meet his children, but she demanded of them that they never tell him who they really were. She told Father that my sisters were guardians of the lands, rather than his daughters, and he never suspected. Why would he? He saw them as goddesses and called them the Faia. He revered them, and they flocked to him.

"I was her second attempt, more than a year later. This time, she corrected aspects of her first attempt. Sadly, she did not correct them all. She carried me for months, but my body was inhuman and she sensed it. She realized this halfway through the pregnancy and fled. She took me here, created this place for me, and birthed me. Then she left me as she had my siblings and returned to Father.

"Finally, two years later, Mother succeeded in giving Father an heir she deemed acceptable, a human heir, by all accounts: my youngest sister, Thiazin. By all appearances, she was mortal, and for a time, my mother's human love story thrived. I think Mother was truly happy during those years, but it was not to last. Father declared war upon the Benascans, and the fights between he and Mother began. I believe every time she saw his intolerance for the Benascans, she displaced that onto me and my sisters. The arguments became more heated until—"

"The Night of Raining Fire," Grei interrupted.

"You have read about it," Saebin said.

"Regent Veldenus wrote an account of it, as did Empress Thiazin."

"The Night of Raining Fire was Velak. While my sisters flocked to Father, content to play the role of his personal goddesses, Velak watched Father from a distance and nursed his rage. It galled him to think he was not "good enough" for Father to accept him as a son. Then, after Mother

and Father's fight about the Benascan War, I suspect she shared Velak's rage. In a fit of pique, she told him to burn down Father's precious city, teach Father a lesson. Velak happily agreed and began his grisly work. But Mother is as fickle as a spring storm. When she saw the devastation, she changed her mind and told Velak to stop. He wouldn't. He burned her, and continued his rampage, slaying father's followers.

"That was when Mother created the sword, that blade you carry that radiates death. Saebin pointed at Baezin's Blade. She focused all of her anger into it; it was made to be Velak's bane. For him to even touch it is agony. It breaks the bonds of magic."

"Is that part of what is fouling up my magic?" he asked, though he'd begun carrying Baezin's Blade long after his magic became wild and uncontrollable.

"No. You are not of Mother's bloodline."

"Why would that matter?"

"Because Mother made it to kill Velak, to give Father protection against him, but I suspect she didn't want it fouling up the magics she used upon Father. Healing spells and the like. I think she has even kept him from death once or twice."

More than twice, Grei thought, but he stayed silent. Obviously Saebin didn't know that his mother had been resurrecting Blevins for centuries.

"So," Saebin said. "While the sword is anathema to Velak, deadly to my sisters and me, and even potent against the foul magics of the the the god Venisha, it would not harm any spells of healing Mother used on Father. And apparently, it doesn't harm you either."

"So your mother made this weapon. And she could have killed Velak if she chose. She's more powerful than you, than the Faia."

Saebin snorted. "Mother is as powerful as she wants to be. She is the steward of these lands. She knows where the source of magic is, with access to all of its limitless power."

"Then why didn't she kill him?" Grei asked.

Saebin took a deep breath and let it out through his nose. Grei thought it must be Saebin's version of a sigh. "Because Mother is insane. One minute, she rages. The next, she is as timid as a mouse. She thinks one thing and does another. She creates a grand vision, then breaks it in half and tacks on her whimsy of the moment. Once she had that sword, she couldn't bear to kill Velak with it. So she enlisted the help of my sisters and imprisoned him instead. Now he is breaking free; he finally has a vessel through which he can act. He can reach us through her, can kill my sisters, kill me. And you." He shook his big head. *"We can spend no more time on this. We must be about the business of getting your magic back. You must establish your haven."*

"Haven. You used that word before. What does that mean?"

"Come." Saebin bowed his head and led Grei out of the library, past the underground meadow of eternal spring and eerie sunshine, back into the tunnel through which they'd come. Saebin stopped in the platform room with the pool with the ten different tunnels.

"Each tunnel represents a different one of my sisters and, of course, my brother. He indicated each of the tunnels with their smear of color at the top of each arch. My sisters drew from different aspects of the land."

He pointed at the brown streak of color.

"Besni, the Brown Faia, was the first of us to die. Emperor Qweryn found her in the Tullawn Mountains, deep under the earth, and he took her with Baezin's Blade, the very sword you carry with you." He nodded at the hilt protruding from the opening of Grei's cloak.

"He killed her...with this?" The thought made him sick, and he was suddenly very conscious of the steel strapped to his hip.

"Oh yes. It was made to slay Velak, but it has the power to kill any one of us." Saebin pointed at the next tunnel.

"Deilli, who you called the Yellow Faia, loved sunlight. She drank its rays and there were times when she could see the future. Unfortunately, she did not see her death coming. Emperor Qweryn captured her with a net he made from Besni's death."

He pointed at the purple smear. *"Lankoli, who you would call the Purple Faia, loved the twilight. She spent her thoughtful moments in that ambiguous space between light and dark.*

"Pyll, whom you call the Green Faia, loved wild things. It is why the Jhor Forest drew her with its dangerous trees and giant creatures. Like Mother, she was also fascinated by human love, how it was birthed and

how it thrived. She and Mother both believed it was the key to balance in the lands.

"Jevare, the ones humans call the Blue Faia, is the most powerful of my sisters. I suspect this is because she took the place where she and her sisters were born as her haven. There is power at Fairmist Falls, and she draws from it. He nodded at the blue smear. Likewise, perhaps more than any of my other sisters, she is bound to it. I have never known her to leave her haven.

"Sherim is the Orange Faia. If she has survived the wrath of Velak, she would make a strong ally. She lives north, near the black shores of Cliffgard."

"The red is Velak," Grei said. A god of fire…

"Yes."

"And the rainbow is you."

"Yes."

"And the colorless rainbow is Thiazin?"

"Thiazin and all of her descendants were deaf to the voices of the land. They were as human as Mother could make them."

"And taking a 'haven' will help me regain control of the whispers?"

"My sisters and I rely on our havens. We draw power from them, and, in turn, feed them. Once we form the bond to a specific piece of the land, we do not leave except at great personal cost and risk. Your injury has twisted your connection to the lands. To regain it, you must choose a haven. The bond will give you the strength you need to undo what was done. You must let the voices own you. It will take time, and you will be bound to it once you have done it."

"So to heal myself, I have to claim a haven. I have to let the spirits of that…bit of land…become part of me?"

"Yes," Saebin said.

He thought of the desperate spirits of the Jhor Forest, longing for him replace the Green Faia and the vicious spirits of the Dead Woods, bitter and twisted after years without their Faia. He shuddered at the thought. Neither seemed appealing.

"The Faia and their havens are intertwined?" he murmured.

"Inextricably."

"What about the Black Faia? Why didn't you mention her?"

Saebin shifted uncomfortably. *"Because Uriozi is…different."*

"Different how?" Grei had heard of no legends of the Black Faia.

Saebin shook his head. *"It is not relevant."*

Grei's anger rose again. "Your decision to hide things from me put us in this situation in the first place. I'll judge what is relevant."

Saebin gave a soft snort. "I believe Uriozi found a way to escape binding herself to a part of the lands."

"So maybe I don't have to."

Saebin shook his head. "That is why I didn't want to tell you."

"Why? If there's another way, why not—"

"Because Uriozi is Uriozi, and you are not."

"How did she do it?"

"If I knew, then I would be Uriozi. And, in truth, she may have deceived us all for reasons of her own. She may, indeed, have a haven. But if she does, she has kept it secret for centuries. Even I do not know where it may be. But if she truly has none, she has kept herself unbound, has done what I and all of my other sisters have not managed. Unlike the rest of us, she moves freely through all the lands."

"But if I bind myself to the lands, I can't chase Velak. He isn't going to stay still."

"You can. It will simply…hurt. And the longer you are away from your haven, the weaker you will become."

"But the Green Faia left the Jhor. She saved Adora from the slinks, then brought her here."

"And she slept for a year after."

"So how do I…connect with something? Do just pick a place?"

"It must be a place that resonates with you."

Grei immediately thought of the glade where Ree currently waited for him, frozen in time. "Where I met Adora, the Forest Girl, for the first time."

Saebin nodded. "When I opened your ears, the voices were small. You could listen to them, but they barely noticed you. But you have grown in the last year. The voices of the lands recognize you now, very much like they do my sisters. I think if you gave yourself to your glade, we could heal what was done. But it will take time."

"Time? How much time?"

"A day. Maybe two. And you will be tired afterward."

"Two days!"

"It is the only way to—"

Saebin cut himself off. He suddenly shuffled to the side and snorted. He peered into the hovering mist above them.

"What is it?" Grei asked, following Saebin's gaze. He couldn't see anything.

Saebin twitched like he wanted to run back into his tunnel, but he didn't.

"He is here."

Grei leapt to the first step jutting out from the side of the circular wall.

"Stop."

Grei ignored him and scrambled up to the next step, wincing at the pain in his belly.

"Grei, you cannot wield the power of the lands. You are injured. You must bind yourself to a haven. If you face Velak now, he will kill you."

"I have this." He patted the sword.

"Velak knows that weapon and what it can do. He will incinerate you before you can raise it."

"Ree is still out there."

"You must plan your fight with Velak, not rush headlong at him. This gives him every advantage."

"So I let her die?"

"You cannot help her as you are!"

"I have to do what I can. I'll make Adora stop somehow." He jumped to the next step.

"She is Velak's vessel. She will not listen to you!"

"I'm not sitting in a cave while Velak kills Ree."

"Then you will die."

"Then I'll die doing what's right, which is more than I can say for you!"

Grei felt the scrape of hooves on stone. He spun as Saebin

left the ground in a mighty leap and landed on the step behind Grei with a great boom. Saebin balanced deftly on the step and reached out to grasp Grei's arm.

Grei spun, drawing Baezin's Blade and leveling it at Saebin's long nose.

Saebin drew up sharply.

"Don't," Grei said.

"I'm trying to help you."

"I'm not your puppet. From what I can tell, every decision you've made has been a bad one. And I think I know why. You're a coward, cringing in your little timeless glade. If you hadn't been afraid to tell me the truth when I was younger, I could have helped. I might have stopped all of this. I'm not going to cower in a pit while Velak kills my friend simply because *you* say I should."

"It is the only way."

"I doubt that," Grei said as he leapt to the next step and the next.

"Grei, wait!"

Grei ignored Saebin's calls and climbed out of the hole.

Chapter 27

GREI

GREI CLENCHED BAEZIN'S BLADE in his hand while he raced up the remaining steps and onto solid ground. His ridged scar burned at the abuse. Grei felt like a hunchback, his teeth clenched and one hand on his side as he hunched over and loped west, retracing his steps back to the glade.

Saebin did not give chase.

After barely a minute, Grei smelled smoke. Fear spiked through him, and he pushed himself faster, then he realized the smoke wasn't in front of him, wasn't in the direction he'd left Ree. He hesitated, wanting to get back to her, but instead he turned toward the smell.

Mist gave way to a charcoal haze, and the smoke thickened as he drew nearer. Grei pulled his shirt over his mouth

Then he saw the flames.

He slowed as he came to a clearing he had never seen in the South Woods before. Every breath sent a lightning shot of pain down his scar.

Enormous lumps of black stone—what he guessed had

once been buildings—had melted, bubbling down into rivers that cut burning grooves through the forest floor. He watched as one of the molten rock streams reached a tree, touched its roots, and the trunk burst into flames. Burning corpses littered the charred ground between the buildings, some looking as though they had been running when they were incinerated.

Through the smoke, in the middle of the carnage, stood Adora. He coughed, and she turned, a dress of flames swirling about her. Smoke curled up from the edges of her burning eyes.

His heart hammered. She was horrific, some twisted combination of a slink and the Adora he once knew. Her hair was flame, her skin a reddish color, and her fingers ended in translucent claws, the same as Kuruk's fingernails. Her eyes were swirling red and yellow, like molten lava.

He swallowed down the ache in his heart. "Adora... I'm...I'm so glad I found you," he said.

Her glowing eyes narrowed. "Grei?" She peered through the smoke.

He pulled his tunic down so she could better see his face. A waft of smoke blew past him, and he coughed again. "Are you... Are you okay?" he asked.

She looked at the smoldering wreckage. "Why are you here?" Then her brows furrowed in a deep frown. "Have you been with *them* all along?"

"Them?"

"I told Velak that you were in league with Lyndion. But here you are."

He suddenly realized what she was saying. He looked around at the molten lumps of black. This must have been Baezin's Order, hidden in the trees of the South Forest all this time. This was where Adora had grown up, where Baezin's Order had indoctrinated her with their prophecy, trained her, manipulated her... This was where she had come for revenge.

"I'm not here for them," he said.

Her lava eyes narrowed.

"Adora," he added. "I didn't know about this place."

Her smile was thin and full of wrath. She raised a finger and pointed it at him.

He flinched, flinging his arms up as if that would stop a bolt of fire. But nothing came. He opened his eyes and looked at her. Her lips pressed together and her arm trembled.

"Adora, please. I'm not here to protect Baezin's Order. I'm here to protect you. Just let me talk. I just want to talk to you."

She cocked her head, as though she was listening to something Grei couldn't hear. Some silent voice in her head. Velak.

"You say you're not Lyndion's puppet," she said suddenly. "You say you're not trying to deceive me."

"Lyndion wanted me to kill you at the Temple of the Faia. I refused. Even when *you* begged me to do it. Why would I side with Lyndion now?"

"Then answer this," she said. "Did you know that Lyndion manipulated me? Back in Thiara, did you know what he was?"

He opened his mouth to speak, but the words stuck in his throat. His mind raced madly to frame his answer. At his hesitation, her lips pulled back in a snarl, revealing her teeth.

"You knew…" she whispered.

"I…was going to tell you."

"And yet you didn't."

"I didn't have a chance! There was—"

"You had *days* to tell me."

"You were dead! And then I was dealing with the aftermath of the Phantom War. I barely even saw you. And then…and then we were making love. And you—"

"You deceived me."

"You said you wanted… You said we deserved to be selfish. You didn't want to think about the war or the empress or anything besides the two of us."

"So it's *my* fault…" she said in a deadly tone. "I *made* you lie to me. Is that what you're saying?"

"No! I only wanted what you wanted—"

"Lyndion came for me, Grei," she said. "He appeared in your room. He led me through a magic portal. Do you think I would have let that villain touch me if you'd told me the truth?"

"I couldn't know… I didn't know he would come into the palace."

"He beat me bloody. He split my skull. He cut open my chest," she said as though she was enumerating daily chores.

Tears welled in his eyes. "I didn't know…" He held out his hands. "I'm so sorry…"

"He sliced me until I died."

"I never would have left you if—"

"But you *did* leave me. I begged you to stay, and you left me," she whispered. "He tore me apart because I didn't know what he was. But *you* did.…"

The tears slid freely down his cheeks now. Adora… Beaten and cut by that savage bastard. "I didn't know… If I'd known, I would never have left—"

"Weep now, Grei. Weep for what you did to me."

"I didn't do that to you! I…didn't tell you about Lyndion, but by the Faia, if I could take it back—"

"How noble," she said sarcastically.

"Velak is worse than Lyndion. He's manipulating you right now."

"I know."

He stopped, stunned. "You know?"

"He told me the price. He told me everything, that he wanted to use me for his revenge, but also that I could use him for mine." She waved a hand at the destruction.

"But, why would you do that…?"

"Lyndion will be brought to justice," she said.

Which meant she hadn't found Lyndion here. Had the old emperor escaped somehow? "Did Velak demand you kill the Green Faia, too?" Grei asked. "Was *that* justice?"

Adora's head twitched.

"The Green Faia saved your life. Look at yourself! Look at what he's done to you, what he's made you into, what he's made you do." Velak had his hooks in her so deep, she didn't know what she was saying. Grei didn't want to use the whispers, but he had to make this right somehow, or Adora would just commit more atrocities. If he could just find whatever magical bond Velak had made with Adora, Grei might be able to unravel it.

He opened his mind and let the warbling whispers come to him. The whole forest seemed to vibrate. When he'd faced the girl with the white lock of hair, he'd found Velak's fire within and pulled it out. He had to do the same with Adora. Take Velak out of her. She'd see clearly then. And they could flee this nightmare together like he should have done that night they'd made love.

He listened to the edges of her body with the whispers, heard the crackling, laughing sounds of Velak all throughout her. But within them, he also heard Adora's own whispers: smooth, sonorous like a flute and a summer breeze. But by the Faia, they were so intertwined, how could he separate them?

Adora's eyes widened. "I hear you in my head, Grei. Whisper, whisper, whisper. I feel you eating at my mind."

"I…I want him to let go of you. I want to talk to the real Adora."

"The real Adora?" She sneered. "You mean the Adora more to your liking?"

Grei couldn't speak over the lump in his throat. "That's not what I mean. Please… I love you."

She gave a dry laugh, and it withered his heart. "Love is the word liars use to make pawns of the ignorant. It hangs on your lips like a sweet sheen of blueberry jam," she said. "But it is poison." Her flickering flame eyebrows lowered over her glowing eyes. "My father said he loved me in a coward's whisper the night he sacrificed me. Jorun Magnus claimed to love me, and he wept, they say, when he threw me to the slinks. And Shemmel, here at Baezin's Order, he held me when I was scared, when I cried because of Lyndion's petty tortures. He rocked me gently and said he loved me." She nudged a charred skull with her toe. "Meet Shemmel."

"And what about evil?" Grei retorted. "Do you remember what evil is? Or did Velak convince you there is no such thing?"

"You keep trying to put Velak between me and my choice. This vengeance belongs to me. Baezin's Order deserved to die. Do you call *this* evil?" She waved her hand at dead bodies and molten buildings.

"I don't call it evil. It *is* evil."

"These men pinned me to a board like a butterfly. They used me and then they tried to sacrifice me. I only regret I cannot kill them twice." She raised her chin.

"The Adora I knew," he said softly. "Would never have killed a Faia, let alone two. She wouldn't justify murder. She dedicated her life to save the empire."

"That woman died."

He held out his arms. "Then add me to your pile of corpses. I won't stand here and let you murder another Faia."

"You'd rather I bat my eyelashes and swing my hips for you, Whisper Prince? To be the willing bar wench? To dance for you and whisper words of love?"

"I want *your* vision," he said. "The little house. The sheep in the yard. Our daughter on my shoulders. I want *you*. Velak is a villain. And if you don't free yourself…" He shook his head. "Adora…I can't let you kill another Faia."

She lowered her head, peering up through her lashes of flame. "Can't let me? You don't get to *let* me do anything."

A wall of fire erupted in front of him. He whispered to the air, trying to transform the flames. Surprisingly, the warbling whispers obeyed him. The flames turned cool and flickered past him like a sea breeze.

But the warbles reverberated, growing loud like a hundred giant bells struck by sledgehammers. His magic exploded outward, and it threw him into the air. He landed in the mud and ash. Trees to the left and right of Adora melted, pooling on the ground and hissing as they touched the molten stone of the buildings.

She strode through the flames, glancing at the melted trees. "Velak says you're broken…" She gave a wicked smile. "That you cannot control your magic."

Grei listened for the warbling whispers, but the hundred huge bells still rang. He could not distinguish between any of them, didn't know if they were the whispers of the ground or the air or the trees or Adora herself.

Then the ringing became screams. Grei shouted, putting his hands to his ears, falling to his knees and writhing in the mud. He tried to block them out, but they howled through him until he felt like he was going to burst.

Then the screaming stopped. Grei groaned, face down. His arms felt like limp reeds. With shaking effort, he raised his head.

Adora stood over him. "Velak has been listening to the whispers of the land since he was born. He taught me how to stop you, if you should try to get your hooks into me. I told him it wasn't necessary, that you would never try to hurt me. That you told me you loved me."

He pushed himself to his knees, his arms trembling. "I do," he whispered.

"That's the last lie I'll ever believe." She raised her arm to strike.

"Adora!"

She brought her flaming fist down on his head, and fire exploded all around him.

Chapter 28

ADORA

ADORA STARED at the prone Grei. Soot smeared his now placid face. The hair on the side of his head was singed where she had struck him. Not enough to kill. He'd jerked to the side at the last moment. Her fist still flamed, and now he was helpless. He wouldn't move this time. One more strike, and she'd never have to think about him again.

"Lyndion is still out there," Velak said. *"Finish him. Your revenge awaits."*

Lyndion was still alive. It made her furious. She'd slain every single member of Baezin's Order. Every consul and every acolyte. But Lyndion had not been among them. Lyndion had escaped; he'd somehow known she was coming, and vanished before she arrived. It was intolerable.

"Yes," she said. "We must find him." She turned to leave this blackened and blasted place.

"Grei is still alive," Velak said. *"Finish his punishment."*

She looked back at Grei. His long, brown hair lay matted in the mud. His back slowly rose and fell as he breathed.

She looked at her flaming fist.

"Why do you hesitate?"

"I'm not…hesitating," she murmured. She shook her head. "I…"

"You what?"

"I don't want to kill him." She didn't know why, but even as she had punched him in the head, she had pulled back. Something inside her didn't want to hurt him. Was that weakness? Or…

"He used his magic on you. He tried to kill you. The only reason you are still alive is that you were stronger. Make him pay for attacking you. Make sure he can never hurt you again."

As before, Adora's mind was filled with smoke. Even recent memories quickly faded into the haze. Yes. Grei had attacked her, but… Had he tried to kill her? She couldn't remember. And there was something about the Faia, wasn't here? Grei had sparked a memory, brought it out of the smoke by something he had said. Something about the Green Faia. Something about a twisted thatch of thorny vines. She shook her head, and the vines faded back into the haze.

What did she care about thorny vines anyway? What mattered was that Lyndion must die. That was why she was here, and he had slithered away yet again.

"We need to find Lyndion," she said.

"Kill Grei first. It is unwise to leave your enemies alive behind you."

She looked down again. Her fist was still wreathed in flame, and an image emerged from the smoke in her mind, an image of her slamming that flaming fist into Grei's head, crushing it.

She twitched.

"No, I don't… I don't want to do that."

Velak's voice was a pressure in her head. *"You must. He'll hurt you otherwise."*

"I'm not killing him!" she shouted. She made the flames vanish from her hand and pushed her fists to her head. "Stop it!"

Velak went silent, though the smoke curled even more

thickly in her mind. For a moment, she couldn't remember where she was or why she was here. She was in a forest. Some forest with…

The image of the Order House emerged from the haze.

"Lyndion," she said. "He wasn't here. I have to find him."

"Yes," Velak said. "And I know just where to look."

"Where?"

"There is a hidden place behind Fairmist Falls. Someone with magic could go there to hide, for none other can see it."

A memory surfaced in the haze. Adora standing at the falls, seeing the falls parting like a curtain, and then… The memory submerged, but she had seen enough. Yes, there was a hidden chamber back there. Velak was right. And that was where Lyndion must have gone.

"To the falls, then," she said. As she turned, her gaze fell on the sword strapped to Grei's back. Unbidden, the smoke pulled back, revealing a memory. She knew that sword. It was Baezin's Blade, Jorun Magnus's sword, bound with Faia magic and the only weapon to ever have killed a slink.

She reached down to pick it up.

"Do not touch that blade."

"Why?"

"It is cursed. That steel cuts the ties of magic. If you touch it…"

"What happens?"

"You would die."

"Die?"

"It would cut me from you like a knife paring a potato's skin. And you would return to the state in which I found you."

The horrific memory of Lyndion carving into her belly, of him opening her flesh and leaving her bleeding came forward through the smoke of her mind. She burned hotter, thinking about how foolish she had been, trusting Lyndion, walking through that doorway to the Night Mountains holding his hand. How weak she had been! How foolish!

"You trusted him, just as you trusted the Green Faia who delivered you into Lyndion's hands."

She paused, and Velak's words rolled over her.

"Lyndion must die."

"Lyndion must die," she said.

He's hiding from you.

"At Fairmist Falls." She forgot the sword and walked east, toward the Wet Woods, toward Fairmist Falls, illuminating the trees around her as she burned with hatred. She wended through the trees, and each turn reminded her of when she'd gone back and forth, reporting to Lyndion and the other Consuls, during her fake life as Adora the bartender. All a charade. All for—

"Stop," Velak said suddenly.

Adora halted, looking around.

"There is something here."

"Lyndion?" she asked, clenching her teeth.

"It could be, he said. *"There is great magic here."*

A glow appeared in her vision that had not been there before. To her right, the grass and trees paled like moonlight shone on them.

"That way."

She followed the lighted path and came upon an empty glade.

"Look."

She squinted, but where the lighted path ended, there was only grass and weeds.

"I see nothing."

"Clever…"

"How am I clever?"

"Not you. Him. Give me a moment, please."

She waited in silence.

She felt a tingle throughout her body, like power moving through her. Suddenly, the glade shimmered. A yawning pit opened up in its center like a mouth. Adora watched in amazement. A stairway of thick stone slabs spiraled down around the edge of the pit.

She felt her blood race, bringing heat to every part of her body. Flecks of fire burned and fell from her hair and arms, singeing the grass as she walked closer.

"It appears Lyndion found a different hiding place," Velak said.

"Is he down there?" she breathed, stepping to the edge of the pit. Rage, heat, and desire for vengeance pushed at the inside of her skin like she was going to burst. Mist swirled in the pit so she could not see the bottom, but on the steps, just above the mist, a beast with mismatched horns and a deer's face stared up at her with wide, rainbow eyes.

"Do you remember that creature?" Velak asked her.

"The slink. The one that emerged from the trees and took Grei away, just before Lyndion and his acolytes arrived. I begged them to save Grei. They said they would send out acolytes to kill the slink and bring Grei back."

"Another of Lyndion's lies. That is no slink. It is a creature named Saebin, and it works for Lyndion. It was Saebin who led Lyndion to you."

The beast snorted, backed down a step, and suddenly she could feel its voice in her mind, different from Velak's. There was no fire, only soft insistence, like a quietly flowing river.

"Do not listen to Velak, Princess Mialene," the beast said in her mind. "He lies to you."

"Where are you hiding Lyndion?" Adora asked in a low voice.

"Velak," Saebin said. We must discuss—"

"Where is he?" Adora demanded.

"He's down there," Velak said, confirming Adora's guess. "His loyal creature is protecting him."

"Velak," the beast pleaded. "Don't do something that you can't undo—"

Fire exploded from Adora's hands, and she leapt over the expanse of air. The creature turned. Hooves scrabbled on rock as it ran down the steps.

But it couldn't run faster than fire.

Chapter 29

GREI

"GREI…"

The voice pulled him up from unconsciousness.

"Come on," the voice said again.

Grei coughed and opened his sticky eyes.

Ree let out a long breath. "By the Faia, I thought you were dead."

He ached all over. Ree assisted him. He sat up, groaning softly.

"Ree…" he said, weak with relief. He grabbed her, hugged her to him. She went stiff for a second, then patted his back.

"Easy now," she said. "You're burned and…I don't know what else. You're covered with so much mud and ash it'll take an hour of washing to discover where you're hurt. Move slowly."

"I thought she was going to kill you," Grei said. "I thought she already had."

"Adora?"

"How did you escape?"

"I didn't escape. I didn't even see Adora. You vanished, I tracked you. I was running through the woods when I smelled smoke. So I raced here. I found you like this."

Grei let out a breath of relief. That was a near thing, and a lucky one. If Adora had seen Ree, the Ringblade would surely be dead now. He hugged her tighter. "Thank the Faia…" he murmured.

Ree patted his back again, then extricated herself from his embrace. She picked up the sheathed Baezin's Blade, which was so slathered in mud it looked like a branch that had been dragged through a pig pen.

She shook her head ruefully. "This is a crime. No way to treat a sword," she murmured. She wiped it on the edge of her cloak, knocking off most of the caked-on mud.

"Velak's taken Adora," he continued. "She's not the woman I knew. He's transformed her into a killer, and convinced her what she's doing is right." He waved a hand at the dead lying in the mud. "She said she only wished she could have killed them twice."

"After what you told me about Baezin's Order, maybe they deserved it," Ree said.

"She's killing!"

"Not indiscriminately. She left *you* alive."

That struck him speechless.

"Maybe there's more of her left than you think."

Grei pushed himself painstakingly to his feet.

"Baezin's Blood, Grei!" Ree moved to him and grabbed his arm to steady him. "I tell you to move slowly, and you do the opposite."

He felt like someone had beaten his legs with cudgels, but he managed to stay upright. "We can't waste time. We have to chase her."

"And get burnt up like these?" Ree gestured at the incinerated corpses. "What's your other plan?"

"She's going after the Blue Faia next. Velak wants all the Faia dead, and no matter how much Adora is left, Velak is in control enough to get her to kill."

His head throbbed. There was a continuous ringing in his ears, and the side of his face felt like the skin had been peeled from it. He winced as he touched it. It was gummy and his hand came away with dots of pus and pink. He glanced around.

"And if you run right back into her arms, what then?" Ree asked.

"I tried to talk to her. I won't make that mistake again."

"And you'll do what instead?"

He took Baezin's Blade from her and buckled it around his waist again.

She frowned. "You're no Highblade."

"I won't have to out-fence her. Baezin's Blade was created to slay Velak. I think I'll only have to hit her with it, or maybe cut her to get him out of her."

"You *think*?"

"I have to try."

Ree's frown deepened. After a long silence, she muttered. "Dammit. Come on."

She led him through the trees like a hunter, and they returned to the glade of the blue rose to recover the horses. Not for the first time, he was grateful for Ree's expertise and clear head. He would not have thought to come back for their mounts, and it made all the difference.

They rode through the woods. Soon, the smoke began to thin. Then, after another couple of minutes, tendrils of smoke began to filter through the trees again. Had they gotten turned around, circled back to the site of Adora's slaughter?

"Wait, stop!" he said, looking to his right where the smoke was thicker. He dismounted and padded that way.

"Where are you going? The falls are that way." Ree pointed.

He reached the edge of the clearing. Another gout of smoke rose up from the ground, but there wasn't anything there to burn. It was coming up out of a hole in the ground.

"No…" he whispered. He staggered forward, trying to make his numb legs move faster.

"Grei!" Ree whispered harshly, cursed, then dismounted and ran after him.

His heart sank as he neared the edge of Saebin's pit. He could only see the first three steps of the circular stone stairs. The rest vanished into smoke and mist. "Saebin…"

"Who?" Ree asked, squinting into the hole. "What is this place?"

"The home of the dream-beast," he said numbly. "His name is Saebin." Smoke coming up from that pit could only mean one thing. He hoped against hope that he was wrong, but started toward the first step nonetheless.

Ree caught his arm. "What are you doing?"

"I…I have to see."

"What if she's still down there?" Ree grabbed his arm.

"Then there might be time to save Saebin." He shrugged off her arm and leapt to the first step, ignoring the tight pulling and flash of pain from his ridged scar.

Ree sighed and followed him.

Grei hunched over, held his side, and leapt down the steps into the haze. It was hard to breathe, even harder to see, but he pulled his tunic over his mouth and pushed forward. Blast marks scorched the walls at the bottom, obscuring some of the colors on the arches. Grei ran down the rainbow tunnel, which billowed smoke, and burst into the glade.

Sun shone down from above, and he coughed. A haze of smoke hung over the once-beautiful spring glade, but he didn't see Adora.

Ree looked around, awestruck. "What is this place?"

"Saebin!" he called. He tried to peer through the haze that stung his eyes. A breeze blew throughout the glade, and, for brief moment, he could see. In the distance, smoke roiled up from the ten windows of the domed library like they were chimneys.

"No!" He ran to the burning dome and charged through the archway. Saebin's beautiful library was destroyed, all the books burnt and smoldering. And in the lighted center of the room lay Saebin's charred body, unmoving.

"No, no, no..." Grei raced forward and crashed to his knees next to the giant dream-beast. He choked on a sob, touching a patch of unburnt fur on Saebin's leg. "By the Faia..."

Saebin had been here for centuries. He hadn't hurt anyone. He wasn't the bravest creature Grei had ever met, but Saebin had wanted peace in the lands. He'd wanted it so much he'd awoken Grei's mind to the whispers so that humans could have a champion who might stop Velak.

Now Saebin's vast knowledge was gone. The volumes of his collected histories, gone. The knowledge of how to restore Grei's magic, gone.

Coughing, Grei stood and staggered back. Ree caught him, steadied him.

"I'm sorry, Grei," she said solemnly.

He looked around. Smoke drifted up from the books, seeking the holes in the ceiling.

"This is the shape of things to come," he said.

Velak would burn all the lands. Everything would be like this: charred, smoke drifting everywhere. "This is just a taste. He'll do this everywhere."

Ree didn't say anything.

He clenched his teeth and backed out of the destroyed library, his rage for Velak building.

"We have a Faia to save," he said tightly.

Without waiting for her, he started back to the tunnel. She followed. Together, they jogged through the smoke-choked corridor, then up the wide steps as fast as they could.

They remounted and raced through the South Forest as fast as they could. Spikes of hot pain jolted into Grei's side with each thudding of the horse's hooves, but he ignored it. This was all a nightmare. Faia dying. Saebin dead. Blevins dead at Grei's hand.

All he could think of was getting to the Blue Faia in time.

They soon reached the first of the tributaries, and they clopped across a small bridge, then galloped upstream. Every beat of his heart told him he would be too late again. He was cold, hurt and exhausted, heartsick and full of fear, but he pushed himself to go faster still.

As they went farther north, he skirted the Wet Woods, guiding them to the bridges, and avoiding the ferries.

After another fifteen minutes of galloping around the edges of the marshy trees of the Wet Woods, Grei's belly felt like someone had jabbed a hot poker inside him and was twisting it. He hunched over even more and labored for breath. As they neared the falls, Ree maneuvered her horse in front of him and got his reins. "Ease up, Grei. Catch your breath. We're close."

They slowed to a walk, and the horses snorted, breathing hard.

"Okay," he huffed. "We walk from here."

"No. I was saying take a break. You don't look good."

"I'm fine." He dismounted and tethered his horse to the nearest tree. With a sigh, Ree did the same, but she watched him. Grei used the pain in his belly and chest to drive him. Together, they crept to the top of the slope overlooking Fairmist Falls, and Grei let out a helpless growl.

They were too late.

The waterfall rushed over the crest of the Highward, falling into the pool below. But the curtain of water had parted with a gravity-defying gap in the center. Smoke poured out of it. He remembered when he had come here to supplicate the Blue Faia, to beg her to teach him. The Blue Faia had created a magical passageway through her waterfall just like that. It had been the most fantastical thing he'd ever seen at the time: a tiny goddess emerging through an enchanted waterfall.

Now the passage gaped like an unholy mouth, smoke billowing out. The little fyds flew like crazed bugs all about the pond. The strange little creatures always clustered around Fairmist Falls, drawn to the power of the Faia. Each was two inches tall and humanoid, heads sloping backward to a point. They flew through the air on flipper-like wings, dodging floating droplets. They had no noses, no mouths, and their eyes were bulbous and huge.

Red light flashed inside the cave's opening. The battle had begun, but thank the Faia it wasn't over. They weren't too late.

"Go!" he yelled at Ree. Grei went to the edge of the ridge that overlooked the pool below. Grabbing his side, he leapt onto the steep slope. The mud slipped under him, and he fought to keep his balance, pain firing through him.

"You crazy idiot…" Ree blurted, jumping after him.

Grei slipped and slid, but somehow, he managed to stay upright without tumbling down and cracking his head on the rocks below. He reached the bottom, and his legs finally gave way like they were filled with jelly. He staggered between the scattered rocks and fell into the pool.

He surfaced and gasped. Ree stood at the edge.

"Miraculous buffoonery," she said.

"Come…" he huffed. "Come on." He unclipped his heavy, waterproof cloak and threw it on the shore, then swam toward the opening in the waterfall. Every stroke of his left arm shot lances of pain through his chest.

"Oh, I'm to believe that your tumble into the water was intentional?" she asked, whipping off her own cloak and laying it beside his.

He didn't say anything, just kept swimming, keeping his eyes on that smoky portal. A moment later, he heard her splash in behind him. She caught up with him just as they passed beneath the falls. Water crashed all around them. Just beyond, steps rose out of the shallows, snaking back and forth to a huge opening in the cliff. Grei had inched behind Fairmist Falls a hundred times as a child, and this had never been here. He wondered if it was some kind of magical "other" place like Saebin's glade. He raced up the steps to the opening.

Craggy, wet granite walls shaped the oblong room. Smoke and steam billowed everywhere, and Grei could not see the end of it. A column of water shot past them, smashing into the wall. Fire roared in response.

"It's difficult to see," Ree murmured.

"Let me go first," he said, adjusting the sword belt.

"Why don't you give me the sword?" Ree said.

"You're trained with a sword?"

She gave him a withering look.

He hesitated, then shook his head.

"Grei—"

"I don't want you killing her," he said.

"I know you don't want to hurt her, but if you can't save her…" She hesitated. "What I'm saying is—"

"I know what you're saying. We save her."

"If it's you or her, I'm going to choose you," Ree said.

"We save her," he said adamantly.

Ree gave a tight-lipped frown. "Fine. Let's split up. If she throws a fire blast, I don't want it hitting both of us at the same time. I'll go this way. You go that."

He nodded.

She vanished into the mist and smoke, following the edge of a pool set in the floor.

Another blast of fire roared deep in the cavern.

The warbling whispers rose in his mind, but he wasn't trying that again. Turning a swath of trees to water was dangerous enough. Turning the stone all around them to water…? He could destabilize the entire cliff, bury them all.

He pulled Baezin's Blade free of its scabbard and padded cautiously along the edge of the water. For a moment, the smoky haze cleared, and he caught a glimpse of the Blue Faia.

She was tiny, hunched in the shallows on the far side of the great pool, nearly in the same spot where he'd seen her bathe in his dream. A wall of water rose suddenly to her left just as a jet of fire struck it. Steam and smoke exploded outward. Twenty feet away, Adora grimaced, teeth showing, holding both hands out like claws and sending the ceaseless bolt of fire from her fingertips. Steam and smoke swirled, and Grei lost sight of them.

He'd only gotten a glimpse of them, but Adora had been standing just below a rise in the irregular floor. He sprinted around the edge of the pool and up a jagged stone ramp. With every step, he expected to stumble and fall, but somehow, he kept his footing. He reached the end of the ramp, just above where he'd glimpsed Adora, and he leapt off it. As he sailed through the air, the haze parted and Adora came into view. She saw him at the last second. Her glowing eyes went wide in shock, and he swung Baezin's blade down on her wrist.

She yanked her hand back just in time. He missed, but the sword swept through the fire stream shooting from her fingertips. It exploded as he struck it.

Adora screamed.

The explosion blew Grei sideways into the pool, and he plunged beneath, tumbling end over end. Disoriented, he swam upward, managing to hang onto the sword, and he gasped as he surfaced. He couldn't see Adora anymore, or the Blue Faia or Ree. He didn't even know which way he had been facing.

He thought about calling out to Adora, baiting her into attacking him instead of the Blue Faia, but he hesitated. Baezin's Blade had done something. He hadn't even struck her directly, only the flame coming from her hands, and yet she'd screamed.

That had hurt Velak somehow.

For the first time, he felt hope. If he could hurt Velak just by attacking the fire lord's handiwork, that gave Grei an advantage. If Velak couldn't even stand the touch of the blade to a flame spurt, how much worse would it be if he hit Adora with the flat of the blade? Could Grei shove Velak out of Adora's body with a good strike?

He picked a direction and swam quietly, listening for anything that might let him know where she was. The granite shore appeared through the haze and beyond it, sunlight. The waterfall. He was where he and Ree entered the cavern. He lifted himself out of the water as quietly as he could, setting Baezin's Blade on the stone until he got to his feet. He picked up the sword and followed the shore to the left.

He moved as quietly as he could, but still his boots scraped against the rock. Five steps... Ten...

He found the Faia huddled against the back wall. Her light blue skin was an angry red in half a dozen places, as if boiled by steam. She watched him approach warily. He knelt, putting the sword before him quietly, then held his own hands up.

He heard no sound from Adora, but he knew Velak wouldn't have given up this easily. Adora would be circling, trying to get closer, now wary of Baezin's Blade.

When Grei had met the Green Faia, she had been able to hear his thoughts as well as speak back to him in his mind. So had Saebin. He imagined his words floating to the Blue Faia.

"Can you hear me?" he asked.

"Whisper Prince." The beauty of her melodious voice filled his mind. *"Thank you for helping me. He is more powerful than he once was. I did not realize..."*

"You have to flee," he thought to her. *"Is there a back way out of this cave? You have to run and keep running. I'll distract her long enough for you to get away. Find a place that isn't here. And don't come back. Velak knows that you are tied to your haven. He'll count on that to trap you. You must cut your ties and never return."*

Her eyes widened in fear.

Grei glanced over his shoulder nervously. He'd surprised Adora with his first attack. He doubted he'd get that lucky a second time.

"I can't...leave," the Blue Faia said.

"Velak will kill you. You don't have time to think about it, Jevare," he said, using the name Saebin had called her. *"Please. There isn't any time."*

Tears slid down her blue cheeks, as if he'd asked her to cut off her arm.

"Live," he said to her. *"Go now."*

With her little jaw clenched, she got to her feet, then floated above the granite floor. With one quick look back at him, she vanished into the mist.

He waited, and decided to listen to the whispers. He might not be able to use his magic, but he could still tell the difference between rock and water. He might be able to tell the difference between the air and the homicidal woman he loved.

The whispers warbled. He heard the pool, the mist, the...

Grei spun, hearing Adora right next to him, a mere six feet

distant. He snatched up Baezin's Blade and dove into the water just as flames burst out of the haze. He went deep, and the surface lit up orange as another flame blast followed him. He stroked hard for the far side of the pool, hoping that the Faia had somehow managed to escape. When he reached it, he pulled himself out and lifted Baezin's Blade in front of him. He had to give the Blue Faia time.

"Were you really going to cut off my hand, love?" Adora's voice floated out of the smoke and steam.

"Were you really going to kill the Blue Faia?" he called back, then moved instinctively to the left. A bolt of flame shot through where he had been, and he shied away from the heat. Carefully, he inched his way around the pool, holding the sword up in front of himself. His ribs and stomach were a constant agony.

"She abandoned you when you needed her most," Adora said. "I'd think you'd want her dead."

He didn't respond to that.

"Jevare is a selfish creature who exists only for herself," Adora continued.

"As selfish as Velak?" he asked. "He wants to kill everyone, keep all the lands for himself." This time, he dove right. Fire roared where he had been.

"The Faia must be removed before there can be peace in the lands," she said.

"Peace," Grei grunted. "Let me know when you're speaking and when Velak is moving your lips." This time he dropped flat. The bolt of flame shot over his head, heating his back. He rolled to the left quickly as a second bolt struck where he'd been lying.

Gasping, he ran into the mist.

"I left you alive before," Adora said, her voice closer than before.

"Did Velak tell you to?"

She said nothing to that, and this time, there was no fire bolt.

Every minute Grei stalled was another minute he gave the

Blue Faia to escape. He crept around the pool. His back was now toward the light of the opening. He stayed low to keep from giving her an easy silhouette to target.

"The Faia delivered me into Lyndion's hands," Adora said. "They turned their backs on you when you needed them. They stood by for seven years while Kuruk murdered our people. They deserve to die. Don't stand in my way. Help me."

Grei's heart turned sour inside his chest. He didn't know which words were Adora's and which were Velak's.

"How can I help you, Adora?" Grei said. "How can I make things the way they were?"

"Tell me where Jevare is."

"Listen to yourself, to how you're speaking. Jevare? You didn't know that name until Velak told you. Tell me who is speaking right now? You or Velak?"

Grei inched his way toward the opening, toward the light, hoping to draw Adora further away.

"I don't think you even know," he continued. "And I think Velak wants it that way. He doesn't want you to know how much of you he's controlling. He wants you to stay confused." He inched his way backward. Sunlight glimmered through the sapphire curtain of the waterfall, illuminating the wet walls of the cavern.

"I *was* confused." Adora's voice made him jump. She was right on top of him! He turned, and she leapt out of the haze. "I'm not confused anymore." She pointed her finger and flames erupted toward him.

He threw the sword up in front of himself, but the blast blew him backward over the cliff. He screamed as his arms and legs burned, and he arced over the expanse of air. The winding steps sailed below him, and he hit the rushing waterfall.

The sheet of water threw him downward, shooting him into the lake below. The force drove him deep into the pool below, spinning him about and tearing Baezin's Blade from his grasp. It glowed bright red as it spun away. He could see the surface far above him, a glimmer of daylight, but he couldn't reach it. His clothes were thick and heavy, pulling on his limbs.

He tried to swim upward, but it was so far away. He needed air. His mouth opened to suck in a breath, but he forced it closed. His vision blurred, and the bright surface darkened. He couldn't breathe. He couldn't…

His vision faded, and the last thing he felt was his chest spasming. His mouth opened, and he pulled water into his lungs.

Chapter 30

LYNDION

Lyndion looked disdainfully at the bramble shack, which hunkered crookedly in the mud. Some poor outcast from Fairmist had obviously thrown it together in these forsaken woods, believing that this was an acceptable way for a person to live.

Immortality... His quest for immortality had led him to this hovel.

Lyndion had possessed everything a mortal could possess. Health. Vigor. Experience. He had possessed women in droves, satisfying every desire of the flesh that could be had. As emperor, he'd possessed the political and military power to crush anything before him. As a student of the Slate Wizards, he possessed more magical might than all but the Faia through the artifacts he owned. But immortality stayed tantalizingly out of his reach. It was the one thing that had eluded Lyndion during his life, and once again, his wretched mortal body hampered him.

He gave a tight sigh and glanced down at his hands. He

wore four rings, each with a different stone set in its top: ruby, onyx, sapphire, and slate. His fingers were gnarled, veined and so wrinkled it seemed like his flesh would slough off the bones. His muscles were feeble, his bones brittle. Making the climb from the South Woods to the Highward had almost been beyond him, and he was sure he looked ridiculous. He did not have a looking glass to consider his appearance, but he knew this stage. To an outside viewer, he was a bent and feeble old man.

And this was as far as his old body would take him. Once again, mortality hung on his shoulders like a cloak of rotting meat. Already, a rattling had begun in his chest as he breathed. It was the foulest insult, being born human. Aging. Dying. Lyndion reviled his own flesh. Great souls like his should be immortal, like the Faia were immortal.

Yes, the idea of stepping into that ramshackle hovel sickened him, but he could not risk looking for a more suitable opportunity while his body died around him. When a storm strikes unexpectedly, the wise man seeks shelter; the fool seeks a palace. He could not afford to be choosy.

He must do what was needed, collect his thoughts, and decide what he must do next. His use of magic these past days—traveling to Thiara, transporting himself and Mialene to the Night Mountains, transporting himself back to the South Forest—had stripped his remaining youth from him. He had intended to revive himself with one of the newest group of acolytes, but Velak's minion had struck too swiftly, forcing him to flee.

He growled at his loss of the *argarakth*. Mialene had kicked it through the portal before he'd wrung his prize from her, depriving him of an easy escape. He'd had to use his levitation ring to get down from the Night Mountains and the last lick of vigor from his onyx ring to speed him home. Now, with his onyx ring spent, he was forced to walk through the mud like a beggar.

He suddenly realized he'd been standing outside the hovel for a full minute. He sniffed. Sitting inside that wretched hovel and taking stock of his shattered life was better than doing it in the cold and mud by a tree.

Shuffling the short distance to the hut, he pulled open the door.

Inside, a man and woman were humping each other like animals. They jumped, startled at his appearance, and their soiled, rough-spun sheet fell to the ground. Both of their eyes were comically wide.

A light haze hung in the air from the poorly built fireplace. The room smelled of their rutting, such that even the smoke couldn't completely mask it. Lyndion wrinkled his nose. But it also smelled of life, too…

Lyndion amused himself by imagining the poor couple's story. The man, obviously a Benascan with his fair skin and blond hair, could find no place among the prejudices of the Thiarans. So, he'd made his home in the woods of the Highward, where no one ever came if they could avoid it. Lyndion mused that the Benascan chopped and sold firewood in the city twice a week for his living.

The woman, on the other hand, was likely a Fairmist native who had broken ties with her family to indulge in this forbidden love of a northern savage. Lyndion had seen her kind before, drunk on her sopping, romantic ideals, thinking the lust of youth would somehow see her through the hard years ahead. Two decades from now, when she realized she'd traded luxury, security, and the flower of her youth for this squalid disappointment, she'd despise the man she now rode with such vigor.

But Lyndion was going to save them from all that.

The Benascan immediately roared and came to his feet. The woman cursed, rolling off the bed onto her knees.

The man's initial roar petered out like a mewling cat as he assessed the threat and found it lacking. Only one old man had doddered through his door. A flicker of pity crossed his face, and he hesitated.

Lyndion felt that pity like a hundred needles poking into his skin, and he hated it. He decided that the man must suffer most of all.

But while the man hesitated, the woman's eyes narrowed. She sensed that Lyndion was not all that he seemed. She grabbed an axe from the wall.

Smart, Lyndion thought. Smarter than your lover. One wonders how someone so perceptive could have chosen such a dullard for a mate.

She stepped toward him, axe held high, and Lyndion touched his onyx ring. The artifact's magic twisted his stomach and, as always, there was the sensation that his bowels would release right here. Then the sensation was gone, and the ring's power reached out from the ring like oily smoke. It touched her and sank into her pores, into her muscles, into all of her vital organs, and then it grew hooks.

The woman gasped, and Lyndion sighed in pleasure. His soul pierced hers in a hundred places. He felt her lungs breathing, her heart pumping and… Ah! The couple's carnal attempts had borne fruit. The woman was with child. There were *two* of them to bolster his vitality.

He smiled. So, it was not to be just an ample meal, but a feast of three. He pulled at the warmth of the woman. Her heart stuttered its last beats. Her blood stopped moving, and her vitals shrank, the juice of them stolen away. He yanked the life from her and her unborn child like he would yank a taproot out of soft mud.

The light vanished from her eyes. She shrank, curling into herself as she aged a hundred years in an instant. Her plump cheeks sank to bone, and she fell against the wall, her body making a crackling sound. The fingers of her dried-out hand broke like twigs and the axe fell onto her foot.

Everything she had been now belonged to Lyndion. The wash of vibrant life filled him, and he sighed as he grew. His stooped back straightened. His muscles filled out, and his bones felt as if they had been reforged from steel. The wash of her memories and talents filled him, too. The woman had been the daughter of a baker in Fairmist. In addition to her rebellious and lusty nature, she knew how to make the most exquisite breads and pastries. Lyndion could feel her hands kneading the dough, could smell the bread rising. Now, *he* knew how to do this as well.

"Klyra!" the man wailed, leaping over the bed and breaking Lyndion from his reverie. The Benascan clutched her desiccated body, but her bones crunched to powder at his touch. An animal rage mottled the man's face. Spittle flecked his lips as he spat words in broken Thiaran. "What have you done?" he shouted, leaping to his feet.

"You don't see a doddering old man *now*, do you?" Lyndion asked.

With an animal howl, the man charged Lyndion, who touched his ring again. Oily smoke twisted out of it and into the man, who gave a gurgling cry...

And then gave everything else.

The shriveled Benascan fell to the floor with little more weight than a leaf.

Lyndion swelled with the man's vitality, growing ever younger. The Benascan's cowardly memories flowed into him. He felt the man standing in snow, awaiting an assault from the Thiaran army. The rudimentary sword in his hand burned him, it was so cold. Frost collected close to his stiff fingers. Fear and anticipation warred in the Benascan, and he ran. He deserted his army and fled here.

It had been a long time since Lyndion had taken two lives at once, let alone three, and his body grew more robust and youthful than he'd been in decades. His beard and hair remained white; he'd come to learn that hair was already dead and so could not be transformed, but his body held the shape and vigor of a twenty-year-old. Because of the triple dose of life, he would age at thirty times the normal speed. It was an unfortunate side-effect of the ring and why he preferred to take only one life at a time. But it was worth the risk. He suspected the coming days would require him to be as powerful as he could manage.

Lyndion could not rely on the ring forever, of course. The rate of aging increased with every usage, and after maybe another dozen uses, the ring would put him in the ground as surely as anything else. It was why he'd stolen Velak's life essence, to experiment with it and find a true path to immortality, rather than the increasingly failing promise of the onyx in the ring.

When he had sufficiently recovered from the dizzying high of his new youth, he looked around the shack. There were almost no civilized amenities. He supposed the couple was overjoyed to have even a real bed, rather than a pallet of barn straw. Aside from that, the room included only a crude circular table with two roughhewn chairs, no doubt made with pride by the Benascan wood cutter.

Pathetic, but Lyndion would make do.

He set the casket down, then took the leather satchel off his shoulder, unbuckled the curved Venishan sword at his waist, and placed them both on the table.

"The spoils of my life," he muttered, enjoying his deep, youthful baritone. All laid out no better than an alley thief's filthy haul. You were supposed to be the culmination of my carefully laid plans, Mialene, not their ruination.

But somehow, even in death, the bitch had thwarted him. Her sacrifice was supposed to be clean, but obviously Velak had noticed Lyndion's appropriation of the gift inside Mialene.

The only reason Lyndion had built Baezin's Order was to find the keys to immortality, to have a safe haven to plumb the secrets of these lands, to find a way to harness the power of the Faia, most especially that of Velak, trapped in his other-dimensional prison. Now he was going to have to do his experimenting elsewhere.

However, first things first. He opened up the casket, revealing a half-dozen other rings, two amulets, a little wooden box the size of his palm, a tiny dagger for breaking wax seals, a feather wrought delicately from steel, a bit of frayed rope with a knot on one end, a cylinder made of rough iron ore with four tiny doors that opened four tiny compartments, a squirrel sculpture made of tin, a rolled-up piece of velvet tied like a scroll, and a single silver spoon.

He removed the small jeweled box and opened it. Music

floated out, delicate and so light it could barely be heard. That meant the danger was over. Velak's minion had moved on, or, if it was still pursuing him, it was going in the wrong direction. The box would have vibrated anxiously if the minion was coming his direction.

He thought of the others in Baezin's Order, most likely dead now. It was a shame, a loss of good resources. He'd spent the last century relying on them, Shemmel most of all.

But, a great soul did not lament setbacks. Lyndion had learned long ago that almost anything could be rebuilt. He would find new lackeys. There were always more lackeys.

Lyndion's stomach rumbled, and he sighed. His new body was ravenous, the downside of youth. He went to their cupboard, looking for food. There was a burlap bag of assorted vegetables with dirt still clinging to them, some stale bread, and half a roasted chicken on a silver platter. Klara's memories identified it: a treasured keepsake from her previous life, stolen from her parents.

He swung the door shut on the cupboard without taking any of the unappetizing food. The door slammed and rebounded open, and he left it. Sitting down at the table, he took a silver spoon out of the cask and put it in his mouth. His mind had been thinking of roast chicken—well-prepared and fresh from the oven—so that was what the spoon tasted like. When he pulled it from between his lips, it actually felt like a chunk of chicken was left in his mouth. He chewed it thoughtfully and swallowed, then took another bite.

As with all of the Venishan artifacts he had collected over the years, there was a price to pay for using the Banquet Spoon. Once a popular toy among the Venishan elite, they no longer used them due to a sudden outbreak in cannibalism. While the Banquet Spoon assuaged hunger and nourished the body like a normal meal, there were side effects. Hunger quickly grew acute the more one used it, and it gave way to…peculiar appetites.

Lyndion had learned this when, after several days of exclusively using the spoon to feed himself, he'd taken a bite out of a courtesan's shoulder while he rode her in the throes of passion. She'd run out screaming and bleeding, and he had begun to take the matter more seriously. Now, he only used the spoon in emergencies.

He took another invisible bite: soft, cooked potatoes churned with butter and salt. He could even smell them.

While basking in the pleasure of a good meal, he looked at his treasures and thought about what must be done next. He had emerged from disaster. His wealth of resources lay in ruins, as did his plans. The Whisper Prince had shattered his prophecy and deprived him of the link he'd hoped to establish with Velakka. And to add insult to injury, once again mortality nipped at his heels like a wolf driving him toward a cliff. The new overflow of life from the onyx ring would begin to fade soon enough. His body was already aging, and it would be visibly noticeable within the week.

But great souls pulled victory from defeat, and he kept his outlook from souring overmuch. There were opportunities here, too. He must simply open his eyes to them.

Lyndion let go of his past disappointments, enjoying a bite of soft, white bread with butter. What could be leveraged from this sudden new world?

First, the great powers of the world were rising, clashing like a lightning storm, and the rain from their struggle would fall like gems from the sky.

Second, Velak was either free, or he could exercise vast power in this world through some flaming minion. Either way, it boded ill for Lyndion. He'd spent years trying to steal Velak's power and use it for his own immortality.

Third, Kuruk's plans were in ruins. The Benascan boy roamed the land somewhere, looking for new purpose. Perhaps looking for petty revenge upon Lyndion himself for sending the boy to Velakka in the first place. Hah. Kuruk should praise Lyndion. He'd made the boy immortal. What a cruel twist of fate that was. If only Lyndion could get his hands on Kuruk, subdue him, perhaps find a way to pull that immortality from him…

Lastly, though the Whisper Prince had wrecked Lyndion's prophecy; he was now as powerful as a Faia. Possibly powerful enough to don the mantle of immortality *like* the Faia...and have it be stripped from him.

The Banquet Spoon seemed to warm in agreement at that thought. A slow smile spread across Lyndion's face, and he took another bite. This time, a cherry tart with sugared cream.

"Yes," he said. The spoon hummed as he pulled it between his lips. The key to immortality was now Grei.

Lyndion untied and unrolled the velvet. Inside were eighteen long, thin pockets. Tucked within each pocket were strands of human hair. Lyndion's fingers moved across the soft fabric and found the pocket with five of Grei's hairs, clipped from him when he lay unconscious next to Mialene seven years ago. He pulled one long strand out, rolled the velvet back up and carefully tied it. He picked up the knotted rope. With precise movements, he wove Grei's hair together with several strands of the frayed rope. As he did, the rope twitched. Lyndion quickly finished his weaving, and the rope slid across the table. Before it could slide off, Lyndion grabbed it above the knot. It tugged gently, beseeching him to go almost straight west, vibrating with excitement.

With his free hand, he put his treasures back in his casket, loaded it into the woodcutter's simple travel sack, and slung it over his shoulder.

"Take me to him," he murmured, and left the shack.

Chapter 31
REE

REE NEARLY CRIED OUT as Adora blasted Grei off the cliff. The tongue of flame hissed as Grei hit the waterfall and plunged instantly downward. Ree slunk through the concealing mist, daggers ready.

Grei wouldn't want her to kill Adora, but Ree had warned him. She was far too outclassed to be merciful. If she had a kill strike, she was going to take it. Besides, what Grei didn't understand was that this creature wasn't Adora anymore. If Ree could take it down, it was her obligation as a Ringblade. Baezin's Blood, it was her obligation as a defender of humankind.

Adora appeared ahead, the mist clearing a path between them. The woman's fiery hair created a red and orange nimbus around her. She pointed at Ree, a single flame flickering up from the tip of her finger. Ree's stealth hadn't been enough. Now she was going to die.

But Adora didn't blast her.

Ree hesitated. Her training begged her to leap forward, not

to waste Adora's hesitation, but the fifteenth dance rose in her mind. It trained a Ringmaid that things were not always as they seemed. It trained her to listen to her intuition, to silence her mind, her fears, and seek truth behind an appearance. Ree searched Adora's strange face, looked past the fierce flames and at the body of the woman beneath. The hand at Adora's side was clenched tight in a fist, straining, like she was trying to lift a great weight. Meanwhile, her pointing finger threatened. But it also trembled. Ree's gaze flicked to Adora's face. It glowed, giving her a wrathful appearance, but there was… Was that regret?

Adora lowered her finger, and it seemed like she struggled to do it. She looked at the waterfall and the pool below, then back at Ree. The two of them stayed frozen like that, staring at one another, then Adora turned on her heel and strode toward the back of the vast cavern, vanishing into the mist and smoke.

What. Was that?

Stunned, she hesitated before she realized she was just standing there, doing nothing. Grei was likely dead, true. That flame blast would have killed anyone. But he was the Whisper Prince. If there was a chance, he'd be the one in a million who could have survived.

Ree ran toward the cliff. In a fluid motion, she sheathed her daggers and dove off the edge.

She hit the waterfall as Grei had done, took the momentum of the falling water, made it her own, and shot into the pool like a spear.

The water was crystal clear, sunlight filtering down into it. She spotted Grei instantly, drifting like a piece of seaweed near the bottom. Baezin's Blade leaned against a rock beside him, burning a bright red. Unbelievably, Grei was unburned. Only the edge of his cloak was singed. She kicked her legs, shot toward him, grabbed a fistful of his tunic and hauled him upward.

They surfaced and Ree gasped. Grei didn't. His head lolled forward, mouth almost in the water. She adjusted her grip, sliding her arm underneath his armpits to keep his head out of the water. No cough. No breath.

"Dammit, Grei…" she murmured. "Come on." She swam for shore and pulled him out.

Ree called upon the twenty-eighth, the Ringdance for just after exiting the Water Door. It taught a Ringmaid how to swim, and it also taught her how to take care of the drowned. She pushed on his stomach, and water sluiced out of his mouth.

"This would be stupid," she said, pushing again. More water came out. She scooted up to his head, put her hand underneath his neck and pinched his nose. She leaned down and breathed into his mouth. "Stupid," she reiterated, taking a few deep breaths. "For you to get hit with a fireball…" She breathed into his mouth again, then took a breath. "And die of drowning." She pushed again on his stomach, breathed again into his mouth. "Stupid. As the Whisper Prince, you're forbidden to die in such a ridiculous—"

Grei coughed, his chest spasming.

Relief flooded through her. "Okay… Okay then…" she murmured, leaning over him and putting her cheek against his chest. "Thank the Faia…"

He coughed again, and river water shot from his mouth. He turned instinctively to his side and coughed again. Water drained from his mouth.

"Baezin's Blood." Ree sat back. "I spend more time hovering over you while you're half-dead, Whisper Prince."

Water dripped on his face, and he blinked, peering up. Ree's wet hair hung down over her face, dripping onto his chin. "How…" he began. "Adora? How… What happened?"

Ree hooked a thumb over her shoulder. "She blasted you. She left."

"Just left? Left you alive?"

Ree was still reeling from that. "We faced off. I waited for her to incinerate me, but she didn't. She just…"

"What?"

"She glanced over the waterfall after you, then back at me, then she left. I think she… I think she wanted me to save you.

275

I think…there's still some Adora left in there."

"You didn't try to kill her."

"No. I didn't try to break open a boulder with my head, either."

"What?"

"I don't think I could have killed her if I'd done my very best. She's too powerful."

"Her blast would have killed me, I think, if not for Baezin's Blade," Grei said. He twitched, reaching to his empty scabbard in a sudden panic. "The sword! I dropped it! I—"

"Calm yourself." She put a hand on his shoulder. "It's down there. I will get it." She stood up, removed her boots this time. Swimming with boots was stupid. "Stay here. Breathe."

She dove back into the water. The pool churned by the thundering falls, then calmed farther away. She pulled deep with her hands and kicked with her legs, fighting to return to the spot where she'd found Grei just a short distance down from the falls.

There it was.

The glowing blade was easy to spot amidst the mossy rocks. It burned red, though the glow was fading. It had been like a firebrand when she'd yanked Grei out of the water. She snatched it up, somersaulted in the water, and pushed mightily against the rocks, propelling herself upward. She broke the surface and drew a deep breath. With one hand gripping the sword and the other cupping water, she pulled for the shore. The red glow had nearly faded by the time she emerged onto land, dripping wet. She laid it on the ground next to Grei.

"Thank you," he said, coughing.

"You're welcome," she said.

"I was going to…" He trailed off, and he squinted up at the bright sun. His gaze suddenly shot from the waterfall to the other side of the river, then to the west.

"The droplets are gone," he said.

The falls shimmered in the sunlight. Sunlight. She hadn't noticed it in the rush to save Grei's life, but the droplets thrown up by the furious falls fell back in the pool like normal droplets. They didn't hang in the air, didn't float gently downstream, imbued by Faia magic. The fyds, always flitting around the lake and the waterfall, had also vanished.

"What does that mean?" she asked quietly.

"She left her haven…" He marveled. "Like I told her to."

Ree sighed. "And what does *that* mean?"

"I… Sorry. You were…frozen in time when I learned about that. It was something Saebin told me. If the Blue Faia leaves her haven, she's weaker…" He trailed off. Ree followed his gaze. The western horizon looked red, like the sun was about to set.

Except the sun was high overhead.

Grei tried to stand up. His legs were wobbly. She put her arm around his waist and helped him up. Together, they staggered to the rocky edge of the lake. The land dropped away another ten feet, the water twisting as it fell. The panorama of Fairmist and the lowlands came into view.

Red mist hung over the lowlands, flowed over the wall, spilled into the city. The nearest tendrils moved sluggishly uphill through the streets.

"No…" Grei whispered. He began breathing in rapid, short little gasps.

"Slowly now," Ree said, but her own heart sank at the scene below. That was the red mist from the city of Thiara. How had it traveled so fast? It was a three-day ride from Thiara. Mist couldn't possibly move that fast.

Grei sagged in her grip.

"Easy, Grei," she said.

He slipped to his knees, and she let him go. His gaze stayed locked on the grim horizon.

"I've killed us all," he whispered.

Chapter 32

GREI

DESPAIR OOZED across Grei's scalp and shoulders. It sunk through his skin and chilled his heart.

"It's not over yet," Ree said grimly.

He shook his head. And even with his magic working, he couldn't stop something that could spread that fast. He'd wrapped himself in a cloak of arrogance, thinking he was a match for the empress, the slinks, the Faia... But the truth of it hit hard. Grei thought himself a match for Velak.

Instead, Grei was bumbling about, destroying the ones he loved and assisting the fire lord. The city of Thiara was enslaved. Fairmist would be enslaved by the end of the day. Terror coursed through him. He couldn't do this. He'd been a fool to think he could do this. All he could do was more harm.

"I..." he said. "We have to... We have to run. We...we warn people in Fairmist, get them to...I don't know. Get them to run to Moondow."

"And you think the red mist won't be in Moondow?" Ree asked.

Grei looked up sharply. "What?"

"If Velak could bring it here, why wouldn't he bring it there, too?" she asked in a flat tone.

"By the Faia…" He blinked. She was right. It was even worse than he'd imagined. Everywhere he turned, disaster. He was a curse. "I have to stop trying to fix things. I just make it worse… We can't… I can't… We have to run. I have to get away from this."

"Run?" she asked with that quiet deadliness in her tone.

He looked at her and he saw that her eyes glittered with anger.

"Ree, I have failed. I am making things worse—"

She seized him by his wet collar and hauled him to his feet with incredible strength. Putting her nose to his, she spoke through clenched teeth. "Listen, Whisper Prince. You're going to fight."

"Ree—"

"You wanted to find out," she interrupted him. "You crawled into my Lateral House and you demanded secrets. You brewed this storm, and by Baezin's Blood, you're going to fight it. You're going to give every ounce of yourself to finish this."

He gaped at her. Ree had been doggedly persistent in keeping them alive, protecting him, cautious about danger, and calmly supportive since the moment he had awoken in the Slate Temple. To see this sudden fury directed at him knocked the wind out of him. "Ree, you said so yourself. I'm going to create another catastrophe—"

"Shut up."

"I killed Baezin! I killed Saebin! The Blue Faia is probably dead, too, because I couldn't do anything to stop Velak!"

"You spat in the faces of powerful people," she retorted. "Did you think you'd smack them around and walk away? That they wouldn't hit back?" She shook her head. "They were going to try to tear you down from the moment they knew what you were. And here we are."

"What else can I do!"

"You can keep your promise."

"My promise for what?"

"Of a better world, Grei. You wanted a better world. You wanted it so bad you brought down the slinks and the whole damned Thiaran empire. You made your dream real. And now you want to abandon it."

"*Look* at what has happened—"

"Because you can't stop halfway," she interrupted. "I believed in you. *Adora* believed in you."

He felt a stab of pain. Adora *had* trusted him, had felt safe with him. He'd let her down. She'd come to him softly in the night, made love to him, and told him her dreams. He'd let her get snatched by Lyndion.

She had begged him to stay....

"Without my magic, I can't... I'm a kid with a wooden sword trying to fight a Highblade. Just look at it!" He waved a hand at the red mist below.

"Yes, you made a mistake. Velak knocked you down, and he wants you to stay down. Get up. Fight." She released his tunic roughly, and he stumbled back.

He looked despondently at the red mist. He'd failed at every single thing....

"How?" The word stuck in his throat.

"Somehow," she said. "You have the answer. It's inside you, and you're going to find it. Because we need you to."

Her words took him back to the Temple of the Faia in Thiara, how he'd struggled to find the answer. He didn't know how he was going to defeat the thousands of slinks. He'd told Adora he'd find a way to beat them without the prophecy. "Somehow," he'd said.

And he had. In the end, he'd found another way.

He watched the red mist creeping up the slope, through the city. For a moment, he stopped thinking about every person caught by it, infected by it, transformed into a puppet by it, all because of him. Instead, he thought of Adora, torn from her chosen life to serve another's purpose. Again. Rage at the injustice filled him.

No, he couldn't quit. He might create catastrophe after

catastrophe, but he couldn't walk away. Adora needed him. He had to fight until he had no strength left.

And he had two advantages. He had Baezin's Blade, which might be even more important than his magic. Cavyn had designed it specifically to slay Velak, and it could obviously hurt him even if it just swiped close.

And Grei had Ree. Thank the Faia for Ree and her oath. She had saved his life so many times he'd lost count. This entire quest would have died if not for her.

He clenched his fist in resolve.

"That's right," Ree murmured. "Eyes on the path, Grei. Light the way. A Ringblade who doesn't focus on her current step stumbles. You cracked open the world, and danger spilled out. If you stop now, that's where it stays. If you fight, we can change it, undo what you've done. We're in the Web of Blades now," she murmured.

"Web of Blades?" He'd heard of the contest, something having to do with Highblades battling each other.

"If you enter the Web, you win or you die. There's no going back."

Grei felt so horrible he *wanted* to die.

"I'll fight," he said.

"I know," she said, as though she'd never had a doubt. She clapped him on the shoulder. "First things first. We need to leave this place. You're not ready to undo that mist, and we can't get caught in it. I'm going back for the horses, and I'll bring them down to the Darkspan Bridge. You catch your breath, then meet me there in ten minutes. Keep an eye on that mist. If it gets too close before I get back, bolt. Don't wait for me."

"How will you find me?"

"I'll find you, Whisper Prince." She dragged her thumb sideways across her tongue. "A kiss and a cut, remember?" She reminded him of the Ringblade spell from their first meeting when she'd pressed her lips to his and sliced his ear.

She winked, then dove into the lake and swam to the other side. He watched her pull herself out on the far bank, grab both of their cloaks, then begin climbing the slope.

He let out a long breath and watched the red mist creep slowly up the streets of the city of Fairmist.

Chapter 33

REE

REE SCRAMBLED UP the slope, a moist mix of rocks, mud, and moss. It made for treacherous footing, each handhold giving way almost as soon as she grasped it. But the sixth dance taught resiliency, how to move confidently on uncertain ground. It taught that all things were transient. You could not rely on the solidity of any single thing forever, and must be ready to adapt, to leap. So Ree took what stability was offered, launching gently and quickly from the rocks least stable, pulling hard on the handholds she deemed solid. It was slower going than climbing a granite cliff face, but she made it to the top in good time.

She rolled over the lip of the slope onto flat ground, then rolled to her feet. As she rose, she took a deep breath of the clean air, let the sunshine warm her skin as the burst of physical effort warmed her. Her body felt alive again. These past days had been a harrowing journey, rife with danger and hardship, but this was what she'd trained for. With her heart aligned to her task, her body had responded. It had only been a week since Grei broke Kuruk's hold on her. The slink's powerful mind had battered her, nearly driving her mad and forcing her to ignore everything except resisting his call. She'd not slept and she'd barely eaten, even while in captivity at the Ringblade sanctum.

But every day she'd lain in the infirmary, eating three meals a day and sleeping in between, her body had been rebuilding. Her health had been like a seed beneath a blanket of snow, waiting for winter's end. The moment she felt Selicia's dagger cut into Grei, the seed had taken root. Her body had begun its journey back to her original strength. Now, after three days on the road, eating voraciously and pushing her body for a noble purpose, her muscles were becoming toned again. A thin layer of fat insulated her. The Ringblade she had been was emerging once more.

She turned and gave a protective glance to Grei, who sat slumped on the far side of the pool. He looked up at her, spent, and she held up ten fingers for him.

Ten minutes, she mouthed silently. He nodded.

The young man was foolish, idealistic, and pig-headed. He, too, had been beaten down, and his idealism had finally been buried underneath the snows of defeat. If she could scoop a couple of handfuls of snow away to reveal his pig-headed idealism again, then that was her job. Grei's stubbornness had driven him to expose the Debt of the Blessed, had driven him to face a god like Velak with no magic. That same stubbornness would drive him to succeed, if he could stay alive long enough.

She softly flexed the fingers of her wooden hand, thinking of how his pig-headedness had healed her, too. For all the world, it felt like her actual arm. Only when she looked at it, tapped it with a knuckle, did she get that chill, remembering it was actually solid wood.

Grei was the only person she'd ever met who so casually defied reality, and who was wholly uncompromisingly good. He was naive, but maybe it was that naiveté that transformed the impossible into the possible.

She believed in Grei.

Her pragmatic mind scoffed at the naive statement. It was the kind of thing a starry-eyed maiden breathlessly declared to herself as she clutched a love letter to her chest.

Ree was not a starry-eyed maiden, but she had seen Grei change the world. Within him was the possibility for miracles, and as long as she could keep him alive, she believed he would find a way. The boy had an intuition that reached deeper than fear, deeper than despair. Anyone could look at hardship and call it impossible, but only Grei looked beneath the filth, beneath the betrayal and violence inherent in every person, and saw something worth saving.

She smiled ruefully and began jogging toward where they'd tethered the horses. Perhaps she would soon spout bad love poetry and clutch letters to her chest, but never had she felt more right than she did now. Grei's pig-headed vision was worth dying for.

She reached the horses in short order. The animals cropped happily where they'd been tethered, as though they had no inkling of the battle that had just raged within the Blue Faia's cave or the red-misted death that slowly approached. They were good mounts. She untethered them, taking both sets of reins in one hand and—

A shadow moved on the ground next to her.

Ree spun and crouched, two daggers in hand—

A tall, broad-shouldered woman stood before her, and she threw back her cowl to reveal her ebony face, tightly curled hair and lavender eyes.

"Liana," Ree whispered incredulously.

The Shalaran woman was garbed in Ringblade black leathers: soft boots made for stealth, tight breeches, and tunic belted at the waist. And, of course, the telltale ringblade rested in its catch at her waist.

Powerful, conflicting emotions rose within Ree. Relief. Caution. Love.

Liana held up both hands up in a pacifying gesture at Ree's hostile pose. Liana held no weapons, but Ree didn't let that fool her. Dances fourteen and fifteen taught a Ringmaid how to set her opponent at ease while maneuvering for a strike.

Liana's lavender eyes became sad. "You greet me this way?" she said in her lovely accent.

"Depends on why you're here," Ree said, giving no ground.

"Spirits, Ree, the world is collapsing! And it is *me* you doubt?" she asked plaintively.

"Why are you here?" Ree asked bluntly, giving quiet thanks to the Faia that Liana stayed where she was. If she moved, Ree would have to act, and Ree knew how fast that woman could move.

"For you, of course," Liana said. She put her tongue upon her thumb, gently, then swiped it to the right. "A kiss and a cut," she said softly.

Ree's heart hurt. The sixty-ninth dance taught how to create the blood bond, to take a person's blood into you and thereby connect their body to yours. As a Ringmaid neared the end of her training, she had been required to partner with one of her Ringsisters and together perform the blood bond. Liana and Ree had been lovers by that time, so the choice of a partner was a forgone conclusion. And when they had made the blood bond, they had shared a kiss at the same time. "A kiss and a cut," Liana had called it. They were the same words Ree had murmured to Grei in the Lateral House when she had marked him, an inside joke that only Liana would have understood.

The blood bond was made for tracking, for a Ringblade to mark an important person so that she could find him or her later. There was a myriad of side effects to the blood bond, and no two people experienced the same ones. With Grei, Ree had felt it when he was stabbed like someone had punched her in the belly. With Liana, the side effect had been pleasure. When Ree concentrated, she could feel a stroke against Liana's dark skin like a stroke on her own. Liana's pleasure became Ree's. It had made their lovemaking exquisitely intense. Though they were supposed to have cleansed the blood bond after making their practice connection, they hadn't. Against the regulations of the order, Ree and Liana had secretly kept it.

Ree felt her eyes prickle with tears. Liana represented the heart of what Ree had lost when she'd been banished from the Ringblades. Fellowship. Family. Love. But she blinked her emotion away and steeled herself.

"I need more of an answer than that," Ree said, still crouching and holding her daggers at the ready. There was only one reason Liana could be here, now: Selicia had sent her. "There's too much at stake."

"Too much? Everything is at stake, *baiben*." She used her pet name, "treasured one," in the Shalaran tongue.

Liana's full lips twisted, pressing together, and the right corner of her mouth turned down. It was a mannerism Ree had seen before; it was how Liana stopped her lip from trembling, stopped herself from crying. To anyone else, it would look like a disapproving frown, but Ree knew Liana like she knew her own heart.

"Please," Ree let a little softness into her voice, "tell me how you came to be here. Tell me quickly."

"Or you will do what?" Liana asked. "You will attack me?"

"Please."

"I fled the horror, Ree! Thiara is gone. There *tyendal* are everywhere."

"*Tyendal?*" Ree wasn't familiar with the Shalaran word.

"Those who…" Liana struggled to find the word in Venishan. Finally, she shrugged. "Those who are dead, and yet walk. I fled the red mist, sister."

"Who sent you?"

"There is no one left to send me! The world has changed, and all in moments. We heard that Selicia died. So Zela took command, and then the mist took them all. Ree, our sisters are all *tyendal*."

"How?"

"It was Syvet. She returned to the sanctum, telling of a battle above. She was urgent, gesturing wildly, and she stumbled like she was near to collapse. The sisters rushed to help her, Zela included, and then the red mist poured from Syvet's mouth. It took them all, one to another, their eyes all going red."

That was exactly what had happened to Princess Vecenne at the palace. "How did you escape?"

"Because the others rushed forward to assist Syvet, and I did not."

"Why?"

"I sensed something. Something was not right about her. It...chilled me. Many little things told the tale. You know Syvet. She is quiet as a stone most times. When has she ever gestured urgently? That was my first clue that something was amiss. Then I saw a flash of red in her eyes." She brushed her arm absently with her hand, like she was cold. Ree concentrated, and, through their blood bond, felt the gesture as though Liana's hand had brushed across her own skin. In turned into a tap, and Ree tensed as she felt it. That was a message in the code of Silent Fingers, one of the secret languages by which Ringblades communicated when they could not speak aloud.

No... Ree thought as the message became clear, but she tamped down her emotions, kept them off her face.

"So when the others rushed forward, I did not," Liana continued as though she hadn't just tapped out a message on her arm. "Then I saw the red mist pass to Zela, and her eyes turned red also. She opened her mouth, and red mist flowed out of her as well, and two more of our sisters breathed it. Then again, and the rest were taken quickly. The sanctum was breached." She let out a sigh. "We are taught never to fight our sisters, and certainly not in the sanctum, so I fled. I went straight to the Water Door and swam out. From the beach, I saw the city consumed in mist, so I avoided it altogether. I spent a day in the fields of a nearby plantation, watching the mist devour everyone. That is when I reached into the blood bond, to see if you still lived. That is when I came looking for you." Liana still kept her arms crossed, and her little finger tapped her skin absently. Ree could feel it like a heartbeat.

"Were you the only one who escaped?" Ree asked.

"Jylla was still herself when I leapt away. She, too, had held back, but we were separated by those who had become *tyendal*. If she was lucky, she might have made it through the Poison Door or the Main. I do not know. If she went through the Main, I have little hope for her. The red mist was everywhere."

"I'm so sorry, *baiben*." Ree echoed Liana's term of endearment, and she stood up, sheathing her daggers. "I'm so sorry." She rushed to Liana's arms, and the tall woman enveloped her in a soft, warm hug, her face pressed to Ree's hair. They clung to each other, and Ree felt Liana's finger twitching again, scratching frantically against Ree's shoulder....

Ree struck the base of Liana's skull with the pommel of her dagger, quick and certain, while at the same time pinching a nerve on the tall woman's neck. The strike was a part of the fourteenth dance, and it caused temporary paralysis.

Liana's arms went limp. Ree pressed the edge of her wet tunic tightly against her mouth as Liana slid to the ground and fell onto her back. Her eyes were glassy, but now a fiery red glow filled them. A puff of red mist rose from her mouth and hovered there, reaching like a thin, palsied hand. Ree backed away carefully, watching the mist, watching her lover. Tears stood in Ree's eyes.

"I'm sorry, *baiben*," she whispered. Ree quickly searched Liana's pouches, found what she sought. A pair of soft black gloves and two vials of liquid, one clear, one a bluish color.

"Will...get...you..." she rasped, low and menacing, and her voice was completely different now, with no trace of a Shalaran accent.

Ree put on the gloves, then broke the waterproof seal and uncorked the bluish liquid, which made a person blind for as much as a day. She held Liana's head gently and peeled back one of her eyelids, carefully dripped one drop into her left eye, then her right as she avoided the little puff of red mist hovering near Liana's head. It began to move toward Ree, spreading out, but she stepped away and approached Liana from the other side.

Ree dumped the contents of the other vial into Ree's mouth, followed it with a bit of water. Liana reflexively swallowed. That would knock her out for most of a day. It wasn't the head start Ree wanted, but it was something. Velak's other minions would have to search the hard way, without Liana's blood bond.

"Kill…you…" she gargled.

"Not today, Velak," Ree said. "But I'll see you soon."

The thing inside Liana hissed back, but if Velak spoke words, they were unintelligible.

While avoiding the questing, but slow, red mist that had escaped Liana's mouth, Ree stripped Liana of everything she owned save her clothes and her cloak, then donned them all. It felt good to have a ringblade at her side again, not to mention the rest of the order's complement, complete with waterskin, ration squares, vials of poisons, healing items, and maps. Once Ree was outfitted, she grabbed the horses' reins and started down the slope. She made a stone of her heart, leaving her lover behind. Ringblades were trained to walk away from sentiment when required.

Her heart longed to return and help Liana, but Velak would prey upon her soft human foibles if he could. He wanted to twist Ree's emotions as he'd twisted her lover, and that wasn't going to happen.

She kept jogging, the horses clopping behind her. There was only one man who could make the world right, and she had to get back to him. The carriers of the red mist were in the city, and they would be searching for him everywhere. They were probably running in Grei's direction right now.

As she hurried toward the Darkspan Bridge, Ree cradled the precious piece of knowledge she'd just gained, perhaps the most important piece she had yet learned.

Velak was weaker than he seemed.

He wanted the world to believe he was unstoppable, so he made a spectacle everywhere he went. But whatever prison the Faia had put him in, Velak had not yet escaped. He could only do as much as his limited vessels allowed him. Liana had resisted him, had done what she could to betray him. While Velak was speaking through Liana's mouth, using Liana's body, her little finger had tapped a message on her arm. One message, over and over:

Run, baiben, run!

Though Velak had enough control over Liana to make her walk and talk and sound as he pleased, a part of her still fought him. The same was likely true of Adora. She could have killed Grei twice. But both times she'd let the defrocked Whisper Prince escape alive.

Ree moved as swiftly as she dared, angling for the first and closest of the great bridges built by the Faia long ago.

We must flee, Whisper Prince. We know Velak's weakness. We must live long enough to discover how to use it.

Chapter 34

GREI

GREI SHEATHED BAEZIN'S BLADE and started downhill. The sun warmed him, and the chill in his chest slowly faded. But the brightness here, the sun overhead…it was wrong in this place. There shouldn't be sun in Fairmist.

It only took him a few minutes to reach the Darkspan Bridge, a beautiful mahogany bridge with Baezin's early adventures carved into its arch. Grei sat down on a wide rock, set Ree's cloak beside him, and contemplated the bas-relief story. It started with Baezin arriving on the shores of Devorra, where Baezin founded the Thiaran Empire. The next carving was of Baezin meeting the Faia here in Fairmist. They surrounded him, little hands up to greet him.

There wasn't a carving of Baezin's meeting with Thiara, though, no indication that the Faia were his daughters. And there was no Velak, either.

"Do you see the lies in that story that I see?" a child said from behind him.

Grei leapt to his feet, spinning about.

Kuruk stood uphill, his boyish face dappled in shade. He wore a noble's clothes: a fine blue tunic with laces at the cuffs of the billowing sleeves, a black belt, brown breeches, and black boots. He took another step forward and the sunlight gleamed on his golden curls. He narrowed his eyes at the light, but made no move to attack. His hands hung simply at his sides, looking for all the world like a little boy. Only his long, translucent fingernails and his monster's red eyes betrayed him.

Grei couldn't breathe.

"You freeze. You pale," Kuruk said. "At the Temple of the Faia, you were fearless. You screamed defiance in my face." He walked slowly downhill, but not directly at Grei. Instead, the slink began a lazy circle around the bridge like a predator.

Grei tried to find his tongue, but no words came. This was the moment he'd feared since he'd awoken after the Phantom War. Grei had barely kept the slink from killing him the first time, and that was with the full power of his magic, as well as Vecenne's and Blevins's help.

Kuruk strolled in that slow semicircle. "Yes…" he hissed the word slowly and then, as if reading Grei's mind, the slink said, "You've been stripped of your powers, stripped down to a bare mortal. What will you do if I attack?"

Grei's blood turned to ice in his veins. Kuruk knew.

"Surprised?" Kuruk said. "I've been following you. I've seen…everything."

Slowly, Grei moved his hand to the pommel of Baezin's Blade. Kuruk watched the gesture like a cat watches a mouse that hasn't yet bolted.

"Why don't I kill you?" Kuruk said softly. "Is that what you're asking yourself?" He clenched one of his tiny fists. "I visited you in Thiara," he said. "I came into your room as you slept, that first night after you brought my plan crashing down, I stood over you, and I seethed as you dreamed. I imagined the many ways I would slice your body apart for what you've done." He paused in his circuit and faced Grei. "In the end, it was your thoughts that saved you. I'd had long hours to ponder my position, and to look at what I'd seen in your head the day you brought my illusion down."

Grei drew Baezin's Blade with a shaky hand, held it in front of him.

"You long to protect those you love," Kuruk said, ignoring the sword. "The princess. The people of Fairmist. Even the ones who hurt you, surprisingly." Kuruk cocked his head. "Thiarans are petty and selfish. But you are not. You don't dream of greater wealth and greater power. You dream for others." The boy leaned his head forward, his eyes smoldering beneath his blond brows. "So do I."

Kuruk began his walk again in that wide arc that trapped Grei against the bank of the river. "It seems that you and I, despite the fact that you are a Thiaran, have something in common. That's why I left instead of killing you. I intended to watch you until you proved that you were just like every other selfish Thiaran. I watched the Ringmother stab you, followed you down the canal until Ree pulled you out. I watched as you melted the walls inside the palace. I saw you create the red mist trying to shake loose Velak's hold. I saw you race to the Jhor Forest, and I saw you fight Velak's puppet in the forest and at the falls."

Grei cleared his throat. "You *followed* me?" He felt like a blind man in a maze, crashing into one wall after another.

Kuruk's voice dropped to a whisper. "Seeing you bumble about… It made me hate you even more…that *you* could have thwarted me. I had planned so meticulously. I waited a hundred years to free my brothers. And then seven more, here, toiling in this world, carefully holding a monster at bay while I built my plan. You cannot understand the hope, the pain, the thin slices of my soul that I cut away for my brothers.… And yet, in a matter of minutes, you tore everything down." His eyes glowed hotter, splashing red light on the ground. Kuruk stopped his pacing, his gaze flicking to the sword, then to Grei's face. With a snarl, he stepped toward Grei.

Grei raised the sword.

But Kuruk stopped, his fists clenched, then he continued his slow, casual stroll around Grei as though he hadn't ever been angry. He reached the edge of the Darkspan Bridge in silence, then turned and started back the other way. "Shall we hack at each other then?" he said, and his voice was calm again.

Grei's heart thundered in his chest.

"Eviscerating you would give me great personal joy, Whisper Prince, I assure you. But I am not here for myself. I am here for my brothers. My only care in this world is to see them freed. Until then, my actions do not belong to me. My original plan was to pry them free from Velak. But, thanks to you, that plan is in ruins and Velak no longer has need of me. If vengeance was all I craved, I'd rip you apart. But I have seen what you can do; I have glimpsed your thoughts, and that brought me to an unavoidable conclusion. The quickest path to what I want is through you."

"What?"

"I need your help," Kuruk said.

Grei's arms had begun to ache from holding up the sword. He adjusted his grip and kept the point in Kuruk's direction. He thought of Julin, of the innumerable other Blessed ripped from their homes and sacrificed to this monster, given over to Velak and his mind domination. He thought of The Garden in Fairmist, where the emperor's Highwands had turned people to stone because of Kuruk and his Debt of the Blessed. Grei thought of the hundreds slain in the first Slink War, the hundreds more compelled to run to the north, driven by Kuruk's mental lash, there to die of starvation or exposure. Kuruk had gutted the empire, and now he wanted a partner. "Best kill me then," Grei said. "I will never help you."

"Then help yourself."

"There's nothing you have that I want."

Kuruk gave the barest hint of a smile. "You speak with passion, but not with sense. I have so much that you want."

"You're a killer. My brother—"

"Julin," Kuruk interrupted, daring to say his name.

"You…" Grei growled. "You took him. You twisted him into a fiend."

"I made him into a vessel for Velak. And I can undo it."

"You— What?"

"And your lover the princess. If we kill Velak, we can save Julin, save Adora. We can save all of them."

Grei's mouth opened, but his words tumbled out awkward. "You..." he said. "You can push Velak out of Adora and Julin?" Hope filled him, but he pushed it down. This was a trick. This slink had sunk Thiara into a mass of lies for seven years. Surely he was lying now.

"So can you," Kuruk said. "You nearly did it in Thiara. It is about the *dasha*. I am strong in manipulating the *dasha*. So, apparently, are you. I did not think it possible for you, what you did to Aylenna. Together, we might free your princess from Velak's hold. That is what I could do for you. And as to what you can do for me—"

"Why would you turn on your master?"

Kuruk made a little sound between his teeth. "Velak killed me, Whisper Prince. He burned my body and made me into this." He gestured at himself with his clawed hand, letting the sunlight glint off the glass-like fingernails. "Then he held my brothers hostage and pushed me back into this world to do his bidding. He promised to give my brothers back when I completed his work, but I knew he never would, not unless I had the upper hand, not unless I threatened him enough to force him to let them go. He wanted only to use me and my brothers. So I made a plan to use him first. That is the plan you destroyed. Now, the only way to get my brothers back is to kill Velak. And this, I cannot do this alone." He paused, watching Grei with those burning eyes. "But with you, I could. Together, we would be a match for Velak."

"There's no way I can trust you. You could be Velak's agent right now, waiting for the right time to strike."

"The right time?" Kuruk said, then he moved so fast he was a blur. Grei barely had time to raise the sword before he hissed and pulled his hand back. Baezin's Blade thumped on the wet grass by the river bank. Three shallow cuts sizzled on the back of Grei's hand. Kuruk stood at arm's length, and he showed his teeth.

"If I wanted to kill you," Kuruk said. "The right time would be now."

Grei opened his mind and let the warbling voices blare into his head. He had no hope of matching Kuruk with magic, but maybe he could get one of those wild ripples to turn the slink into water.

"Don't," Kuruk said. "Let your mind settle. Look with clear eyes and see the truth. Apart, we die, and everyone we love dies with us. Together, we may succeed." After a moment, Kuruk held out his little hand.

It all seemed like one of Saebin's jolting dreams. Impossible… And yet… If Kuruk was telling the truth….

Grei had almost no knowledge of Velak or Velakka, but Kuruk had lived there for a hundred years. Just that information was valuable, let alone the power Kuruk could bring in a fight against Velak. Could Grei afford to throw away such an advantage?

"I hate you for what you've done," Grei whispered.

"Your hate is a candle next to my bonfire. Let us agree that we loathe one another. And when we have what we want, then let us rip at each other to our heart's content. But for now, together, let us save those we love."

Grei clenched his teeth. "Very well, slink." He reached out, took the little hand—which was as hot as a rock in the sun—and he shook it.

"Very well, Thiaran." Kuruk's eyes smoldered, little trails of smoke rising from the edges.

Chapter 35

GREI

ONCE THEY'D CLASPED hands, Kuruk's gaze flicked to Grei's neck. In a blur, Kuruk raised his free hand alongside his head. The warbling tones of magic blared in Grei's mind, and a ringblade struck Kuruk's hand with a metallic bang, rebounded and splashed into the shallows of the river.

Kuruk hissed, stepping away from Grei.

Grei spun, looking for the source of the attack, and he spotted horses across the river. He heard Ree's footsteps thumping across the Darkspan.

She leapt upon the bridge's rail and dove at Kuruk, two daggers out. Kuruk blurred, moving to the side and deflecting one of the blades with his palm. Ree hit the ground, turning her dive into a roll and popped up. She hurled a dagger at Kuruk's head.

"Ree, stop!" Grei shouted.

Kuruk batted the dagger away.

"We've struck a bargain," Grei shouted again. "Stop it!"

Breathing hard, Ree paused her furious attack. Kuruk

walked calmly toward her.

"Kuruk, you kill her and we have no deal," Grei said.

"If I hadn't spared her the first time, my plan would not now be in ruins," Kuruk said.

"And you'd be Velak's slave," Grei spat.

Kuruk stopped his advance. He turned to face Grei and crossed his arms over his chest.

"You made a deal with this creature?" Ree asked incredulously, breathing hard.

"Yes," Grei said.

"He's a slink. Grei, he's *the* slink! He ate my arm!"

"He can bring them back," Grei said.

Her mouth opened to retort, but she closed it. Then she said, "The Blessed?"

"Yes."

"He's lying," she said.

"What if he's not?"

She glared at Kuruk.

"We have enough enemies, Ree," he said in a quiet voice. "If there's a chance he's not lying, don't we have to take it? For my brother. For your sister. For Adora."

Ree's gaze went flat. She hesitated, then sheathed her remaining dagger and stood upright. In a toneless voice, said. "You're right, of course."

She acquiesced so abruptly that Grei blinked. She turned her back on Kuruk and strode down to the river.

Grei's befuddled mind caught up a second later. Ree hadn't actually agreed. Of course she hadn't. She was a Ringblade. She was simply playing the part. It was better to seem harmless while waiting for a moment to strike. Playing the friend to an enemy for the time being must be as easy as breathing for her. He'd have to talk to her later when Kuruk wasn't around, convince her that they must play in good faith with Kuruk.

Ree stooped and picked up the ringblade from the shallow waters, then washed the mud from it. A ringblade. Where had she found a ringblade?

"Where did you get that?" he asked. If Ree had suddenly

produced a third arm, it wouldn't have been stranger. Only Ringblades possessed their namesake weapon. She couldn't have bought, stolen or bartered for that.

"My Ringsisters are here," she replied. "They're looking for you, and they're infected with the red mist. They brought it to Fairmist." She glared at Kuruk. "We have to leave. Now."

Grei absorbed that, glancing over the valley. The red mist was halfway through the city now. His heart quailed. "Ree... I'm...I'm so sorry."

"We don't have time to discuss it now," she said. "Come on."

Reluctantly, he nodded and walked toward his horse. Something brushed against his leg, and Grei glanced down. A fyd tugged on the edge of his breeches.

"Ah!" he said, and glanced around. The fyds had returned, and they clustered thickly over the rushing water.

"A Faia attack?" Kuruk asked as the fyd flew up and circled Grei's head. He pointed a finger at the fyd as if he would incinerate it.

"Don't hurt it!" Grei said. The fyd did a little dance on the air and whisked away to the river. A dozen fyds joined it, then dozens more. In seconds, over a hundred fyds clustered over the water, then flew toward Grei.

He took a surprised step back. The fyds whirled around him, a cloud of clicking, whirring wings.

"What are they doing?" Ree said.

"I don't know," Grei said. "I don't..."

And then he felt it, the same pull he had felt at the Jhor Forest.

"...Mother..."

The fyds circled him faster, blurring together.

"...he hears us..."

"...Mother..."

The warbling whispers got louder, and he felt the immense force of the waterfall higher up, the magic that resided in that pool just outside the Blue Faia's cave. It was different than the Jhor, where everything hovered in the trees and the animals, like a pressure from all directions moving inward. This felt like Grei was being pulled into a whirlpool. Here, the immeasurable power was concentrated only in the waterfall, not spread through an entire forest. And it hungered for him.

"It's happening again," Grei said.

"What is happening?" Kuruk asked.

Ree flicked a gaze left and right. "Like the Jhor?"

Grei stumbled, taking a step backward like he was facing a fierce headwind. "It's not animals this time," he said. "It's the water. It wants to draw me in."

Ree grabbed his arm and pulled him away from the water. The fyds flew furiously around her, kicking, grabbing her hair and pulling. More appeared over the river and flocked to her in a frenzy, grabbing and yanking at her clothes. Ree's feet came off the ground, and she winged her arms, trying to get her balance.

"Dammit," Grei growled, grabbing Ree's leg.

A cluster of the fyds exploded in a blast of fire. The horses spooked, whinnying and bolting into the woods.

"Kuruk!" Grei snarled. The flaming fyds dropped, contorted in pain, bodies and wings burning. Some fluttered awkwardly away, hitting the water with little hisses. Ree dropped to the ground and rolled back to her feet. Grei rounded on the slink. "I said don't hurt them!"

Kuruk narrowed his eyes and pointed his finger at Grei, which brought him up short.

"Once you succeed in freeing my brothers," Kuruk said, eyes flickering. "You can sacrifice your life in whatever manner you wish. Not before."

"...Mother..."

"...stay with us..."

The powerful vortex yanked at Grei again, and this time his feet almost jerked out from under him. He slid toward the water, making gouges in the soft earth. His instincts screamed to fight it, to run, but he hesitated.

Saebin said Grei had to bind himself to one location to restore his magic. Why not this one? This was a perfect opportunity. The water spirits wanted him. They would open the path for him. He could have his magic back!

And do what with it? Stay hidden in his cave like the Blue Faia?

No. It couldn't be here. It couldn't be now.

Saebin, for all his knowledge, had made few right choices. He withheld information when he should have shared it. He hid when he should have fought. If Grei and Saebin had confronted Adora together, they might have prevailed. But if Grei bound himself to Fairmist Falls now, he would be overrun by the red mist.

He leapt away from the water. The jump was pitiful, like he had ropes tied to his ankles. He managed a scant six inches, then he fell on his face and began sliding back toward the water.

With a grunt, he got his feet underneath him, lowered his head, and pulled like an ox against a yoke. One step. Two steps.

The water of the river stopped flowing downhill, swirling right next to the bank. In seconds, a huge pool formed, spilling over the banks and creeping into the woods toward Grei. The depths sloshed like a sea serpent thrashed in it. A tentacle of pure water formed on the surface and shot forward, coiling around Grei's leg and yanking him onto his face.

"...Mother..."

"...we need you..."

"...stay..."

It dragged him between the trees, toward the swelling pool. Grei made a desperate grab for one of the trunks, but couldn't hold on.

Kuruk shot flame, breaking the tentacle. Water and fire hissed, and it released Grei. He rolled, scrambled hastily to his feet, and lurched away from the river. Another water tentacle shot at Kuruk. He spun, cried out as it hit his skin. Steam went up from his shoulder like he was a stove. Fire blasted from his mouth, turning the water tentacle to steam. He leapt deftly backward. More tentacles rose.

"Run!" Grei said. Though the tentacle had lost its grip, the invisible force still pressed thickly around him, and again, it felt like he was trudging through mud.

Then Ree was there, Baezin's Blade in her hands. She swiped it through the air between Grei and the river, and suddenly he stumbled forward.

"...Mother..."

"...stay..."

"...stay with us..."

"Thank you," he huffed. She grabbed him by one arm and Kuruk took the other. Together, they propelled him, stumbling, into the forest.

They sprinted. The fyds flicked after them in pursuit. Ree unclasped her cloak and wrapped one end around her fist. She spun around and ran backward nearly as fast as she'd been running forward. "Guide me," she said tersely to Grei, laying a light hand on his shoulder as she flicked the cloak out like a whip, knocking three fyds from the air. Kuruk ran next to them, keeping up easily. He eyed the fyds emotionlessly, but he didn't try to burn any more of them.

Grei picked their path through the trees, making sure there was enough space on his left so that Ree wouldn't run into a tree as she ran backward. They ran this way for fifteen hard minutes, Grei weaving through the trees with Ree in tow, Ree flicking fyds away with her cloak.

They ran until Grei could barely breathe, until all but a few persistent fyds had fallen behind. He could still hear the water spirits, but they were whispering echoes.

"...Mother..."

"...stay..."

The invisible force no longer grabbed at him. Huffing hard, Grei stumbled to a stop against tree. The few remaining fyds flitted about, disoriented. They didn't try to attack him, but looked more like they had forgotten why they were so far into the woods. Many looked back the way they'd come, then at Grei in indecision. Perhaps they couldn't remember what they were supposed to do now that they were so far from the water.

Kuruk walked calmly around the little glade, unfazed by the desperate run. He wasn't winded, didn't even seem to be breathing at all, really. But his skin glowed red in the shadows.

Grei pointed a finger at Kuruk's face. "You don't *kill* things!" He gestured at the remaining confused fyds, which fluttered around Grei's head. "If you travel with us, you don't do that."

A jet of fire shot from Kuruk's fist, striking the ground at Grei's feet and turning it to molten soup. Grei slipped and nearly fell into the deadly lava as he scrambled backward. The heat wafted up, forcing him to close his eyes. The edges of his boots smoked. Ree drew her daggers and bounded to Grei's side.

"Don't push your shabby morality on me," Kuruk hissed. "Your arrogance is barely tolerable as it is. I will kill what needs killing until my brothers are returned to me. The only reason you continue to breathe is because I need you." The slink turned his dead-eyed gaze on Ree. "And you, Ringblade… You, I *don't* need."

Grei wanted to snarl at the monstrous little boy, and he barely kept his temper.

He held up a hand for Ree. "Put the daggers away, Ree," he said. Then he looked at Kuruk. "Threaten us again," Grei said in an iron voice. "And I'll show you what I can do with my broken magic."

Little tongues of fire ran over Kuruk's body. Grei felt a tingle in his shoulder and neck, and the little fyds flew down out of his vision. Kuruk lifted his chin and glared at Grei, as still as a stone.

"Do we understand each other?" Grei pressed. Kuruk said nothing.

Grei narrowed his eyes. "Kuruk, do you…" He trailed off. Kuruk wasn't moving *at all.*

Grei turned to Ree. "Did he just—"

Ree was also frozen. Her flinty eyes focused on Kuruk. Her hands clenched on the pommels of her daggers, but her arms were rigid. Wisps of her hair moved lightly in the breeze, but nothing else did.

Grei glanced down at the fyds that had clustered around him. They all lay on the grass at his feet, stiff as painted wooden figurines.

His beleaguered brain finally caught up. They were being attacked!

He put his hand on the hilt of Baezin's Blade and spun just as the paralyzing spell hit him. It started in his stomach and reached into the rest of his body like twisting wires working through his veins. He opened his mouth to shout, but nothing came out. Even his throat had ceased working. He couldn't move.

A powerfully built man stood up from behind a cluster of bushes. He wore the brown breeches of a Fairmist native, a gray tunic and an expensive gray cloak. Though he had long, white hair and an equally long white beard, he looked to be in the prime of youth. He strode toward Grei.

Grei tried to struggle, but only his frantically racing mind seemed to work. Aside from that, the only place he could feel anything was in his right hand where it clasped the pommel of Baezin's Blade. Tingles danced in his palm and fingers.

The muscled, white-haired man worked his shoulders in a circle, then absently massaged his chest. He pulled an amulet from underneath his shirt and laid it over the top of his tunic. It was made of gold, carved with elaborate designs, and it bore a kaleidoscope stone in the center

The man grunted, wincing and glancing sharply at the frozen Kuruk. "Even now, he fights," the man murmured, seemingly impressed. He touched his amulet, which jumped against his chest. "Must tend to that right now, I suppose. Excuse me." Businesslike, the man reached into his satchel and withdrew a little wooden box the size of his palm. He carefully faced the box toward Kuruk, then opened the tiny wooden doors.

Kuruk vanished. The tiny doors of the box snapped shut, and it grew five times its previous size. It thumped to the ground and lay there, now a wooden box a foot wide by two feet long. The man let out a relieved breath.

"That was...invigorating," he said. He faced Grei and Ree, and Grei noticed with shock that the man looked suddenly older. He'd been as hale as a twenty-year-old Highblade when he strode into the glade. Now the fullness of his cheeks had diminished. There were lines at the corners of his eyes and mouth. "My apologies," the man said. "The Still Amulet stops the body." He tapped the amulet with a finger. "But not the mind. Kuruk was trying to break into my head. Best to box him up." He let out a breath as though he'd just done a full day's work. "What a treasure trove we have here. The mighty Kuruk, the fallen Ringblade Ree, and the mythical Whisper Prince." He came forward, close enough to take Grei's chin in his strong fingers. "I spent so much time on you," he said softly. "What a disappointment. But here, at the end, perhaps not a complete waste. We will squeeze some use out of you yet."

Grei's heart hammered as he realized who this man must be. This was Emperor Lyndion! This was the fiend who had tortured Adora, manipulated the empress, and sacrificed Kuruk and his brothers in an attempt to buy his own immortality.

He tried to shout, but no sound came. Not a single muscle in his body moved except his pinkie finger.

"Oh, you want to say something?" Lyndion touched the amulet, then touched Grei's throat.

Suddenly, Grei's head could move. He could speak, but the rest of his body might as well have been encased in a block of wood.

"Bastard!" he exclaimed hoarsely.

Lyndion gave a throaty chuckle. "Unique you may be, Whisper Prince. Eloquent you are not."

"Filth," Grei spat.

"You should sing my praises, Grei. I orchestrated your heart's desire, the desire of every young man, and I gave it to you: the sway of a barmaid and the confidence of a princess.... Did you think such a creature just drops from the sky? No. She was built brick by meticulous, frustrating brick. I prepared her, trained her, shaped her. I made her into your ideal woman. I *gave* you true love." He smiled thinly. "I even made sure she was well-seasoned by the time you sampled her wares. As skilled as a Venishan courtesan—"

Grei shouted fury into Lyndion's face, a feral howl. "I'm going to kill you!" Flecks of saliva flew from his mouth.

Lyndion shrugged, unfazed by Grei's outrage. "You know, even her current elevation is thanks to me. She would never have become Velak's vessel if I hadn't intervened," he mused wistfully. "I've made her a goddess."

"She didn't want to be a goddess! She wanted to live a life with me."

Lyndion grabbed Grei's chin and yanked Grei's face to his. His jovial manner vanished and rage flamed in his eyes. His breath smelled like a rotting corpse. "Oh, I'm sure she did," he hissed. "But she owes me, boy. I poured my most precious resources into her, and she will repay me before the end."

"You're insane," Grei growled.

Lyndion let go of Grei and ignored him like he no longer mattered. Instead, Lyndion moved to stand in front of Ree.

The raving mad emperor touched her softly, tracing the curve of her cheek with his finger. Her eyes flashed, but she said nothing, did nothing.

"Not all lives are meant to endure," Lyndion said quietly. "The purpose of a worm is to feed the sparrow. The sparrow's purpose, to feed the falcon. The falcon serves the falconer. And so on. All the way up to those who were meant to rule, to those rare great souls. And the greatest of these are meant to endure forever." He brought up his left fist, which bore two rings. He touched a black ring to Ree's cheek. "You have been an effective servant of the empire, Ree. Even I have heard of your prowess, just as I heard about your betrayal. But here, at the end, there is one last service you can render your empire."

Grei struggled, painstakingly moving his pinkie along the pommel. The warmth in his hand increased, and suddenly he could move all his fingers. He clenched them around the hilt, and Saebin's words came back to him.

...the blade breaks the bonds of magic...

Now his wrist was free. He twisted it, touching the pommel to his forearm. Suddenly, his entire arm could move. He drew the sword in a quick motion and slapped the flat against his chest.

The paralysis shattered.

Lyndion spun, yanking his fist away from Ree. His mouth opened as he saw the sword in Grei's hand. "Where did you get that?"

"Eloquent you may be. Perceptive you aren't." Grei lunged, swinging. Lyndion stepped to the side, and the strike missed.

But Lyndion wasn't Grei's target. At the end of the swing, he flung the sword. It spun so that the pommel hit Ree in the chest. At four feet away, even Grei couldn't miss.

Ree gasped and stumbled backward, free of the paralysis. She dropped to a crouch, blinked for a half second. Then a snarl twisted her lips, and she grabbed Baezin's Blade from where it landed in the grass.

Grei hadn't wanted Ree using Baezin's Blade against Adora, but she could gut Lyndion for all Grei cared. She could gut him twice.

But Lyndion was already running. He lunged at the wooden box containing Kuruk and snatched it up with one arm. At the same time, he pulled an iron cylinder from his satchel. The rusted chunk of metal was as thick as his wrist. With a flick of his thumb, he opened a tiny hatch in the cylinder.

Abruptly, the ground opened up beneath him, and he dropped into a hole.

"No!" Grei shouted, furious that Adora's tormentor was going to escape. He lunged forward and threw himself after the man. He slid through the hatch just as it began to close.

"Grei, no!" Ree shouted. Her voice cut off as the hatch slammed shut over Grei's head, plunging him into darkness.

Chapter 36

GREI

GREI DROPPED INTO A TUNNEL, and instantly, there was a loud hissing in his mind, just like at the Slate Temple in Thiara after he'd been stabbed. The hatch slammed shut above him, leaving no sign there had ever been an opening at all. The sudden darkness seemed total, but after a moment, it softened. It wasn't pitch-black. The roughhewn ceiling and walls were illuminated by a faint blue light ahead, and Grei could make out Lyndion's silhouette moving quickly away.

"Baezin's Blood," he cursed quietly, dropping to his knees. He glanced up. Solid rock curved overhead. Whatever artifact Lyndion had used was powerful enough to either transport them to this tunnel, or to create it.

"...*sssssssss...*"

The hissing was so loud! Grei clenched his teeth and held his hands to his ears. Slowly, the hissing changed into a sound like someone trying to form a word.

"...*ssssssswwwwwhisper prinssss...*"

Grei spun, but there was no one behind him. Lyndion was

almost gone down the tunnel, taking the light with him.

"Whisper Prince..." The hissing suddenly became clear. It was that an old man's voice, the same one Grei had heard in the Slate Temple, but this time it was articulate. Was it the spirit of the ground? He hesitated, waiting to see if it tried to pull him like the voices at the river.

It didn't.

He chased after Lyndion, who didn't yet seem to know Grei had followed him into the tunnel. Grei had the element of surprise; he had to use it.

"Whisper Prince..."

Grei ignored the voice. Far down the tunnel, silhouetted in blue light, Lyndion stopped at what appeared to be a crossroads in the labyrinth, tossed something to the ground, then turned again to the left. Grei snuck forward, slowing as he neared the little round room with three tunnels forking away from it.

In the center, Lyndion had dropped what appeared to be tiny stone sculpture of some kind, segmented and curled like a human finger. Grei approached cautiously. He could hear the warbling whispers coming from it, marking it as one of Lyndion's artifacts.

Lyndion retreated down the left-hand tunnel, and the blue light grew dimmer.

Grei came a little closer and could see, thankfully, that the object wasn't a finger. It was a stone sculpture of a scorpion's tail. Tiny filaments of copper wire sprouted from it, creating little glimmering dome over it.

Hesitating, Grei decided to open his mind to the warbling whispers. Even as jumbled as they were, they might give some clue as to what this—

The filaments around the scorpion's tail shot out at Grei, lengthening and growing into thin ropes.

Grei leapt back, but he wasn't fast enough. The filaments lashed around his ankles, wrists, and thighs like whips. They yanked him onto his back. They dragged him slowly toward the center of the room.

The stone scorpion's tail suddenly came alive, flopping back and forth. It split into two tails, and both grew. In seconds, they were as long as Grei's forearms. They split again, growing larger as Grei slid toward them. Four deadly tails, stingers in the air, were now rooted to the floor. They swayed as though smelling prey.

Grei struggled mightily, his heels scrabbling on the dirt floor, but the filaments dragged him inexorably up to the swaying, segmented tails. He expected them to lash out and drive a stinger the size of a stalactite into his body.

But they didn't.

The tails, each as tall as Grei and as thick as his arm, split again into eight tails. Seven of them snapped together over Grei's head, creating a seven-sided cage with him inside. The final tail continued growing until it was twice as long as the rest. It bent over at the top of the cage, then hung down inside, twitching, its stinger dripping with a black liquid. The whips that had dragged Grei into the cage let him go and retracted into the center of the cage.

Grei spun to find Lyndion emerge from the tunnel down which he'd gone. He held his fist aloft, the blue light emanating from a sapphire ring on his finger.

"I wanted this to go a different way," Lyndion said, walking into the room. He still carried the wooden box containing Kuruk. "But you just can't resist sticking your nose where it's not wanted." He shook his head. "You were a bad investment, Whisper Prince. Like Adora, you've cost far more than have given in return." Lyndion had aged further in the last few minutes. His body was far past middle-age now, his exaggerated muscle mass gone. Deep lines spiderwebbed away from his eyes, mouth, and across his forehead.

He stepped nearly to the opening of the tunnel, but he seemed careful not to step into the little room.

"The stinger will strike if you move too fast," he said. "It remains still if you do. Try to cut the bars, and it will sting you… It's also triggered by magic use… So if you try to use your whispers, Whisper Prince…" He made a stabbing motion with his finger. "Well, you get the point."

"Lyndion—" Grei gripped the bars. The stinger twitched.

Lyndion gave a mocking wince. "Careful. That poison will kill you in about ten seconds." A drop of that dark liquid fell onto Grei's boot, and he slowly let go of the bars. "Speaking is even more than you probably ought to do." Lyndion took a deep, satisfied breath, hands on his hips.

Grei had never hated anyone more than he hated this man. There was a red tinge to Grei's vision, and his hands shook at his sides. It was all he could do not to leap at the bars.

"Now," Lyndion said. "I have to go. I would stay and talk, but Kuruk is a prize that cannot wait. Do me a favor for once. Don't move and stay alive, will you? You are still valuable to me." He turned and started up the hallway again. The blue light slowly faded.

Grei swallowed his rage and carefully turned his head. The stinger vibrated like a hunting dog spotting prey.

"He's going to kill you either way. You realize that, don't you?"

The sudden words stunned Grei. It was the old man's voice again. The Slate Temple voice.

"Who are you?" he said back within his mind. It was like talking with Saebin, except this voice was much softer, much weaker. Saebin's had been so powerful, it had filled his head.

"Ah, so you can hear me. I wasn't certain. You didn't respond at the temple in Thiara. And then again, here."

"Are you a Slate Wizard?" Grei asked.

A soft, rasping chuckle seemed to come from the walls and ceiling of the room. Grei looked up, trying to find the source—

At Grei's movement, the stinger struck, arching down to impale him…

…but it stopped an inch from his chest.

He stared at it with wide eyes, breathing hard. The stinger had become stone, now a gray sculpture with a single stone drop of poison dangling from its tip.

The chuckle continued, eventually subsiding. *After a fashion.*

Grei slid out from where the stinger sculpture practically

pinned him to the bars of the cage. He moved to the far side of his prison.

"Did you do that?" he asked.

"It is my creation. I can do what I wish with it. I am the Slate Spirit. The wizards are my… kin."

"Are you…? You're like a Faia?"

"Not a Faia. But I can be of more use to you than they can. Especially now. I can affect this cage and everything else in the thief's pack."

"The thief. Lyndion?" Grei asked.

"We were…associates a long time ago. He made promises to me. He failed to keep them. But he kept my artifacts."

Ree's brief story about the Slate Wizards flashed back to Grei. She'd said the holy men, the Slate Wizards, of the Slate Temple had tried to establish a following in Thiara a hundred years ago. They'd been run out of the city, but Ree hadn't said why. Grei suddenly realized that Lyndion would have been emperor at that time.

"Why would you try to help me?"

Again, that dry chuckle. "There are some who do not wish to see Velak break the world."

The cage suddenly sprang open, three of the seven stingers pointing at the ceiling.

Grei leapt out, and the cage immediately began to shrink. In moments, it was the single, stone scorpion tail the size of a finger. And the little copper filaments, attached at its base, hovered over it in a dome, so fine they looked like hair.

Grei felt the need to go chasing after Lyndion, but he hesitated. This mystery Slate Spirit had just saved his life. Questions abounded in Grei's mind.

"I have done you one favor. I offer you two more," the Slate Spirit said.

"Why?"

"To fight Velak, of course. Don't you want your magic back?"

Foreboding and hope rose together as Grei's heart caught in his throat.

"You can help me get my magic back?"

"Yes."

"How?"

"You couldn't heal yourself at the temple because you had not yet chosen a place of power. A place of power keeps a piece of you within it, even as you keep a piece of it within you. You strengthen each other. If you'd had one, it could have shown you how to sew yourself up correctly. Without it, well, you saw what happened...."

That was exactly what Saebin had said, but with different words. *"I've heard it called a haven,"* Grei said.

"That is a Faia term, but it is short-sighted. A haven is a place of power, yes, but not all places of power are havens. The Faia think in terms of the lands, and only the lands, so when they think of their place of power, they think of only one spot. A waterfall. A forest. A hole in the ground. A patch of berries. Limited. The Faia fear to leave their havens. But if your place of power is an object, something you can carry, it goes with you wherever you go."

"Is that possible?"

Again, he chuckled drily. *"Not just possible, but preferable. But it must be an object of great puissance. I would not recommend bonding yourself to an ordinary stick. As with the Faia, you define your place of power, and it also defines you."*

"You talking about an artifact," Grei said. He glanced back at the scorpion's tail, and his heart sank. That sinister thing made his flesh creep. *"Like that?"*

"The Scorpion Cage? Do you have an affinity for scorpions or cages?"

"No."

"Then it would be a poor bond for you. You came into your power listening to the streams, the trees, the earth. You need something attached to the lands, and Lyndion carries The Root."

"The Root? What's the Root?"

"We are inside it."

"We're inside an artifact?"

"It is the nature of The Root."

Grei suddenly realized the Slate Spirit was talking about the artifact Lyndion activated just before he jumped into that hole in the ground. He had flipped open a hatch in that rusted cylinder, and a similar hatch had opened in the ground beneath his feet.

"That…that rusted iron cylinder Lyndion used before he jumped into the ground. It creates tunnels?" Grei asked.

"It is the tunnels. The Root creates a labyrinth beneath the ground of wherever it is opened. So in a sense, you are just below where you were in the forest. In another sense, you are inside the 'iron cylinder', as you put it."

"How can it be both?"

The Slate Spirit chuckled.

"So I'm actually underneath the North Forest?" Grei asked.

"These tunnels would look different if Lyndion had, say, opened them in the Court of Pyramids in Venisha. The magic of the artifact and the lay of the land blend together."

"And if I bond to The Root, I can get my magic back, the way it was meant to be?"

"Yes."

Grei hesitated, and the Slate Spirit remained silent. After a long moment, Grei finally asked the question.

"How do I do it?"

Chapter 37

GREI

THE SLATE SPIRIT explained how to bond with The Root and urged Grei to do it quickly. If Lyndion returned before the bond was made, he would destroy the process and Grei would have nothing.

Grei clawed into the tunnel the wall. After digging for a moment, he found a thin filament of rusted iron running vertically just as the Slate Spirit had described it. Next to it was another and another, as though a million of them sheathed each tunnel he'd run through. He pulled hard on one of them, and a piece snapped off. Once he had the sliver of rusted iron, as thin as a needle and twice as long, he opened his tunic at the front and pressed the rusty piece of metal flat against his chest.

"It will burn," the Slate Spirit said. "It will feel like someone is poking a hot iron into your chest, but you must accept the burning until it stops. If you try to break the bond in the middle, it will not work, and all your suffering will be for nothing."

"Saebin said creating a haven would take two days. You're saying it's going to take only moments?"

"Bonding to an artifact requires less time. And remember, this is my artifact, and you have my assistance."

Grei did remember that, and he wondered what it would mean in the long term. If this artifact belonged to the Slate Spirit and Grei bonded to it, would Grei, in turn, belong to the Slate Spirit? He hesitated, his heart pounding.

"Why did Empress Lymeera chase away the Slate Temple followers?" he asked. *"Why did they drive you out of Thiara?"*

"You wish a history lesson now? We don't have much time, Whisper Prince."

"Tell me," Grei said.

"The story is long."

Grei set his jaw and didn't respond, and the Slate Spirit waited. After a long silence, it spoke again.

"The god Venisha sent the Slate Wizards to this land to spread His word. In Venisha, anyone can use magic. In Thiara, only the Faia. He wished for all Thiarans to taste magic, but the Faia did not like this. They would rather keep magic to themselves. So they allied themselves with Empress Lymeera and pushed His servants out."

"He wanted to give people magic."

"Yes."

"You're lying," he said.

"And you are out of time, Whisper Prince. Lyndion is using my artifacts to rip Velak's influence from the little changeling boy. Once he does, you won't be able to defeat him even with your magic. Is that what you wish?"

Grei clenched his teeth.

"You have only dipped your toe in the ocean of power available to you," the Slate Spirit said. *"You will be a match for Lyndion, perhaps even a match for Velak. And most importantly, you will have a chance to save your lover, Adora."*

"And I will be bonded to one of your creations."

The Slate Spirit went silent for a moment. When it spoke again, its voice lacked the encouragement it had had before. *"Yes,"* it said.

"And what does that mean?"

"There is a price, but it is far preferable to your current predicament. Without a way to defend yourself, Lyndion will use you until you wished you were dead, then he will kill you. And without you, Adora will die. Is that what you want?"

"What is the price?" Grei asked.

"You will be bound to fulfill six of my requests. Not immediately, but when I require something of you. In the meantime, The Root is yours, and you may use it at will. Once you have fulfilled my requests, your debt will be paid, and The Root will be yours with no further obligation."

Cold sweat seeped into Grei's palms and along the back of his neck. A request could mean anything. If Grei agreed, he was agreeing to be this thing's pawn at an unspecified time.

"I will warn you, Whisper Prince. If you think to bond with The Root and then later break our bargain, if you refuse even one of my demands, The Root will hold you accountable. There will be no escaping it."

Grei swallowed. "Is that what's happening to Lyndion?"

"That thief will come to a foul and painful end."

"So that's a yes."

"He broke his promise. That is the price."

"But he's been around for a hundred years. Why isn't he dead yet?"

Silence.

"He has figured out a way around your curse, hasn't he?" Grei asked.

"Temporarily."

"A hundred years is hardly temporary. You want me to kill him. That's why you're helping me."

"I make no secret of it. But I was honest when I said I have no wish to see Velak destroy these lands."

"Because Venisha wants to invade," Grei said.

"I am not your enemy."

Grei felt ill at the idea of making himself beholden to this creature with a shadowy agenda, likely a violent one....

But the Slate Spirit was right: Grei was out of time. He had no weapons against Lyndion. This was the end, right here, right now. If Grei didn't find a way to beat the ancient emperor, he would die in these tunnels. As insidious as this

Slate Spirit might be, his assistance would give Grei an edge. Lyndion's power came exclusively from his artifacts.

Ree's words came back to him: do every damned thing you can to follow through on your promise…

Grei had squandered his chance to run away with Adora. Now she was enslaved. He'd squandered his chance to have Saebin teach him. Now Saebin was dead. Grei had backed himself into a corner with one last choice: he could sell his soul, or he could die here and fail everyone who depended on him.

"Three favors," Grei said.

"Excuse me?"

"If you want me to bond with The Root, then I will do you three favors."

Silence.

"We don't have much time, Slate Spirit." Grei said aloud, throwing the creature's words back at it.

"Very well."

Grei nodded. That, at least, was something.

"How do I do it?" he asked.

"Open your mind to your whispers. When they come, imagine that sliver of iron sinking into your skin, down to your heart."

Grei did, letting his mind open to the discordant, warbling whispers. As the Slate Spirit predicted, the thin iron sliver burned his skin, but Grei envisioned it going deeper.

He gasped as it pushed into his chest like a knife.

Grei fell to his knees, gritting his teeth so he didn't cry out. He clenched the rough dirt of the wall, his fingers digging in and feeling a half-dozen of the other thin iron filaments in the wall. The iron sliver in his chest pushed deeper like a hot slash of fire. He choked back a sob, clenching his fists.

"It is almost done," the Slate Spirit encouraged.

Grei fell onto his back, blinded by pain, and he arched. An anguished hum came from between his teeth. He fought to keep himself quiet, but a ragged wail burst from him. His legs and arms shook.

Inside his chest, the iron shaving elongated into a string,

ripping through his insides with white hot agony. The string coiled around Grei's heart, and he thought he was going to die. He thrashed on the ground, flipping to his side and curling into a ball.

Then it was done. The searing pain slowly faded, then vanished altogether.

He sucked in a sobbing breath, trembling and covered in sweat. He lay there, curled against the wall, as echoes of the torture faded away. But the whispers…

The whispers rose in his mind, and they became voices so sweet and melodic that he almost cried. They were just as they'd been before, and he hadn't realized how precious they had become to him until now, until they had been snatched away and returned in all their glory. They resonated throughout his body, and he felt like a silent hall that had suddenly been filled with music. There were no warbles, no twangs or tinny clangs. The voices of the land were all around him: the dirt of the walls, the wafting air, even the hissing whispers of the inert Scorpion Cage, hoarding its secret power within the tiny finger-sized sculpture. For a moment, Grei let himself float upon the voices.

Soon, through the music in his mind, he realized the Slate Spirit was speaking to him.

"…in my land of Venisha," the Slate Spirit was saying, *"the holy number is three. Two favors I have already done for you, but a third remains."*

With great effort, Grei managed to pull himself away from the glory of the voices and formulate a thought to send to the Slate Spirit. *"A third favor?"* he said.

"The Root knows you now, knows the shape of your heart. There are some things that will be much easier for you, such as healing your wound."

Grei pulled up his tunic to expose the ridged, inhuman scar along his belly.

"Reach into the Root, Whisper Prince. You can feel it as it feels you. Let it know what you want, and it will assist you."

As the Slate Spirit spoke, Grei realized he *could* feel the Root. It was part of the voices all around him, part of the

320

voices in his body. Simultaneously, Grei could feel the location of the artifact, the nexus of the magical hallways all around him, paradoxically within itself at the end of the hallway, stashed in Lyndion's satchel. It made a sound like a harp with rusted strings, melodic but…husky.

"Good. Yes. Now ask it to put your body right," the Slate Spirit said. *"To make it the way it was meant to be."*

Grei whispered to The Root, asked it to heal him.

The Root heard his request, and the coil around his heart grew warm. It radiated out pleasantly to all the extremities of his body, and also to the badly stitched wound in his belly. It seemed to instantly recognize the hack job he'd done of sewing himself up, and the will of The Root began rearranging the muscle and tissue. There was pain, but it wasn't anywhere near the agony of the bonding he'd just done. Mostly Grei felt queasy and odd at his flesh being rearranged inside his body. But in moments, the unpleasant sensation subsided, and he drew a deep breath and straighten up fully for the first time in days. Even the hand that Kuruk had scratched had been healed.

He reached down, touched his stomach. The ugly ridged scar was gone. It was smooth skin over muscles, gloriously normal.

"Thank you," Grei whispered his heartfelt thanks to The Root. It didn't respond, but its happy harp continued strumming throughout his body.

"A final word of warning for you, Whisper Prince. Lyndion holds The Root in his satchel. If he escapes with it, he will hold great power over you, especially if he knows you have bonded to it," the Slate Spirit said.

"Find Lyndion," Grei responded. *"Get the satchel. I understand."*

"Farewell, Whisper Prince. I look forward to our next meeting."

And with that, the voice of the Slate Spirit was gone from Grei's mind.

Chapter 38

GREI

GREI STOOD UP to his full height again, glorying in the ability to stretch out and feel no pain in his abdomen. He took a deep breath and let it out. For the first time since he'd fled Thiara with Ree, he felt equal to his task. The whispers were with him. The magic was at his command.

He heard the solid earth, intoning its permanence. He heard the metallic harping of The Root, the happy swishing of the air. He closed his eyes and reached out. Through the voices, he heard the whispers of Lyndion down the hall, and they were horrifying. The man's skin, his muscle, his bones spoke of decay and death, over and over.

Grei walked closer, whispering to the earth to make his footfalls absolutely silent. No scuffs rose from his boots. No dirt crunched under his feet. Soon, he neared Lyndion's glowing blue light and saw the man in a small, circular room that the Root had carved out for him.

He knelt over the wooden box in which he'd trapped Kuruk, a bulky satchel slung from his shoulder, and he pressed an amulet against its small doors. Grei tried to pick up on the buzzing of Lyndion's emotions like he sometimes could with people, but Lyndion's thoughts were maddeningly indecipherable, as if spoken in another language. Still, Grei didn't need to read Lyndion's mind to know that the old man was bent on doing something to that box.

First things first.

He could feel The Root nestled within Lyndion's satchel, as well as a number of other artifacts. Grei whispered to the seam at the top of the satchel's strap.

Become water, he gently asked of it. With gleeful abandon, the thread complied.

At that same moment, Lyndion's head shot up, and he saw Grei. The ancient emperor spun to his feet, shocked. The satchel, bereft of its necessary stitching, shot off his shoulder with his sudden movement. The shapeless bag dumped its contents in mid-air before it ever hit the ground. A small wooden box hit the ground with a hard thunk, the lid flying open and scattering items into the dirt. Rings, a tiny dagger, a short length of rope, a velvet scroll, a spoon, a metal sculpture of a squirrel, and of course, The Root.

"No!" Lyndion lunged at his treasures, but Grei had already asked the air to turn solid in front of the man.

Lyndion's head and shoulders smashed into the invisible wall, and he dropped to his knees. Grei whispered again, and The Root leapt from the ground, lifted on a sudden breeze. It shot across the distance into his hand, and he tucked it into a pocket. Once he had it next to him, practically touching his flesh, Grei felt immeasurably better.

With a howl of rage, Lyndion staggered to his feet and flung something at Grei. It was a metal spider the size of a thumbnail. As it tumbled across the dirt, it came to life and grew impossibly fast, just like the Scorpion Cage. By the time it rolled to a stop in front of him, it was the size of a hunting dog.

"Arrogant boy!" Lyndion snarled. "I was going to keep you alive, but now you die!"

"I'm not your boy," Grei said. "I'm the Whisper Prince. And you're fucked."

The spider bared metal fangs and lunged.

He held up a hand and murmured. No Scorpion Cage was going to trap him and no damned metal spider was going to bite him. He heard the voices of the artifact, and he sent his own desires into their monotonous repetition.

The spider gave a metallic screech and stopped a foot from Grei. It shuddered, then collapsed in on itself like hastily folded paper. A crumpled piece of tin the size of a melon rolled awkwardly toward Lyndion, finally settling on a flat edge.

Lyndion's mouth hung open.

"That's right," Grei said. "Now drop your—"

Lyndion's onyx ring flashed with a dark light. Oily smoke shot toward Grei, but he was quicker. He whispered, encasing Lyndion in a cylinder of hardened air from floor to the ceiling. The emperor cursed and dropped his fist. The oily smoke hit the barrier and swirled within the contained space. It hovered, as if confused.

Lyndion looked at the oily smoke, trapped inside the invisible barrier with him, and his eyes widened in horror. "Okay, open it!" he commanded, shrinking away from it.

"Not so eloquent now, are you?" Grei growled. "You look and sound more like a frantic chicken."

"I'm not kidding. If that smoke touches me—"

"You'll die?" Grei guessed. "The fate you conjured for me? For Ree?"

Lyndion crouched, staying below the oily smoke, which had begun questing about its container. "Fine. You can have the damned Benascan boy. And I'll show you how to get out of this place."

Grei walked up to the barrier. He pulled The Root from his pocket and flicked open one of the hatches. A square of light yawned above them and blinding brightness lit the room. "I don't need you," Grei said.

Lyndion squinted. His thin gaze flicked frantically to the smoke and back to Grei. "There are...are other treasures

beyond compare in that pile you scattered across the ground."
Lyndion pressed himself flat against the ground. The oily
smoke drifted lower, seeking. "I'll tell you the secrets of each!"

"Even if I believed a single one of your lies, I don't want
your grisly toys."

"If that smoke touches me, it will *kill* me!" Lyndion
pleaded.

Grei slammed his hand against the barrier and it boomed
in the little chamber. "You tortured Adora," he shouted. "You
cut her apart! Shriveling in your own poison is the justice you
deserve!" Lyndion's eyes practically bulging from his head as
he fought to stay away from the oily smoke. It was almost
upon him. Grei raised his hand, ready to constrict Lyndion's
cage, to force the smoke into his lying face, but he stopped.

All his life, Lyndion had done nothing but murder and
manipulate. He'd done nothing but perpetuate his gross
existence. It would be a blessing to be rid of him. Grei would
be doing everyone a favor. If Lyndion had never existed, if
someone had had the ability to slay him before now, Adora
would be happy; she'd be herself.

And now Grei had the power to pay the man back for
every horrible act he'd committed. Ree would tell him to do it.
She'd say he was naive not to, that the world was better off if
Lyndion was dead.

But he remembered what he'd told Ree back in Thiara
when he'd healed her arm. Grei wanted to heal, not destroy.
He didn't want to be Ree with her calculated violence, or even
Blevins who blatantly disregarded human life.

Clenching his teeth, Grei fought down his rage. Instead of
constricting Lyndion's prison, he readied himself to turn the
solid air into a breeze that swirled the oily smoke up and safely
out of the open hatch, but before he could, Lyndion snarled at
him.

"I'm going to peel the skin from your skull, boy!" The
sapphire ring on his fist flashed, and Lyndion screamed. Just as
the oily smoke touched him, the emperor's body warped like a
reflection in a sheet of tin. His scream became long and thin,

and then so did his body. The man transformed into a shimmering twist of blue light, shot through Grei's barrier and through the hatch.

It happened so fast Grei barely had time to blink.

Lyndion was gone.

Suddenly, Grei wanted to curse himself for not closing the trap while he'd had the chance.

But no. He couldn't start thinking like that. Lying and killing… Grei had striven to stop such things by unmasking the slinks, by forcing the end of the Debt of the Blessed. He'd had no power then, just a dream to stand up for the weak, for the people who couldn't stand up for themselves. Now that Grei had power, he couldn't just throw that dream aside and act like the emperor or Kuruk or Velak. If he slew whomever he deemed dangerous, then he was no different than they were.

He turned around slowly, listening to the whispers, making sure Lyndion wasn't close by, ready to ambush him. Once he was certain, he went to the box that held Kuruk and knelt beside it. Grei hesitated with one hand on the small cabinet style doors, then opened them. He half-expected Kuruk to leap out, reforming in reverse just as he'd been sucked into it.

Instead, the interior was a tryptic of Kuruk's life. The left-hand picture, painted on the inside of the left door, was Kuruk as a Benascan boy, holding the hand of his mother and surrounded by his six brothers, all of whom had blond hair and pale skin, but none of whom particularly looked like Kuruk aside from those obviously Benascan traits. In the center of the shallow wooden box was a painting of Kuruk and his brothers surrounded by flames, each in agony. The third painting on the inside of the right-hand door showed Kuruk the Slink Lord, his hand out with marionette strings connecting them to a hundred tiny human figures below.

Grei was stunned by the meticulous detail of the paintings; each Kuruk figure stared at him like it was alive, though none of the paintings actually moved. He listened to the voices of the tryptic, and he heard Kuruk's, a carefully modulated tone in the timbre of the young boy, but the words were unintelligible.

Singing around that lone voice were a dozen others, rising and falling next to each other, speaking a dozen other things. It was a dizzyingly complex melody, and Grei couldn't sort it out in an instant.

He glanced over his shoulder at the hatch, and with every second that passed, he feared Lyndion would return with some new trick to stab Grei in the back. He needed more time with this tryptic to understand how it worked.

Carefully, he shut the doors, then went to the empty satchel. He picked it up and beseeched the unraveled strap to weave together as one piece of cloth. Quickly and cautiously, Grei picked up each of the scattered artifacts. The carved box that had spilled its contents sang a happy wood song, but the bands of brass were magical, talking of corrosive death for anyone who tried to open the box without a key. Fortunately, the key rested snugly in the box's lock.

For once, a bit of luck. Apparently Lyndion had meant to use something from this box just before Grei showed up.

He touched the key, listening intently to see if there was some nefarious booby-trap involved in closing it. There wasn't, so he closed the lid and locked the box. It gave a solid click. His fingers didn't hiss or begin to dissolve, and the whispers of the brass sang a tinkling melody of satisfaction. Once again, he opened it and began putting Lyndion's artifacts back inside.

He paused as he picked up the metal feather and looked at it. The craftsmanship was exquisite; it looked like it had been a real feather dipped in steel, capturing every detail permanently. After admiring it, he went to put it back and accidentally tapped the lid with the feather's tip.

Gentle whispers rose from that touch.

The box floated an inch off the ground.

Grei murmured with pleased surprise. A levitation spell? He tapped the box again. It dropped to the ground. He tapped it a third time, and it hovered once again, just an inch above the ground. Grei lifted the box, and it weighed nothing at all. He lifted it higher and let it go. It stayed there, hovering in the air where he'd left it. He pushed it down and it went, drifting to a stop. Amazing.

Grei loaded all the artifacts into the box except the feather, which he put in a pocket. He put the light-as-air box into the amorphous travel bag, pushed it to the bottom, then added Kuruk's tryptic box as well.

"Grei?" Ree's voice suddenly jolted him.

Startled, Grei squinted upward. Ree crouched next to the hatch, looking down, the sword in her fist. "Baezin's Blood!" she cursed. "What happened? Where is Lyndion?"

"Fled," he said. "Did this open in the same glade?"

She laid flat on her belly, reaching down her hand to hoist him up.

Instead of grasping her hand, he whispered quietly to the air, this time doing it only in his mind. The air responded just as if he'd said the words aloud. An invisible platform of solid wind formed beneath his feet, and he slowly rose. "He brought Kuruk down here to do something horrible to him," Grei said. "I stopped that at least. And some other things have changed."

"Your magic!" She rose, pivoting gracefully away from the hatch as he emerged and alighted on the grass.

"Among other things." He pulled The Root from his pocket and flipped the hatch shut. The square hole to the tunnels slammed shut like a sliding slab of rock.

"Faia!" she exclaimed. "You did all that in a few seconds?"

"What do you mean?"

"You jumped into that hatch, then this one popped open across the glade."

"I was down there for a quarter of an hour," he said. "At least."

"You were down there five seconds. You jumped in the hole, then I saw a spear of blue light shoot up from across the glade. I ran to it. That's how long you were there."

Grei suddenly thought about Saebin's glade. "Time," he said. "I was down there much longer than that. When I was in Saebin's glade, underground, no time passed for you. Maybe The Root is the same way."

"Tell me everything," she said.

They sat down on the grass and Grei relayed the story. After he was done, Ree told him about her encounter with Liana, how she'd been taken by the mist, and how Liana could track them through their blood bond.

Ree let out a breath when she was finished, and they sat in silence for a time. Finally, she said, "The Slate Spirit? Really?"

"That's what the voice said."

"Well...I have to say it's is nice to have a victory for a change," she said. "I was beginning to wonder if our journey would just be one harrowing flight after another."

He stared thoughtfully at the grass, thinking about the time difference in The Root and Saebin's eternal glade.

"You look like you had a thought, Whisper Prince," she nudged him with her elbow, a smile curving the edge of her mouth.

"I think we have a few advantages on Velak at last," he said. "And I'm trying to come up with a way to exploit them. He's had all the advantages since Thiara. The mist. Adora. By the Faia, just plain information. He knows how this all came to be, and I've had to stumble about in the dark like an idiot, looking for pieces to this puzzle. And because of that, time has been on his side. He knows what he wants and how to get it. He's been planning this for centuries. But now, finally, we have a couple things."

"Like your magic?"

"My magic. Cavyn. Kuruk."

"And Cavyn is in Benasca," Ree said.

"And that's where we're going. It might even be where Velak is going. If Saebin's stories were right, Velak hates his mother as much as the Faia." Grei remembered the enormous, frost-rimed trees, the people surrounding Cavyn in their white cloaks with their white faces and blond hair. "Velak may attack another Faia first, but he's going to Benasca sooner or later. We could be there waiting for him."

"That's a five-day ride by horse, and probably half a day searching for them in these woods."

He held up The Root. "Maybe not."

She narrowed her eyes. "Those tunnels go all the way to Benasca?"

"I haven't explored everything they can do, but I suspect they will go anywhere I tell them to go. And if they do, we could make it there in maybe as little as a day.

"Because of the time...thing."

"Because of the time thing. We could get there before Velak."

"Magic makes my head dizzy," she said.

"It could work," he said. "While Velak marches on Benasca for his final revenge, we set a trap for him."

"How?"

"I don't know yet." He held up The Root. "But let's put some distance between us and this place while we think on it."

"That," she said. "Is the best idea I've heard all day."

He concentrated on the song of The Root, then flicked open a hatch. A square doorway dropped open in front of them.

"After you, my lady." He made a deep bow.

She rolled her eyes and shoved him into the hole.

Chapter 39

GREI

WHEN THEY DROPPED through the hatch, they were in the same room Grei had left before. He had imagined it would look just like Lyndion's creation, and it did. But as he concentrated on the wall, envisioning a new tunnel, the wall crumbled away, falling downward and upward, left and right, compressing dirt into all sides until a new passageway formed. The Root felt warm in his hands.

"To Benasca," he whispered.

Nothing else seemed to happen, but he could sense that the tunnel went for a long time in that direction. It had extended into the darkness so far that he couldn't see the end of it. They began walking, and Grei envisioned what he had seen of Benasca in Saebin's dream about Cavyn: the tall, frost-covered trees, the Sere Plains that her spirit had flown over, the wooden walls of the room where her heart had stopped.

Ree followed him, glancing behind to the source of light as the hatch slowly fell behind them. After a time, even the bright sunlight was too far away to illuminate much.

"Light's going to be a problem," Ree said.

Grei stopped, keeping his fluid connection with The Root, and he flicked the hatch shut.

Absolute darkness fell over them.

"You said you had good night vision," Grei murmured.

"Night vision, yes," she said. "This is not night. This is being buried alive."

He flicked open the same hatch. A square hole opened above them, blinding sunlight shining down.

Ree squinted. "Maybe some warning next time?" she asked.

"I wasn't sure it would work."

"Were you sure we wouldn't be crushed to death by a collapsed tunnel when you shut the last one?" she asked.

A chill ran down Grei's spine. He hadn't thought of that.

"Remember when we first met?" she asked.

"When you threatened me, threw your ringblade at me, kissed me, cut me, and shoved me out the door? All while you were stark naked? Yes, I remember."

"Remember when I asked you if you were brave or just stupid?"

"Nice. Look, the tunnel didn't collapse. We aren't dead."

She frowned. "Just don't use up all our luck here, Whisper Prince. We're likely to need some later."

They continued walking, and Grei explored his connection with The Root. At first, he thought the only tunnel they could make were these dirt tubes, but he found he could make square tunnels if he wanted. Then he made them as smooth as polished stone. The changes didn't happen instantly, and not right in front of him. But if Grei concentrated, envisioning what he wanted while letting the whispers of The Root fill his mind, he and Ree would soon walk into a tunnel just as he'd pictured it. The more he used it, the more quickly he could effect the changes.

Ree noticed the differences as she walked, but she didn't say anything.

"This is an amazing artifact," he finally blurted, feeling the excitement of the bond with this place. He felt more secure than he had in a very long time. The Root gave him power, even as he filled it with his own.

She nodded.

They walked for hours and finally, when Grei's stomach began to rumble, he called for a stop.

"All of the food we bought in Fairmist was in our horses' packs. But I took this from Liana." Ree brought out two paper-wrapped squares. The gray paper was cunningly folded, sealed with wax and tied with silver thread. She opened one and handed it to him.

"What is this?" he asked. The square inside was as dark as oil with little seeds in it, and it was sticky.

"Travel rations. Ringblades take this with them when they're on a mission. It doesn't spoil, and it'll keep you alive for an entire day." She bit into hers.

He took a bite. By the look of it, the thing should have tasted like charcoal, but instead it was thick, chewy and sweet. It stuck to his teeth. "What's in it?" he asked around the bite.

"Ground seeds and nuts. Molasses. Other things."

He was ravenous, and it seemed like he'd never tasted anything so good. "Do you have more?"

She smiled. "I do. And you can have one tomorrow."

"This is all we're eating? One square?"

"Welcome to your first Ringblade lesson."

"I'm not going to be a Ringblade."

"That is certain."

"Hey!"

"If we are traveling in dirt tubes," she said. "I imagine the hunting will be sparse. We'll ration what we have. When we reach Benasca and there is a banquet of food before you, you can eat as much as you like."

"We could go above ground to hunt."

"We'll do whatever you want, Whisper Prince, but even if time is skewed in this place, we're still too close to Fairmist for it to be safe for us running around above. Liana will be asleep for a good many hours, but Velak will have his mist-infected servants scouring the forests for you right now."

He nodded. "Okay."

"Are there any other creatures in these tunnels we need to worry about?"

In the back of Grei's mind, he could feel the shape of The Root, could feel the tunnel they'd been walking in like it was an extension of his arm. He could feel Ree's presence in that extra "arm" like a warm stone placed on this new arm's skin. He felt no other warm spots like that. "No," he replied. "Not that I can feel."

"Feel?"

He described the sensation to her.

"Okay then," she said. "If you don't feel like we're in imminent danger, close that hatch and sleep. You look horrible."

Grei suddenly realized how exhausted he was. They'd been running full tilt since they'd awoken this morning next to the Fairmist River. He was wet, sore and there had been one danger after another.

Strangely, his bond to The Root made him feel utterly safe here.

"You might not be wrong about that," he said, and leaned back against the wall, liking the feel of the compressed dirt. A lassitude crept over him, and it felt like the wall receded a little, conforming to the contours of his back and head.

He fell asleep in an instant.

WHEN REE WOKE HIM, he had no idea what time it was. She tapped him affectionately on the shoulder, then settled herself on the floor. She went to sleep almost immediately, and Grei sat in the dark, thinking.

He was grateful for the dark. There were no distractions, no sunlight or chirping birds, no wind or animals scurrying in the undergrowth. It allowed him to sort through everything that had happened. He let the images of Adora's glowing eyes, the snarl on her face, Velak's domination of Thiara and now Fairmist through the red mist, Grei's slaying of Blevins, the loss of at least two Faia and possibly Jevare as well…

He let it all roll over him and, as Ree had suggested before, he set his failures behind him and turned his attention forward. What he needed was a plan. He thought about what Kuruk had said.

Grei had pulled Velak out of the girl: Kuruk had called her "Aylenna". That had almost worked. The result had been disastrous, but if Grei had been in command of his own magic, it might have turned out differently. He'd wrenched Velak away for that critical second. Kuruk had seemed certain that, together, they could free Adora.

Grei listened for the voices immediately around him. The solid intoning of the earth, the rusted harp of The Root, the multitude of voices that comprised Ree's body, the slithering whispers of her clothing, of his own clothing. And he could hear the voices of the satchel and its artifacts. He leaned over, pulled the sack to him, and withdrew Kuruk's tryptic. He laid it on his lap.

He opened the doors and, though he couldn't see the pictures in the dark, he remembered them. He listened for the voices, and he began to form a plan.

I'm going to start with you.

Chapter 40

GREI

IT WAS HARD TO TELL time inside The Root, but Grei figured around two hours had passed when Ree's breathing changed and she awoke. There was a soft rustle as she sat up in the absolute darkness.

"You can rest more, if you like," he said, though he was excited to talk to her about what he'd discovered.

She took a deep breath. "I'm fine," she said.

"Good."

"Oh?"

"I know how to open Kuruk's tryptic," he said. In the end, it had been fairly simple. It had only taken him probably half an hour of listening carefully to the voices of the spells bound within the wood. The artifact, like The Root, was operated by a trigger. If the box was empty, opening it would suck in whomever or whatever stood in front of it, trapping them like Lyndion had trapped Kuruk. If it was full, opening it only showed images from the occupant's life. To bring the person out again, the trigger was more complicated. The right door must be opened and closed four times, then the left door twice, then the right door once more. Once that specific sequence was made, whomever was trapped would re-emerge.

"Why would you do that?" Ree asked, tense.

"Because he can help us—"

"No," she cut him off. "He can only betray us. He's a fiend, Grei. He's wholly Velak's creature."

"He hates Velak as much as we do."

"Is that what he told you?"

"Ree—"

"Kuruk is a bloodthirsty monster. He took my sister. He chewed off my arm. He would happily kill every single Thiaran if he could. Once he has freed his brothers, what do you think he's going to do? I only agreed to have him join us at the Fairmist River because I knew if I fought him then, I'd lose. I've been waiting for the moment I could kill him when the odds were in my favor. Now we don't have to. Leave him in the box."

"He can give us information that could—"

"There is nothing you could gain from him more useful than keeping him imprisoned."

"With his help, we can—'"

"No," she interrupted him again. Annoyed, he flipped a hatch on The Root. The sudden sunlight blinded both of them, and she held up a hand against the light.

"Would you shut up a moment?" he said.

She crossed her arms.

"You told me to do everything I could to win this battle," he said. "This is everything."

"Not this."

"Kuruk has power to help us. And he has the knowledge." Grei bulled forward as though she hadn't spoken. "More knowledge than we can get anywhere else. More than all the histories in Thiara. Kuruk lived in Velakka for a hundred years. He knows about that red mist I pulled from Velak. He called it the *dasha*. If I'm going to save Adora and defeat Velak, I'm going to need Kuruk's knowledge."

She glared at him grimly.

"We don't have options, Ree. I don't think I can beat Velak alone."

"What about Cavyn?"

"The woman who tortures her lover by ruthlessly resurrecting him over and over, who abandoned her sons and daughters in the woods to fend for themselves? Saebin called her crazy. We don't know her. She might kill us as soon as look at us."

"But we do know Kuruk. He *will* kill us if he gets the chance."

"I don't think so. I think we are incidental. I think he only hated us because we stood in his way. He wants to save his brothers, will do anything to save them. I saw how he came to be in Velakka in the first place; I saw it through the eyes of the Green Faia. And this…" He patted the tryptic. "I have a plan for it, too. If it can trap Kuruk, why not Velak? If I can pull him out of Adora, then stuff his *dasha* in this…" He let her finish the picture in her own mind.

She shook her head. "That is an enormous if," she said skeptically.

"We have to use everything we have. I don't see a better way."

She let out a frustrated breath, then reached into her pack, took out two of the paper-wrapped Ringblade rations and flipped one to him. "By the Faia, I hope we don't regret this," she murmured under her breath. "Open the damned thing up."

Grei put the tryptic on his lap and opened the doors in sequence.

Part IV

The Eighth Faia

Chapter 41

GREI

KURUK ARRIVED IN A FLASH OF FLAME. The flickers flared then vanished. Curls of black smoke rose toward the open hatch then left the Benascan boy standing in sunlight, his golden hair shining. The tryptic shrank again to a palm-sized box of wood, and fell to the ground at Kuruk's feet. He looked around the tunnel, up at the hatch, then turned his red gaze upon them.

He seemed about to sneer, then he said, "You freed me." He glanced at Ree, then back at Grei. "Does this mean you have your powers back?"

"I do."

"And where are we?"

"Can you walk?" Grei asked.

Kuruk snorted. "Of course I can walk."

"Then let's walk, and I will tell you where we are and my plan for Velak."

They continued their journey underground, and Grei shared the trap he planned for Velak, to free Adora, then trap

Velak's dasha in the tryptic. To his surprise, Kuruk didn't sneer at the plan. After some thought, he nodded and said he thought it would work.

They continued on and, using Vecenne's map, Grei visualized Benasca's capital city, Iceward. On the first day of walking, he stopped every couple of hours and opened a hatch to see if they were actually heading in the right direction. They were every time, unwavering, and soon he began to trust The Root.

That became their routine, walking for hours and hours in the dark, their only illumination Kuruk's glowing body. Twice a day they would stop, rest, and open a hatch to the real world. Ree would hunt, bring back food, but they would always eat it in the tunnels. Every time they opened a hatch, the sun seemed just a little closer to the western horizon, and Grei dared to hope the time difference in the tunnels was that pronounced.

So the days went. A brisk walk. Open a hatch. Hunt. Eat. Walk more. Sleep.

Every time they opened a hatch, the sun had only moved slightly in the sky. It seemed like they were still in the same day that they'd first entered The Root. If time in the real world was passing that slowly, they were actually covering the ground from Fairmist to Iceward faster than a horse at full gallop.

Grei thought he would tire of being in the tunnels after the first few days. He'd never been much for confined spaces, but being in The Root felt like being home.

On the ninth day they had been underground, Grei called the second halt of the day and opened the hatch. Snow fell into the tunnel, just as it had for the last two days. This time, the pile was half as tall as Kuruk, who wrinkled his nose and stepped back. The slink lord didn't need to sleep or eat, but he didn't like touching anything having to do with water, including snow.

Grei lifted Ree up on a platform of solid air, and she went on her daily hunt, bearing homemade arrows and a bow she'd made days ago from a fine ash branch and Vecenne's spare bow strings.

He left the hatch open, enjoying the sunlight streaming in. In the world outside The Root, the sun was just rising on the third day. Kuruk stood in the shadows, glowing red and watching Grei without any expression. For the first five days, Kuruk had trained him with the *dasha*, but no longer. Everything Kuruk could show him, he already had. On the sixth day, Kuruk had waved him away, telling him to practice on his own.

So Grei did. To his surprise, every living thing had a slight bit of *dasha*. In a normal tree, the *dasha* was just a thin wisp at its center. In a squirrel, it was a curl of colored mist the size of its spine. Since it had gotten cold outside, though, Grei had begun to practice with the roots that protruded from the corridors.

He sat down, reached out with his mind, blending with the voices of the earth all around him, finding some nearby roots that had sunk low enough to use for his *dasha* experiments. For about an hour, he played with the roots' *dasha*, and then he heard a faint chorus of voices.

Behind him, back toward the hatch, Kuruk slumped against the wall, sending focused jets of flame at the pile of snow, cutting precise symbols in it.

That wasn't the source of the voices. He turned the other way, looked deeper down the tunnel. It was as black as night. Grei went back to the hatch and rummaged around in Vecenne's satchel, found the candle and the onyx artifact, then went back to where he'd heard the voices. He lit the candle as he went. The voices became louder, and they sounded similar to the spirit voices of Fairmist Falls and the Jhor Forest, protectors of a specific place. But these voices were softer, gentler, deeper.

"Where are you going?" Kuruk's childlike voice said.

Grei turned to tell him about the voices, then stopped. He was so far down the tunnel that Kuruk was tiny, and the light from the hatch was barely the size of Grei's fist at this distance. He'd wandered much farther than he'd meant to, but he had to find out what was making that chorus of voices. They sounded…sad.

"When Ree returns, follow me. I'm just going to explore a little."

Kuruk stood perfectly still, then went back to his slump against the wall and shot flame spurts at the snow.

Grei continued down the tunnel, the candle light wobbling against the walls, throwing shadows from every tiny imperfection in the walls and floor.

The voices rose, touching his mind like the smallest edge of something enormous, like the tentacle of a leviathan moving beneath the depths of the ocean.

He continued, commanding The Root to follow the voices. Soon, the tunnel ended, opening into a cavern that hadn't been made by The Root. This cavern had always been here. A tumble of rocks descended from where Grei stood down to an enormous underground lake that looked as black as tar in the dim light of the candle. The voices pulled him forward to the dark water. As he approached, he realized there were bumps all over the surface of the lake. They were…dead fish, hundreds of them floating to the top of the pool. The air was thick with the smell of decay. Something horrible had happened here. Some…poison in the water?

The voices continued to pull at him, as though this wasn't the source, just a…stop along the way.

Grei remembered the blue rose he'd found at the Temple of the Faia in Fairmist, when he first heard the whispers transform into song. He remembered Meek crushing the flower under his heel, and the bile that rose in Grei's throat at the injustice. This felt like that. This tragedy was so stark he wanted to vomit.

He went to the far side of the cavern, just along the edge of the lake. The wall had the same blackened, rotting roots as he'd seen in the tunnel above, but many more and much closer together. A trickle of black sludge crept down from the wall of the cavern into the lake. He held the candle high, illuminating as far as he could. The entire wall created sludge rivulets that leaked into the lake.

The poison…

He pulled The Root from his pocket and bid it create a tunnel. Dirt fell away and packed itself into the ground, the ceiling and the walls. The newly formed corridor plunged into the dark. He entered and began walking into the dark. The blackened, rotting roots with their dripping poison became thicker the farther he went. Soon, the corridor had a thin film of black poison along the floor. He could feel it sticking to the bottom of his boots.

The sonorous voices became more and more powerful, as though he was following the tentacle of the leviathan to its enormous source. Finally, he stopped.

The rotten roots surrounded him, spiraling out from a point overhead. Each was as thick as his waist, dividing and dividing again as they left that central spot.

Grei backed up to a point that wasn't solid footwork, then he opened a hatch. Snow fell as it had before every time they'd surfaced in Benasca, but this time three jagged sheets of ice also fell, shattering when they hit the ground. Icy wind blew into the hole, and Grei floated up through the hole.

Before him stretched an ice field, perfectly flat, covered with a sheet of ice and dotted with roses. Many were vibrant blue like the one he'd seen in Fairmist, and the song they sang was…overwhelming.

But about a third of the roses were withered, blackened, and fallen. No song came from them.

The thick poison roots had come from one of these roses. The roots were enormous, and they stretched…how far? The strength of the voices made him think that those roots went…as far as they wanted to go. The thought was so foreign to him. How could something so small have roots so large?

A chill passed through him as he suddenly realized where he was. This had been the place Cavyn had gone in his first dream of her. She'd reached one of her ethereal hands to this place and destroyed a rose to bring Blevins back from the dead.

She had caused this decay, this willful poisoning of the

lands.

Grei reeled with the power of the place and the shocking revelation of Cavyn's abuse of it. Such magic filled the valley, a chorus of voices. It was so powerful that he could barely stand here. The magic filled him, so loud he could barely hold himself together without flying apart. He reached into the celestial song of the remaining roses and pulled a little from each of them.

It was like putting a cup beneath a waterfall.

The voices of the elements flowed through him and around him. This was a place of power, like the haven of a Faia, but indescribably vast. He'd not felt even a hundredth of the strength at the Jhor Forest or Fairmist Falls as he felt here.

A cold thought grew in Grei's mind and spread throughout his entire body. Velak could never know about this place. This much magic would turn a Faia into a super Faia. If Adora came here, Grei had the horrible suspicion it would be enough power for Velak to break out of his prison.

His mind raced.

And Kuruk couldn't know about this place, either. Grei had told them to follow him. He had to get back. Anyone who knew how to come here would either abuse it...or they might lead someone here who would.

Grei sprinted to the hatch and jumped through it, slamming it after himself. He raced back through the tunnels, closing them after himself and burying the poisoned roots of the dead black rose. He passed the sad, dead lake, scrambled up the tumbled rocks and leapt into the tunnel. With barely a whisper to The Root, the tunnel closed behind him.

And not a minute too soon.

Kuruk's red glow illuminated the tunnel ahead, and he and Ree appeared around a curve.

"Grei?" Ree said. He realized he'd dropped the candle at some point and had run purely by listening to the whispers of the elements around him.

"Yes," he huffed.

"Why are you breathing hard?"

"Just…decided to run."

"Where did you go?" She peered down the tunnel, and Kuruk followed her gaze.

"Nowhere. I thought I…heard something."

"Did you?"

"No. Just…the whispers of the rock."

She narrowed her eyes a little, just enough to let him know she saw his lie, but she didn't say anything.

"Well don't run off like that." She shook her head and turned around, walking back toward the pinpoint of light where he'd opened the original hatch.

Grei tried to slow his breathing as he followed them, but the location of the field of blue roses burned in his mind.

Chapter 42

GREI

BARELY AN HOUR of walking past the cavern of the dead fish, Grei, Kuruk, and Ree emerged from The Root into Benasca. Grei's heart was weighted down with yet another responsibility that was beyond him. Knowledge of that powerful bastion of magic was a terrible privilege. Those blue roses saturated the lands, possibly all the lands with those enormous, far-reaching roots. He wouldn't be surprised if those roots laced throughout the entirety of Benasca and the Thiaran Empire alike.

Seeing what one group of root tendrils from one withered black rose had done to that lake of fish, Grei wondered if that field held the beating hearts for the lands. Kill one of those hearts, and an arm or a leg of the lands died.

And the roses were being destroyed by Cavyn. For someone who felt the life of the lands, who could hear the whispers of magic, it was an unthinkable crime. Cavyn had been killing the lands one heart at a time by resurrecting her Beloved. Grei had hoped to team up with Cavyn to drive Velak back to Velakka, but Cavyn might be a villain herself.

Grei, Ree, and Kuruk floated up on the wind and gently landed in the knee-deep snow. The cold attacked Grei's hands and face like a barrage of needles. Snow covered the ground as far as he could see, laying in drifts against stolid pine trees and white trees Grei had never seen before. They had thick trunks, scaled like they were wrapped in white snakeskin, and looked like they were covered in frost. Branches reached outward a third of the way up the trees, and their leaves were wide, jagged, and translucent with a blueish tinge along their edges, as though they were made of ice.

"Frost Trees," Ree murmured, her breath making a white cloud in front of her. "These are the Whitening Woods."

Kuruk's legs hissed in the snow, raising tendrils of steam. He growled, then ran a distance away from Grei and Ree to a small clearing in the trees, his feet making hissing holes. He glanced over his shoulder at them, perhaps to gauge if he was far enough away, then flame erupted around him. Grei and Ree threw up their hands against the light, and the icy air turned warm for an instant. The snow around Kuruk hissed, turning to water, then to steam, creating an aisle of dry, burnt ground extending toward the distant city.

"Why don't you blow a war horn and announce to the entire country that we are here!" Ree growled at him.

"Iceward." Kuruk pointed, not acknowledging Ree. The grandeur of Benasca's capital city rose against the horizon. The Frost Trees around Ree, Kuruk, and Grei were small by comparison to the mighty Frost Trees of Iceward. They had to be three hundred feet tall, monolithic giants with structures attached to the sides of their trunks like pouches.

Once upon a time, Grei might have marveled at their grandeur, but after discovering the field of blue roses, the rot at the heart of the lands, he could barely think of anything else.

He had to save Adora. That had not changed, but everything else had spun on an axis. Grei had begun his journey as the Whisper Prince to set right all the wrongs perpetuated by the Thiaran Empire, to hold those in power accountable for their horrible decisions. He'd believed that there was justice at the heart of the lands, and that it had been perverted by the emperor.

But Cavyn was at the heart of the lands. She was to all of Benasca and the Thiaran Empire what Pyll had been to the Jhor Forest, what Jevare had been to Fairmist Falls.

Even if Grei managed to find Cavyn, to join forces with her against Velak, even if together they won the day and sent Velak back to his prison, how could Grei condone Cavyn's treatment of the lands? She was slowly killing them for her own personal…obsession or revenge, he couldn't tell which. What made Cavyn preferable to Velak, who wanted to destroy the lands in fire, except that Cavyn's destruction was slower?

He couldn't bear to think that the rot and corruption went all the way to the center of the lands.

"Hey," Ree said, touching his shoulder.

He started from his reverie.

"I…" he said, faltered. "Sorry."

She came around, stood facing him. He always forgot she was so much shorter than him until she stood right next to him. When she leapt into action, Ree seemed a giant, fierce and unstoppable.

She tugged his cloak closed over his shoulders like a mother securing her child against the cold. For a few seconds, she stayed engrossed in the task. He felt warmer and, strangely, safer.

"Heavy thoughts?" She looked up at him.

"Gods and goddesses," he said. "Against me and you, and…you know. Him." He tipped his head at the distant Kuruk, who was literally blazing a trail to Iceward.

She gave a tight smile. "Don't feel sorry for Velak. He deserves the thumping you're going to give him."

"Feel sorry for Velak…" That drew a rueful chuckle from him. "I wish I could joke about it. Even with my magic, I wouldn't pit myself against a single Faia and expect to win, let alone Velak. And Cavyn is a completely different creature altogether."

Ree's brow wrinkled. "Cavyn? Why Cavyn? She's on our side, right?"

He waved a hand. "Yes. I mean, that's what I meant. I mean, she will help us."

She cocked her head. "Baezin's Blood, but you're an awful liar. You've been holding back since that moment I came back from hunting. You put something together. Do we have two enemies now?"

"It's not that. Really, it's not. I'm…sorry I said anything."

She let out a breath, shook her head.

"The plan remains the same," he said. "Just like we talked about, just like we practiced."

"Okay," she said skeptically.

Whatever Cavyn was, he'd have to deal with it afterward. He had to keep his focus. Only one thing mattered right now. Save Adora. That, at least, he was sure of. Once that was done, then he could think about Cavyn, her transgressions, and what to do about it.

He glanced ahead. Kuruk was now just a figure in the distance, a tongue of flame rising a dozen feet in the air and a cloud of steam rising from him.

"We're going to have to tell him to stop doing that," Grei said. "All of Benasca's going to know we're coming."

Ree clapped him on the shoulder encouragingly, and they ran after Kuruk.

AFTER AN HOUR'S WALK, Grei, Kuruk, and Ree entered the city of Iceward. The sky was overcast, but the tree city shone still like a landscape of diamonds. Ice walkways arced from the giant trees to the slightly smaller trees at the edge of the woods. Some walkways curved around, solidly attached to the trunks. Some spiraled to the ground like curling locks of white hair, dangling from thick branches.

Pathways of crushed black stone laced together on the

ground, and the ramps and walkways among the trees bore the same black gravel. The city was eerily quiet, and they were watching a group of three white-skinned, blond-haired Benascans standing in the center of one of the paths. They wore white garments thinner even than Grei's and Ree's clothes, and yet none of the Benascans seemed the least bit cold. Grei wondered if magic wasn't involved with those clothes. He and Ree would have been an icicle by now if it wasn't for the heat radiating from Kuruk.

"They're not moving," Ree whispered. Those three were the first Benascans they had seen in this seemingly-deserted city, and they hadn't moved since Grei and his companions had spotted them. Only the white puffs of their breathing marked that they were alive. "And they're not talking."

Kuruk watched them intently, eyes glowing. "Their *dasha* has been taken."

Grei reached out tentatively, listening to the whispers of the tall Benascans. Kuruk was right. The flaming, crackling sound of Velak's presence hovered around them.

"Then the red mist is here, too," Grei said. Ree had been right. Velak hadn't just sent the red mist after them in Fairmist. He'd sent it everywhere. Except…Grei didn't see the red mist anywhere.

"Why aren't they moving?" Ree asked. "Those the red mist caught in Thiara didn't stop like that. Liana didn't stop like that."

"I think he is taxed," Kuruk said.

"Taxed? What do you mean?"

"I have manipulated the *dasha* of hundreds of Thiarans before," Kuruk said. "It is crushing to the mind, a constant battle for control. Velak took Thiara. He took Fairmist. He has taken Iceward. He would have taken other cities, too," he said, confirming what Grei had suspected. "He may be at his limit."

"So he has them, but you think he doesn't have the strength to make them do anything," Grei said.

"Yes."

"Or maybe his focus is elsewhere," Grei said, thinking

about what that might be. "And he told them to stand still until he needs them."

"Let's not find out if they'll move by letting them see us," Ree said.

"He's trying to break the barrier," Grei said, realizing there was only one thing that might pull Velak away from domination of the lands with the red mist. "He's killed enough Faia, and he's trying to break through. That would take his focus away from the rest of this."

Both Kuruk and Ree looked at him.

"We need to get to Cavyn's room. Now. In my dream, she was in the largest tree in the city. That's where Velak would be."

"That one." Kuruk pointed. "That is the Elder Tree, where the elders of Benasca gather and where they live."

"Let's go."

They snuck through the city to the wide walkway at the base of the Elder Tree, passing two other Benascans who simply stood in plain sight, doing nothing but breathing. No alarm was raised, and they quickly ran up the winding walkway. As they ran, Grei gently listened for the use of magic. They'd gone fifty feet up the side of the massive trunk before he stopped, breathing hard, and said, "It's there. Up there. The doorway." Another hundred and fifty feet above them was a wide, circular platform. "And so is Adora. Be ready."

They ran up the walkway until they reached the platform. Kuruk glowed with his exertion, and Ree and Grei stopped to rest a moment. The platform was made of wooden planking that had then been covered with ice and black gravel. Grei took the moment to whisper to his body, to Ree's body, and prepare them as they had practiced.

The door Grei had seen Cavyn enter in Saebin's last dream stood before them. It was seven feet tall, arched at the top, and made of thick, white wood bound with iron bands. He heard the burning, crackling voices of Velak beyond the door.

"Be ready," he said, then threw the door open.

A blast of sweltering heat hit them. The room was just like

Grei had seen in his dream: the red velvet couch and its chair, the glass table between, the autumn-colored paintings on the wall. But the air was so hot that it seemed the entire thing was about to burst into flames.

Adora stood before the wide pillar in the center of the room just as Cavyn had stood in the dream, right before she opened the doorway which Saebin said went to Velakka. Adora was trying to break into the room. Her hands pressed to the wood where Cavyn had touched it, but the portal didn't open. Instead, a circular spot glowed red. She was so focused on her task that she had not heard them, had not seen them enter.

"Kuruk," he snapped. "Pull the heat!" During their days in the tunnels, Grei had asked a great number of questions about Kuruk and what he might do to fight Velak. One of the things Kuruk could do was manipulate the *shkat*, the physical form of fire, specifically heat and flames. He could increase heat, of course. But he could also pull it away.

Adora's head snapped up, craned to look at the group, but she didn't take her hands from the pillar.

Kuruk raised his fists. The swelling red heat in the wood immediately began to fade, drawing away the pillar and swirling into Kuruk, who suddenly glowed a brighter red. The fierce temperature in the room plummeted.

"Ree!" Grei said.

Ree charged across the room, leapt into the air, and kicked Adora in the shoulder. Adora spun away, losing contact with the pillar. Kuruk continued sucking the heat from the pillar and the room. It became as frosty inside as outside. A plume of white leaked from Grei's mouth as he let out a breath.

"Kuruk!" Adora snarled as she careened across the floor, but it wasn't her voice. It was deeper, darker. Velak's voice. "I am opening the rift. Your brothers are but a moment away."

"You never intended to give them to me," Kuruk growled, holding onto the fire. "Now, I will take them after you are dead."

"Fool!"

Then Grei did his part. He listened to the voices: the air

between him and Adora, her skin where it touched the air, the muscles underneath, then deeper.... He heard the muscle of her heart beating. He heard and felt the crackling flames throughout her, the rage that overwhelmed her beleaguered *dasha*, a combination of her anger at Lyndion and Velak's boundless fury. Velak had completely saturated her.

"Get out of her!" Grei snarled and, as he had trained with Kuruk over and over, Grei reached inside Adora and took hold of Velak's *dasha*.

After training with Kuruk and learning the nuances of the *dasha*, Grei realized he had, many times in the past, unwittingly grabbed the *dasha* of others. It was how he saw their thoughts, their emotions. He'd looked into Adora's heart in Fairmist, during their first awkward meeting. He'd also done it with Selicia at Fairmist Falls, just before she'd knocked him unconscious, then with her again after he'd made a bridge out of the Fairmist River. Some people's *dasha* was easy to read. Others had training to block him from seeing within them, like Empress Via and Lyndion.

Velak's *dasha* was like grabbing the whipping tail of a sea serpent, almost too big to wrap his arms around, nearly impossible to hang on to. Grei had caught Velak by surprise in Thiara, and the lord of fire was ready this time. Velak was tightly intertwined with the fibers of Adora's being, twice as entrenched as he had been with Aylenna. Like a cat with a thousand claws, Velak clung to Adora's insides, her muscles, her vital organs, and he wasn't about to let go easily.

But this time, Grei wasn't broken. He could hear the voices of the elements clearly, and they told him what he needed to know. Secrets came in clear voices, rising in harmony, just like the song of Jhor Forest the first time Grei had entered it and met the Green Faia.

Grei spoke with the flames. He spoke with Adora's skin, her muscles, her bones and organs, and the water throughout her body. Like he had done when he'd transformed Selicia and her Ringblades back from stone to flesh, he split his attention so that he could hear every single voice within Adora's body.

Blood rushing, rushing, bringing nutrients. Heart pumping, pumping, sending life. Muscles flexing, flexing, giving strength. He listened to all of them, then he made a gentle, powerful request.

Reject Velak. Push him out.

Sweat beaded on Grei's forehead as he strained to pull Velak forth. His concentration burned as he beseeched Adora's body to do his bidding. Velak fought him, trying to shake off Grei's unceasing words he spoke to Adora's body. Grei didn't let up. He knew if he paused even for a second, Velak's *dasha* would sink back into Adora, grabbing hold tighter than ever.

Then Velak attacked Grei directly, sent a tendril of his *dasha* across the air and into him, trying to dominate him.

That almost broke Grei's concentration. If he'd not been prepared for Velak to try just that, it might have worked. But Grei had whispered to his muscles and skin and bones, talking to them before the fight, beseeching them to reject any foreign *dasha* they felt. He'd done the same to Ree's body, and so, when Grei felt Velak's *dasha* invade him, it took only a little extra attention for him to remind and reinforce his standing request.

"Get...out..." Grei grunted. Painstakingly, one at a time, he pulled Velak's claws out of Adora. But as soon as he'd pulled out the hundredth of Velak's claws, the first would escape his attention and sink back in. Each one he failed to hold sank deeper, became stronger.

Then Kuruk was there, his powerful *dasha* joining the fight. With unbelievable might, Kuruk yanked out claw after claw, and he made sure the claws Grei yanked out stayed out.

"Nooo." Velak's sepulchral voice seeped from Adora's mouth as the red mist rose from her skin. "Kuruk...stop!"

But Kuruk continued about his work, grim-faced.

The red mist seeped out of Adora's skin. She shuddered, head thrown back, mouth open. Then her head whipped up, lava eyes glaring at Grei. With movements as stilted as a newborn colt, she staggered at him, fingers extended like claws, hoping to break his concentration.

But Ree was there, as they'd practiced. She interposed herself, took Adora's arms like they were beginning a ballroom dance. Ree pushed her body against Adora's, took her center of balance, spun, and sent Adora stumbling away.

Adora crashed to her knees next to the room's center pillar.

The red cloud grew around her, and Grei, sweating profusely with the effort, bid the air to contain the foul mist. It was almost completely out of her.

"We are at the limits…" Kuruk said between his teeth, hands up and clenched as he fought to keep Velak's *dasha* claws from getting back into Adora. "Sever it, Whisper Prince. Cut…him…free…"

Grei's mind and attention were already overtaxed, but he somehow managed to whisper to the air around Adora.

"Cut it…" he grunted. "Cut the…"

But his attention was suddenly yanked way. The room was suddenly sweltering again. His gaze snapped to the pillar. The same area Adora had been working on was glowing red hot again.

The air around Adora, poised to do something, hesitated at Grei's vague command. Grei lost control of some of Velak's *dasha*, and their claws sunk back into Adora.

"Kuruk," he yelled, sweat dripping down his face. "The pillar! Take the heat away!"

"Don't let him go, Whisper Prince," Kuruk growled through clenched teeth. "Don't—"

The glowing circle exploded. Flaming bits of wood shot out from the pillar. Kuruk lifted a fist, and chunks bounced off him. Ree threw herself into a roll, narrowly avoiding being skewered by the flying shards, but Grei barely had time to move. Searing pain shot through him.

He fell to his knees, concentration shattered, and looked at a wooden shard the size of a dagger sticking out of his shoulder. Another stick the size of a sword had impaled him clean through his thigh.

The multitude of voices he'd been feverishly concentrating

on vanished from his mind. The red mist sucked back into Adora.

Gaping, his hands quivering over the jagged wooden spear, Grei looked up at the black smoke roiling out of the hole in the column.

A tall, slender man emerged, framed in the archway, smoke flowing around him. From head to toe, he wore tight-fitting armor, made from glowing squares of lava. His skin was a burnished copper, and his handsome face was long, with a straight nose and chiseled jaw. Horns curled back from the edge of his hairline, sweeping over his head along with his hair, which was coal black and streaked with glowing embers. In one elegant hand, he palmed the head of someone he had dragged up the stairs. Blood-streaked blond hair spilled from between his long fingers. Cavyn. The man flicked his wrist, letting her body fall next to Adora's.

Kuruk growled in helpless frustration, like a cat that had watched its prey tumble over a cliff, out of reach.

"Whisper Prince," Velak said, his voice deep and smooth. "We meet at last."

Chapter 43

GREI

"GREI!" Ree shouted, leaping toward him. She landed at his side, but as fast as she was, she was only human. In a blur that made Kuruk look slow, Velak shot forward. Ree barely got her hands on him; her fingers fluttered about Grei's pouch for a scant second, then Velak swatted her away like a fly. She flew through the air, hit the wall with a terrible thud, and collapsed to the floor, unmoving.

Velak snatched both of Grei's wrists, slapped them together, and held them with one long-fingered hand, pinning them over his head. Then, Velak closed his free hand around Grei's throat. The fire lord's fingers were like hot iron, and Grei's skin sizzled. He struggled to listen to the voice of the air, to somehow force a wall between them, but he couldn't concentrate. The pain from the wood shards had blown Grei's concentration apart. In the end, the most he could do was gasp for breath to keep himself from blacking out.

Kuruk took a step forward, but Velak looked in Kuruk's direction and shook his head like he would to a naughty child.

"Stop now, or your brothers die," Velak said.

Kuruk hesitated.

"My errant son," Velak chuckled. "We have had our differences in the past, but this rebellion is over."

"You aren't my father," Kuruk growled.

Velak grinned, showing pointed teeth as clear as Kuruk's fingernails. "I hate my father, too. Let's not bandy bitter titles back and forth. Instead, focus on the truth. You've lost this battle, just as you've lost every battle with me over this past century. You know you can't beat me. Your new ally is likewise overmatched." Velak shook Grei for emphasis.

Kuruk clenched his teeth, his small body as tight as a wound spring.

"But," Velak said, "you could still win. What you've always dreamed of can still be yours."

"You said once you were free, you'd free my brothers," Kuruk growled.

Velak gave Kuruk a toothy grin. "Exactly." He drew the word out. "And I am free now." Velak's voice dropped to a deadly tone. "But if you attack me again, I will suck the life from them like you sucked the heat from this room."

Kuruk remained completely still for several heartbeats. "And if I do not attack you?" he asked.

"You walk out of here with your brothers."

"No! Kuruk—" Grei choked out the words. But Velak squeezed, cutting off Grei's wind. Grei grappled with the immovable fist.

"Choose," Velak said.

"You've lied before," Kuruk said.

"I'm not lying now." Velak looked toward the smoking opening in the column. Three figures appeared, rising on the stairs. They were small like Kuruk, but none looked as close to human as him. The only telltale features that set Kuruk apart from a normal Benascan boy were his glass-like fingernails and his glowing eyes.

Each of the boys had vaguely human faces and flaming hair, and flickers rose from time to time from their reddish skin. One of them had three arms and three legs like a tripod. Another had a head that was two times normal size, and arms as thick as a blacksmith's. One was hunched over, leathery wings sprouting from his back. Also, each of his inhumanly long fingers had an extra digit. They all had grins that mirrored Velak's.

They moved cautiously forward, stepping over Cavyn's inert body.

Grei tried to shout denial, but he couldn't breathe. The room was starting to go dark. Little dots filled his vision. He brought up his uninjured leg and kicked at Velak feebly. The strike bounced off the fire lord's chest like it was made of rock. Velak ignored it.

"Very well," Kuruk said, and bowed to Velak.

Panicked, Grei used the last of his consciousness to try to talk to Baezin's Blade, sheathed at his hip. He tried to make it rise up. If he could just get it to touch Velak, maybe he could startle the fire lord, break his grip, disrupt his magic.

But Grei couldn't concentrate. He couldn't hear the voices.

His vision fading, Grei watched as Kuruk's brothers entered the room, looking up and around in amazement.

"Come," Kuruk commanded them. "Quickly." The three flame fiends leapt to the door obediently. And just like that, Kuruk and his brothers left the smoky room.

"No…" Grei gurgled.

With the last of his strength, he craned his neck to look at Ree, but she was as still as a corpse, slumped exactly as she'd fallen after Velak had viciously struck her.

Grei's vision darkened, and Velak brought his face close to Grei's. "Now, that's better," Velak said. "Just the two of us. I can't tell you how happy that makes me. Now that we've taken each other's measure, Whisper Prince, let us talk. I've been *longing* to talk to you."

Velak dropped him unceremoniously to the floor. Grei cried out as his injured leg hit first, and he collapsed. Pain exploded through him, and he lost consciousness.

Chapter 44

GREI

"Not yet, Whisper Prince. No, no…"

Velak's matter-of-fact voice filled Grei's ears, dark and silky and certain. A searing fire burned into Grei's thigh. He screamed.

"Not finished quite yet," Velak said.

Grei sat upright and clutched at his leg. The bloody spear of wood lay on the floor next to him. Velak crouched with one long, coppery finger stuck into the wound, shooting fire into it.

"There we go," Velak said, rocking back on his heels, eyes glowing. "If you pass out, this is less satisfying for me."

Grei clutched his leg with his right hand, but his left shoulder blazed from the dagger-sized stake still jammed into it, and his left arm hung useless at his side. He clenched his teeth, dizzy with pain, and gave Velak a defiant stare. But despair sloshed inside him. The battle was over; he had failed. Again.

"You," Velak said calmly. "Have been a thorn in my side. You stopped the Debt of the Blessed. You recruited Kuruk to your side, and that is no mean feat. You stopped me from slaying Jevare. And you interfered with my vessel." He gestured a long arm at unconscious Adora, sprawled by the center pillar, unmoving. Her hair still burned, a torch of flame that slowly blackened the wood of the pillar. The flaming dress still flickered over her body, so Grei assumed she was still alive. "She simply wouldn't let me kill you." He raised his hands, palms up in a helpless gesture. "Those are too many affronts to overlook, and I want to look into your eyes as you become my slave...."

Suddenly, Grei felt his body being invaded. It was so abrupt that he didn't even know it was happening until Velak had already soaked into Grei's own *dasha*.

Grei fought. He closed his eyes, left the pains of his body and leapt inside himself. He braced the invasion, his *dasha* and Velak's *dasha* clashing like two serpents made of smoke, one red and one blue. Grei tried to shove Velak out, but he couldn't. Velak's serpent was enormous, filling all the spaces within Grei, crushing the life from his smaller, smoky serpent.

The red serpent tore at Grei's mastery of himself on every level, tore at his ability to control his own body, tore at his ability to think clearly. Grei knew with sudden terror that Velak outclassed him. Grei was a talented amateur at manipulating the *dasha*. Velak was a master, perhaps the *original* master. Grei simply didn't have the strength to push this fire god back.

But he slowed the domination, as Velak slowly seeped into his muscles, his organs, his mind, and his very memories.

Suddenly, Velak gasped.

"The roses..." he suddenly whispered. "You know about the roses."

Grei's heart went cold.

"Did you find them?" Velak asked.

He had touched on the memory, but he didn't know where they were, and Grei couldn't allow him to know. Velak was already unstoppable. What would he be if he had all of that endless power at his fingertips? Grei had to keep that information away from Velak at all costs.

"No…" Grei said through clenched teeth.

"Oh, I hardly think that's true." Velak grabbed the stake in Grei's arm and twisted it. Grei screamed again. Sweat dripped down his face. Spots floated in his vision, and he felt himself losing consciousness again.

Velak yanked the stake out of Grei's arm, jerking Grei forward and sending another lightning bolt of pain through him. The hot air smelled like burning hair.

Velak's invasion of Grei's *dasha* continued, and with the pain of the distraction, Grei was slow to resist. Velak grabbed another memory.

"A lake…" he said. "Is it near a lake with dead fish?"

Grei tried to think of a plan. He needed to use Baezin's Blade. He fought with all his might, but he couldn't hope to do more than slow Velak down. He had to draw the sword, to hit Velak with it. But the sword was sheathed and twisted behind Grei, trapped behind his back, the hilt sticking out sideways from his waist, and his left arm could barely lift, let alone wield a sword. He'd have to reach across his body, then pull it three feet out just to draw it. And with Velak's supernatural speed, Grei would never have a chance. He had to get Velak to step away from him.

Velak's *dasha* dove deep into Grei's mind, ravenously seeking the location of the blue roses.

Grei abandoned his attempts to keep control of his own body and threw himself solely into protecting his memory. He dredged up everything he could except the location of the blue roses, flinging random images to the top of his mind. He couldn't beat Velak toe-to-toe, but perhaps he could do what Selicia had done with him while they were traveling companions. When Grei had tried to read Selicia's *dasha*, she'd constantly fed him a banquet of confusing, unrelated thoughts.

Grei did that now, creating a sphere of confusion around his memories. Bridges over the Fairmist River. The cliff cat he'd seen stalking on that autumn afternoon when he was seven. Fern's voice as she read to baby Julin. Hunting for a Midnight Lily for Adora. He threw street name after street name up at the red *dasha*: Bullbend. Milkmist. Faia Lane. Ferryman. Clapwood…

Velak's *dasha* infected every other part of Grei's body and mind, and he could feel the fire lord's hundred cat claws sink into him.

"Stand up," Velak ordered.

Grei stood up. Pain lanced up from his leg, and he hobbled.

"Ignore the pain," Velak ordered.

Grei stood still. His eyes watered at the agony, but he made no sound, and he didn't move. Baezin's Blade hung loosely at his hip now, easy to draw. He strained, trying to make his right arm move, but it wouldn't.

"You're a tough one," Velak said. "Let's make this easier. Give me what I want, and I will let you live. Tell me where the blue roses are."

The compulsion twisted inside him, as though all his muscles were being flexed at once. It demanded he pull the information from his memory. Grei reached into the confusing maelstrom he'd made of his memories, grabbed whatever was on top, and began speaking. "Skybridge… The Lance… Shieldbridge… The Darkspan… The Blacktale…" he murmured.

"Clever," Velak said. He turned toward Adora. She jerked like she'd been poked with a pitchfork, then sat up. She blinked her glowing lava eyes, rose and walked halfway toward them. Her gaze was sleepy.

"St-stop it!" Getting those two words out was like pushing a boulder out of his mouth. Spit flecked his chin with the effort.

Velak chuckled. "Set your mind to at ease, Whisper Prince. I'm going to give you exactly what you want. You chased us all over Devorra, trying to get me to release her. Here, at the end of your journey, I shall grant your wish."

Velak waved his hand, pulling the flames from Adora. The fire of her hair winked out, leaving the shaved scalp she'd had in Thiara. Her flaming dress vanished to reveal her naked body. The lava drained from her eyes, and they returned to her natural deep blue color. She blinked, her gaze fell on Grei, and her eyes connected with his for one breathless instant. He could see *his* Adora, the woman he loved, the woman he'd crossed the lands for.

Then her face twisted in pain. Red lines opened on her belly. Blood welled up. Her intestines spilled out. She grappled with them, fell to her knees, trying to hold herself together.

"No!" Grei gargled the word. "Adora!"

"You see…" Velak said in a low, ruthless voice. "I found her just one step from death. Behold, Whisper Prince, what your beloved is without me."

The light left Adora's eyes, and she collapsed.

"Nnnnnooooo…" Grei gargled, struggling to get free of Velak's hold.

"Beg me…" Velak said softly to Grei. "Offer me everything I want. The location of the blue roses. Your beloved's life. Beg me."

"Nnnnggg! Grrrrnnnnnggg!" Grei spat unintelligibly. He let go of his effort surrounding the field of blue roses. He let go of the confusion sphere in his memories. Velak closed his eyes, feeling the loss of resistance. He let go of Grei's body, of everything except diving deep into Grei's mind, and his *dasha* swirled around the precise location of the field of blue roses.

Grei made use of that one, single moment. He threw his rage and the entirety of his own *dasha* into gaining control of his right arm…

…and broke free of Velak's control.

His right hand jumped across his body, grasped the hilt of Baezin's Blade and pulled it free.

Velak spun lightning-fast, dancing back as Grei swung. The sharp tip swiped within an inch of Velak's chest, but it didn't cut him.…

With a snarl, Velak yelled, "Stop!" And his powerful *dasha* overwhelmed Grei's body again.

Grei froze, the sword poised overhead.

"That cursed sword!" Velak hissed, genuinely spooked at

how close Grei had come to slicing him. "Throw it out the door!" he commanded, and his *dasha* wrung Grei's soul like a wet rag. Grei's body turned, aimed and threw the blade. The sword spun end over end, sailing through the doorway, over the walkway's rail and into the wide expanse of air, glimmering suddenly in the sunlight as it fell from sight.

Velak laughed.

Grei knew he should try to think of something else, some other way to fight Velak, some clever thing that Velak hadn't thought of, but all he could do was stare in despair at Adora's lifeless, ruined body. Hope was gone. The fight was over. He'd lost.

That was when Ree made her move.

Chapter 45

GREI

VELAK'S LAUGH CEASED when Ree launched herself at him. With that same blurring speed, he stepped away from her attack.

But Ree wasn't attacking.

She dove at Grei. In her fist, somehow, she held The Root. How had she gotten that? In mid-air as Velak stepped away, she flicked open the hatch, and Grei dropped through the floor just as she slammed into him.

Velak charged, full of rage and surprise as he suddenly realized Ree's objective was escape. His long arm lanced out, fingers reaching for her ankle.

The hole slammed shut over Grei's and Ree's heads. Velak's howl of pain erupted and was cut off. His long, coppery index finger fell into the hole, severed from his hand by the slamming hatch. The finger flamed for an instant, illuminating the white wood tunnel.

Ree, her body on top of his and her eyes tight with pain, rolled off Grei onto her back, breathing hard.

Velak's severed finger flickered, then the flame slowly died. The tunnel plunged into utter blackness.

Velak's red *dasha*, still hooked into Grei with its cat claws, suddenly came alive, demanding that he grab the artifact from Ree and reopen the hatch. Against his will, Grei groped for Ree, found her arm, and yanked it toward him.

She twisted, escaping the grab.

"Give that to me," Grei growled in Velak's voice.

"Resist him," Ree said, her voice tight with pain, but calm.

Velak's *dasha* twisted inside Grei. Those thousand cat claws pulled his muscles like marionette strings, forcing him to lurch to his feet, to make another grab for her. But the compulsion was weaker now, strained and desperate and losing strength fast. Here, inside The Root, Velak's control was fading.

Grei howled, pulling strength from the white wooden walls of his haven. The artifact pulled life and power from the Frost Tree, tapping into it and the life of the earth beneath it. Sudden, sweet nourishment flowed into him.

Within Grei's mind, he once again saw his *dasha* and Velak's as intertwined, battling serpents. The red serpent of Velak's *dasha* shrank, but Grei's blue serpent grew. The blue serpent squeezed Velak's *dasha*, choked it, and finally, painstakingly pushed it out of Grei's body.

The red serpent turned to mist and vanished.

Velak was gone. He was out. Grei could control his own thoughts, his own actions…

"Adora!" he shouted, turning. He had to get back to her. He turned, looking for Ree. His injured leg flared with pain, and he stumbled, hit the wall of the tunnel, then went down to one knee. "Ree," he called. "Give me The Root. We have to go back."

A sudden light flared, and Ree stood with Vecenne's onyx artifact pressed to the wick of a candle. The candle burned bright, and she held it aloft, squinting at Grei's face. The candle shook in her hand, and the light wobbled. She leaned to the left, her left arm cradled against her side.

"Don't…" she huffed. "Be stupid."

"Adora's dying!"

"No, she's dead," Ree snapped. "The light was gone from her eyes before she hit the ground."

Grei let out a thin keen and hunched into himself, falling to his knees. Ree was right. He knew she was right. He saw Adora die, still standing up, and he knew there was nothing he could do for her, not like he'd done for her before, even if she was right here inside The Root with them.

When Adora had died at the Temple of the Faia, her *dasha* had seeped out of her body with her blood, laying in stasis in the enchanted water. That water had been designed to take and hold *dasha*. Grei had caught her *dasha* and brought it back to her body. In combination with his own magic and the rest of his strength, he had restarted her heart, kept her *dasha* inside her body and revived her. That unique combination of resources was the only reason he'd been able to bring her back.

But not this time. There was no Faia-ensorcelled water. Adora's *dasha* was gone to wherever dying *dasha* went.

"She's gone…" Grei whispered through numb lips. Adora was gone. He'd failed her.

Ree spat a string of curses and limped toward him. "Dammit, Grei! She's gone but *you're* not. The rest of us are not. You have to stop Velak. You're the only one who can—"

"I have no reason to try anymore," he said, looking at the wooden floor.

"You selfish bastard," she spat. "You had him. You almost pulled his influence from Adora."

"He has the blue roses now," Grei murmured. "It doesn't matter anymore. Nothing matters anymore."

"The what? What blue roses?"

"We are just ants to him!" Grei shouted.

"Don't let him…make you small…" Ree swayed, caught her balance. The candle lowered, as if she couldn't hold it up anymore. She shook her head as if to clear it. "You can stop him… He came after you…you first. Not Kuruk. Velak is…afraid of you…. He sent Kuruk away. He didn't want…to face both of you at the same time. I think…he couldn't. So he…divided you. Divide and conquer. A god…a god wouldn't do that. He's…still vulnerable." Ree slumped to her knees, and the candle touched the floor. "You're…a threat to him. He…lost a finger trying to get you. He wants you to stay down. Get up… Fight…" Her eyes rolled up into her head, and she fell over. The candle clacked to the ground and rolled toward Grei.

Numb, he looked at her. He felt like he should go to her, try to help her, but he could barely move. His chest and back were wet with the blood leaking from his shoulder wound. He felt light-headed. His thigh was a thudding, burning agony. His insides felt like they had been raked with razors. All he wanted to do was lie down and die, to lie down alongside Adora and just die.

He and Adora had reached for one another, but they'd had never had a chance. Their fingers had touched for one magical moment, then they'd been ripped apart. Again and again.

And now there was nothing. There would be no little house, no chicken-scratched yard, no laughing little girl on Grei's shoulders. The only hope for that dream had died with Adora. Grei was going to just lie down here with Ree, just let it end.

With his good arm, he pulled himself to Ree and slumped against her. Velak had the location of the blue roses. He'd killed Adora. He would enslave all of Devorra, or burn it. But it was someone else's responsibility now. Not Grei's.…

He lay his head against Ree's shoulder and closed his eyes.

Chapter 46

GREI

"YOU GAVE ME HOPE....

Grei stirred.

It was Adora's voice. Dark colors drifted by him, and he saw her, lying next to him. She was propped up on her elbow, talking to him like she had during that sweet moment when they lay together In Thiara, wrapped in their own warmth, skin to skin, happy.

But it wasn't her. It was a dream, the last happy moment they'd spent together. Those were the words she'd spoken after they'd made love.

Please... I want to die, he thought.

You gave me hope... You gave hope to everyone. She continued, relentless, as though nothing was wrong. As though they were back in Thiara during that wonderful moment when they imagined they were safe, imagined they could actually have a life together. His heart ached. He wanted that back. He should never have left her....

We didn't need Highblades to protect us or a prophecy or an emperor, Adora continued. *We needed you.*

You're gone. He felt himself rising to consciousness, and he struggled against it. But her words carried him upward.

We needed you...

Grei reluctantly opened his eyes to darkness. The candle had gone out. His thigh throbbed, and his shoulder flamed in pain. He lay across Ree, whose breathing was ragged and wet.

The dream of Adora faded, and The Root's voice, that gentle harp, played in his mind.

He levered himself to a sitting position, leaned against the smooth wood of the tunnel wall. He let the song of The Root sink into him and then, after a moment of reluctant hesitation, he asked it to fix his broken body. He made the request subtly, silently, and he truly didn't care if his body listened.

The elements leapt to fulfill his request more quickly than they'd ever done. The power of Grei's haven flowed through him, and its half-sentience knew exactly how Grei's body ought to be. With barely any pain, the burned hole in his leg closed. The wound in his shoulder stopped bleeding and knit together. Invigorating energy rushed through him.

He was going to try because Adora would have wanted that, because she made her life entirely about serving the people of the empire. Grei could do no less. His spirit had died when Adora's body had fallen, lifeless, but if this was what her echo, reverberating through his dream, demanded, then he would spend whatever life he had honoring that.

His passion was spent. His desires, gone. But he was going to kill Velak.

After that, Grei could die.

He went to work on Ree, reaching inside her body, listening. Her arm had been broken when Velak had struck her. Her ribcage had been caved in. Splintered bones punctured her lungs and her organs.

He healed them all.

She sucked in a deep, healthy breath, but as she was about to open her eyes, he whispered to her mind. He listened to the

373

voices within her that wished to rest, and he encouraged them to speak louder...louder...

Her eyelids flickered, then she fell into a deep sleep.

At Grei's request, Ree's candle and Vecenne's onyx artifact floated to his hands. He touched the black stone to the wick and the candle flared to life again. The tunnel curved sharply to the left and down as though it was following the shape of the Frost Tree's trunk. Grei whispered, and the candle and Ree's unconscious body floated into the air.

He envisioned The Root forming a tunnel to his destination, to the icy valley of the blue roses, and Grei began running. The candle floated in front of him, lighting the way, and Ree flew behind him.

Velak was going to the field of blue roses.

And Grei would be waiting for him.

Chapter 47

URIOZI

FATHER SAT on the craggy rocks by the sea, sobbing. His wide, muscular back shook. Neither Uriozi nor Sherim had ever seen Father cry, but he had been like that for an hour now, mourning a hundred years of tragedy.

Sherim stood in her orange dress next to Uriozi, wringing her hands. Uriozi could feel her sister's desire to do something, to heal Father somehow. Sherim wanted to heal everything. Uriozi also saw Sherim's exhaustion, the strain around her eyes, the way her muscles were always just slightly flexed now. The deaths were affecting both of them.

Uriozi felt the barrier pulling at her. Mother's pocket dimension was cracking. The strain of upholding the barrier had multiplied. Either Jevare was dead now, too, or she had released her part of the barrier.

The barrier was now only being held together by the magic of Uriozi, Sherim, and Mother. That could not stand for long. Velak would break free soon, then they would all die.

She turned her focus back to Father. The tide had come in

and, as waves crashed, water rushed up to soak into the boots, breeches, and tunic that Sherim had made for him. Suddenly, Sherim's voice moved outward to the elements like a ripple. She beseeched Father's clothes to—

"Don't." Uriozi put a hand on her sister's shoulder, interrupting her concentration.

"I was only going to make his clothes waterproof. He's cold," Sherim said.

"He's not cold. He's sad. And he *should* be sad."

"You should not have told him," Sherim said, her lips twisted with compassion. "It hurts him so much."

It had taken days for Sherim and Uriozi to reconstruct Father. Sherim had returned all the memories Mother had stripped from him. But Uriozi gave him more, the secrets Mother had never told him, the truth about his family: that Thiazin wasn't his only offspring, that Baezin had two sons, one named Saebin who had lived in the South Forest—a gentle creature who appeared to be a monster to human eyes—and one named Velak, who was a actually monster in every way, who was going to rip the world apart if they let him.

Then Uriozi had gone further, had told Father that the "goddesses" called the Faia were his daughters. She'd told him that, in his ignorance, he'd helped Emperor Qweryn kill two of them.

"It is too much for him to know," Sherim said, twisting the edge of her dress in her hand. Sherim felt the pain of others more strongly than any of her other sisters, and Uriozi felt bad for that. Sherim was a sweet soul. But Uriozi didn't feel bad for Father. She had come to the disappointing conclusion that her parents, so long revered, were deeply flawed. Father had been unrealistically stubborn. Mother had been volatile and vengeful. Uriozi wished she'd seen this three hundred years ago.

"Just imagine if he had known from the beginning," Uriozi said. "If Mother had told him long ago. How would the history of this land be different?"

"Mother said he could not handle the truth, that it would

be worse for him to know."

"We only need to look at our lands, ripped and bleeding, to see that she was wrong."

Sherim went silent. Each of Uriozi's sisters held a reverence for Mother. Who else could they look up to? Who else could have taught them how to behave? Speaking ill of Mother felt like blasphemy. After a moment, Sherim asked, "What will you do now?"

"We fight Velak."

Sherim looked at her in shock. "We cannot!"

"We must."

"He killed Pyll. He killed Lankoli. He—"

"There is no other way," Uriozi said. She could see the story of her family like a half-drawn circle, never finished. It had been cut short, a force of nature now forever out of balance. Father and Mother began that circle together. Father needed to close it now, one way or another.

When Velak first burned Thiara, it should have been Father who braced him, educated him, or brought him to justice for his crimes. But Mother had said no, and Uriozi and her sisters had followed her lead.

Uriozi was finished with that.

Unlike her sisters, Uriozi had traveled far and wide. She'd not only watched nature and humans in Devorra but also in the lands far to the east, beyond Fairmist and Benasca. She had learned much that her sisters did not know. While her sisters had turned their gazes inward, burying themselves in their little havens, Uriozi had gained experience. There was much to know beyond the sphere of Mother's volatile tantrums and peevish desires.

"Mother does not want this—"

"Mother is insane," Uriozi said.

Sherim gasped.

"Do you remember feeling aligned with the lands? We were once, you know." Early on, Uriozi and her sisters were extensions of the land, aligned with its magic. They were innocent and blessed. They traveled the lands freely, and luck followed wherever they went. "We helped Father, and his people prospered. Do you remember?"

Sherim didn't say anything.

"That's what luck is, Sherim. It is being one with the lands. It is serving them, all of them. Not hiding in one small part of them. We forgot that as Mother slowly poisoned Devorra. She had a responsibility to the blue roses, and she forsook that responsibility. When we are aligned with the lands, when we give to them, they give back. But we abandoned that, and luck abandoned us. There has only been tragedy since."

"You can't beat him," Sherim said in a small voice.

"Not alone. But there are some who will fight. The Whisper Prince will fight for his love. Father will fight because he is a fighter, but also to make amends. I will fight to serve the lands. And there is the sword…"

"The sword…" Sherim's voice quivered. None of her sisters liked the sword. It had been crafted specifically to kill Velak, but that also meant it had been crafted to kill any one of them, too. They were his sisters, after all.

"I want to be aligned with the lands again," Uriozi murmured, and she felt her heart ache for it, an ever-expanding need. When one lived without balance for so long, it eventually seemed normal. But as Uriozi looked down the trail of history and at Mother's many mistakes, she felt the imbalance in the lands like she had swallowed a poison, thick and greasy and foul. She wanted to feel clean again.

"We will feel the luck again," Uriozi said.

Sherim shook her head, both hands now wringing her dress, and Uriozi knew that Sherim wouldn't be coming with them. Even now, at the end of the world, Sherim planned to hide in her haven. This was why Velak had been able to pick them off one by one.

There was nothing left to say, and the two sisters stood side by side for another hour until Father finally stopped crying. He stood up, eyes red, and looked at them. That fierceness was back in his eyes, but behind that was a haunted depth that would never go away.

"Where is he now?" Father asked.

"Mother is in Benasca," Uriozi said. "He will go there, if he isn't there already."

Sherim, looking hesitantly between Father and Uriozi, turned without a word and floated up to her rocky haven. Father watched her go, then focused on Uriozi.

"I need my sword."

Uriozi gave a little smile, but there was no joy in it. It was time to slay. And that was what Father did best.

"Come," she said. At her request, the air lifted them both. They flew northeast from the mountains surrounding Cliffgard. It took them half the day, but as the sun set, they could see the Frost Trees of the Benascan city of Iceward. Despite the fear that thrilled through her, Uriozi felt drawn to the center of the city. Velak was there. She could feel it. He was in Benasca already. And she could feel…something else.

They landed on the ground next to the largest of the Frost Trees. There, gleaming in the sunlight, was the sword, flakes of snow glittering on steel.

Father knelt and came up with Baezin's Blade in his fist.

How in the world had the sword come to be here, just lying in the snow in this place?

Uriozi smiled. Luck. It was the lands talking to her, approving of this deadly gambit. They were doing right. Now, for better or worse, it was time to fight.

Chapter 48

GREI

IT TOOK HALF AN HOUR of running in The Root to get back to the field of blue roses. He saw the blackened roots twisting through the walls as he neared, heard the sonorous, mournful voices. Grei took a deep breath, and Ree floated gently to the ground at his request. He knelt next to her and spoke to her *dasha*, asking it to wake soon. Soon, but not right now. Ree had done everything she'd promised. She'd taken him to this final moment, and he wasn't going to risk her life in a fight where she could only be another casualty.

He flipped the hatch on The Root. Snow fell through, creating a pile in the center of the tunnel. The smell of winter followed, cold and ice.

"You were true to your word," he whispered. "I'll be true to mine."

He looked up and asked the air to lift him through the hatch. For the first time, he didn't worry about failure. Death was his ultimate goal, but first, he was going to spend everything else on killing Velak.

Grei rose, and the vast field of ice stretched out before him, dotted with vibrant blue roses and withered black roses.

In the center of the field stood Velak. His feet had created two perfect, melted circles in the vast sheet of glimmering ice.

Even with the time difference in The Root, Velak had arrived first. He must have flown here. Grei felt fear, but it was dull and small. He acknowledged it like he would acknowledge the sky was blue. Fear didn't matter now. Only one thing mattered.

"Ah," Velak said without facing Grei, "I knew you would return. I admire you for that. You never give up. I, too, have never given up hope that I would come to this moment." He let out a long breath, and a white cloud floated up from his head. "You know, Whisper Prince, I was not permitted friends in my life, but I think you could have been a friend, in some other life, some other version of history." Finally, the fire lord turned. "We have much in common. Betrayed by our parents. Caged by those who were supposed to love us—"

"You can stop talking. I'm just here to kill you," Grei said.

Velak chuckled, bowed his head like he'd heard a good joke. "Then you're a bit late. Mother is dead. Her haven is now my haven. The blue roses belong to me." He raised his hands. All of his fingers—save the one he'd lost—curled up like he was holding a pair of invisible spheres. Blue lighting crackled around them. Slowly, the missing finger regrew amidst sparkling blue light. "I'm truly a god now."

"Show me," he growled.

He heard the ripple of Velak's voice in the air, lancing toward him, a split-second before the fire erupted at him. The sheer power of it shook the world.

Grei flipped a different hatch on The Root, dropped into the tunnel, and shut it just as the fire incinerated the place he had been. He sprinted up the hallway, envisioning coming up just behind Velak. The hallway ended, The Root letting him know where to stop. Grei flipped open a third hatch, launched upward, and burst through the snow before it even had a chance to fall.

No time had passed during his feverish sprint. Velak was still pointing where Grei had been, and he didn't realize Grei had emerged behind him.

Grei reached out to the blue roses. Let's see just how tightly you've bound yourself to your new haven.

The roses gave him everything. Either Velak had not put any barrier to keep another from pulling from the power of the roses, or he could not. Pulling from the blue roses wasn't like drinking from a river. The magic, the power, was so plentiful that Grei felt it could do anything. He birthed a whirlwind, wind swirling, snow lifting to join.

"Water." Grei pointed at Velak. The whirlwind transformed into a floating river, thick, swirling, and moving faster than a horse at full gallop. Surprised, Velak spun with his inhuman speed—

Just as the column of water slammed into him. Steam exploded from his sizzling body, and Velak roared. He shot straight upward, trying to get out of the way.

Grei let the power of the blue roses flow through him again. Focusing so much it felt like his mind was burning, he did two things at once. He reached out with one hand, whispering to the air around Velak's steaming body, to the steam itself, to the burning skin of the fire lord, and jammed his ethereal fingers into Velak's *dasha* and yanked. With his other hand, he asked the air high above Velak to create five more columns of water. They formed like a tornado and lanced at Velak.

Velak raised his hand to send another bolt of fire at Grei, but the flames flickered and died as Grei yanked his *dasha*. Growling in rage, Velak abandoned his *shkat* attack, yanked his *dasha* back from Grei and pointed his finger again—

Just as the five new columns of water slammed into him. They were so heavy, so powerful, that they knocked him out of the air like a fly. Velak plummeted amidst a waterfall, impacting the snow so hard he caused a crater.

Ice cracked; steam billowed upward.

Grei reached out to the air around the crater, requesting it to form a fifty-foot sphere of ice all around—

Then the unlimited power of the blue roses vanished.

Velak lunged out of the pool of water, scrambling over the rim of ice and snow. His skin looked awful. Once it had been smooth and reddish. Now it was mottled, like half of it had been turned to bubbling stone and the other half had become deep, red wounds.

Grei tried to access the blue roses again, but they were closed to him. Velak had closed the hole.

Grei reached out to the air, asking it to change into water around Velak using only his powers as the Whisper Prince, but the little particles of magic in the air, without the aid of the blue roses, seemed so small and paltry. So slow. The transformation had barely begun when Velak's fire blast hit Grei in the chest.

He barely had time to turn the air solid and keep himself from being incinerated. But the blast lifted him off his feet, carrying him several body lengths backward before he fell into the snow.

"Whelp! This is my birthright!" Velak roared, and he didn't even point his hand this time. Fire exploded from every part of him: his chest, his arms, his legs, his face.

Grei threw up a barrier, but didn't have time to make a proper request of it. The air turned solid, and Grei's thoughts went muddy and sluggish. Velak's fire slammed into him, driving Grei into the ground again, smashing his body and head so hard that it knocked him senseless.

Bright lights swirled around him. Grei thought he could see the blue sky, but it was fuzzy. He thought he should do something, but Velak appeared above him, his mottled body hunched over the hole, before Grei could decide what that something should be.

"This is my haven," Velak rasped through his bubbly stone lips. "Who do you think you are, human?"

"I'm...the Whisper Prince," he growled, realizing how badly he was hurt. His ears rang, and he smelled something burning. Hair. His hair, probably, maybe even his skin. He tried to concentrate, but he could barely hear the voices of the elements over the ringing in his ears. It didn't matter. Nothing mattered. He would fight. He would die. That was what he wanted, anyway…

Through his fuzzy vision, Grei thought he saw two people high in the sky above Velak, one large and human-looking, one small and charcoal black. The big one seemed to be getting larger. Was that a man falling from the sky? Was that…Blevins?

Velak pointed a finger at Grei. Fire swirled around his fist—

Then Velak jerked his head up just as Blevins arrived, Baezin's Blade chopping down at Velak's head. Velak lurched back in a blur, blindingly fast. The blade clipped his horn, missed his neck…

And chopped through his arm at the elbow. Blevins hit the ground with a *thoom* like some giant, ferocious god.

Velak keened like a wounded cliff cat, scrambling backward in the snow. Snow hissed around him as his stump gouted flame.

Blevins rose up, all thick muscles, dark hair and eyes of death.

"Son," he said. "We need to talk."

Chapter 49

GREI

"FATHER," VELAK SAID in a low, grating voice. His cracked, stony lips had peeled back so far it made his entire head seem like a mouth of tall, translucent teeth. "So they finally told you."

With a painful grunt, Grei levered himself up on his elbows. He tried to stand up, but his legs were too shaky. Above him, the Black Faia hovered, watching Velak with tense anticipation. Grei shook his head. Everything hurt, but he had to get himself together, get back into the fight.

Blevins strode toward Velak like he had when the Highblades had come for him in the Badlands, certain, intent. Baezin's Blade floated out to the side, gleaming and deadly, a quiet promise of violence.

"Stop," Blevins growled darkly. "Stop, and you and I can talk. But this horror ends now."

"Horror…" Velak spat. He backed away one cautious step at a time, holding his flaming stump. Snow hissed and melted around his feet. "That's exactly what Mother was afraid you'd say when you saw me. My son, the horror. That's why she never told you about me. And she was right to keep it from you. I can see the *horror* in your eyes! Talk to you? Why would I want to do that?"

"Because this can change. *You* can change."

"Or what?"

"I'll kill you."

Velak gave an ugly laugh. "That was why she hid me. That's why Mother asked me to burn your precious city. If something doesn't pass your righteous judgement, it simply has to die.…"

"It wasn't the first mistake I've made. But I've changed. So can you—"

"I don't want to change," he said. "I don't want to be anything like you. I burned in a hole for a hundred years because of you. But at last, my tormentors are nearly dead. I have come into my inheritance." He waved his good hand at the field of blue roses. "And not that abomination in your hand, my weak little sister up there, or this pathetic human are going to stop me."

"Last chance," Blevins growled.

Velak burst into the air on a pillar of flame. Fire blasted out below him, and Grei could feel the rising voices of the blue roses. Velak shot fire down at them, a catastrophic blaze big enough to engulf half the field. The Black Faia above screamed, but it wasn't from pain. Grei could feel her own whispers on the air, shielding Blevins from the fire, pushing back more power and rage than Grei could even imagine.

I have to do something. This is the moment. I can't overpower him, but I can…

Then he knew what to do, because he knew Blevins. Blevins did not slide sideways, seeking advantage. He attacked. It was the only thing he ever did. Blevins, as he was in all things, would be direct. He'd go for the kill. And Grei had to make sure he succeeded.

The flame cleared around Blevins, and he was unharmed. The Black Faia, though, had spent everything she had to throw

386

off that unbelievable assault. Unconscious, she fluttered down from the sky like a broken butterfly.

Blevins threw Baezin's Blade with all his enormous strength at Velak. It flipped end over end, straight and true.

Contemptuously, Velak lurched to the side, blurring with inhuman speed—

And smacked into Grei's invisible wall. It stopped him, held him in that one spot for a flickering half a second.

Baezin's Blade impaled him. Velak gasped. For a moment, he hovered there, looking down at the sword buried to the hilt in his chest.

Velak screamed, dropping from the sky like a comet trailing fire.

The terrible boom of his impact shook the earth, and Grei could feel the ripple of Velak's anguish through the voices of the snow, the air, the blue roses. Fire burst upward, and Grei shielded his eyes. It flared, white-hot, and snow turned to steam in a thirty-foot radius around Velak.

The tortured scream twisted, splitting the air. Grei clapped his hands to his ears.

Then the flare of fire vanished. The scream stopped, though its echo reverberated in the whispers of the lands and within Grei's mind.

When it finally felt like someone wasn't stabbing ice picks into his ears, Grei took his hands away.

Blevins appeared, standing over Grei. He waited a moment, grim-faced, then extended his hand.

"I…have to see. I have to listen to his body," Grei said.

Blevins grunted, then lifted Grei out of the hole like he weighed nothing. Together, they walked to where Velak had fallen. The fire lord's entire body had turned to mottled stone, and Baezin's Blade stuck up from the center of him. The stone of Velak's chest had grown up around the blade like a snowdrift against a tree, as though Velak's body had grabbed onto the sword even as it had killed him.

Grei listened for any whispers that might indicate Velak was faking, that he was still alive, and perhaps this was a feint to lure them closer. But his body was actually stone. The mantra it whispered over and over was the same mantra Grei had heard from every stone he'd ever listened to.

"He's dead," Grei said.

Blevins drew a long, shuddering breath. He clenched his fists, then released them.

Grei staggered, caught his balance, and barely managed to stay standing. He felt like he'd been scooped out with a giant spoon. His heart, his organs, everything important to him had been scraped away. There was nothing of substance left.

He'd done what he'd come to do. That was the end of it.

"Come on," Blevins said.

"The sword," Grei said absently.

Blevins gave a baleful gaze to the sword, then started walking toward where Uriozi had fallen.

"Don't you want it?" Grei asked.

"Leave it," he said over his shoulder. "I don't ever want to touch it again." He never broke stride.

Grei nodded, then slowly slid to his knees. This was as good a place as any. He could lie down in the snow and let the cold slowly take him.

Blevins paused, looked back. He fixed Grei with that intense gaze, then he said, "Ah... Mialene. Velak killed her."

Grei lay back in the snow, letting the despair and exhaustion crush him. "Go..." he murmured. "Go help the Black Faia. Go do whatever you do when you're not killing people. This is my end. Right here. Right now." He stared up at the sky, feeling the icy cold beneath him, letting it seep into his skin, his muscles, his bones.

Blevins boots crunched through the snow toward him. Then the big man's iron grip caught Grei's arm, hauled him roughly back to his feet.

"Bullshit," Blevins growled. "Get up. Help Uriozi now. Kill yourself later."

Blevins dragged Grei to where Uriozi lay sprawled in the snow.

Epilogue

GREI STOOD ONCE AGAIN in the midst of the field of blue roses, nearly a day later. The full moon sent streaks of silver across the sheets of ice, and across Adora's pale face. Her body lay next to him, beautiful and utterly without life.

Velak was dead. The field of blue roses was free of him, and the field craved a new steward. The voices of the roses called to Grei just like the spirits of the Jhor Forest and Fairmist Falls had done, but with a key difference. These voices were not desperate, not violent; they didn't grab at him. They were simply…compelling. They threatened to overthrow his reason with an achingly beautiful, sonorous invitation.

If a user of magic wanted to be powerful, there was no better haven. The blue roses connected to every part of Devorra. They flowed throughout Benasca, the Thiaran Empire, probably even farther south than the empire stretched and farther north than Benasca claimed.

Both Grei and Uriozi had felt this thrumming compulsion the moment Velak had died, and Grei had suggested that Uriozi take up her mother's mantle.

Uriozi had instantly declined. She said her mother's

stewardship had been a disaster, and felt a new stewardship would end the same. Cavyn had used the roses for her own selfish desires, to hide from the world, to resurrect Blevins over and over because of some horrible combination of infatuation and revenge. She had put the lands in jeopardy, had started a rot at their very heart. Uriozi had said the blue roses were better left alone to serve the lands naturally, the way they were originally intended.

So Uriozi had fled the compulsion, only reappearing when Blevins, Grei, and Ree returned to the Elder Tree through The Root. The four of them tidied up the site of their battle with Velak. Between Grei and Uriozi, they'd shut the portal in Cavyn's eerie basement room, then walled it off from the normal room above in the same fashion Cavyn had done. When they were finished, the center pillar of the room looked once again like the white wood of a Frost Tree. No normal person would ever know that basement room, with its bloody secrets, had ever existed.

Grei thought they may as well have not even bothered. Let the Benascans see the evidence. Let them wonder at it, meddle with it. Grei didn't care.

The pocket dimension of Velakka no longer held anything dangerous. It was an empty little prison with no prisoner. Everything Velak had been, everything he had created, had vanished with his death. His Velakkans, which Uriozi had explained were thousands of insane little facets of himself, were gone. The mind-dominating red *dasha* mist was also gone. The Benascans who'd fallen prey to Velak's *dasha* attack had wandered around the city bewildered, no doubt with nasty memories like the echoes of a nightmare. Grei assumed that the same had happened in Fairmist, the city of Thiara, and every other place Velak had managed to infect. But again, he didn't really care.

But Blevins had insisted, so he had helped cover up the aftermath of the battle.

Once they'd shut Velakka away forever, they had retreated into The Root before any of the Benascans discovered them.

The Benascans would have undoubtedly reacted violently to any Thiarans in Iceward, much less magical ones, especially after a mystical red mist had so recently attacked their people. Blevins, who had taken on a much more commanding air since he'd regained all of his memories, had told everyone the plan. They would rest for a night, then make their way west to Cliffgard. There, they could bury Cavyn and Adora in private and decide what they would do next.

Decide what to do next....

So they had descended into The Root, walking south for a few hours, the bodies floating behind them at Uriozi's command, before creating a cozy place for everyone to lie down. They hadn't even posted a guard. They had all simply slept. Humans side by side with a Faia. Highblade next to Ringblade.

All except Grei. He had waited until everyone was asleep, then set about his work. He listened to the voices of Adora's corpse, then healed her wounds, kept her flesh and organs from decaying. Once that was done, he had lifted himself and Adora on the air and moved silently backward into a new tunnel. He had floated quietly for half an hour before he bid The Root to wall off the tunnel behind him, separating him from his friends by a thousand feet of earth. Then he had flipped a hatch over their campsite, giving Blevins, Ree, and Uriozi a way out when they awoke.

And then, Grei had returned here to the field of blue roses.

The sonorous voices reached out to him, swirled around him like sparkles of snow in a breeze. He felt their offer, their power, and the vast responsibility that went along with it. Becoming the steward of the field of blue roses would make him more powerful than either of the remaining Faia, more powerful than both of them together. And it meant Grei would be responsible for the well-being of an entire continent, responsible for healing the wounds Cavyn had made.

He let it all rush through him...

...and he accepted.

He shuddered as the roses bonded to him. His body felt

electrified, connecting to every living thing in Devorra. His *dasha*, a silhouette of misty blue in the shape of his body, rose above his physical form. The arms of his *dasha* silhouette grew, expanding and extending all the way to the icy shores of Cragmouth, all the way to the warm waters of Trimbledown, all the way to the shadowy city of Moondow and beyond. They went farther, reaching and reaching. He saw the shape of things. He saw the glittering magic on the air. He saw the *dasha* within every tree, every living creature, every human that scuttled about their mundane lives.

His physical body shook like a leaf in the wind. So... Much... Power...

Grei suddenly realized he'd been inhaling for a very long time, and he painstakingly pulled his *dasha* back into his physical body. Looking at the lands through his human eyes, they seemed faded, dull. His vision was horribly limited. It was so...mortal. All he could see was light and physical shapes. No glittering sheens of magic, no flows of power wafting through the air. He remembered the dream back in Thiara, when he had been Cavyn for an instant, had watched her resurrect Blevins, and now he knew exactly how she had felt coming back into her mortal body after being one with all the magic in Devorra.

Cavyn had committed horrible crimes, destroying the *dasha* of the lands—its very soul—one piece at a time, over and over, for her own personal needs. Those transgressions opened like mouths within his own body, festering wounds that hadn't been tended.

After a long moment of swirling in the vast power, Grei finally pulled his focus together. He clenched and unclenched his fists to ground himself, to be in his physical body. The words he'd spoken to Ree the day before Adora had been snatched, before the horror of Velak became gut-wrenchingly real, returned to him.

I want to heal the wounds they've made....

He let the phrase float in his mind. He'd never been so passionate about anything when he had spoken those words to

Ree.

"But I want you alive more," he said in a ragged voice, and he turned his gaze to Adora's body.

With his new, expansive *dasha*, Grei reached out and destroyed a blue rose. The power roared through him, ripped free of the lands, wild with need. As he had seen Cavyn do in his dream, he channeled that life-giving power into Adora's body, and willed her back to life. He demanded that her *dasha* return to her body. He gave the wild power free rein to complete his command, no matter the cost.

Adora's body rippled like a mirage, then became solid again. He fell to his knees next to her, hands on her cold shoulders.

For a moment, he thought he'd failed, that nothing had happened.

Then Adora's eyes snapped opened. They were bright, blue as sapphires…

…and filled with horror.

Mailing List/Social Media

MAILING LIST

Don't miss out on the latest news and information about all of my books. Join my Readers Group:

https://www.subscribepage.com/u0x4q3

FACEBOOK

https://www.facebook.com/todd.fahnestock

AMAZON AUTHOR PAGE

https://www.amazon.com/Todd-Fahnestock/e/B004N1MILG

Author Letter

THIS ONE TOOK FOREVER. By the Faia, it took forever! The first book in this series, *Fairmist*, was published in February of 2015. That's four years! Yeesh.

But there's a story behind this great lateness. It all started with the best of intentions....

Back in February of 2015, I had assumed I'd leap right into *The Undying Man* and have it out by February of 2016. I had the plot in mind, had half the story roughed out before *Fairmist* hit the shelves. I even had an alternate cover that is nothing like the final cover you see now (Ask me about it; I might let you see it....).

Then *The Wishing World* arrived. That little middle-grade novel, based on stories I told my children to get them to go to sleep, grabbed my attention and stole my time. I conceived of it, wrote it, and got a contract from Tor for it. Suddenly, it became all about prepping for the launch of *The Wishing World*.

The Undying Man sat neglected.

I intended to get back to work on it. I really did. But *The Wishing World* needed a sequel in order to keep with Tor's timeline. So I got to work and wrote *The Wishing World II: Loremaster*.

The Undying Man sat neglected.

Once *Loremaster* was off to my editor, I finally returned to *Fairmist's* lonely sibling. But most of my energy still went to *The Wishing World* marketing efforts. There was a contest to promote. Entries to judge. There were over fifty elementary school classrooms to visit. And, of course, I was certain *The Wishing World* was going to be my *NY Times* bestseller, and once it took the world by storm, I was going to be writing *Wishing World* books for a decade. Dreams and plans floated into the air like a unicorn with rainbow wings. I figured *The Undying Man* could wait just a little longer....

Then those lovely plans crashed to the ground in flames.

In April of 2017, I got the news from Tor that sales for *The Wishing World* weren't robust enough for Tor to purchase the sequel. They wouldn't be publishing *Loremaster* or any other books in the series.… I was crushed.

As fate would have it, I got that news two days before my happy return to the Pikes Peak Writers Conference in Colorado Springs, where I'd gotten my start as an author. I called up my friend and avatar, Chris Mandeville.

"I don't want to go," I said. "My book is a flop. I'm humiliated. I want to stay home."

"You're the emcee," she said. "You *have* to go."

"I don't wanna. Make it go away," I said, not unlike a two-year-old throwing a tantrum.

"You know you're going to love it when you get there. You'll be surrounded by creative people who love you and love what you do. It'll inspire you."

"I don't want to be inspired. I want to crawl in a hole and sleep in my own vomit."

"Put on your f*#king big boy pants and pack your suitcase!" she barked. (Chris can turn it on when she needs to.)

So I packed my suitcase. I went to the conference with my heart flopping despairingly in my shoes.

As I sat at my faculty table during lunch, surrounded by people asking me questions about how to be a successful author, I wanted to yell, "I'm not a successful author! I'm a horrible failure of an author!"

But after lunch, in the lobby of the Marriott Hotel, I sat with Donald Maass, agent extraordinaire and the most inspiring man in the world, and he gave me hope. Over the course of a mere half an hour, he rekindled my love of Story, reminded me that it's not about the sales, not about the highs and lows of the industry; it's about creating an unforgettable story. And he inspired me to throw all of my energy into…

Charlie Fiction, my barely-born idea for a time-travel novel. I blazed through the rough draft in record time and spent months on revisions.

And *The Undying Man* sat neglected.

After *Charlie Fiction*, the *Threadweavers* novels roared into the world, an inspiration that rode on the coattails of *Charlie's* success.

And *The Undying Man* sat neglected.

But finally, after the dust of the incredibly prolific 2018 settled, I turned my gaze back to the tragic, magical world of *Fairmist.*

I dove into *The Undying Man* with vigor. It was like coming home after my own tragic, magical adventures. I fell in love with Grei and Adora all over again, two indefatigable lovers trying to mend a broken world. I felt the story in my skin, in my blood: the noble Highblades, the saucy Ringblades, the slinks, and the Thiaran Empire's twisted history.

In the end, rather than being neglected, *The Undying Man* received the best of what I can do. The skills I honed in *The Wishing World, Loremaster, Charlie Fiction, Wildmane, The GodSpill, Threads of Amarion,* and *God of Dragons* came spilling onto the pages of this epic quest through Devorra.

I hope you enjoyed it as much as I enjoyed creating it. I apologize for the long wait. *The Slate Wizards*, Book 3 of the series, is already in the works.

Thank you for reading! I look forward to seeing you again when we return to Devorra….

-Todd

ALSO BY TODD FAHNESTOCK

Tower of the Four
Episode 1 – The Quad
Episode 2 – The Tower
Episode 3 – The Test
Episode 4 – The Nightmare
Episode 5 – The Resurrection
Episode 6 – The Reunion
The Champions Academy (Episodes 1-3 compilation)
The Dragon's War (Episodes 4-6 compilation)

Eldros Legacy (Legacy of Shadows)
Khyven the Unkillable
Lorelle of the Dark
Rhenn the Traveler (Forthcoming)

Threadweavers
Wildmane
The GodSpill
Threads of Amarion
God of Dragons

The Whisper Prince
Fairmist
The Undying Man
The Slate Wizards (Forthcoming)

The Wishing World
The Wishing World
Loremaster (Forthcoming)
Spheres of Magic (Forthcoming)

Standalone Novels
Charlie Fiction
Summer of the Fetch

Memoirs
Ordinary Magic

Short Stories
Urchin: A Tower of the Four Short Story
Royal: A Tower of the Four Short Story
Princess: A Tower of the Four Short Story
Pawns of Magic: A Tower of the Four Short Story
Here There Be Giants: *Fate's Dagger*
Talons & Talismans 2: *The Darkest Door*
Parallel Worlds Anthology: *Threshold*
Fantastic Realms Anthology: *Ten for Every One*
Dragonlance: The Cataclysm – *Seekers*
Dragonlance: Heroes & Fools – *Songsayer*
Dragonlance: The History of Krynn – *The Letters of Trayn Minaas*

ABOUT THE AUTHOR

TODD FAHNESTOCK is the award-winning, #1 bestselling author of fantasy for all ages and winner of the New York Public Library's Books for the Teen Age Award. Threadweavers and The Whisper Prince Trilogy are two of his bestselling epic fantasy series. He is a winner of the 2022 and 2021 Colorado Authors League Award for Writing Excellence for Khyven the Unkillable (2022) and Tower of the Four: The Champions Academy (2021) and two-time finalist for the Colorado Book Award (2022 and 2021). His passions are fantasy and his quirky, fun-loving family. When he's not writing, he teaches Taekwondo, swaps middle grade humor with his son, plays Ticket to Ride with his wife, plots creative stories with his daughter, and wrestles with Galahad the Weimaraner. Visit Todd at www.toddfahnestock.com.